As Robin turned in a circle taking her on a magical moonlight ride, she brought him up short by hammering his chest with her fists and demanding, "What if I couldn't swim?"

"You can swim."

"You didn't know that! What if I couldn't?"

"Then I would have rescued you, and you would have been indebted to me for saving your life."

Beth gave him a dubious look. "But you're the one who threw me in to start with!"

"Only because you said you wanted to cool off."

"This wasn't precisely what I had in mind," she admitted squirming against his chest, "but it worked."

Beth wiggled her legs free and stood up clinging to his wet, musk-scented body as she placed her feet on top of his. "I'm not hot anymore."

"I am."

"Oh!"

"Is that all you have to say?" Robin asked.

"No."

But before she could say anything more, Robin pulled Beth toward him and lowered his head toward hers, delighting in the feel of her lips on his. It was a kiss of passion that overwhelmed them both as they stood together beneath a lover's moon caught up in their own undulating waves of ecstasy. . . .

KATHY WILLIS

WARRIOR'S WOMAN

ZEBRA BOOKS
KENSINGTON PUBLISHING CORP.

To Ron and Ronda, my real hero and heroine.

ZEBRA BOOKS

are published by

Kensington Publishing Corp.
475 Park Avenue South
New York, NY 10016

Copyright © 1992 by Kathy Willis

First printing: December, 1992

Printed in the United States of America

Chapter One

The Florida Territory, 1837.

The tall sun-bronzed Indian tensed as he heard the thundering hoofs of a single horse beating a path toward the spot where the trail narrowed, banked on either side by low hillocks dotted with pine trees and underbrush. Corded muscles rippled across his naked back as he crouched low, nodding almost imperceptibly to his companion hunkered down in similar fashion a short distance away. As the pounding grew louder, each man drew his end of the rope taut and wrapped it twice around the base of a sturdy sapling.

The forest held its breath. Not so much as a bird twittered or a squirrel cavorted in the trees overhead. And the only breeze was created by the onrushing horse kicking up a cloud of dust in its wake. The steady rhythm drummed louder and louder. The animal raced forward as though the devil was at its heels. In less than a heartbeat it was over. The slender buckskin-clad figure, who but a moment ago had seemed one with the powerful steed, now lay sprawled on the ground as the horse continued toward Fort King apparently unaware that its burden had been lifted.

Beth Townsend blinked up into the bright afternoon sun and then closed her eyes tightly. Surely even in her worst nightmare she had never seen such a hideous face as the one she thought she had seen peering down at her. Shaking her head in an effort to clear her befuddled brain, she dared to peep out from beneath thick rust-colored lashes.

Oh, God! It was still there! The threatening prick of the knife point, poised against the smooth skin of her neck, scarcely registered as she shut her eyes once again. The grotesque image of her assailant implanted in her mind's eye. He was a monster with rough, scaly skin, a wide slashed mouth, and two empty holes where his eyes should have been.

"Kill him!"

The pitiless command startled Beth into opening her eyes, and she took care to focus on the harsh voice coming from somewhere over the shoulder of the miscreant straddling her prone body, as she lay upon the hard-packed earth. Why hadn't she heeded Davey's advice and taken the more circuitous route to the fort? If by some miracle she lived to see him again, she would be sure to tell her cousin how right he had been before she strangled him with her bare hands; just recompense for Davey's breaking his leg thus necessitating her making this trip alone.

Beth and Davey had worked as a team for over a year riding dispatch between Fort Brooke and Fort King keeping the soldiers advised of Indian activities in the area. And now, the first time she had been forced to ride alone, *this* had to happen. She would never live it down, if she lived at all, which looked doubtful at the moment.

Beth felt the weight of the heavy male body pressed down upon her long, slim legs. Her attacker, too, wore tight-fitting deerskin breeches but his upper torso was bare. One powerful deeply tanned arm held her shoulder pinning her to the ground; in his other hand he wielded a wicked-looking knife. Beth wondered how many scalps he had taken and fleetingly imagined what a trophy her long, red hair would prove to be gracing this ugly warrior's lance.

Praying for a miracle to even the odds, she struggled to free herself using her well-toned leg muscles to try and buck the repulsive fiend off. Her efforts would have been laughable if her situation had been less catastrophic.

"Kill him!" The order broke the silence of the woods once again.

Damnation! Was that the only English the savage knew? Beth fumed inwardly as she glared at the second Indian now positioned directly over her head. He looked for all the world as if he would like nothing better than to stomp her face into the dust.

From somewhere behind the cavernous mouth of the deformed visage holding her in his steely grip, a distorted voice answered, "Did the darkness of the white man's prison blind your eyes so that you can no longer see what is in front of you?"

So mesmerized was Beth at hearing the words spoken through a lipless opening that did not move, her own mouth fell as she gaped at the loathsome brute holding her helpless beneath his rigid frame.

His compatriot was quick to respond. From between clenched teeth he snarled, "You had best have a good reason for questioning my authority, brother!"

The tension was palpable between the two men as each fought to control his own emotions. Finally the eerie voice of her captor broke the strained silence.

"I am pledged to fight for the freedom of my people, to restore their hunting lands, and establish for them a place where they can live in peace. I am willing to surrender my life for such a cause and if necessary I will shed the blood of the white man. But heed my words, Asi-yahola, I do not kill women!"

With that he swiftly snatched off Beth's hat which had remained in place, thanks to the chin strap, even through the indignity of her unseating. She winced when the leather thong scraped her tender skin. A mass of thick, titian hair swirled out and about her head, settling to frame the delicate features of her face. Her lightly tanned complexion was the color of rich creamy butter. A smattering of freckles dusted the narrow bridge of her nose above a pink mouth with a full bottom lip that appeared sensuous despite the firmly drawn expression with which she regarded the two men arguing over her fate.

Beth sensed it would be to her advantage to encourage the sympathy of the ghastly cretin atop her, but as she stared into those empty black sockets an uncontrollable shiver coursed through her. She felt him stiffen and knew he was aware of her revulsion, yet his countenance remained frozen.

Frozen! The truth suddenly dawned and Beth chided herself for not having realized it sooner. Blaming her slow-wittedness on the fall she had taken, she focused her gaze on the inhuman face a mere breath away. Of course there was no change of expression. *The man was wearing a mask!*

Strangely enough, Beth felt more curiosity than fear, and without conscious thought she lifted her arm running her hand over the rough wood of the grotesque facade. It was made from bark! Cypress, probably. She had no idea how it had been molded in such a fashion for she could see that it covered his entire head.

The Indian jerked back. It was almost as if he had felt her touch beneath the disguise. He caught her wrist in a viselike grip and Beth thought for a moment she could detect a spark of anger behind the dark hollows that hid his eyes. Or was it confusion?

Her attention was drawn to the man called Asiyahola as he uttered an unintelligible oath and backed several paces away, beating one tightly clenched fist against his thigh in a gesture of frustration. He was of medium height with a lean and sinewy build that loaned grace to his movements. He had the prominent high cheekbones of a Seminole yet his features were finely chiseled, leading Beth to wonder if he were a "pure-blood." Dark, angry eyes surveyed her from a distance. They rested briefly on the swell of her breasts rising and falling beneath her soft buckskin shirt. When he had completed his slow perusal of her body, he turned and spat into the bushes beside his moccasin-encased feet.

Beth wondered what she had done to warrant such a display of disgust. Surely it had nothing to do with her sex. According to the soldiers, the Seminole had slaughtered countless women and children in their war against the United States. Why should either of these savages hesitate to kill her?

Before Beth could utter a word of protest, the masked man astride her lowered his knife and, in one deft motion, severed the cord around her waist from which a leather pouch was suspended and tossed it to his cohort. Beth groaned, not knowing if the reports the pouch contained from the commander at Fort Brooke to the commander at Fort King, would cost more lives now that they were in the hands of the enemy.

"Go now! I will meet you at the camp after I have seen the woman safely to the fort," the masked Indian ordered.

How, Beth mused, were the Seminole able to organize so much resistance against the whites when they all seemed equally bent on issuing orders? What, in heaven's name, was their chain of command?

"Have you lost your mind?" the other objected, his face incredulous. "Leave her! The soldiers will find her soon enough when the horse arrives at Fort King."

The grisly wooden head swiveled around searching the dense woods just as the high-pitched scream of a panther seeking its mate rent the still air.

"No! I will not leave her!" came the ghostly reply.

The smaller of the two Indians must have realized that to argue further would be pointless, for he turned without another word and melted quietly away among the trees. Now that Beth was alone with her captor her tension eased. Not only was she to be allowed to live, but apparently the man intended to escort her safely to Fort King. It made no sense, but she was not so foolish as to question her good fortune.

The Indian stood up and waited for her to rise, not offering her any assistance. Beth couldn't help but wonder what was hidden beneath his elaborate disguise. Had he been so disfigured in battle that the horrid mask was less repugnant than his own face? Despite the warm rays of the afternoon sun filtering through the branches overhead, she trembled at the possibility.

As she suspected, he was taller than his friend by several inches and much wider from shoulder to shoulder. His broad chest tapered to a narrow waist and as the muscles of his upper body rippled, the only sign of his impatience, Beth was awed by the sheer magnificence of the man. The mask probably added to his height yet she was still only eye level with where she imagined his chin should be. She let her eyes wander over his deeply tanned skin which showed not a single blemish. What could have happened to scar his face so badly without leaving a trace of the tragedy on the rest of his beautiful flesh? Damn, she scolded as she brushed pine needles from her backside. Here she was in the middle of nowhere with an unpredictable savage who could change his mind in a heartbeat and plunge his knife into her gut while she stood admiring his virile body. Still, he was impressive in a primitive sort of way. She shook her head to clear it of such fanciful thoughts, raising her eyes to stare into the twin hollows of the mask. She felt his own eyes looking back. Then he shrugged his broad shoulders and grunted as he pivoted and strode off into the woods.

Aloud Beth said, "Just as I expected . . . all brawn and no brain!"

The tall Indian missed a step and then continued on his way. Beth, not knowing what else to do, trailed along behind. Some hundred yards into the forest, an enormous black stallion stood placidly cropping tender shoots of grass. He wore no saddle but had a bridle from which the reins dangled to the ground. The horse raised his head and whinnied as they approached, then seemingly satisfied, went back to chomping the tender blades.

Effortlessly the Indian gathered the reins and leaped upon the horse's back then held out his hand to her. Beth looked around seeking an alternative. Finding none she placed her hand tentatively in his. He strengthened his grip and hoisted her up behind him as if she weighed no more than a feather, then kicked the animal into motion. They skirted the perimeter of the trail staying hidden among the dense foliage. The animal moved steadily forward undaunted by the tangled brush which at times was so high the Indian had to hold it over his head to prevent Beth from being scratched by the rough brambles. That he would do so took her by surprise as did the thick swirls of dark hair adorning his naked chest, something she had not noticed until she found it necessary to wrap her arms around him or risk falling. Most of the Indian braves she had seen had no body hair. Glancing down at the hard-muscled arms guiding the powerful steed, she saw that they, too, were liberally coated with a healthy amount of black thatch.

"Who are you and why are you taking me to the fort?" she dared ask when the silence grew unbearable.

He responded with another grunt that spurred Beth into recklessness.

"Damn it! Stop acting like an ass! I know you can speak English!"

She pounded one fist against his back to show her exasperation. She felt him tense then heard the all too familiar deep short sound characteristic of a hog. Given no choice she entwined her arms about his massive body once more as he kneed the horse forward. She silently seethed resenting her dependence on this uncouth barbarian who seemed determined to rescue her from a predicament for which he and his *brother* were responsible.

Beth promised herself she would not give the savage the satisfaction of asking him more questions she knew he would not answer. Soon he drew the horse to a stop reaching around to lower her none too gently to the ground. Pointing toward what appeared to be an impenetrable barrier of muscadine vines and clumps of palmetto, he turned the big black around toward the shadowed forest from where they had come.

"But . . . surely you're not going to leave me now?" she stammered, hating the pleading note in her voice.

Again he pointed toward the heavy underbrush and grunted. She looked at the jungle of vegetation before her, then turned to berate her captor for allowing her to believe he would deliver her safely to the fort. But he was gone, disappearing like a specter into the dense woods. Beth stared at the spot where she had seen the warrior only seconds before and fought the tears of helplessness she felt welling up in her eyes.

She never cried. It was a silly feminine trait that she didn't possess!

"Damn you to hell and back!" she cursed angrily, determined not to give in to her fear. Swiping at a tear she would never admit was there, she heaved a sigh then pushed aside the leafy bush where the Indian had motioned. To her amazement, there in the wide clearing beyond stood the familiar walled stockade of Fort King. He had brought her to safety after all. "Well what do you make of that?" she asked herself but could find no ready answer.

"This is an outrage!" roared a nearly apoplectic Baker Caldwell, the newly appointed commander of Fort King.

Elizabeth Townsend leaned up against the wall in a straight-backed chair balanced precariously on two wooden legs as she listened to the bewhiskered military leader rant and rave over the latest atrocity perpetrated by the elusive Seminole Indians. Safely within the confines of the fort, the danger she had felt while in the hands of the two renegades faded into a mild misadventure. Having been on the trail for nearly three days, the boyishly dressed dispatch rider stifled a yawn pulling the brim of her hat down over her eyes as the major continued to vent his spleen consigning all Indians to the fires of hell. Caldwell was a squatty little man whose uniform seemed too big for him. Beth, who was used to the tall rugged frontier type, was not impressed by his blathering.

"Let me assure you, Miss Townsend, we will catch

the two villains who dared attack you, and they shall be hanged!"

Beth leaned forward peeking from beneath the felt rim of her hat to watch a pulse in the major's temple throb. For over three years the Seminole had been at war with the United States, striking with lightning speed at the army's most vulnerable defenses then disappearing without a trace into the dense woods and impenetrable swamps of the Florida Territory. As she saw the vein gradually slow its pumping, she eased back against the wall and closed her eyes. She decided a stroke was unlikely for the time being—not that she wished the little man ill. He was just one more of a string of military misfits sent down here from Washington to put an end to the war with the Indians. It wasn't Major Caldwell's fault that he was equally as inept as his predecessors. Thank God, "Old Hickory's" term as president was at an end for Andrew Jackson's hatred of the redskins had certainly clouded his judgment in handling the relocation of the Seminole people.

Beth was wrested from her musings when she heard the door open. She cracked her lids as Sergeant Rourke entered. He left the door open as if to assure a quick means of escape. He saluted the fort's commandant then remained at attention even after Caldwell bid him "at ease."

"You sent for me, Major?" inquired the baby-faced soldier unable to disguise the quiver of apprehension in his voice.

Beth snorted in derision at the youth's subservient manner. Brian Rourke had turned nineteen more than a month ago, the same age as she and her twin

15

brother, Edward. Yet to Beth's way of thinking he was still a little boy kowtowing to old "Baker, Baker, the Blunder maker"! For all his fancy uniform, Brian had no backbone. Thank God, the soldiers at Fort Brooke knew how to stand tall. Without their determination to make the Territory of Florida a safe place to live, the settlers might just as well head back North and leave this land of promise in the hands of the Indians.

"Damn right I sent for you, Rourke! Thirty minutes ago to be exact!" the major reprimanded pulling his large round watch from his pocket and glaring at its face. "Don't you realize we are at war? Time is of the essence!"

Sergeant Rourke cast a nervous glance in Beth's direction, disbelieving that the unladylike noise he had heard could have come from her. Caldwell seemed oblivious to any sound other than that of his own voice as he continued his diatribe. Puffing up like a pouter pigeon the commander approached his subordinate tapping him on the chest as he spoke. He reminded Beth of the way her diminutive Aunt 'Becca gained attention when she wanted a point made clear.

"Tell me, Sergeant Rourke," Caldwell sneered into the frightened face of the young officer. "Did or did not Miss Townsend's horse appear at the gates of this fort over an hour before she herself staggered out of the wilderness?"

Beth rolled her eyes heavenward. Her entrance could hardly be described as "staggering out of the wilderness." Actually she thought her arrival was rather "plucky" all things considered.

"Y . . . yes, sir," Brian stammered focusing his gaze

somewhere over the major's shoulder. "Yes, sir," he repeated with a little more confidence. "You see, sir, we were in the midst of trying to decide the direction from which the horse came so we could send out a search party when Beth . . . I mean, Miss Townsend, ran out of the woods."

Major Caldwell's face changed rapidly from ruddy to beet red. The telltale vein took up its wild beating once again. Beth pushed her hat back and stared openly. Finally, this had to be it! At the least it was a seizure of moderate proportions.

Rourke cringed as Caldwell shouted in response to his explanation. "You spent an hour discussing where to begin the search knowing Miss Townsend was out there alone in the damned woods?"

Beth watched the fort's leader rise up on his toes while his chest swelled with indignation. She half expected him to ascend like a balloon until he hit his head on the rafters above. Before the younger man could stammer a reply in his own defense, a large shadow blocked the open doorway.

"Excuse me, Major, but I need to talk . . ."

The deep voice broke off as the newcomer noticed the other occupants in the room. Beth leaned forward to look up at the tall stranger whose huge frame blotted out the last rays of the late afternoon sunshine. The front legs of the chair thumped against the hardwood floor.

Taking a deep breath, Caldwell sought to bring his temper under control. "Yes, Hawkins! Come in! Come in!" He motioned the visitor inside, unable to hide his irritation at the interruption.

The man called Hawkins had to duck his head beneath the doorjamb to enter the room, but Beth paid scant heed to his above average height. Her attention was caught by the impeccable cut of the black frock coat hugging his broad shoulders then tapering to a lean waist. Her gaze traveled the long length of his body past tight-fitting black trousers down to a pair of highly polished knee-high boots. The only relief to his somber attire was his snowy white linen shirt and neatly tied cravat decorated by a gold, ornamental pin.

Beth snickered, her lips curling with distaste as she wondered what this dandified fop could be doing at Fort King. He looked as out of place as a gator up a live oak tree.

"I can see you are busy, Caldwell," came the strong, baritone voice. "What I have to say can wait until another time."

In no way could the stranger's words be interpreted as an apology for his intrusion. His tone denoted the self-assured arrogance of one not used to biding his time. Obviously, he had little regard for the man to whom he spoke. Surprised that a visitor would talk to the major in such a manner, Beth looked up into a pair of the coldest eyes she had ever seen, eyes not gray and not green but an unusual combination of both. Raven-colored hair was drawn neatly back and tied with a ribbon at the nape of his neck. He had a thin, aristocratic nose and a wide mouth held firm in a way which made Beth doubt his ability to smile.

In all fairness she had to admit that his face was put together rather nicely, but there was about it a decided lack of warmth. For some unaccountable reason he brought to mind the Indian who had

18

concealed his face behind the hideous wooden mask. She wondered if this stranger might also have something to hide taking refuge beneath a veil of indifference.

"Not at all, Hawkins. Sergeant Rourke was just leaving and I'm sure Miss Townsend would like to rest after her long journey from Fort Brooke. We'll discuss this later, Rourke," he said accompanying his curt dismissal with a look that promised the matter would not be forgotten. Brian saluted then made a hasty retreat.

Beth stood up and rubbed the aching muscles in the small of her back. Baker Caldwell had not spoken to her directly, but she knew she too had been dismissed. Her curiosity was piqued for she had never known the gruff little commander to buckle under to anyone, yet in the presence of this elegantly dressed, inscrutable gentleman, the major acted positively obsequious. Who the hell was this man?

As if she had spoken aloud, Caldwell held out his arm to halt her progress toward the door. "Miss Townsend, I would like you to meet Mr. Hawkins who has been sent here from Washington to look into the Indian situation in the Territory."

That the major would have preferred to let her slip away unnoticed was apparent by the resignation in his voice. His introduction also explained his attitude toward Mr. Hawkins. Beth knew enough about the conflict between the Indians and the soldiers to understand why Baker Caldwell was worried. Things had not gone well for the army and Caldwell's entire military career could depend on what this haughty politician told the "bigwigs" up in Washington.

"Ah, yes. Miss Townsend," Hawkins acknowledged.

Beth would have sworn his long nose lifted slightly before he nodded his head in her direction then turned back to Caldwell.

"This is a coincidence since Miss Townsend is precisely what, or should I say whom, I wish to speak to you about."

The major flushed beneath the larger man's sarcasm as Beth felt her hackles rise. Before either could speak, Hawkins went on. "I would like an explanation as to why, with all the money Congress has appropriated to fight this blasted war, the army is so hard pressed for couriers that it has become necessary to use women?"

The commander seemed to shrink under the cold hazel eyes of the disdainful informant. To Beth's way of thinking Hawkins was no more than a spy sent here to find fault with the efforts being made to relocate the Seminole west of the Mississippi. Though she had little confidence in the military leaders sent to Florida by President Jackson and President-elect Van Buren, she took his criticism as a direct insult to her family who had lived in the territory for more than a decade. She thought of her father and her Uncle Lance who had played an important role in the establishment of Fort Brooke and the little settlement the Indians called Tampa. There was her twin brother Edward, who though born in England, was now as dedicated to this land as Davey, her handsome, half-breed cousin by marriage. Her crystal blue eyes snapped with defiance as the major did what he could to make matters worse.

"I take it you are aware that Miss Townsend narrowly escaped an Indian attack today?" he replied feigning nonchalance as he tried to downplay the near tragedy.

" 'Narrowly escaped'?" Hawkins ground out between clenched teeth.

After glaring at Baker Caldwell for a long moment, Hawkins rounded on Beth, his expression forbidding. "And what have you to say, *Miss* Townsend? Did you indeed 'narrowly escape' attack?"

Beth's first reaction was to take a step backward but she forced herself to stand firm. "Actually, *Mr.* Hawkins, I narrowly escaped *death!*" she clarified to the major's chagrin.

Why did she have the feeling Hawkins already knew all of this? Damn the man for prying!

"What I mean is that I *was* attacked but the Indians chose to let me go unharmed."

The nose of her inquisitor lifted once again and this time there was no mistaking his contempt. "Is that a fact?" he asked mockingly. "And just why do you suppose the bloodthirsty savages *chose* to let you go?"

Beth was momentarily at a loss for words. "I . . . I really don't know," she stuttered truthfully for the same question had been plaguing her since her release.

"Oh come now. Surely there has to be a logical explanation." He paused to consider, bracing his right elbow with his left hand as he stroked his clean shaven chin. "Perhaps it was your feminine attire that so attracted the heathens they could not bring themselves to do you injury." Frigid gray-green eyes drifted over her dusty buckskins and well-worn boots. "Or could it be they were captivated by the color of your hair while it was cleverly concealed beneath that sweat stained excuse for a hat."

Beth seethed as he continued his ruthless assessment. Though he dressed like a gentleman, his manners were reprehensible.

"Then again, maybe fierce warriors are enamored by girls who look like boys."

Now he had gone too far and Beth's temper took over. Raising her arms with claws outstretched she lunged toward the man who would dare belittle her with his cruel words. She was unprepared for the speed with which he grasped her wrists as she tried to scratch his eyes out. Before she could inflict the damage she intended, her wrists were caught and she was yanked against an iron-hard chest. Their eyes locked as Beth struggled to pull free, her rapid breathing pushing her small breasts against his coat.

The major rushed in to separate the two. "Here now, Hawkins! Unhand Miss Townsend this instant!"

Beth staggered backward as she was quickly released. Something electrifying had happened when she and the brutish lout had touched. She knew he had felt it, too. Surprised by the strength in the hands that had held her, she stared into eyes as cold as a Cornish winter.

"You bastard! Damn you to Hell and back," she cursed daring her tears of rage to fall for she was certain the stone hearted troublemaker would gain enormous satisfaction by any show of weakness on her part.

Hawkins merely laughed, an evil sneer tilting his

lips. "Could it be the red devils were entranced by your eloquent vocabulary?"

Beth drew her hand back to slap the smirk from the face of this man whom she recognized as her adversary. Again he was ready for her, grabbing her arm he held her away from him as he clacked his tongue in disappointment. "Some people just never learn," he jeered.

God, how she hated him. Somehow she would make him pay for the humiliation he had put her through. Damn! She almost wished the two renegades had kept her! Even they had treated her with more courtesy than this spawn of Satan. But they had let her go. Again the unanswered question rang through her mind. *Why?*

Without another word for either man, she stomped to the door and slammed it shut behind her.

Chapter Two

Beth lay neck-deep in the warm water taking pleasure in soaking off the grime of the trail. The five-mile ride out to the farm of her friends, the McAfees, had done little to defuse her temper. The nerve of that city-bred dung heap insinuating that she had failed to deliver the army dispatches from Fort Brooke because she was a woman. She was certain a man would have suffered the same fate. Why she and Davey together would not have stood a chance against the two savages who had accosted her!

She closed her eyes and saw again the macabre mask of the man who had captured her then set her free. As she raised her arm toward the lamplight, studying the iridescent coating of suds, the door burst open and Maggie McAfee rushed in without knocking.

"Did you see him, Beth? But of course you must have," she replied answering her own question. "Isn't he the most gorgeous man in the whole world? A Greek god only more perfect. Everytime I look at him I'm afraid I will just melt right away and end up a puddle at his feet."

Beth groaned and sank deeper into the metal tub until the water tickled her earlobes. Next to Davey Logan, Maggie McAfee was her best friend even though they had little in common. Maggie was everything Beth was not and hoped she would never be. She scowled at the yards and yards of ruffled blue dimity, a shade exactly matching the girl's cornflower blue eyes, as Maggie twirled around the room then came to an abrupt halt leaning against the tub's rim. Curly blond hair framed her delicate heart shaped face. Her rosebud lips pouted as she waited for Beth to say something.

"Thanks for warning me, Maggie," Beth replied sucking in her cheeks. "If you disappear on a sunny day and I hear a splash I'll know what happened."

The blond girl looked down nonplused. "What do you mean by that? Why must you always talk in riddles?"

Unable to keep the laughter from her voice, Beth explained, "You just said you were going to melt at the feet of some Greek god. Afterward I imagine Zeus or Apollo or whomever you're talking about will have to step on you to get by. Splash!"

Maggie stood up and turned her back on her friend. "I swear, Elizabeth Townsend! You haven't got a romantic bone in your body."

Beth lifted a long, slender leg and rubbed the lather into her skin. "You really shouldn't swear, Maggie. It isn't ladylike."

Maggie swung around, her eyes nearly popping

from her head. "Oooh! Talk about the pot calling the kettle! You know more cuss words than the soldiers and the trappers combined. I swear I don't know where you pick them all up!"

"There you go again. Your momma's going to wash your mouth out with soap, Margaret Mc-Afee," Beth declared shaking her head as she massaged her other leg.

"Will you be serious?" implored Maggie spinning toward the tub once again. "I'm asking if you met Robin while you were at the fort." She clutched Beth's slippery arm and gave it a shake. "I swear, Elizabeth, Robin is the kind of man dreams are made of," she gushed.

"Jesus, Maggie! Will you stop swearing? And no, I didn't meet any robin at the fort. Sounds like a bird that flies South for the winter. A sure sign of weakness. No stamina! No fortitude!"

"That's it! I am never going to speak to you again!" Maggie vowed stamping her dainty, little blue-slippered foot. "Do you know what you are, Elizabeth?" she went on immediately forgetting her promise of silence.

Beth sighed. "No, but I'm sure you are about to tell me."

"You are a cynic, Beth Townsend. Yes, that's exactly what you are. A cynic!"

The husky laughter that filled the room was hardly what Maggie had expected.

"God almighty! Where did you hear a word like that?" Beth asked sitting up a little straighter as she reached a hand to rub tears of mirth from her

26

cheeks and ended up getting soap in her eyes instead.

Hands on her hips, Maggie retorted sharply, "For your information I read it in a book and it describes you perfectly! When it comes to men you are skeptical, suspicious, disbelieving. . . . Oh, just forget it! Besides, I'm not speaking to you anymore," she repeated flouncing toward the door. "Anyone who doesn't recognize Robin Hawkins as the most handsome man God ever created is hopeless! Totally hopeless!"

Her words hung in the air as she left without a backward glance. Beth stared at the closed door dumbfounded. Robin Hawkins? Dear God! Her capricious young friend was infatuated with the man Beth detested above all others. She slid down into the metal tub until her head was submerged beneath the water's surface. Bubbles floated through the air as she voiced her opinion of Maggie's latest heartthrob.

Beth pushed back from the table and patted her full belly. "Martha, you have to be the best cook in the whole territory," she said sincerely, addressing the plump little figure coming out of the kitchen.

"Now, Elizabeth. You know the only thing that kind of talk is going to get you is another piece of apple pie," Martha McAfee smiled as she wiped her hands on the apron tied around her ample middle.

Beth groaned shaking her head. "No, please. I couldn't eat another bite."

"Tsh! You're nothing but skin and bones."

Beth, who had known the McAfees for nearly five years and regarded them as family, chuckled at Martha's scolding.

"You sound just like Rachel and 'Becca," she answered, her cinnamon brows drawing together at the memory of how worried her stepmother and her aunt had been when they found out she was making this trip alone. "I reckon they're the next best cooks in the Territory, though they would have to combine their efforts to come up with a fare equal to this," she qualified taking in the remains of the succulent roast pork, baked squash, new potatoes, and fresh greens left on the plate.

As a rule Beth was stingy with her praise, but it did her heart good to see Martha McAfee's face light up with pleasure over well deserved compliments.

From the head of the table Patrick McAfee interjected good-naturedly, "I'll bet the problem is getting this firefly to light long enough to sample what is put before her." He grinned at their slender, copper-haired guest.

Maggie and Abigail, her younger sister, giggled and Beth joined in the laughter. "That sure wasn't the case tonight, Patrick. I feel like one of those prize hogs you're readying for market. Have you heard from Peter lately?" she asked steering the conversation away from herself.

The jovial atmosphere changed abruptly.

"Far as we know he's still with an army patrol somewhere south of here," Martha offered.

28

Patrick McAfee frowned. "Ought to be home helping with the crops and the livestock, not off in the swamps chasing Injuns," he muttered.

"Now, Pa. You know Peter's only doing his duty." Maggie looked pleadingly toward Beth. Apparently her brother's enlistment in the army was a subject not to be broached at the supper table.

Beth lifted her hand to cover a yawn, and Martha was immediately by her side placing a comforting arm about her shoulders. "Just listen to us going on," she clucked. "Why you must be exhausted, child! Maggie, you take Beth off to bed right this minute while Abigail and I see to the dishes," she ordered like a general marshaling his troops. "And mind you, don't stay awake all night gossiping," she admonished hurrying the two of them toward the stairs.

I doubt anything will keep me awake tonight, Beth thought as she snuggled beneath the light-weight quilt.

Beside her Maggie whispered, "Beth? You still haven't told me what you think of Robin Hawkins."

Beth rolled over and began making soft snoring sounds.

"Where the devil have you been, Hawk?" There was accusation in the voice of Asi-yahola as he tossed aside the half-eaten rabbit leg and rose to greet the man who had quietly entered the camp where a dozen or so braves sat around an open fire.

"The fort," came the brisk reply.

29

"Did it take you two days to deposit the woman at the gates?"

The tall, fierce-looking warrior answered with a question of his own, "You call that foulmouthed boy-girl a woman?"

Asi-yahola chuckled, his good humor quickly restored by his friend's mounting irritation. "As I recall, it was you who pointed out that she was a woman, and it was you who took it upon yourself to see her safely to the fort."

Hawk glared at the other man. "There is no need to remind me of my foolishness."

"I didn't say you were foolish, my friend. Our war is not with women and children. Come and have something to eat. Then you can tell me what punishment the fearless white major has decided to mete out on us as payment for sparing the life of his little courier."

He slapped the taller man on the back as together they joined the others around the campfire.

Later that night Hawk lay awake beneath a blanket of stars trying to erase the memory of sparkling blue eyes as clear as the water of the little spring the Indians called Weekiwachee. Why couldn't he forget the young hellion? It wasn't as if he hadn't had his share of women. There was no conceit on his part in admitting that more than one of the fair sex had begged for his favors. Elizabeth Townsend had about as much appeal as a gelded stallion. Why should he be thinking of her when he could dream of one of the many buxom wenches he had bedded over the past ten of his twenty-seven years? Yet he

30

could still feel her supple young breasts pressed against his chest begging for attention, see the stubborn jut of her chin and her moist pink lips trembling beneath the onslaught of his unbridled tongue as he did his best to undermine her self-confidence.

Damn her for making him feel guilty! Knowing there would be no sleep for him tonight, Hawk stood up and walked quietly across the silent clearing to throw a handful of sticks on the smoldering embers. The wood crackled as flames sparked to life—reddish flames the color of her hair.

"Rarely have I known the Hawk to lose sleep over a woman."

Asi-yahola moved to take a place beside the troubled warrior. Hawk saw no point in denying what they both knew to be true. "Your perception is as sharp as ever, 'Black Drink Crier.'" He had purposely used the English translation of the other man's name. It was a useless attempt to try and come to terms with his own identity.

Asi-yahola studied the rough chiseled planes of the halfbreed's face silhouetted in the firelight. "I sense there is more that troubles you besides the woman." He waited patiently not wanting to intrude where he wasn't welcomed but ready should his friend need a willing listener.

For a long while the two men sat in companionable silence watching sparks shoot skyward. Finally Hawk spoke, "I was only twelve summers when my parents died and my uncle came to take me to live with him in the North. He gave me everything money could buy. A fine home, the best schools

31

and, in addition, he gave me love and understanding. Never once did he ask me to forget the part of me that was Indian."

The story was familiar to Asi-yahola who had known Hawk before he had been uprooted and taken to live in the nation's capital. He knew how hard it had been for the wild young buck to adjust to a life not of his own choosing. Now Hawk was tearing himself apart trying to reconcile the differences between his two worlds and there was little he could do but lend an ear.

"Your mother was a princess, the daughter of a tribal chief."

"And my father was a trapper who felt more comfortable among the Indians than with his own people," Hawk finished.

"We became his people as we are yours."

"Only time will show me the right road to follow," Hawk sighed. "But enough talk of the past. It is time to plan for the future. Was there anything of importance in the dispatches we intercepted?"

"Much of importance. I wish we had not prevented their delivery."

Hawk arched thick black brows. "Why?"

"The pouch contained a letter written by Colonel Worth at Fort Brooke encouraging Major Caldwell to initiate a meeting with our chiefs so that together they could try to work out a plan for peace."

"Do you believe his intentions are honorable?" Hawk asked hoping against hope that it was not too late for a compromise that would enable the Indians to keep the lands they had claimed as theirs.

Asi-yahola considered carefully before answering. "I trust no white man, but unlike the soldiers at Fort King who were sent here to wage war, most of the men at Fort Brooke came as settlers to the Territory long before the present conflict began. I have heard of a man there who may even be sympathetic to our cause."

Hawk gave his companion a doubtful look. "Who is this man?"

"His name is Lance Logan. He came to Florida before Fort Brooke was established as an outpost. He lived with a woman of the Calusa tribe. A few years after her death he married an Englishwoman."

Hawk's interest was aroused. "What makes you think we can count on this Lance Logan to help us?"

"He has always treated the Indians fairly offering them the protection of the fort when times were hard. To my knowledge he has never killed a man unless his own life was threatened. He has a halfbreed son who, like you, has been allowed to retain his Indian heritage."

"You seem to know a lot about the man," Hawk acknowledged. "It never hurts to have a friend in the enemy camp."

Asi-yahola stood up, paused, then added, "There's one more fact about Logan that may be of interest to you."

"And what is that?"

"He has quite a large family at Fort Brooke including a niece."

Hawk stared up at his tribal brother, his forehead

33

creased. "Why should I concern myself with his niece?"

"No reason at all," the Indian grinned, "except that the lady in question is a redheaded firebrand named Elizabeth Townsend."

Robin Hawkins took a deep breath before knocking on the door of the commander's office. He had done all he could for the moment. The next move was up to Baker Caldwell.

"Come in!" came the brusque response to his sharp rap.

The major paused in his pacing, his ruddy face registering surprise as Robin entered. "Oh, it's you, Hawkins. I sent for Sergeant Rourke twenty minutes ago," he fumed glaring at his watch. "Where the Hell is he?"

"You sent for me, sir?" Brian answered running into Robin's back as he skidded to a stop just inside the door.

The commander looked ready to explode. "Where did this come from, Rourke?" he demanded thrusting several pieces of paper in Brian's direction.

Nervously the young officer tried to get a look at the sheets of vellum being waved in his face. "Wh . . . what is it, sir?"

Caldwell continued to shake the pages in the air. "It's a letter from Colonel Worth at Fort Brooke. Where did it come from?"

Brian's expression was blank. "Wh . . . what does it say, sir?"

"It's none of your business what it says! I want to know how it got here!" The major's words echoed from the rafters.

"I . . . I have no idea, sir."

Robin turned toward the window unable to keep his lips from twitching at the baffled expression on Sergeant Rourke's face.

"Well you had damned well better find out right quick unless you prefer swamp patrol to acting as my second in command. You have exactly one hour to discover how someone could have gotten into this office during the night and put this document on my desk! Do I make myself clear, Sergeant!"

"Yes . . . yes, sir," Brian stammered, saluting sharply as he backed out of the office.

Caldwell collapsed in his chair as the door closed, seeming to have forgotten that he was not alone. He jumped when Robin spoke.

"Excuse me, Major, but if that letter is from Fort Brooke, it must have been brought by courier."

"The only courier to arrive at this fort within the past week was Elizabeth Townsend. This letter is dated five days ago. It had to be the document stolen from Miss Townsend by those damnable redskins. So how the hell did it get on my desk?" Infuriated, Caldwell waited as if daring his unwelcome visitor to come up with an answer.

"Hmm. . . ." Robin puckered his brow thoughtfully. "Is it possible the Indians might want you to have whatever information is contained in the letter?"

Baker Caldwell looked up in surprise. "As a matter of fact, Colonel Worth is urging me to try and arrange a peace conference with the tribal leaders of the Seminole," he answered, leaning back in his chair to consider Hawkins's suggestion. He slammed his fist against the desk. "But that doesn't explain how the document got here! By God, if there's a leak in the security at this fort, I'll plug it with somebody's bottom!" he blustered.

"Surely, Caldwell, you don't mean to imply that one of those murdering savages might actually have sneaked past the guards and entered the fort last night?" Robin managed to look properly horrified at the notion. He rubbed his jaw contemplatively. "I hesitate to think what they might have to say about this in Washington."

The major leaped to his feet. "Now just wait a minute!" he exploded. "I never said the Indians were responsible for putting this on my desk! That was your idea!"

"Well it's as good as any you've come up with," Robin countered, taking advantage of the opportunity to nettle the pompous little tyrant. "Perhaps you could get them to do it more often. With the enemy acting as courier you would have no reason to use a woman."

The major's jaws opened and closed like a steel trap but he was too angry to speak. Just then they were interrupted by a hesitant knock.

"Enter!" Caldwell screeched, his voice an abnormally high-pitched falsetto.

Wide blue eyes peered around the edge of the door.

"Sorry for the intrusion, Major," Beth apologized for she had heard Caldwell bellowing long before she reached his office.

Seeing Robin Hawkins standing by the window was explanation enough for the commander's ill temper. Beth felt her lip curl contemptuously and spared only a glance at the impudent outsider as she strode across the room and stood before the desk. What could Maggie possibly see in the obnoxious son of a warthog?

"I'll be heading back to Fort Brooke this morning, Major. Have you any messages for me to deliver?"

"I'll have a letter ready shortly. I wouldn't want to delay your departure." He shifted his eyes toward the tall man leaning against the far wall.

Robin jerked to attention, the quickness of his movement putting Beth immediately on guard. "Caldwell! If this is your idea of a joke, it isn't funny!"

"A joke?" Baker spluttered. "What do you mean?"

"Surely you don't intend to allow Miss Townsend to leave the fort after what has already happened to her?"

Allow indeed! Beth was about to remind the conceited jackass that she needed no one's permission to take her leave when the major came to her rescue.

"Mr. Hawkins! Whether you like it or not, Miss Townsend is a courier between this garrison and Fort Brooke. If I had the manpower available I would offer her an escort but it so happens most of my men are out on patrol right now. Even if they were here, they would only slow her down."

Beth smirked knowing the truth of the major's words.

"Besides," Caldwell went on, managing to undermine his own argument, "since Miss Townsend has decided to leave us, I assure you there is nothing I can do to detain her short of locking her in the guardhouse."

"Then do it!" Hawkins barked.

Caldwell looked down as if something about the tips of his boots required his immediate attention and Beth felt suddenly uneasy. Just who was this man with the power to intimidate the fort's chief officer?

"Enough!" she shouted into the silence that followed. Rounding on Robin, she planted her fisted hands on her slender hips. Challenging him with her eyes she said defiantly, "No one holds me against my will, Mr. Hawkins! If I am not back at Fort Brooke day after tomorrow my family is going to come looking for me. And when they find the culprit responsible for my delay, my uncle is going to chew him up, spit him out, and leave the pieces for the buzzards while the others cheer him on!"

Their eyes met and held. Never had Robin witnessed such a sight. Sparks fired by determination shot from nearly translucent blue crystals drawing him like a moth to a flame. What was it about this ill-bred hoyden that made him want to protect her? Here she was promising an abomination even the

Indians would find distasteful and all he wanted to do was pull her into his arms and shield her from any who might cause her harm.

Robin was the first to drop his eyes. Somehow the situation had gotten entirely out of hand. Priding himself on his iron control, here he was trading insults with a fiery termagant who looked more like a boy than a girl. If he wasn't careful, this she-cat would jeopardize the outcome of the well laid plans which had brought him back to the Territory.

He forced himself to calm down and even managed a rueful smile. "My apologies, Major Caldwell. I seem to have overstepped the bounds of propriety in my concern for the young lady's welfare."

While the major looked decidedly relieved, Beth eyed Robin suspiciously. He didn't appear to be a man who backed down easily and his reference to her being a lady, young or otherwise, hinted at devious motives.

"If possible I would accompany Miss Townsend myself. However, I must journey to Tallahassee to meet with the governor. I can only urge you," he said looking at Beth, "to use the utmost caution. We can only hope that will be enough."

His sincerity rang false to his own ears, but the room's other two occupants seemed willing to accept his words at face value. Caldwell smiled broadly unable to hide his delight over Hawkins's imminent departure while Beth was already moving toward the door.

Speaking to the commander, she said, "I'll be

waiting at the stables when the dispatches are ready."

"May your trip prove uneventful, Miss Townsend," Robin bade to her rigid back.

The door closed behind her, but not before he heard a most unladylike snort.

Chapter Three

It was the same trail she had ridden dozens of times before, a narrow ribbon of hard-packed earth lined with scrub brush and clumps of palmetto. Pine trees grew straight and tall upon the hillocks while just ahead lay the swamplands where cypress domes dotted the horizon like giant mushrooms. One dared not stray from the beaten path for unexpected dangers lurked among the waist-high marsh grass. Beth reined in her horse as she rounded a bend in the road and stood up in the stirrups craning her neck to survey the land. She was jittery despite the cloudless blue sky overhead and the natural noises of wild woodland creatures scurrying among the bushes.

Close by a flock of egrets took flight startling her mount and causing him to sidestep. Beth muttered an oath. She had stopped so often it was no wonder the animal was nervous. At this rate it would take her a week to reach home. And it was all *his* fault! That damned Hawkins!

"May your trip prove uneventful," she mimicked

aloud. Oh, his words sounded innocent enough, but to Beth they were as good as a curse for she knew he wished her nothing less than the plague.

She wondered how two people could become so antagonistic toward each other on such short acquaintance. After all, he wasn't a bad looking man. He was big and despite his fancy clothes he was not at all like some of the dandies she had met when her Uncle Lance had taken her to Tallahassee a few years ago. On the surface he was everything she admired most in the few men she thought worthy of admiring at all. Yes, on the outside he reminded her of her uncle and Davey. But on the inside he was an opinionated bully who would smother a woman with his highhanded ways. Beth wondered if he were married. She pictured a mousy little woman hanging on her husband's every word and never dreaming of speaking her own mind.

The sun dipped lower in the western sky. Beth was exhausted but her tiredness was more mental than physical for she was used to being in the saddle for long periods of time. She would make camp at Big Bass Creek, get a good night's sleep, then start out fresh in the morning. The knowledge that while she moved south, Robin Hawkins was traveling northwest toward the capital, gave her sagging spirits a lift. Yes indeed! The more miles between the two of them, the better she would feel. She hoped her peace of mind would increase with each yard that separated them.

* * *

Hidden among the trees, the hooded eyes of a lone figure watched the girl as she drew her horse to a halt. Hawk knew that Asi-yahola and his warriors were on their way to Payne's Landing to meet with the great chief, Micanopy, bringing him news of what was contained in the letter from Colonel Worth. There was little danger of Elizabeth Townsend running into trouble on this trip. So why was he here? he asked himself disgruntledly. And the answer came more readily than he cared to admit. Since the moment she had first opened those startling blue eyes and stared in horror at the hideous mask he was forced to wear, he had come under the spell of the red-haired spitfire. She was unlike any woman he had ever met. Instead of fainting or screaming in terror, she had reached out to touch the rough wood that covered his face. In doing so, she had touched his very soul.

She was too daring for her own good, he scowled as he watched her standing up in the stirrups to study the terrain. What she needed was a firm hand . . . liberally applied to her backside, he added as his mouth curved into a wry grin. Gazing at the aforementioned part of her anatomy as Beth twisted first to the left, then to the right, he wondered how his blood brother could possibly have mistaken her for a boy. He remembered the swell of her breasts as she fought to free herself

43

from his grasp, the slight rounding of her hips caught in a vise between his knees. A contradiction of innocence and experience, she was journeying alone along a trail fraught with danger.

Hawk balled his fists as Beth kicked her booted heels into the horse's side and took off at a reckless gallop. Experience, Hell! She was just plain stupid! What kind of upbringing could she have had in a fort filled with ragtag soldiers? Surely she had been exposed to a modicum of feminine influence! But if so, the women in her life must have been very poor examples for Elizabeth Townsend obviously preferred to look, act, and talk like a man. Hawk's anger surged as he remembered the gleaming red tresses falling about her shoulders when he had snatched that unsightly hat from her head. What a waste! Knowing of only one person with whom she was connected, he cursed Lance Logan beneath his breath. The man may believe in justice for the Indians, but for what he had allowed to happen to his niece, he should be horsewhipped. It was time the little hoyden learned the difference between a man and a woman. He might even be willing to show her the pleasures each could give to the other.

God! What was he thinking? Surely he had not become so crazed from this damnable war that he would force himself on an innocent young woman then justify his actions by saying it was for her own good! Common sense warred with the growing ache in his loins. No! He had never taken a woman against her will and he didn't intend to start now. But somehow he had to make her see that she didn't belong out here in the woods alone. She should stay at home, find a man to protect her, have some children.

Suddenly he knew what he would do . . . how he could discourage the little hoyden's solitary sojourns. And he wouldn't have to lay a hand on her. He stroked the ugly mask hanging by his side as a smile of satisfaction played upon his narrow lips.

Beth sat cross-legged upon her bedding, watching the flames from the fire leap into the air releasing tiny sparks that flared then disappeared into the black, moonless night. Leaning closer to the heat, she wrapped her arms around her to ward off a chill of apprehension that had nothing to do with the warm nocturnal temperature.

Hawk moved from the shelter of the trees on silent moccasin-clad feet until he stood directly behind her. Thick titian hair hung loose about her slender shoulders shining like polished copper in the light. His hands itched to feel the silky softness flow through his fingers. He wondered what it would be like if she ever allowed her fiery temperament to blaze with passion instead of anger, to see those intense blue eyes burning with desire instead of defiance.

Sensing his presence, Beth turned her head and

45

stared up at the masked man looming over her, his naked chest bronzed by the glow of the fire-light. She was neither surprised nor frightened by his appearance though she could not say why. She turned back toward the fire as if he wasn't there.

"Why are you not afraid?" he asked, his bewilderment evident despite his distorted voice.

Beth answered with a shrug, then said, "You will not hurt me." And she knew it was true.

Instead of confirming or denying her words, Hawk lashed out harshly, "You deserve to be hurt! You beg to be hurt for you deliberately place yourself in dangerous situations. Do you not value your life?"

For a man who had scarcely spoken to her at their previous meeting, he was now unaccountably verbose, but Beth hid her confusion by answering with another shrug.

"Can you do nothing but shrug your shoulders?" he growled.

"You grunt, I shrug," Beth retorted, pleased at her ability to irritate the man. whose face she could not see. "I'd say we match in our choices of expression."

His voice softened perceptibly. "I agree that two people can often communicate best without words."

Beth wondered what the rogue hoped to achieve with his muted, ambiguous talk. She felt more comfortable when they were sparring.

His manner became curt once more and she relaxed beneath his hollow gaze. "Why do you endanger yourself by traveling alone at night?"

Impatiently Beth repeated, "I'm not afraid of you."

Hawk chose to ignore what he could not understand. "You had no way of knowing who was stalking you. It could have been anyone," he challenged.

Beth had no ready reply. How could she tell him that she had felt his presence close by ever since she had ridden through the gates of Fort King this morning? If she could not explain the magnetism that seemed to be drawing them together, how could she possibly enlighten this savage stranger who chose to keep his identity a secret?

"There is no point arguing about what might have happened. You are the one who has invaded my camp and disturbed my solitude. Why did you follow me?" she demanded intending to put him on the defensive.

She gasped as powerful hands reached down and pulled her to her feet pivoting her body around until she was faced with his broad bare chest. Her heart began to beat a rapid staccato within her breast but again her reaction had nothing to do with fear. Her arms tingled where he touched her, and she found herself leaning toward instead of away from his muscular body.

"I'm disappointed in you, Miss Townsend. Even a half-wit would realize I am here to relieve you of the document you carry."

The amusement in his voice served to snap Beth out of the trancelike spell he seemed to have cast over her. What had she expected? Did she really think he had followed her because he felt some attraction for her as a woman? Angry and humiliated, she tried without success to pull from his grasp.

"You bastard!" she spat.

"Not really, but my family history is not important. The letter, if you please," he commanded, his voice as cold and as brittle as ice.

Beth remained rigid in his arms. "How do you know my name?"

"I have ways of finding out what I want to know."

And ways of sneaking documents inside the fort, Beth decided, remembering the mysterious reappearance of the stolen dispatch. The man was more dangerous and more powerful than she had suspected but she could be just as cunning.

Hawk loosened his grip as she reached for the pouch secured to the belt encircling her trim waist. With deliberate slowness she unfastened the clasp and handed the leather bag to him. "If you are determined to steal the major's letter, I can't stop you. But you're making a big mistake." Beth tried to sound impassive but it was impossible. Too many lives were at risk.

The supplication in her voice plus the fact that he resented being called a thief forced Hawk to reconsider his actions. In truth, he placed little significance in what Caldwell had written. Any man with a smattering of intelligence would know better than to rely on information provided by that ineffectual fool. His reasons for following Elizabeth Townsend had nothing to do with what was in the leather pouch he now held in his hand. The motive behind his pursuit was to scare the pants off her, figuratively speaking of course, so that she would stay home where she belonged and stop trying to be something she wasn't.

"And just what is in here that would benefit my people were I to allow you to take it to Fort Brooke?" he asked, tossing the bag lightly in the air.

Beth hated his condescending manner yet she forced herself to swallow her resentment toward the offensive heathen. If there was the slightest chance that she could convince him to give her back the letter, she had to take it. She knew that the only way of persuading him was to tell the truth.

"Major Caldwell has agreed to do what he can to arrange a meeting between the leaders of the Seminole and the army."

"Caldwell has more wisdom than I gave him credit for."

"He had little choice," Beth countered. "The men at Fort Brooke wield a great deal of influence in the Territory, and they're not about to see this land destroyed by senseless fighting."

"I'm relieved to know that Fort Brooke has produced a few intelligent people."

Enraged by his insinuation, Beth let her arm fly in the direction of his face but it was caught in a cruel grip long before her open palm could connect with its target.

"You little fool!" he hissed. "You could have shattered every bone from your wrist to your elbow!"

Only then did she remember the hard, wooden mask that he wore, and the knowledge that he had probably saved her from a painful injury fueled the flames of her temper.

"Go to Hell, you low-bellied snake! You have what you came for. Now get out of my camp!"

Beth had never experienced such blinding rage. She wanted to lash out at him and hurt him. Knowing she hadn't the strength to do so brought tears of frustration to her eyes, illuminating their crystal depths until they sparkled like the clearest cut diamonds.

"You're wrong, little spitfire." Hawk released her arm and placed the leather case in her hands. "I don't have what I came for . . . yet!"

Beth took an involuntary step backward as her heart skipped a beat. She had meant it earlier when she said she was not afraid of the towering warrior, but now she was not so sure. How could one predict the behavior of an uncivilized redskin? Looking up at the crudely sculpted headcovering, she willed her voice to remain steady. "What is it you want from me?"

She held her breath as all sorts of horrifying possibilities flitted through her mind. Would he take off his mask and force her to look upon his ravaged face? Would he compel her to kiss his twisted lips? Or would he demand the ultimate sacrifice . . . her innocence? He seemed in no hurry to answer, allowing her to squirm in her own imaginings until she wanted to scream at him to do his worst and get it over with.

Finally he spoke. But in the wake of all the despicable mental pictures Beth had conjured, she was more disappointed than relieved when he said, "What I want is your promise never again to ride unescorted through these woods."

Beth's mouth gaped open. Then she began to laugh, a sweet melodic sound that seemed to float among the branches overhead. And once started she could not stop. Hawk grasped her shoulders and gave her a firm shake.

"I'm not leaving here until I have your solemn oath."

Beth sobered at once. "No one tells me where I can or cannot go!" she railed. "No one!"

Never in his twenty-seven years had Hawk butted heads with such a stubborn female. His first impulse was to continue shaking her until her teeth rattled but he knew she would only dig in her heels. He had to come up with a way to make her see reason. He let her go and turned to search the dark shadows surrounding the clearing.

"Where would you be right now if you had been followed by Asi-yahola or one of his braves?"

Ignoring his words, Beth admired Hawk's smooth, well-muscled back. She wondered again what could have marred his face so badly without leaving a blemish on the rest of his beautiful body.

"Answer me!" he roared whirling to face her once again.

"I suppose if *your friend* had followed me, I would be lying by the fire with a knife in my belly," Beth replied, remembering the hatred she had seen in the eyes of the other Indian. "If it had been one of his followers, I would probably be lying in the same spot with my legs forced apart."

Her accurate appraisal of what could easily have happened stunned even the imperturbable Hawk while her indifference infuriated him. He knew she was trying to shock him with her worldly-wise attitude. In truth, she most likely believed herself invincible. Well, two could play the game.

"I'm glad you have no delusions as to your fate should you again be caught by the infamous Asi-yahola."

Beth scoffed. "Infamous? You must be joking? Why, I've never even heard his name."

"Are you so sure?" Hawk's words seemed to issue a challenge. "Think about it carefully, little spitfire. Then perhaps you will realize that to continue these daredevil missions could result in a painful death . . . your death!"

Surely he didn't believe she would be frightened by his absurd warnings.

"The pronunciation of his name may have been corrupted by your people, but you have heard of him and to underestimate his power would be a grave mistake."

Hypnotized by Hawk's soft, silky voice, Beth closed her eyes and let the name beat a rhythm in her mind. Suddenly her eyes flew open as she felt the blood drain from her face. Looking around she discovered that the masked Indian had once again disappeared as though he had never been. With the realization that she was now alone and defenseless, the fear she had so heatedly denied became a living, breathing thing. Every night creature that scurried through the bushes became a potential attacker. Was that really the hoot of an owl she heard or something more sinister? Beth collapsed upon her pallet, her legs refusing to hold her upright as the name that brought dread to soldiers and settlers alike sounded like a death peal clanging in her head. Asi-yahola . . . Asi-yahola . . . Osceola!

Beth stood grimacing at the full-length mirror taking stock of the reflection frowning back at her. She tried to flatten the layers of petticoats beneath the delicate white dress patterned with pale blue roses, its low rounded neckline emphasizing the swell of her bosom.

"Whoever heard of blue roses?" she muttered in disgust.

The idea was as fanciful as Rachel's belief that dressing her stepdaughter like a lady would change what was underneath all the frills and falderals. And her father, a coward only in his refusal to thwart Rachel, would not say one word in her behalf! Why, if it weren't for her Uncle Lance, Beth would have to spend her days doing needlepoint or baking cookies.

"Damn!" she wheezed. "How was one supposed to breathe trapped inside these blasted stays?"

Why did fashion demand that women try to mold themselves into something less than the Good Lord made them? Men didn't try to pour themselves into clothes two sizes too small. And women only did it to impress men. But since there was no one at Fort Brooke Beth cared to impress, except Uncle Lance and Davey who both thought she was much more suited to buckskins, the whole idea of dressing for dinner seemed ludicrous.

She had been home little more than a week and already the walls of the fort were closing in on her. She longed to saddle Senabar and ride across the meadow with the wind in her face. But even Uncle Lance had turned against her, agreeing with her father that she must not venture away from the fort after hearing of her encounter with Osceola and the mysterious masked Indian. As if to pour salt in her wounds, Davey's leg had healed sufficiently to enable him to travel to Fort Drum with Edward while she was forced to stay at home playing dress up in her Maggie McAfee look-alikes! It was not to be borne. She knew something had to be done or she would go stark raving mad. Wrinkling her nose as she gave the mirror one last critical look, Beth vowed that tomorrow she would have a private talk with her Uncle Lance and make him see reason.

The family was already seated at the long linen-covered dinner table when Beth came down the stairs.

"Where is everyone?" she asked, surveying the empty seats.

Andrew Townsend waited impatiently behind Beth's chair to assist his daughter into her seat. Not that she needed assistance, but Beth had long ago given up arguing over the silly custom.

Her twin half brothers, Johnny and Jeremy, were playing some type of under-the-table game with their feet that only ten-year-old boys would find amusing. Their mother cleared her throat sharply snapping them to attention.

Andrew answered Beth's question as she felt the chair push against the backs of her knees. "Edward has gone to Fort Drum with Davey. They should be back in a few days."

Knowing only too well where her own twin was off to, Beth stifled the urge to debate the injustice of parental restrictions which allowed Edward his

55

freedom while she was imprisoned within the stockade. She knew there was no point in bringing up the issue for her father would continue to adhere to Rachel's wishes.

Beth looked down the table at her stepmother who was spooning small portions of meat and mashed potatoes onto her youngest child's plate. Little Amanda, just four years old, was a small replica of Rachel with black curls, sapphire eyes, and the darkest, thickest lashes imaginable. While both sets of Townsend twins had red hair and freckles like their father, this beautiful dark-haired child was such a novelty the others could not help spoiling her despite Rachel's efforts to discourage special treatment. And Mandy seemed to suffer no ill effects from their pampering for she had a sweet and loving disposition that no one could resist.

Beth smiled at the little girl. "I knew that Edward and Davey were gone, but where are 'Becca and Uncle Lance and the boys?"

As long as Beth could remember the Logans and the Townsends had shared their Saturday evening meal together either here or at her uncle's house outside the walls of the fort.

Rachel spoke up. "They have an unexpected guest. A gentleman rode in this afternoon from the capital. He said he had important matters to discuss with Lance."

There was nothing unusual about such an occurrence. Lance Logan knew more about what was

56

happening in the Territory than anyone else around. Often strangers appeared seeking his advice. There was no reason for the tingle of apprehension Beth felt run down her spine.

"He's purty," Amanda giggled, her mouth full of potatoes.

Beth could scarcely draw air around the lump in her throat. "Who's pretty, sweetheart?"

"Mr. Hawkins. He wears white lace up here," said the wide-eyed little girl clutching her throat with a pudgy hand, "just like momma sometimes does."

Damn the man! What could Robin Hawkins be doing at Fort Brooke? Here to stir up trouble, no doubt. A knowing gleam appeared in her eyes. It would be interesting to see how he dealt with her uncle. If he had the sense God gave a rabbit he would not approach Lance Logan with the arrogant disdain he used to intimidate Major Caldwell. Of course, she would not be around to witness whatever took place between the two men. Not for the world would she give Robin Hawkins an opportunity to see her dressed like a rufflewinged butterfly! He would laugh himself silly. No indeed! She would go out of her way to avoid the impudent popinjay while he remained at Fort Brooke!

Robin sat relaxed and replete enjoying the comfort of the oversized, padded rocker as he watched the giant of a man leaning against the mantel over the unlit fireplace. Everywhere he had traveled within the Territory he had heard this man's name spoken with respect and no little awe. Lance Logan was a living legend and after spending a few hours in his company, Robin began to see why.

Logan was a rugged frontiersman not given to flowery phrases; yet his love for this land in which he had lived for nearly twenty years was obvious in his every word. Instead of extolling the accomplishments of the white settlers as one might expect, he talked of Florida's unspoiled beauty. He called the pioneers, himself included, "the privileged few." He claimed it was not foresight but luck that had brought them to this place where the climate was warm, the earth rich, and the game plentiful. He spoke of the need to preserve and protect the Territory from those who would rape its natural resources to satisfy their own greed. Though he didn't say so, Robin felt certain Logan's concern included the fate of the Indians who had cherished this land long before the whites dreamed of staking a claim.

"My boys have a way of monopolizing our guests, Mr. Hawkins. I hope they didn't bore you with all their questions during dinner. They are interested, as we all are, in what is happening in the outside world."

Logan's voice was a rich baritone befitting his large stature. His words were an explanation, not an apology.

Robin smiled. "You have a fine family, Logan. I envy you."

To his surprise, Robin recognized the truth in what he said though he had never given any thought to settling down and starting a family of his own. At dinner he had met four of Logan's five sons, all darkly handsome like their father. When introduced, Benjamin, the oldest of the siblings present, had proudly informed their guest that he was "going on eleven." Then like descending stairsteps came Thomas, Patrick, and the youngest, Andrew, who stated firmly that he was named after his uncle, not the former president.

His mother had promptly taken him by the ear and plopped him into his chair. "That's hardly the thing to say to a gentleman from Washington," she scolded as her emerald eyes flashed while a delicate blush colored her flawless cheeks.

Rebecca Logan was scarcely taller than her ten-year-old son, Benjamin, and a good foot shorter than her towering husband; yet there was about her a strength of character that led Robin to believe she was a force to be reckoned with. As dainty as a porcelain figurine and as pretty as a picture, her jeweled eyes met those of her husband. What, Robin wondered, would it be like to be loved by such a woman? Though he was a man of experience when it came to satisfying his lust, he had never taken the time to encourage a serious relationship with one of the opposite sex. Now something in the way Lance and Rebecca Logan looked at each other caused him to suspect there might be an important element missing from his life.

And having met Elizabeth Townsend's aunt, Robin knew his original assumption, that any woman in the girl's life would have to be weak and ineffectual, was far from true which made her even more of an enigma.

Logan's deep voice wrenched him from his musings. "Now then, Mr. Hawkins. When you arrived here this afternoon you said you had come seeking my help. Just what did you have in mind?"

So much for small talk! Lance Logan was not a man to bandy words and Robin knew he would have to be equally straightforward in order to gain the assistance he sought.

He replied candidly, "As I have said, I was sent here from Washington to assess the progress, or perhaps 'lack of progress' is more apt, in convincing the Indians to relocate west of the Mississippi."

Logan's chiseled features turned as hard as granite. "Let me make one thing clear to you up front, Hawkins. I do not approve of the methods the government is using to *persuade* the Indians to leave the Territory. If you came here expecting me to support this aggression against people who have just as much right to this land as any of us do, then you're barking up the wrong tree!"

"I couldn't agree with you more," Robin stated without hesitation leading Lance to frown in consternation. "While it is true that I have been sent here from the nation's capital, I am not a representative of the president."

His face inscrutable, Lance waited for Robin to explain.

"Not everyone in Washington is in favor of this war. There is a powerful faction in Congress that wants to see an end to it; men who seek to find a way for the Indians and the whites to live together in peace. My uncle is one of those men."

Years of having to use his instincts to survive had made Logan a good judge of character. Not for a moment did he doubt the younger man's sincerity, but he felt inclined to test his instincts.

"I suppose the war is putting quite a dent in the national treasury," Lance remarked dryly, simply to gauge Hawkins's reaction.

Robin came to his feet bristling at the suggestion that the war's cost might be behind his and his allies' opposition. "The men who crave an end to this war are concerned with lives, not money. And I'm not just talking about the lives of the Indians!" he answered heatedly. "Someday, in the not too distant future, this Territory is going to gain statehood. The question is whether it will enter the union as a slave state or a free state. There are plenty of southern plantation owners backing repression of the Indians. Their runaway slaves have found a safe haven among the tribes here in Florida."

Lance pierced Robin with his steely eyes. "Your

61

speech is most eloquent," he said aloud. And there is more to your crusade than you are telling, he thought to himself. "I hope your uncle and those of a like mind have enough influence to put a stop to this senseless war. There is plenty of room in the Territory for all of us: red, black, or white. But I still don't know why you have come to me. I have no say in government policies."

Robin grinned. "You are too modest by far, sir. Your opinion carries more weight with both Indians and whites than that of any man in Tallahassee or Washington. I was at Fort King when Colonel Worth's letter arrived urging peace talks. After this evening I cannot help but believe you were the force behind the pen. Surely Major Caldwell can see the logic in such a proposal."

"Ah, yes. The mysterious letter that seemed to appear and disappear at will." Lance wrinkled his broad brow. "But you are right. Baker did agree to take the initiative in arranging a meeting with the tribal leaders. I will be riding to Fort King next week to discuss with him some possible options to relocation."

Robin breathed an audible sigh of relief. "That's the best news I've heard since my arrival in the Territory. I believe the government underestimated the intelligence of the Seminole people when they sent seven of their chieftains out west to view this reservation they have set aside for them. They seemed to think a few weeks of courting the sagacious elders was all it would take to win them over. And I understand there were some among the seven who were willing to accept what was offered in order to achieve peace. But they soon realized that the young warriors would never meekly surrender the land they consider their heritage."

Again Lance was struck by Hawkins's intensity and knew the young Washingtonian was much more than just a casual observer in this conflict. But damned if he could see how this well-bred gentleman from the North could be personally involved in a war between the army and the Florida Indians.

"I'm sure the men I represent will appreciate any assistance you can provide in bringing the two sides together," Robin concluded unpretentiously.

"I'll do everything within my power to see peace restored to the Territory." But as he gave his assurance Lance could not help wondering just whose side Hawkins was on . . . and why!

Chapter Four

Moonlight guided Robin along the well-worn path from the Logan home to the gates of the fort. Before going to the barracks where he would bed down with the soldiers, he decided to stop at the stables and check on his big black stallion, Satan. He planned to leave at the crack of dawn. Knowing the location of the horse's stall would save valuable time. All was quiet within the confines of the garrison for he calculated it to be after ten o'clock at night. The night songs of frogs and crickets were muted by the sturdy logs encircling the compound.

Robin paused beneath an enormous oak tree to light a cheroot, exhaling a puff of smoke into the balmy late spring air. It was then that he saw a slender woman in white, her head topped with a crown of red-gold curls gleaming in the moonlight like a flame above a candle. Her full skirts rippled in the gentle breeze making it seem as if she were floating, an ethereal wraith not of this world.

He watched in fascination as she reached her arm outward across the top rail of the paddock crooning softly to the roan mare within. The roan nuzzled its nose against her hand seeking and finding the treat hidden there. Robin drew deeply on the small cigar enjoying the unobstructed view of the enchanting creature before him. Just as he drew the pungent smoke deep into his lungs, his mind returned to the day he had seen Elizabeth Townsend leave Fort King riding an identical red-coated mount. He was suddenly bent double by a spasm of coughing and wheezing. It was impossible, he thought as tears formed in his eyes. There was no way on earth this angel could be the same little hellion who had cursed him to hell and back just a week ago.

"Oh, dear! Are you all right?" The vision of loveliness rushed toward him, her gentle voice edged with concern.

If he hadn't been on the verge of choking to death, Robin would have laughed aloud. For a moment he had actually believed the beautiful girl anxiously wringing her hands to be the redoubtable Miss Townsend. But the sweet melodic voice he heard could not possibly belong to the foulmouthed shrew he had hoped to avoid during his brief visit to Fort Brooke. Forcing himself to stand erect, Robin pulled the pristine linen handkerchief from his coat pocket and dabbed at his burning eyes. As he lowered the cloth, he was once again overcome with a long wracking cough that caused the tears to start afresh. There, before him, he saw a pair of crystal blue orbs he remembered only too well.

"Miss Townsend?" he finally managed to voice uncertainly between a sneeze and a gasp. Despite the evidence before him, Robin's mind refused to accept this delicious confection of petticoats and ruffles as the same sharp-tongued virago who had driven him beyond annoyance to full-fledged animosity.

Her look was guarded as she drew back and raised her chin, her eyes searching the semidarkness as if suddenly realizing they were all alone. She reminded him of a doe sniffing the air, poised for flight.

"Why, ye . . . yes, I am," she stammered in that soft husky voice that sent chills up and down his backbone. ". . . but, who are you?"

Robin felt as if he had been doused with cold water. This time it was his turn to take a step backward. Even in the pale light of the moon he could make out the familiar delicate features of her face right down to the sprinkling of freckles across the bridge of her petite little nose. And there was no mistaking those sparkling blue eyes even when they held a look of bewilderment.

"Now really, Miss Townsend. Though I will be the first to admit that we did not exactly hit it off at our last meeting, don't you think your rebuff would be more appropriate if we had an audience to witness your remarkable performance?"

Her face was all innocence. "Sir, if we had met before, rest assured I would remember," she said with confidence. "There are not so many men in the Territory that I would forget one of your . . ." she paused as if searching for just the right word, ". . . arrogance." She smiled seemingly satisfied

66

with her choice.

Ah! This was more like his memory of the sarcastic Elizabeth Townsend even if she did persist in playing out her little scene.

Before she could anticipate his actions, Robin reached out and grasped her none too gently by the shoulders drawing her toward him. "Stop it, Elizabeth! Enough of this ruse!"

She tried to pull away but he held her firmly at arm's length. When she continued to stare mutely he gave her a shake.

"Please! I beg of you," she implored looking for all the world like an abused little puppy. "Release me for I am not Elizabeth! I am her twin sister, Edwina."

Robin dropped his arms and jerked back as if struck by a lightning bolt.

"Her twin?" his voice echoed both relief and disappointment. The sides of his mouth twitched as he pictured how amusing it would have been to confront the abrasive Elizabeth Townsend disguised as a lady. But he was glad to know that his first instincts had been correct. It stretched his imagination to think that the sweet, docile creature calling herself Edwina was even distantly related to the ill-tempered scapegrace blessed with her same lovely face.

Robin bowed to the frightened young woman. "Please accept my apologies, Miss Townsend, as well as my condolences."

"I'm afraid I don't understand, Mister . . . ?"

"Hawkins. Robin Hawkins," he supplied.

"Why, of course. I should have guessed," Edwina said timidly. "You are the gentleman from Washington who is here to see Uncle Lance." Her tentative acceptance warmed Robin's heart though her facial likeness to her sister continued to disconcert him. "Your apology I will accept but I have no need of your sympathy, sir."

"If Elizabeth Townsend is your sister, sympathy seems in order," Robin countered.

For a moment Edwina went rigid, then recovering herself she said teasingly, "Shame on you, Mr. Hawkins. First you ruin my family's dinner and now you insult my sister."

Edwina batted her lashes. Robin could almost feel the embarrassed color flooding the young woman's cheeks as she clasped a dainty hand over her mouth.

"Oh dear! I suppose it's my turn to apologize, Mr. Hawkins. I should never have said what I did about spoiling my family's dinner."

"I will gladly accept your apology, Miss Townsend, providing it comes with an explanation."

Edwina stood silently staring down at the tips of her satin slippers until he thought she would refuse to answer. Then resolutely she raised her chin and her remarkable blue eyes locked with his. "Beth doesn't like you, Mr. Hawkins, and she spent the entire dinner hour itemizing what she considered to be your worst faults!"

Her words came out in a rush, her voice containing what sounded like a trace of satisfaction. But surely Robin must have been mistaken for Edwina immediately ducked her head as if ashamed of what she had revealed.

"And it only took an hour?" Robin retorted.

Edwina continued to study the ground, her manner was unprepossessing. Robin found her guileless innocence absolutely adorable. Indeed, Edwina Townsend was everything a man could want in a woman: attractive, well-bred, malleable. He placed his finger beneath her chin and forced her to look up.

"And what about you, Edwina? Do you like me?"

It was impossible to interpret the myriad changes that took place in the depths of her shadowed eyes.

"I don't know you," she replied, leaning slightly forward in a way that again reminded him of her twin sister, Elizabeth.

Robin could in no way stop what happened next. Without any conscious thought as to his motives, he bent his dark head and captured her partly opened lips with his. She was warm and soft and feminine, and he discovered to his amazement . . . willing. Though obviously inexperienced in the art of lovemaking, Edwina did not draw back but allowed Robin to deepen the kiss. His tongue teased her lips then dipped into the sweet moist recesses of her mouth. Her eyes were open wide staring into his with something akin to wonder as she tentatively touched her tongue to his. It was only when his arms encircled her slender waist drawing her against his aroused manhood that she seemed to remember where she was and what she was doing.

Pushing hard against his chest, she broke from his embrace then had to grab his arms to retain her balance. He could scarcely hear her short rasping breaths above the thundering beat of his own heart. Never had he been so affected by a single kiss and somewhere in the depth of his being a warning signal sounded. Too much was at stake here to permit a personal entanglement to get in the way, yet he knew the young woman looking up at him with an expression of bewilderment on her face was someone very special. Had they met under different circumstances, he would have enjoyed taking the time to teach her the wonders of love. He sensed that lying dormant just beneath her prim and proper facade were raging fires of emotion equal to his own.

Robin shook his head regretfully. His primary objective was to save lives and put an end to a war that should never have begun. He could let nothing stand in his way.

His voice when he spoke was not quite steady. "This seems to be my night for apologies, Miss Townsend. Though I doubt any man finding you alone in the moonlight could have resisted the chance to taste your honeyed lips, that is no excuse for my behavior and I do beg your pardon."

Edwina laughed shakily. "On the contrary, Mr. Hawkins, I can assure you other men have never found me irresistible."

Her reply held no false modesty causing Robin to question the intelligence of the men she had known. "More fools they," he murmured half to himself.

Behind them the horse who had claimed Edwina's

attention earlier whinnied softly. Seeming to welcome the distraction, the fragile young woman turned and glided across the grass toward the paddock. As if unable to break from the magnetic force that drew him to her, Robin followed.

"Do you and your sister share the horse?" he asked from just over her shoulder, his breath tickling the back of her neck.

Edwina laughed again, a musical tinkling sound that raised gooseflesh on Robin's arms. "Beth rides Senabar. I spoil her. All animals need a little spoiling, don't you think?"

"Absolutely," Robin agreed, entranced by the way the moonlight played on her red-gold crown of curls.

But it was a two-legged animal he pictured enjoying the ministrations of her gentle touch. He was amazed that two women who came from the same seed could have such totally opposite natures. Elizabeth Townsend was hard as nails, daring to a fault, with none of the softer qualities that endeared a woman to a man. He was not surprised that she saw a horse as no more than a means of transportation. Edwina, on the other hand, was the epitome of feminine charm and sensitivity. He decided this evaluation as he watched her lightly stroke Senabar's nose.

Without warning Edwina whirled around bumping into Robin's chin.

"Ouch!"

"Oh dear! I really must be going, Mr. Hawkins. My father and stepmother will be looking for me," she protested as his hands went automatically to her shoulders.

He frowned down at her as she glanced nervously around the compound. She was certainly an insecure little creature and he wondered if she could really be happy cooped up within the walls of the fort where one must constantly be on guard against unexpected dangers. Fort Brooke might be all right for someone like Elizabeth but never for a woman of Edwina's delicate constitution. She belonged in a city like Washington where she could attend balls, preside over teas and luncheons, and shop to her heart's content.

"Please, I must be going now," she insisted.

Robin could think of no argument to keep her there but, God, how he hated to let her go.

"I will be leaving at first light tomorrow," he said, hoping to persuade her to stay a little longer.

"Where will you go from here?" Edwina whispered a little breathlessly.

Dare he hope she might be disappointed by news of his imminent departure?

"I'm riding to Fort Drum then on to Fort King."

"Oh dear!" Something in her reaction caused Robin to suspect there was more to her distress than just the fact that he was leaving.

"Miss Townsend, I feel certain my work will bring me back to Fort Brooke in the not too distant future. I would like very much to see you again."

She gave him a winsome smile. "Perhaps by the time you return you will no longer desire my company, Mr. Hawkins."

Before he could stop her, Edwina turned and fled across the moon-drenched lawn, her white skirts billowing out below her tiny waist. What a strange little pixie she was. Of one thing Robin had no doubt. The young lady definitely underestimated her desirability.

Beth flung the white dress to the floor resisting the urge to stomp it into the carpet. What had possessed her to pull such a damn fool stunt? She yanked the pins from her upswept hair and shook her head furiously. Damn the man! Didn't he have eyes? Even an imbecile could have seen through her childish pretense! Robin Hawkins had to be the most stupid human being God ever put on this earth!

As she removed her stiffly starched petticoats and soft lacy undergarments, her temper soared to unprecedented heights. Why, anyone could see that beneath the elaborate dress and the ridiculous simpering mannerisms it was she, Beth Townsend, whose only purpose in pretending to be someone else was to keep the arrogant dolt from laughing at her in her finery. And it had worked! So why, she asked herself, was she so outraged that he had actually been duped by her disguise? The answer was simply too galling to accept. Robin Hawkins liked the mousy little piece of fluff he assumed her to be! The fact that he would go so soft over a demure doormat like Edwina proved once more the incomprehensibility of the male species.

"My Indian would never be taken in by such an obvious charade," she muttered, pulling the plain nightgown over her head.

Now when had she started thinking of the masked charlatan as *her* Indian? She groaned as she climbed into bed and brought the quilted coverlet up to her chin. And why did Hawkins have to go to Fort Drum of all places?

Beth tried to downplay the possibility of Robin running into Davey and Edward on his sojourn, but the likelihood was all too probable. One look at her brother and the game would be over. Hawkins would know immediately who the *real* twin was. Despite the consequences, Beth smiled. How she would enjoy seeing his reaction when he realized what a fool she had made of him! The mental picture was almost worth the humiliation she would feel when he discovered she was, in fact, the woman dressed like an overblown powder puff.

Not until the sky turned from black to gray to mauve did Beth lapse into a restless, troubled sleep. For hours she had fought against acknowledging the effect of Robin Hawkins's kiss, but as she entered that semiconscious state that comes just before sleep, she was forced to admit that the warm, sensual feel of his lips pressed against hers had not been altogether unpleasant.

She was dreaming and soon he came to her again, his dark head moving inexorably toward hers as she lay waiting, her hair spilling across the pillow in wild disarray. His features were in shadow but she could smell his male scent. Closer he came. Her body tensed with anticipation. Impatiently she reached out, her lips opening in welcome to meet his kiss. But instead of the warm softness she remembered, her mouth was crushed against the rough hard bark of the mask worn by the faceless Indian. Beth jerked upright.

"Blast all men!" she cried aloud. "Red and white alike!"

Robin rode the big ebony stallion down the quiet main street of the still sleeping little settlement of Tampa. It wasn't much of a town yet; a few houses, a couple of saloons, and a two-storied structure that passed for a hotel. Most of the activity centered around the docks where pens had been erected to hold the cattle waiting to be loaded onto ships having easy access to the port through the deep, natural channel of the bay.

There were a number of Indians camped along the wharf as well, human cargo that would be transported to a barren tract of land near the far western border of the Louisiana Territory. These Seminoles had managed to elude Osceola and his warriors who were determined to prevent their relocation even if they had to be killed to stop their flight. Not long ago, Chief Charlie Emathla had accepted money from Wiley Thompson, the Indian agent at Fort King, and agreed to emigrate with his band of followers. But before they could reach Tampa, Osceola accosted the group on the trail. Flinging the coins in Emathla's face, Osceola had

75

called him a Judas, accusing the Indian leader of selling the souls of his kinsmen for tainted pieces of gold. Then he had executed the chief in the manner befitting a traitor. Robin wondered how the Indians could possibly hope to win with brother pitted against brother.

As he reached the end of the street and headed eastward, his thoughts turned to his puzzling conversation with Lance Logan a short time ago. The former army scout had been waiting for him two hours before daybreak as he entered the stable to saddle Satan. Robin had spent a restless night driven to frustration by a delicate, freckled face that appeared each time he allowed his lids to close. First the roughshod Elizabeth Townsend had floated before his eyes clad in dusty buckskins, a sneer twisting her lips until in his dreams he had grabbed her slender shoulders and shaken her roughly. Then her mocking mouth had curved into an inviting smile and it was Edwina he was holding; Edwina, dressed in a virgin white gown adorned with blue roses. As he had lowered his head to taste her honeyed sweetness, Elizabeth reappeared pulling away from his embrace, taunting him with her laughter, making him feel the world's biggest fool.

No wonder he had given up any attempt to sleep, deciding to quit Fort Brooke an hour earlier than planned. Robin wondered if the tall man waiting for him in the light of a single lantern had nightmares, too. Remembering the beautiful Rebecca it seemed unlikely.

"Good morning, sir," Robin had greeted Logan,

according the older man the respect he deserved.

Lance cocked an eyebrow noting the shadows beneath Robin's gray-green eyes but made no comment. In truth, he'd scarcely recognized the well-dressed gentleman he had entertained the night before. Today Robin wore tight-fitting breeches and a full-cut white linen shirt open at the neck. His dark hair was all but hidden beneath a wide-brimmed black hat which he hoped would protect his face from the scorching sun he would be facing by mid-morning.

"You seem anxious to be on your way, Mr. Hawkins," the frontiersman had remarked as he watched Robin toss the blanket and saddle across the back of the stallion. "He's a beauty." Logan had looked at Satan closely reaching out to stroke his sleek, black neck.

"I can in no way fault the hospitality at Fort Brooke. I don't know when I've enjoyed a meal or finer company than you and your family offered me last evening. But I feel it imperative that I speak with the commander at Fort Drum as soon as possible. Perhaps I am too optimistic, but with your backing and the grudging support of Major Caldwell, I hope to convince the other military leaders in the area to join in the peace talks with the Seminole should we be able to arrange such a parley. I look forward to seeing you at Fort King within the week."

Logan had appeared to be listening with only half an ear as he continued to glide his callous-roughened hand across the horse's smooth coat. Then he reached to take the bridle from Robin, easing the bit between Satan's teeth. "My niece, Beth, whom I believe you met at Fort King, came home with an incredible tale about a masked Indian who accosted her on the trail, then deposited her unharmed at the very gates of the stockade."

Warily Robin had led the horse out of the stall and through the stable doors into the darkness but Logan was right behind him, the lantern he carried casting wavering shadows about the compound. As they came to a halt, the big man raised the light so that Robin's face was illuminated in its glow.

"She couldn't give us much of a description of the Indian, but she sure got a good look at his horse. Said it was a big black stallion. It must have been a lot like this one, Mr. Hawkins."

As he prepared to mount, Robin turned to face Logan, one hand on the pommel of his saddle. "As a matter of fact I did meet your niece at Fort King and was present to hear of her near disaster enroute. I can't help wondering why you and Miss Townsend's father would allow her to place herself in such danger."

At first he had mistaken the older man's response as an embarrassed cough. Then he realized that Lance Logan was trying to stifle his laughter. "I take it your meeting with my niece was rather brief," he chortled.

Not brief enough, Robin thought inwardly.

Not waiting for an answer, Logan expounded, "Beth is a free spirit, Mr. Hawkins. She thinks, says, and does exactly as she pleases."

Robin couldn't believe what he was hearing. Why Logan actually seemed to condone his niece's harebrained escapades! "And for this you are proud?" he had blurted out, then immediately wished he could recall his question.

Logan's gray eyes turned rock hard. "Proud? You better believe it, son! It's women like Beth who will make this Territory a land fit to live in. It takes courage and self-sacrifice to do what she does. Yes, I'm proud. I'm damned proud of her and Eddie both. They're the future of this land and thank God we have young people like them to mold this wilderness into a place where decent people can live in peace and raise their families."

Robin had found himself at a loss for words; not because of the man's fervid defense of Elizabeth Townsend's unladylike behavior, but because Logan actually seemed to think Edwina in some way resembled her tomboy sister.

Pulling himself onto the saddle, Robin could not disguise his disgust at such a comparison. "I have spent as much time as I care to with Miss Elizabeth, and . . ." he hesitated finding it impossible to call the lovely Edwina, Eddie, ". . . suffice it to say, I have met both of the twins and I must say I find them vastly different."

Without giving Lance an opportunity to reply, Robin had dug his heels into Satan's flanks and raced toward the gates.

Lance quietly removed his clothing then stood naked in the gray light of dawn admiring the outline of his wife's shapely figure beneath the thin cover. He thought back twelve years ago to the day the golden-haired little vixen had arrived by ship from England with Eddie and Beth in tow demanding that her brother-in-law assume the responsibility for his children.

From the beginning Rebecca and Logan had locked horns at every pass. He had thought her completely ill equipped for life in the Territory. She had thought him an uncivilized bully. Only after she had been captured by renegade Indians had Lance realized how much he loved her. And miracle of miracles, when he rescued her and brought her back to the fort, she had admitted that she loved him in return. It was like a fairy tale. Then just as the "happily ever after" was about to begin his new bride had been carted off by pirates, and it had taken the combined efforts of the soldiers, a band of friendly Indians, and the United States Navy to get her out of that mess!

As Lance climbed into bed and pulled Rebecca close so that her back fitted to his front, she squirmed to adjust to the new position rubbing her hips against his manhood in the process. He felt himself harden instantly. He wondered if he would ever get enough of his wife. As he began to gently fondle one breast, Rebecca turned over, her emerald eyes still clouded with sleep.

"Mr. Hawkins left quite early," she said, glancing toward the window.

"Hmm."

Lance worked his hand beneath her gown to idly twirl a nipple between his thumb and his forefinger as he bent his head to nibble her neck.

"He seems like a very nice young man and he is extraordinarily handsome," she continued, pretending not to notice her husband's overtures.

Lance raised himself up on one elbow and frowned, miffed that she could be thinking of another man when he wanted her thoughts centered on him and what he was doing to her. She smiled and caressed his dark stubbled chin.

"Too bad he didn't stay long enough to see Elizabeth dressed in a gown."

"Now, sweetheart, I would have to know a great deal more about Robin Hawkins before I would allow Beth to become involved with him," Lance stated firmly.

It never occurred to Rebecca to remind Lance that he was not Beth's father, for though Beth loved Andrew dearly, the special bond that had developed between the girl and her uncle over the years went beyond the loyalty and devotion of blood kin.

"I thought you liked him. What is it you find disturbing about Mr. Hawkins?"

Lance fingered a lock of his wife's silky hair enjoying the familiar scent of wildflowers. He took a moment before he answered. "I believe what Hawkins says about his uncle and the others in Washington who want to see an end to the war. But I feel that the man is more personally involved in the confrontation than he is letting on. It's a gut feeling I really can't explain. Then there's this thing about his horse."

"His horse?"

"A big black stallion that looks exactly like the animal Beth described as belonging to that masked Indian."

Rebecca scoffed as she outlined her husband's ear with her fingertip. "Now really, Logan. You can't possibly believe the well-bred gentleman we entertained at dinner last night dons an ugly wooden mask and roams through the woods waylaying dispatch riders?"

Hearing her put his vague suspicion into words made the idea sound ludicrous. "Of course not," he shrugged, "but I still think you should curtail your matchmaking schemes until I find out more about the *gentleman*."

"You needn't worry, my love, for it is difficult to matchmake when half of the match is no longer around."

" 'Difficult' perhaps," he replied, kissing the tip of her pert little nose, "but I learned long ago not to underestimate your resourcefulness."

Rebecca bit back a quick rejoinder. "What else is it that bothers you about Mr. Hawkins?" she asked instead.

"It was the strangest thing. He accused Andrew and me of placing Beth in danger by allowing her to ride courier to Fort King."

"There's nothing strange about that. Rachel and I have been saying the same thing for months."

"But when I mentioned something about Beth and Eddie being alike in their allegiance to the Territory, Hawkins said he had met both the twins and that he found them 'vastly different.' "

Rebecca looked perplexed. "That is odd. When on earth could he have met Edward?"

"When Eddie returns from Fort Drum remind me to ask him," Lance murmured distractedly as he traced Rebecca's lips with his tongue while he tenderly ran his hand along the smooth skin of her inner thighs.

"Perhaps Mr. Hawkins was remarking on the fact that one is a boy and one is a girl."

"Who?"

"The twins, of course."

"To be more accurate, sweetheart, Edward is a man and Elizabeth is a woman."

"I know, but I can't help thinking of them as the two little scamps I brought here from England when they were six years old," she sighed, giving herself up to her husband's ministrations.

Knowing that now was as good a time as any to broach the subject, Lance whispered, "I think I'll take Beth with me to Fort King next week."

He quickly covered Rebecca's lips with his to avoid any protest she might raise. Surprisingly, when he released her she nodded affirmatively.

"Good. Perhaps Mr. Hawkins will be there. I shall advise Rachel to make sure she packs a pretty gown and I shall count on you to see that she wears it while at the fort."

Lance groaned wondering how he would ever convince his strong-willed niece to shed her buckskins in favor of more feminine apparel. Then he groaned even louder pulling the pillow over his head, for there was no mistaking the patter of small feet across the floor of the loft above. He and Rebecca had spent so much time discussing their mysterious visitor, they would now be forced to postpone their dalliance until nightfall. Damn Robin Hawkins anyway!

Chapter Five

Davey Logan sat on one of the high-backed wooden chairs placed in a row along the narrow porch outside the barracks at Fort Drum. He rested his recently injured leg upon the railing as he listened to his cousin extol the virtues of a pretty barmaid who served beer and whiskey and anything else a man could afford at the saloon just outside the stockade.

"Come on, Davey. We'll have a few drinks and, if we're lucky, we might find ourselves some softer beds than those in there," Edward coaxed, nodding his head toward the long stark room the soldiers called "home."

"Not tonight, Eddie. My leg hurts like hell. You go ahead and enjoy yourself."

"Good God! You grumble like an old man with the rheumatiz," he argued. "Why, I'll bet Dora has a friend who could move that pain from your leg to a place a little higher up then ease it right out of you."

Davey laughed in spite of himself. Ever since his cousin discovered the second most important function of that thing between his legs, he was randier than a bull in a cowpen.

"And just what are you going to tell Miss Maggie McAfee if she catches you fooling around with a saloon gal?"

Edward gave his cousin a sly wink. "Maggie's a hundred miles away and what she doesn't know can't hurt her . . . or me," he assured with a "devil may care" grin on his face.

"I've heard Miss Maggie can be hell on horseback if you get her dander up," the older of the two warned. "But you go ahead and have a good time. Don't give a second thought to what Miss Maggie might do if she finds out you're cheating on her."

"I won't," Eddie replied with the cocky self-assurance of youth. "Sure you won't come along?"

"I'm sure. I'll just rest this bum leg for a little while longer then I plan to turn in. We have to get an early start for Fort King tomorrow. Can't wait to tell Miss Maggie what you've been up to."

Eddie knew Davey was only teasing him. The two had been as close as brothers for thirteen years and in some ways it seemed they had always been together. When Eddie arrived in Florida with his Aunt 'Becca and his twin sister, Elizabeth, he had been a wide-eyed English lad eager to meet his father and learn all there was to learn about this strange new country in which he found himself. From the very first day, Davey had been his mentor teaching him to hunt and fish. Together they had explored the woods under the watchful eye of Davey's grandfather, Nokomis, chieftain of the nearly extinct Calusa Indians. Davey had taught him everything worth knowing including a wholehearted appreciation of the opposite sex.

Giving his cousin a jaunty salute, Eddie leaped from the porch and headed toward the stable. "Don't wait up for me," he called over his shoulder.

"Evening, Mister. Mind if I join you?"

Davey was still gazing after Eddie's departing figure wishing he felt up to joining the fun when the deep voice spoke beside him. "Make yourself at home," he invited, motioning toward a vacant chair. He watched curiously as the tall, dark-haired stranger took the seat next to him.

"Name's Hawkins. Robin Hawkins."

Robin's outstretched hand was caught in a firm grip.

"Davey Logan."

Davey didn't miss the cool appraisal in the man's gray-green eyes; light-colored eyes that seemed at odds with his near black hair and browned skin. Hawkins's hand, he had noticed, was rough, indicating a man used to hard work.

Meanwhile Robin was making his own assessment of the good-looking young man who had been pointed out to him as Lance Logan's eldest son. Davey Logan was dark like his father though his cheekbones were higher, more prominent, and his eyes were a soft brown, framed with long, thick lashes. Even sitting down, Robin could tell this half-breed son had the same tall stature as his sire.

"Yes, you resemble your father," Robin surprised Davey by saying.

"I take that as a compliment, Mr. Hawkins. But how is it you know my father?"

Robin proceeded to explain how he had just come from Fort Brooke, enlightening Davey further on the mission that had brought him to the Territory.

Davey was impressed and said as much. "I'm sure my father was most supportive of your cause and, for what it's worth, I will certainly help in any way I can."

Again Davey felt the man's eyes on him taking his measure.

"Believe me, Mr. Hawkins. I do not wish to see Indians and white men killing each other for the blood of both runs through my veins."

"Then you know what it is to be torn apart by conflicting loyalties?"

The man spoke as if he, too, had grown up caught between two different worlds, and Davey could only wonder at the background of this obviously well-educated Northerner.

"My loyalties center around this land. I was born here in Florida. Not too many people can make such a claim. It's something I'm proud of, Mr. Hawkins. And I damn sure don't want to see this land torn to pieces by selfish men who have only their own special interests at heart."

Robin chuckled at the younger man's ardor. "You have your father's spirit, too, I see."

Davey grinned sheepishly. "I'm afraid I haven't inherited my father's ability to hold his tongue in check."

"I imagine that is something even your father had to learn, Davey, and please call me Robin."

"What does Major Lewis think of your plan to initiate peace talks with the Seminoles?" Davey asked with interest.

Robin frowned remembering the long afternoon he

had spent with the commander of Fort Drum. "He has reluctantly agreed to attend if they ever get beyond the talking stage. But . . ." He paused.

"But what? Surely it's worth a try!" Davey asserted, bringing his leg down and turning to face the man who was now just a shadow in the waning light.

"Lewis feels the only way such talks would be worthwhile is if Osceola is included in the Council. Even though he's not a chieftain, his influence among the tribes is weighty to say the least. It makes sense, but I wonder if it's possible?" Robin concluded dishearteningly.

Giving a low whistle, Davey leaned back in his chair. "A few years ago Osceola attended what was supposed to be a peace conference headed by an Indian agent named Wiley Thompson. When none of the recognized chiefs showed up, Thompson presented a document supposedly signed by sixteen minor chiefs agreeing to removal. Word has it that when the alleged agreement was placed on the table, Osceola plunged his knife into the paper and disavowed its authenticity."

Robin's dark brows drew together. "I've heard the story. For his actions Osceola was clamped in irons and imprisoned at Fort King until he agreed to put his name on the removal document. Which he finally did."

"Only a fool would have believed Osceola's agreement was anything but a ploy to win his release," Davey said, shaking his head.

"They don't make fools much more naive than Wiley Thompson proved to be. He was so grateful to gain the young warrior's cooperation, he gave him a custom-made rifle."

Davey smirked. "Yeah, and Osceola returned to Fort King three months later and killed Thompson with that very same gun."

Both men sat quietly slapping at an occasional mosquito as they digested the tale that had become a legend.

Finally Davey said regretfully, "I don't think there's a chance in Hell of getting Osceola to another peace table."

Robin shrugged. "Maybe. Maybe not. But as you just said, it's worth a try. Incidentally, your father will be at Fort King in a few days to discuss the matter personally with Major Caldwell."

"Then I will probably see him there," Davey yawned, rising from his chair as he stretched his long arms upward. "My cousin and I will be leaving for Fort King in the morning. But right now I think I'll hit the sack." He looked down at the man he had come to like during their brief conversation. "Where will you be going from here, Robin?"

"I'll be at Fort King day after tomorrow," Robin hedged.

"Guess we'll see you then." With that Davey limped toward the door.

Robin remained on the porch for a few more minutes. *Christ! Another cousin!* He wondered just how many relatives made up the Logan clan. Of course, Davey was not really a cousin to Edwina and Beth Townsend, not by blood at least. For some reason the idea that the lovely Edwina had grown up in a family setting with a virile young man like Davey Logan, who wasn't really related, went against the grain.

Robin was sound asleep several hours later when Edward Townsend staggered into the barracks and collapsed upon the first empty bed he came across.

"Never!" shouted the angry warrior, his dark eyes snapping with defiance. "That you would suggest such a meeting makes me wonder if your years of living among the white eyes has reduced your loyalty to our people to a point of nonexistence."

Hawk jumped to his feet, his fists balled tightly at his sides, ready to challenge Asi-yahola's unwarranted accusation. But he quickly realized that arguing among themselves would be the same as fighting on the side of the federal government. Deciding to try a different tact on the friend he called "brother," Hawk issued a challenge of his own.

"Could it be that you are afraid to hear the words of the white leaders or is it that you have developed a taste for the bloody butchering taking place?"

Asi-yahola looked ready to throttle the larger man who dared to question his bravery and his motives. His chest swelled with indignation and his eyes glittered dangerously. Then suddenly the fight seemed to go out of him. His shoulders drooped. He looked tired and older than his thirty-three years. Hawk was startled by the unexpected change, and he instantly regretted his harsh words of a few moments ago. But before he could say as much, Asi-yahola continued.

"You know I am no coward. I would gladly give my life to restore peace to our people. But meeting with the soldiers is not the way. We agreed to talk once before but what they really wanted was for us to listen while they talked. We were supposed to listen to their demands and agree to abide by a useless document supposedly signed by a number of handpicked lesser chiefs who had no authority to make decisions for the People."

Hawk was troubled by the Indian leader's dispirited countenance. He had expected pessimism over the outcome of a parley but not this attitude of hopelessness. His concern was in no way alleviated by the warrior's next words.

"Perhaps you are right and it's time for us to move on to this 'new and wonderful land' we have been promised." His voice was filled with bitter sarcasm.

Nostrils flaring, Hawk grabbed Asi-yahola by the shoulders and shook him roughly. "Damn it, man! What's wrong with you? I said nothing about giving up! This conference will be different. I trust Logan to mediate fairly. Both sides will have an opportunity to air their grievances and suggest ways we can reconcile our differences. Working together I feel confident that we can come up with a way to live right here in peace. And for the first time the whites seem willing to listen to what we have to say."

A spark of the old spirit flamed in Asi-yahola's piercing eyes. "You put a great deal of faith in the integrity of our enemies."

"Lance Logan is an honest man with the good of the Territory at heart. As for the others, only time will tell. But I think we should take advantage of an opportunity to work things out without further bloodshed on either side."

Asi-yahola shrugged indifferently. "I will agree to meet with the soldier leaders and your friend Logan.

I am tired of fighting. I ask only that I be allowed to live with my wives in peace someplace where my children can grow up unafraid."

Hawk's frown deepened as the man on whom the Seminole People rested their hopes and dreams turned without another word and walked back toward the fire. Several hours later Hawk left the Indian camp. He should have been jubilant for the first steps toward a peaceful resolution of the conflict had been accomplished. Both sides had agreed to sit down and talk to one another. Instead he felt a terrible sense of foreboding. He prayed he was wrong but he could not rid himself of the suspicion that one side had already given up.

On the porch outside the log building housing soldiers and visitors to Fort King, Robin and Davey Logan sat talking much as they had at Fort Drum the day before yesterday. Both men looked up as two dust-covered riders galloped through the gates and came to a halt in the middle of the compound. Though Robin squinted into the sun he could not make out the shadowed features of the new arrivals. Not so Davey. Despite his game leg, he bounded off the porch and limped across the yard to greet the pair enthusiastically.

Robin watched as the smaller of the two slid from the horse's back right into the young man's arms. He groaned audibly as he recognized the lithe boyish figure of Elizabeth Townsend. Squeezing her tightly, Davey lifted Beth off the ground and swung her around in a circle in spite of his injured leg.

A scowl marked Robin's handsome features as he observed the reunion between the cousins who weren't really cousins at all. The muscles in his stomach tightened and for the life of him he could not understand why he found the scene so irksome. He tried to convince himself that his irritation stemmed from the knowledge that the girl had once again ridden the hazardous trail between Fort Brooke and Fort King, but it didn't wash for by this time he had identified her companion as none other than the formidable Lance Logan. If anyone could guarantee her safe passage, it was her uncle. So why did seeing the little hellion in Davey's arms cause such a gut-wrenching reaction? He certainly wasn't jealous of the camaraderie between them. Though, he did consider their public display of affection to be in poor taste. But then what had he expected from one who didn't seem to know whether she was a boy or a girl?

Deciding to ignore the entire affair, he pulled the brim of his hat down over his eyes and pretended to be asleep. He tried to hear what the three were saying but from a distance their words were indistinguishable.

"I'm so glad to see you, Davey," Beth exclaimed laughing up at her cousin as he held her at arm's length, his keen brown eyes running an inventory of her person.

When after several moments his only response was to continue scrutinizing her, Beth began to feel self-conscious. Puzzled and a little annoyed, she asked saucily, "Have I grown another head or did you forget and leave your manners at Fort Drum?"

At that Davey managed a tight-lipped smile. "Neither, little scamp. I'm just making sure you're still in one piece."

Beth glanced down at her well-worn buckskins then tilted her head over one shoulder eyeing her backside. "Yep! I'm all here," she reassured, grinning up at him once again.

"Well it's certainly the same sassy mouth I remember. Howdy, pa," Davey greeted, letting Beth go as he clasped his father's arm.

Logan's mouth twitched as he listened to the banter between the reunited clan. "Glad to see you, son. I take it you've heard about Beth's last visit to Fort King." Lance had read Davey's reaction correctly.

"Major Caldwell couldn't wait to tell me about the attack. I feel guilty as Hell," he confessed putting an arm around Beth's waist and drawing her protectively against his side. "If only I'd been with her."

"God Almighty, Davey Logan!" Beth fumed and pulled away to stand facing him with hands on narrow hips. "You talk as if I were dead and gone when anyone with eyes in his head can see that nothing happened I couldn't handle. And let me tell you," she raved on, "having you along wouldn't have stopped those damned heathens from taking the bloody dispatches, so don't you dare blame their loss on the fact that I'm a woman!"

Davey grinned as he listened to her tirade. He always had admired her spunk.

From his spot on the shaded porch, Robin heard every word Beth flung at the younger Logan. Though he didn't know what had ignited her fury, he raised the brim of his hat an inch or so at her reference to the "damned heathens." "Ungrateful little bitch," he

95

grumbled disgustedly. She didn't realize how lucky she was to be alive.

As soon as Beth stopped for breath, Davey chucked her beneath the chin saying, "Simmer down, little one. I'm sure the same thing would have happened if I had been riding the trail alone instead of you."

Somewhat mollified Beth retorted haughtily, "You would probably have gotten yourself killed, you being only a man."

At this both Logans laughed heartily.

"Can it be?" Davey asked, turning to his father with a look of feigned disbelief. "Has Beth finally discovered there is a difference between the two sexes?"

Stamping her foot, Beth felt the color rise in her cheeks. From out of nowhere came the image of the masked Indian and she felt a flutter in the pit of her stomach as if she had swallowed a butterfly. "Of course there's a difference you braying jackass! Women are much more clever."

Davey was not afraid to rise to the bait for he and Beth had spent many hours debating the merits of each sex, but a sudden pain in his injured leg caused him to grimace. "Shall we continue our discussion on the porch?" he suggested. "Perhaps with Robin on my side, I'll finally stand a chance of winning an argument with you."

"Ah! So you've met Hawkins," Lance remarked, looking at the dozing figure whose face was hidden beneath the lowered brim of his hat.

Neither man heard Beth's startled gasp as they turned toward the barracks.

"I like him," Davey offered. "We spent an evening

together at Fort Drum. Seems sincerely dedicated to helping end this war with the Seminoles. Even thinks we might be able to get Osceola to the peace table. I don't know how he plans to pull it off, but more power to him."

Beth stopped listening at the point where Davey said he and Robin Hawkins had spent an evening together, her thoughts turning inward. Oh Lord! Had Edward also taken part? And, if so, why hadn't Hawkins jumped at the chance to embarrass her in front of Davey and her uncle by forcing her to admit to her charade as Edwina? She would never believe he had slept through their arrival. More than likely he was just prolonging her agony.

As Lance headed in Robin's direction, Beth took a firm hold on Davey's arm preventing him from following his father.

"Wait!" she whispered, urgently causing him to look at her in surprise. "Wh . . . where is Eddie? Wasn't he with you at Fort Drum?"

Davey was bewildered by Beth's unusual stammering and certainly she should know that if something had happened to her brother he would have said so by now. "Of course he was with me. He's here with me now," he answered, drawing his dark brows together.

Beth looked around the compound, her eyes wide with dread.

"I don't mean he's 'here' here. As soon as we got to the fort he rode out to see Maggie McAfee," Davey explained, wondering what the reason was for her wariness.

Taking a deep breath, Beth decided she might as well learn the worst so she could prepare a defense against the man she would be forced to face in a very few moments. "But I suppose Eddie met Mr. Hawkins at Fort Drum?"

Davey hesitated for he could hardly tell Edward's sister how the young rascal spent his evenings when he was out from under his parents' watchful eye. "Uh, no. As a matter of fact, Eddie had business in town the night Robin arrived and the next day Hawkins was gone before your brother woke up."

Ready for a barrage of questions concerning Eddie's "business" which Davey knew was none of his sister's concern, he was taken aback when she gave him a smug little smile and suggested it was time they joined Lance and Hawkins on the porch. Beth knew she was not out of the woods by a great deal. All Robin had to do was ask about Edwina and the humiliating truth would come out. But at least temporarily she had gained a reprieve. Now if only Hawkins didn't bring up the subject of her sibling, and if she could keep the men talking about Indians, and if Eddie didn't return to the fort unexpectedly, and if . . . Oh, hell. She might as well depend on the bright ball of sun overhead setting in the east. Resignedly she looped her arm through her cousin's, thrusting back her slender shoulders.

"Shall we go and rattle the lion's cage?"

As they slowly walked toward where the two tall men now stood talking animatedly, Davey could only wonder at Beth's strange behavior. Climbing the steps Robin shook Davey's outstretched hand, giving Beth no more than a brief nod which suited her fine. The last thing she wanted was to be the center of attention. Her primary goal was to quit the men's company as soon as possible.

While Robin brought Lance up to date on the progress he had made toward finalizing talks between the government representatives and the Seminole leaders, Beth had a chance to study the unlikely peacemaker. There was no denying he was a man to turn the heads of silly women impressed by boundless muscles and a too handsome face. She admired the way the white linen shirt stretched across his broad back while his tight black britches hugged his trim hips fitting like a second skin over long, well-formed thighs and calves. Even his feet were long and narrow, the length exaggerated by the sharply pointed toes of his black boots. At first glance one might assume by his dress that he was a dyed-in-the-wool frontiersman like Davey and her Uncle Lance; yet to Beth there was a subtle but unmistakable difference. Something about the image he portrayed just didn't ring true. Perhaps it was the pristine whiteness of his shirt or maybe the polished sheen of his boots. Whatever the reason, Beth decided he was not a man to be trusted regardless of his seemingly logical explanation for being in the Territory.

Yes, the man would definitely bear watching. Having concluded her perusal and having formed an opinion she deemed worthy of note, Beth exhaled a decidedly unladylike snort which had nothing to do with the conversation taking place among the men. Lost in her own musings, it was not until she glanced up to find three pairs of eyes staring back at her that she realized she had voiced her disfavor aloud. She burned with the heat of the blush that suffused her face as gray-green eyes focused upon her with smug interest. She felt certain the cad knew exactly what she had been thinking and found her ill-disguised aversion amusing. How she longed to slap the smirk off his handsome face!

"What's wrong, Beth?" her uncle asked at a loss as to why she looked both embarrassed and annoyed.

"No . . . nothing." Her stammering only added to her mortification. "I'm sorry. My mind was on something else. Oh, look! Isn't that Brian headed this way?"

Never had she been so glad to see the young sergeant as he strolled in their direction accompanied by two men. How she loathed the way Hawkins always seemed to put her on the defensive without saying a word. However her relief was short-lived when she recognized the other men as Ralph Tillman and his son, Jesse. Tillman had one of the largest spreads in the Territory and a small army of paid ruffians to make certain no one trespassed within his boundaries. He was a notorious Indian-hater who considered both purebloods and half-breeds beneath his contempt which made him one of the few people her cousin, Davey, openly disliked. Even though they were not touching she felt Davey's body grow rigid as he watched their approach. His jaw thrust stubbornly forward while his soft brown eyes darkened with enmity.

The tension in the air was palpable as Robin, too, noticed the suddenly charged atmosphere and pondered the reason behind it. Without knowing why, he took an immediate dislike to the big man sauntering toward them. Ralph Tillman had a barrel chest and a ruddy complexion that Robin guessed was more the result of strong drink than time spent beneath the broiling sun. Small beady eyes were nearly swallowed up in his heavy, florid face; yet they were as cold and ruthless as any he'd ever seen. Stopping at the bottom of the stairs, Tillman stood with his legs wide apart, his thumbs looped around a brown leather belt.

"Afternoon Logan. Miss Beth," he said, nodding toward Lance then fastening his rodent eyes on Elizabeth.

His deliberate snub of Davey was obvious to everyone, but only Robin seemed to take exception to the way the obnoxious rancher leered at the girl who was young enough to be his daughter.

"Tillman," Lance acknowledged grudgingly while Beth silently moved closer to Davey, leaving no doubt as to where her loyalties lay.

Tillman scowled at the two and went on talking to Lance as if no one else was there.

"I understand you're here to powwow with those murdering savages. Waste of time," he vowed, spitting a stream of tobacco into the dust. "The only talk those bastards understand comes from the end of a well-aimed rifle."

Robin marvelled at Davey's restraint for he personally had to fight down the urge to flatten the man's bulbous nose against his beefy face. Sergeant Rourke shifted nervously from one foot to the other as Lance pinned the overblown rancher with a look that would have made a man with more sense take a step backward, but Tillman unwisely stood his ground.

"What I'm doing here is none of your damn business." Logan's quietly spoken words held more threat than a coiled rattler yet the agitator seemed oblivious to the danger.

"A bullet between the eyes. That's the only way to rid this country of the red pestilence. Right between the eyes," he repeated, purposefully looking at Davey.

Faster than Robin would have thought possible, Lance Logan launched himself at the smirking rancher and landed a blow to his heavy jowls that sent Tillman sprawling to the ground. His son, who hadn't said a word to this point, hurried to help him to his feet.

"Get the Hell out of here, you son of a bitch!" Lance roared. "And don't even think about trying to interfere with my plans or so help me God you'll be the one dodging bullets!"

Regaining his footing, Tillman shook off his son's hand and glared at the tall man in buckskins. "You'll pay for this, Logan. You and that half-breed you spawned. I'll get you if it's the last thing I do!"

His eyes gleamed with wicked promise. Then rubbing his sore jaw, he turned and stomped off with his son following in his wake.

"I'm sorry about that, Mr. Logan," Brian Rourke apologized shakily.

Lance followed the heavyset rancher with granite eyes. "Tillman's the one who'll be sorry if he's not careful."

"I should have been the one to hit him," Davey grumbled.

"In line behind me," Elizabeth stated firmly.

Robin chimed in, "I wouldn't have minded throwing a few punches myself."

Relaxing his grim expression, Lance laughed, a deep rumbling sound that erupted from his chest.

"Hell, Hawkins! You haven't even met the man," he barked massaging the knuckles on his right hand.

Robin grinned. "I would have introduced myself just before I hit him," he assured. "But I think I would have aimed lower so all that blubber in his gut could cushion the blow."

"I'd have aimed lower still," Beth spoke up angrily. "Seems a solid kick where his brains hang between his legs would have been in order."

Lance and Davey laughed while Robin winced imagining the pain of such a blow.

As the Logans told Robin how Ralph Tillman had arrived in the Territory several years ago with plenty of ready cash and a deep-seated hatred for the natives, Beth watched the sun arc toward a line of darkening thunderclouds rolling in from the west. Finally she interrupted, "I'd better be heading for the McAfees. Looks like we might get some rain."

Lance looked up at the sky, then frowned as he studied the distant horizon. "Might be better if you stay over tonight and ride out in the morning."

Beth's eyes darted nervously toward Robin and then back to her uncle. As foolish as it might seem, she felt the need to put some distance between herself and this man who caused her no end of confusion. Besides, if she could talk to Eddie before he accidentally ran into Hawkins, there was a slim chance she might convince him to stay out of sight until Robin concluded his business and returned to Washington. She had no idea how she would explain the mess she had gotten herself into. She could only hope Eddie would understand and perhaps see the humor in what she had done.

"I can make it before dark and a little rain will wash off the dust before I get there."

Her laugh sounded strained, her voice almost pleading. Robin wondered why she felt the need to leave in such a hurry. Gazing out to where the sun was now nearly eclipsed by the black thunderheads, he hoped Logan would insist that she spend the night at the fort. But such was not the case.

"Be careful," Lance admonished, "and give my regards to the McAfees."

With a reassuring nod, Beth leaped from the porch and all but ran to where her horse stood waiting. "See you in a day or two," she threw back over her shoulder as she mounted and headed for the gates.

She reminded Robin of a bird set free from its cage. Like one with the animal beneath her, Beth flew through the opening and disappeared just as a rumble of thunder sounded in the distance. After a few minutes, Robin mumbled something about business with Major Caldwell. He made his way purposefully toward the commander's office leaving the two Logans alone.

Chapter Six

Beth had traveled no more than a mile from the fort when a lone horseman appeared blocking the trail directly ahead. Reining in sharply she muttered an oath as she recognized Jesse Tillman. She looked from the man to the ever darkening sky and then back again.

Jesse was lean and lanky with nice enough features, though nothing out of the ordinary. Beth guessed him to be somewhere in his early twenties, yet she thought of him as younger for he always seemed to be standing in his father's shadow. She had only spoken to him on a few occasions, but when they chanced to meet she went out of her way to be pleasant because she felt sympathy for anyone forced to live with the domineering Ralph Tillman.

"Jesse? I'm surprised to see you out here. Is anything wrong?"

"No more than what's been wrong for the last six years," he replied shyly. "I followed you then circled ahead in order to apologize for what my father said back there." He nodded in the direction of Fort King.

Baffled but flattered that Jesse would go out of his way to find her just to voice his regret over his father's deplorable behavior, Beth offered him a smile of genuine liking but couldn't help saying, "It's your father who should be apologizing and not to me but to my cousin."

Jesse hung his head. Though Beth tried to excuse his submissiveness as the result of being under the thumb of a man like Ralph Tillman, she had little use for weakness.

"Never mind, Jesse. It was good of you to seek me out like this. I just find intolerance hard to understand. When it comes right down to it, the Indians have more right to be here than we do for they got here first."

Jesse laughed bitterly. "My father would call that kind of talk 'blasphemy.' "

"But why?" Beth's curiosity as to what had generated such hatred made her speak without thinking. Tillman's prejudices were really none of her business but Jesse seemed not to take offense.

Rubbing his hand over the pommel on his saddle, he looked at her sadly. "My father was never what you would call 'tolerant.' He's always held with the notion that the white male is a superior being made in God's image, you know." He cast a sheepish grin at Beth. "Six years ago we were on our way to Texas. Pa had made up his mind that Texas was where he wanted to settle but on the way we were waylaid by a war party of Creeks. They killed my ma and shot the horse right out from under my pa. I always thought he grieved more for the horse than for ma." Jesse still wore the same shy smile, but Beth was aware of a seething resentment just beneath his surface over a situation he could not change. Knowing he was probably right in his harsh judgment of his father she could think of nothing to say.

"Anyway, pa had a few bullet holes in him and by the time they healed he'd decided the future lay in the Florida Territory. He'd also come to the conclusion that the only good Indian was a dead Indian."

Beth shook her head. "It's a shame he has chosen to condemn so many for the actions of a few." Though she could not condone Ralph Tillman's philosophy, she now had a better understanding of what had made him the way he was.

Again Jesse looked at her timidly from beneath sandy lashes reminding Beth of a little boy. "Things weren't so bad when ma was alive. I've been thinking lately maybe having a woman around the house would make it like it used to be. We have a real fine place. I don't suppose you'd like to ride out and see it for yourself sometime?" Seeming to sense her refusal he hurried on. "There's a stream running right through the property with water as clear and blue as your eyes, Miss Elizabeth. I've always wanted to have a picnic along the bank of that stream, but a picnic's not much fun alone."

Beth didn't like the way the conversation was going. She didn't want to hurt Jesse for she could tell he'd suffered more than his share of grief and was vulnerable. Giving him false hopes, though, would be more cruel than the truth. The last thing she wanted was to serve as a replacement for his mother.

"I'm sorry, Jesse, but I'm afraid I can't accept your invitation."

"It's because of pa, isn't it?"

Beth knew he would not understand if she told him it was not just her dislike for his father that made her say "no," but the fact that she knew Jesse would never stand against him even to uphold his own principles. A jagged streak of lightning followed by a loud clap of thunder saved her from answering.

"I've got to go, Jesse. There's a storm coming and I have to get to the McAfees before these clouds unload."

"Why don't you come back to the fort with me until it blows over?" he suggested worriedly.

"I'll be fine, but I have to be on my way now."

"I wish I could go with you but my father. . . ." he let the words hang.

Beth fought the urge to reach out and shake some sense into him, but she knew it would do no good. Instead she kicked her horse into motion giving Jesse a jaunty salute as he moved aside to let her pass.

Reaching the edge of a wide meadow just as the first fat raindrops fell from the sky, Beth pulled her horse to a stop and scanned the open field bathed in the dusky shadows of the approaching storm. Damn Jesse Tillman for delaying her journey. The lily-livered daddy's boy was no doubt safe and dry back at Fort King right now while she had to brave the elements for a good three more miles. Any sympathy she had felt for him evaporated with the promise of her own discomfort.

Beth's inspection of the flat land she would have to cross in order to reach the McAfees' homestead had been cursory. Who in his right mind would be out in the rain on an afternoon rapidly turning black as night? Then her heartbeat quickened as she riveted her eyes back toward the vague shadowy figures barely discernible through the mist.

"Dear God!" she exclaimed. She wanted to deny what she was seeing but despite a view distorted by a murky haze her eyes were not playing tricks on her. There across the open tract of land was a band of Seminole braves mounted on ponies and cutting a path in her direction. Without a moment's hesitation, Beth tugged sharply on the reins and nudged her horse into the surrounding thicket, ignoring the brambles and brush that tore at her clothes and scratched her face. When her hat snagged on a limb, the leather thong caught around her neck and she thought for a moment she would strangle to death. With one hand she pulled it loose and secured it to her pommel, then using her arm as best she could, she deflected the rough branches that sought to bar her way. She had no idea whether or not the redskins had spotted her, but she wasn't about to wait around and find out. The conversation she'd had with the masked Indian came back to her like a prophesy of doom. She remembered admitting that had she been caught off guard by Osceola or one of his followers she would likely have been raped or killed.

Beth shuddered remembering how carelessly she had spoken, never for a moment believing such a thing might actually happen. How naive she was to think herself invincible. Maybe now she had tempted fate once too often. To add to her predicament the bloated clouds seemed to burst overhead, letting loose torrents of icy rain which soon soaked her to the skin. Lightning flashed and thunder roared while the wind whipped the trees into a pagan dance, their branches reaching out as if begging her to join in. On and on she rode, deeper into the forest, farther away from all that was familiar. Moisture streamed down her cheeks. It had to be rain for she never cried, yet she could not deny her fear as she found herself caught up in a nightmare of her own making and wondered if she would ever see the light of day again.

Had she been riding through this tangled vegetation for minutes or hours? It didn't really matter. Beth just knew she was chilled to the bone and numb from exhaustion. At some point she realized the worst of the storm had passed. Having no idea where she was and only a vague outline of what lay ahead in the mist-shrouded woods, she knew she would have to stop for the night. Hopefully the sun would enable her to backtrack in the morning.

Just ahead she spotted a small clearing beneath a canopy of pine trees that formed a shelter against the light drizzle. With her last ounce of strength she pulled the weary horse to a halt tying the animal to a nearby sapling. As she unbuckled the cinch and let the saddle slide to the ground, she sank to her knees pulling the blanket with her. Her face and hands stung from the scratches caused by thorns and brambles during her flight. She wondered if she would ever have the energy to move again. Wet, hungry, and completely alone, she rested her head against the smooth leather and tried to find some warmth beneath the damp saddle blanket. Too tired to worry about what might be lurking in the surrounding darkness, she stretched out on the forest floor and fell instantly asleep.

Beth knew she was dreaming for nothing in real life could elicit the sensations she was feeling. All at once she was both hot and cold. Every nerve in her body seemed charged as if she had been struck by a lightning bolt. She remembered being terribly cold as she lay cuddled beneath the soaked blanket, but if she had contracted a fever it came without the discomfort one would expect. The world seemed to be drifting around her. Suddenly she felt lighter than air as if she were floating atop a puffy cloud. It was a delicious feeling and if she were indeed asleep she hoped never to awaken. She was outside herself, up above looking down. There was a man kneeling beside her body — a tall, powerfully built man. His head was bent so that she couldn't make out his features but his hair was as black as the moonless night. Beth giggled then clapped her hand over her mouth hoping he wouldn't hear her and look up. But he was far too occupied to pay any attention to a laughing cloud.

She watched as he worked the wet buckskin britches down over her hips and her long, slender legs. He massaged the muscles of her thighs and calves as he went. She could almost feel her aching limbs relaxing. He raised her arms above her head pulling off her shirt, allowing the evening breeze to whisper against her skin. Imagining the feel of such hands on her body, Beth stretched and purred like a well-fed kitten. Never mind that the self she was seeing was naked, for it was only a dream. Everyone knows there is no room for modesty in a dream.

Beth gasped as the man lay down behind her and fit himself to the contour of her body. She hesitated for only a moment before willing herself back to earth, for such things were possible in dreams. And who could resist the promise of warmth and safety being offered? Enfolded in a tight embrace, Beth moaned with rapture as a long-fingered hand stroked her smooth, flat stomach then cupped one small breast as if weighing it against the size of his palm.

The rough horse blanket had disappeared and in its place a soft, sweet smelling cover captured their body heat and cocooned them against the damp, chilly night air.

"Sleep well, little spitfire," a deep soothing voice whispered in her ear.

Snuggling closer to the source of her comfort, Beth sighed, bidding her imaginary lover a silent "good night" before lapsing into a peaceful, dreamless slumber.

The smell of roasting meat along with the growling of her empty stomach awakened Beth to morning sunlight filtering through the thick branches overhead. With a start she levered herself up on one elbow and looked around the empty clearing. Still drugged from sleeping so soundly, she lay back down closing her eyes to savor the dream that was like none she could recall.

"Damnation!" She jerked to a sitting position, for there, in the middle of the clearing, a fire burned low giving off just the right amount of heat to roast the meat suspended above it on a wooden spit. She spotted her buckskins spread neatly over a bush to dry.

Eyes wide with horror, she dared to glance down. She shrieked, realizing she was stark naked beneath the beautiful, brightly patterned quilt she was clutching over her breasts.

Shaking her head to clear the cobwebs, then rubbing her eyes, Beth prayed with all her might that this was just a part of her extraordinary dream. But she knew it was not. What had happened to her while she slept? She remembered feeling tired and cold and wet. She had ridden out the storm then collapsed here deep in the forest drugged by exhaustion and fear. After that the dream had come to give her a sense of well-being allowing her body to renew its strength.

A tremor coursed through her at the memory of strong arms holding her close, of warm lips against her neck. There was no denying the physical evidence around her. Someone had actually been here during the night. Someone who'd had the gall to undress her and put his hands on her in a way no one else ever had. Beth's mind rebelled at such an outrage while her traitorous body tingled in the aftermath of an experience she could not in all honesty describe as totally distasteful. And that same someone who had kept her safe and warm in the darkness had provided food for her breakfast.

The "who" and "why" of it remained a mystery, but the image of the masked Indian appeared unbidden before her. Common sense told her it could not have been him. One thing she knew for sure. The man who whispered softly in her ear just hours ago wore no face covering. She could still feel his breath upon her neck like a gentle caress. His voice, though low and sensual, had been clear. Besides, why would he come to her without his disguise? It didn't make sense. But, then, nothing made sense this morning.

Still pondering the identity of her protector, Beth heaved a sigh and tossed the cover aside. She dressed quickly for it was chilly in the shadowy, dew-dampened forest even with the sun shining above the treetops. She hunched down beside the fire, her mouth watering as the aroma of the tempting fare teased her nostrils and emphasized the rumbling noises coming from her belly.

After devouring the savory meat and licking the juice from her fingers, Beth scooped dirt onto the dying embers, then moved to saddle the mare, crooning soft nonsense words as she tightened the cinch and mounted. She paused to take a last look at the clearing, its dim shadows gradually giving way to the morning light. No trace of the storm or the fear which had nearly overcome her last night remained. She marveled at the beauty of nature here in this peaceful glen and thanked God that she was alive to see the beginning of another new day.

Aloud Beth spoke softly, "Well, my guardian angel, whoever you are, I am indebted to you."

The mare whinnied and nodded her head in agreement. Smiling, Beth nudged her toward a break in the tangled brush, a break that had not been there last night. No doubt whoever had spent the night with her in the clearing was also responsible for pointing her in the right direction. If it was *her* Indian that had come to the rescue, she wasn't at all sure she liked being obligated to him, though there seemed little she could do to change what had already happened. She owed him for preventing Osceola from killing her.

Had he also assured her safety during the night? If so, her debt was mounting and it went against the grain. But life was a funny thing and sometimes even the strongest among men needed a little help. Should the opportunity present itself, Beth vowed she would repay her unknown benefactor. Rational or not, she couldn't help hoping he turned out to be the man she now thought of as *her* Indian. The prospect brought with it both excitement and dread.

From behind a screen of saplings cloaked in wild creepers, Hawk watched as Beth drew rein at the edge of the meadow taking time to search the open field for any sign of the band of redskins who had driven her into the woods the day before. She raised her face to the sun then straightened in the saddle sniffing the air like a hound after a scent. He felt a moment of panic when she swiveled around and stared straight at the dense tangle of brush he had chosen for a cover. But after what seemed eternity, Beth shrugged her slender shoulders and turned away kneeing her mare into motion and galloping at breakneck speed across the open pasture toward the McAfee homestead.

Reckless hoyden! She didn't have the brain of a gnat. Someone ought to shake some sense into her. Or better still, warm her backside! Maybe that would convince her that a female belonged at home doing female things, not spending the night alone in hostile territory.

But she hadn't been alone. And damned if Hawk could understand what had possessed him to follow her. He cursed the day he first set eyes on Elizabeth

Townsend. Even flat on her back with Asi-yahola urging him to kill her, she had shown more curiosity than fear. It just wasn't natural. She was unlike any woman he had ever known, a strange mixture of tomboy dare-deviltry and girlish charm. One minute he wanted to throttle her; the next he wanted to hold her in his arms and protect her from harm as he had done last night.

Ahh! Last night! He was still uncertain as to how such an unlikely situation had come about. He had planned to follow her at a safe distance just to assure himself that she arrived safely. He had seen her startled reaction when young Tillman jumped out at her from behind the bushes. He had been relieved by her surprise, for it clearly indicated that their meeting was no clandestine affair planned in advance. But relief had swiftly turned to anger. Hawk had gone so far as to draw his rifle from its sheath almost hoping the candy-ass would give him an excuse to use it. It annoyed him that Beth seemed on friendly terms with the son of a bigot like Ralph Tillman.

After wishing Jesse to Hell and back, Hawk's wrath irrationally grew to mammoth proportions when he realized the mealymouthed coward was going to allow Beth to continue her journey alone with the sky growing ever darker and the thunder rumbling overhead like an avenging angel. Never had Hawk experienced such conflicting emotions in dealing with the opposite sex and the fact that he was doing so now did nothing to improve his temper. When he needed a woman, he paid for his pleasure and walked away without a backward glance or a twinge of guilt.

Good God! What was wrong with him? The comparison was absurd for in no way did he lust after the skinny little termagant. So why was he wasting so much time thinking about her? Making love to Beth Townsend would be like bedding a boy, not at all appealing to his way of thinking! If he knew what was good for him he would forget her and get on about his business!

While he tried unsuccessfully to put her from his mind, he continued to dog her tracks; thus he was able to get a clear picture of what took place when she reached the meadow and sighted the roaming band of bucks. Cursing her stupidity, he watched as she whirled Senabar and dashed helter-skelter into the dense undergrowth. Had she remained motionless she would have gone undetected by the youngsters, for what Beth had feared was a war party turned out to be nothing more than a group of Indian boys hunting small game. But on spotting the solitary rider they decided to give chase just for the fun of it.

Hawk was tempted to let them pursue the little hellion. Then maybe she would think twice about venturing out alone. Instead he easily intercepted the rascals who were overawed by the presence of the mighty warrior whom Asi-yahola called brother. He warned them not to interfere for he was on the trail of the treacherous white eyes they had spooked, one thought to be carrying important documents which would be invaluable to their leader. The boys were reluctant to let such a golden opportunity pass, but finally Hawk convinced them that he would not need their assistance in relieving the courier of his dispatches.

Though by this time Beth had a good start on him,

she was moving slowly against the storm and Hawk had no difficulty in finding the clearing where she finally collapsed in exhaustion. Shaking his head, he allowed his imagination to envision what might have happened had there been a real raiding party in the meadow. How could he continue to protect her from her own folly. And why the hell had he made it his business anyway?

From that point on he had no time to analyze his motives. Even from where he stood at the edge of the clearing he could see that Beth was trembling with cold huddled beneath the damp blanket. As he came closer he could actually hear her teeth chattering. He knew he had to get her dry and warm or she would likely catch pneumonia. Her cooperation as he removed her boots then peeled off the tight buckskins followed by the pullover shirt caused the perspiration to pop out on his wide brow. Knowing she would never willingly allow such liberties were she aware of what was going on, he felt her forehead fearing she might already have contracted a fever. His hand lingered even after assuring himself that her temperature was normal. Her skin was soft and smooth despite the unladylike tan and spattering of freckles barely visible in the moonlight peeking from behind the clouds overhead. He knelt beside her allowing his eyes to feast on her naked beauty, taking advantage of her trancelike state.

Hawk was astonished to realize that she was indeed beautiful. As sleek and smooth as a young colt, her breasts looked small and firm like ripe peaches. He itched to cup the forbidden fruit in the palm of his hand. His eyes roamed over her flat belly to the triangular mound of reddish-gold curls covering her most private part. Then his gaze traveled down long slender legs coming back to that enticing juncture where her thighs met. He felt his shaft harden and his stomach muscles grow taut. How could he ever have thought her boyish? She was like the bud of a delicate flower just waiting to be kissed into bloom. He wondered what it would be like to watch her blossom into womanhood. A wry grin supplanted his musings for the likelihood of his being anywhere near when the transformation occurred. . . . He let his thoughts trail off.

He was daydreaming in the middle of the night. Elizabeth Townsend and the Hawk? What a laugh! He could just imagine her horror were she to wake up and find him bending over her now, seeing his face without the mask. No doubt she would come up kicking and clawing and calling him a son of a bitch with some justification. Still he couldn't resist running his fingers over her body with feathery strokes, circling her nipples then following a downward path to rest his hand lightly atop the springy mound of curls between her legs. If the weakness of his flesh doomed him to perdition by the white man's god, so be it. He would rely on the Indian gods to protect him from such vengeance.

Beth shivered, whether from his touch or the cool night air, Hawk had no way of knowing. Standing up he crossed the clearing to where his stallion waited contentedly blowing in Senabar's ear.

"Restraint is a great character builder," he whispered softly as he caught Satan's reins and urged the animal a short distance away tying him to a bush out

119

of reach of the mare.

Removing a dry blanket from a canvas protected pack, Hawk returned to the spot where Beth lay trembling, her legs drawn up for warmth. He had every intention of staying aloof as he tucked the blanket around her and squatted on his heels staring down at her sleeping form. But as he watched, the tremors continued to rack her body.

Reluctantly he got up and untied the stallion who wasted no time in closing the gap between Senabar and himself. The mare whinnied in gentle response, welcoming him back.

Retracing his steps, Hawk lifted the cover and slid down behind Beth's restless form fitting the contours of her body to his. He put his arm beneath her breasts and pulled her close.

"The Hell with restraint!"

Chapter Seven

Edward Townsend grudgingly relaxed his hold on Maggie as Senabar leapt the McAfees' fence and raced directly toward them as if the devil was at her heels. Eddie had been enjoying a few stolen moments beneath the crab apple tree just far enough from the kitchen so Maggie's mother couldn't see them should she glance out the window. Though Eddie loved his sister dearly, he thought her timing a little off the mark. As she approached the couple, his glowering expression said as much.

Beth waited until she was almost upon her brother and Maggie before she jerked hard left. Senabar careened in that direction grinding turf beneath her hoofs then coming to a stop.

Blue eyes wide with feigned innocence, Beth looked over her shoulder, "Hope I'm not interrupting anything."

An identical pair of eyes glared back at her. "Damn it, Beth! You nearly ran us down! Have you lost your mind?" Eddie shouted, knowing full well his sister had perfect control over the horse, but aggravated that his little tryst with Maggie had been cut short.

Beth dismounted and walked to where the young couple stood a respectful distance apart. "I haven't lost my mind and I trust Maggie hasn't lost anything of importance either," she retorted, tapping her brother on the chest for emphasis.

Eddie had the grace to look embarrassed while Maggie tittered and covered her face with her hand. The fact that Maggie seemed to understand what she was hinting at made Beth wonder just how far their romance had progressed. She decided it might be time for her brother to declare his intentions or back off. Eddie might think she didn't know what was what but she had heard enough gossip to understand that a *certain kind* of women held him in *high esteem!* Maggie might be a featherbrain, but she was also Beth's best friend and she didn't deserve to be hurt.

"It's so good to have you back, Beth," Maggie said a little breathlessly. "Let's go up to the house and tell ma you're here."

Beth shifted uncomfortably. "Uh . . . Maggie, there's a little matter I need to discuss with Eddie first. Why don't you go ahead and see if your folks feel up to having two Townsends taking advantage of their hospitality. We'll be right along."

"Why, Beth! You know you and Eddie are like family," the girl cooed looking longingly up at Edward.

When Beth showed no sign of following her, Maggie gave an exaggerated sigh. "Don't be too long."

With that she turned and walked slowly toward the house, her rounded hips swaying gracefully beneath her full skirts. Beth had to say Eddie's name twice before she drew his attention away from Maggie's exit.

"Huh? Oh, sorry, sis. Guess I was woolgathering," he apologized halfheartedly.

"Woolgathering, my foot! Your mind was on cotton! You know, the stuff petticoats are made of? And unless you want Patrick McAfee to skin you alive, you'd better make your intentions clear or keep your hands in your pockets!"

Eddie was the most even-tempered person Beth knew next to Davey, but as she watched golden sparks flame to life in his eyes she knew she had overstepped her bounds.

"Damn it all! I'm a grown man, and if I want to kiss a lady I'll kiss a lady!"

"And if you want to sleep with a whore, you'll sleep with a whore! But you'd better not let the lady catch you doing it!" Beth shot back before she could stop herself.

She closed her eyes awaiting the well-deserved rebuke that never came. Instead she felt her brother's arms go around her and heard his amused laughter ringing in her ear.

"Beth, you are incorrigible!" he hooted, burying her face against his chest. "I swear I don't know where you get your information or why you feel the need to impart it at such inopportune moments. But believe me," he assured sincerely as he held her at arm's length, "my intentions toward Maggie are honorable. I would do nothing to bring down the wrath of Patrick McAfee on my head!"

Beth did believe him for Eddie had never lied to her. Smiling up into his face was like looking into a mirror. "Does that mean you've sown all your wild oats?" she asked hopefully.

Chucking her under the chin, Eddie replied honestly, "That means, little sister, that my intentions toward Maggie are honorable. Now, shall we go inside?"

Beth knew that was as much as she was going to get from him and probably more than she deserved since she had butted into something that was really none of her business. Eddie's voice held a note of finality that brooked no argument; therefore, he was surprised when she drew away from the arm he extended.

"Beth, I've said all I intend to say on the subject."

Still, Beth held back. If Eddie didn't know any better, he would think she was the one caught with her hand in the cookie jar.

She looked up at him her face flushing with embarrassment. "Actually, Eddie, your affair with Maggie was not the 'little matter' I wanted to discuss."

Seeing him scowl she amended hurriedly, "I didn't mean 'affair' literally. I meant . . . relationship."

His scowl deepened.

"Oh Hell! You know what I mean."

"I'd better say I do so you can quit while you're behind!"

Seconds ticked by in silence. Growing impatient Eddie glanced toward the house then grumbled, "Well, spit it out, Beth. The McAfees are waiting for us."

Beth knew he meant Maggie was waiting for him. Still she couldn't find the words to broach the subject of her ridiculous masquerade as Edwina Townsend.

"Well?" Eddie repeated.

When Beth remained mute, he turned toward the house, unwilling to stand there under the broiling sun, when his sister seemed to have nothing to say.

"Wait!" she cried, catching hold of his arm. "It's

about a man!"

Eddie looked at her in disbelief. Never had he known her to show any interest in the opposite sex unless it was to prove she could outshoot, outride, or outsmart some unsuspecting male who had been foolish enough to issue a challenge. Slowly his face split into a mischievous grin.

"If you wanted my expertise on how to entice a man, you shouldn't have begun by criticizing my worldliness."

Beth felt the blood suffuse her face but this time her crimson hue was the result of anger not embarrassment. "ENTICE?" she bellowed. "I'm talking about a man I hate, loathe, and despise! Now do you understand?"

"No."

"Of course you don't because you're a conceited jackass just like Robin Hawkins! You're all the same! You think women are only good for fluttering their eyelashes and swishing their skirts for your entertainment!"

To her horror Beth felt the tears well up in her eyes and brim over making twin paths down her cheeks. No one could have been more shocked than her brother who had never known her to cry even when she fell from an oak tree and broke her arm in two places. Helplessly he enfolded her in his embrace, feeling his shirt grow damp. When her sobs subsided, he led her to a fallen log and sat beside her while between hiccups she told him everything that had happened since her first meeting with Robin Hawkins at Fort King.

Edward sympathized, knowing how the stranger's high-handed attitude must have stung Beth's pride, yet her opinion of the man was so at odds with what Davey had told him he felt an overwhelming desire to meet Robin Hawkins so he could judge for himself. He found it hard to contain his mirth as Beth told how she had fooled Hawkins into believing her twin was a genteel young lady named Edwina.

" 'Oh what a tangled web we weave,' " Eddie quoted, rubbing Beth's hand gently as she rested her head against his shoulder.

"I know I dug myself into a hole without bringing a ladder. But couldn't you see fit to stay out of sight for a little while?" she asked pleadingly.

Eddie shook his head. "It won't work, honey. Even if I agreed, someone is bound to mention my name sooner or later. I can't believe Davey or Uncle Lance haven't said something to give it away already."

Beth, too, wondered how she had managed to get away with such an absurd farce up to now.

"Why does it bother you so?" Eddie asked, puzzled by her attitude toward this man he had never met.

"What do you mean?"

"Why don't you want Hawkins to know that you are a beautiful, well-bred young lady who can hold her own at a governor's ball or an afternoon tea? You were the toast of Tallahassee when Uncle Lance took you for a visit. He told us how all the handsome politicians were groveling at your feet and the women were pea green with envy."

"Pooh! You know how Uncle Lance exaggerates."

"On the contrary. Uncle Lance has never been one to overstate the truth and you know it."

Beth blushed in spite of herself. She knew now that her charade had been foolish and she couldn't say why she had pulled such a childish stunt. All she knew was that she couldn't have stood hearing Robin Hawkins's cynical laughter when he saw her dressed in ruffles and lace. It shouldn't have mattered, but it did.

Her down-at-the-mouth expression tore at Edward's heart. He and Beth were closer than most siblings. Perhaps because they came from the same seed they seemed more attuned to each other's emotions. He didn't like knowing that Beth was suffering because of some inexplicable reaction to a total stranger. He wondered why his usually shoot from the hip sister had gotten herself into such a mess. There wasn't a deceitful bone in her body. His lips quirked as he remembered several occasions when she had been most painfully honest. He would have to be the same. On the other hand he would not purposely subject her to humiliation.

"Look, Beth. I don't think there's a chance in Hell that Hawkins won't find you out and my advice is to fess up before this goes any further."

Beth started to protest but he hushed her with a finger over her pouting lips.

"But . . . I will stay here with the McAfees until Davey is ready to return to Fort Brooke. The chores have fallen behind since Pete joined the army and I'm sure Patrick can use an extra hand."

Beth's face lit up as she threw her arms around her brother's neck. She knew his advice was sound and she promised herself she would tell Hawkins the truth at the first opportunity. She just needed a little more time to decide how to go about it. Meanwhile there was always the chance that some unforeseen circumstance might arise which would make her explanation unnecessary. Perhaps she could persuade *her* Indian to shoot the arrogant bastard. With a lighter step and a secret smile she walked arm in arm with Edward toward the McAfees' front porch.

Fort King was bustling with activity as military leaders from throughout the territory came to take part in the peace talks scheduled to begin on the morrow. Representatives had already arrived from Forts Volusia, Call, Barnwell, Columbia, Drum, and Brooke. There were politicians from Tallahassee who would take no part in the talks but wanted to know the results firsthand, for their push for Florida Statehood depended to a large extent on whether or not the internal dispute with the Seminole could be resolved. There were also many settlers who had a more personal reason for wanting to see what happened for their very lives could depend on it. Beth studied the expressions on the faces of the men going in and out of the gates; some hopeful, some skeptical, but all willing to do what they could to bring peace to this troubled land.

True to his word, Eddie had remained with the McAfees though this was scarcely a sacrifice on his part since his romance with Maggie seemed to be progressing toward a probable engagement. Beth had managed to avoid Robin Hawkins by spending most of her time with her brother and her friends. The few times she had come to the fort, Robin had been nowhere in sight. Her uncle mentioned his frequent sojourns into the surrounding countryside to make the final arrangements for the parley, but she knew he would be here soon if he wasn't here already. He had played an important role in bringing the two warring factions together and would not miss the grand finale. For the hundredth time Beth wondered what was really behind his determination to see an end to the dispute between the Indians and the whites in Florida.

As if her thoughts had conjured him up, Robin strolled around the corner of the barracks, stopping abruptly as soon as he saw her.

"Miss Townsend," he acknowledged. "Still in the thick of things, I see."

His words rankled but she smiled tightly. "Of course, Mr. Hawkins. It's not often one gets a chance to see history in the making."

"History is made every day, Miss Townsend. Some events are just more important than others in the total scheme of things. Only time will tell how significant tomorrow's meeting will be."

Beth noticed how tired Robin appeared, the lines beside his gray-green eyes more pronounced than she remembered. He was on the verge of achieving his goal, whatever his reasons might be, yet he lacked the enthusiasm her uncle had remarked upon whenever he spoke of the Washington negotiator.

"And what do you predict will be the outcome, Mr. Hawkins?"

"I make no claim to forecasting the future, Miss Townsend. As I've said, only time will tell."

He started to walk away then paused. "Did the rest of your family come from Fort Brooke to observe the festivities?"

Beth was surprised by the question though with so many settlers attending the meeting as spectators she supposed it was a logical assumption.

"I'm afraid not. My father is needed to help maintain the defenses at home, and my brothers and sister are far too young to make the trip though I'm sure Johnny and Jeremy would disagree."

Robin narrowed his eyes looking at her suspiciously. "Since you and your sister are the same age, I hardly see how you can say she is too young to travel."

Sucking in her cheeks, Beth realized her mistake. She had been thinking of little Mandy when she mentioned her sister, for the moment forgetting completely the nonexistent Edwina. Now would be an ideal time to set the record straight, to admit the only sister she had was a four-year-old darling who didn't look the least bit like her. She took a deep breath but the words simply wouldn't come.

"Ah . . . well . . . it's true Edwina and I are both nineteen. I didn't realize the two of you had met." Beth ducked her head unable to look Robin in the face. "Though we are twins, Edwina and I are very different," she said, studying the tips of her boots. "Edwina doesn't care for riding, you see. She prefers to stay at home helping our stepmother look after the little ones."

"Very different"? Now that was an understatement of major proportions! Robin was disappointed that he would not be seeing the lovely Edwina among the crowd. He was also puzzled by Beth's description of her sister.

"That's strange. Miss Edwina seemed quite fond of your mare. On the night we met she was standing beside the corral talking to the animal and stroking her head as if they were old friends."

Beth shrugged her shoulders. "I've really never been

130

able to figure Edwina out. She's so unpredictable. Flighty, actually. One minute she's up; the next minute she's down. Typical female," she added disparagingly.

Robin looked incredulous. What Beth Townsend was saying about her sister sounded childishly spiteful and certainly didn't fit the impression he had gotten of the lovely young lady.

"Too bad she couldn't make the trip. I would have enjoyed seeing Miss Edwina again."

Beth felt her heart plummet as she was assaulted by a wave of envy foreign to her nature. Hell's bells! How could one be jealous of one's self, she thought irritably. Why should she care if the undiscerning jackass preferred a simpering bit of fluff to a woman able to do things that really counted—like carrying dispatches from fort to fort? She refused to let his preference for the fictitious Edwina undermine her confidence. She hoped, in fact, that he was truly infatuated with *her sister.* What sweet revenge that would be for she would make sure he never laid eyes on Edwina Townsend again!

A tremor of excitement ran through her as she remembered that brief moment when their lips had touched. The stupid man thought Edwina desirable and her, Beth . . . well, who cared what he thought of her! He was too shallow to see beneath the surface. At least she did not judge a person by appearance alone or she might be taken in by Hawkins's handsome face.

She watched his tall, muscular frame as he moved away, admiring his loose-jointed stride. Suddenly it dawned on her what she had done. Pounding her knees with tightly balled fists, she let go a string of oaths beneath her breath. Instead of telling him the truth as she intended to do, she had complicated her deception and the knowledge brought with it a terrible sense of loss. She might not like the man and she might question his motives for being here, but she couldn't see him as someone who would stoop to duplicity in order to save face. Eddie may have laughed at her masquerade as Edwina Townsend, but she doubted Robin Hawkins would see any humor in what she had done.

The next day dawned bright and clear. By eight o'clock the sun was already beating relentlessly down upon the open field which had been selected as the meeting site. Though the heat would be nearly intolerable at midday there was a definite advantage to holding the talks here. Neither side could have hidden forces waiting to attack, should things not go their way.

There was a hint of festivity in the air reminding Beth of a church picnic. Two long tables had been set up with a shorter table at the end to form a "U." There Lance Logan had already taken his seat. Military leaders from the various forts took their places at one table, looking uncomfortable in their heavy dress uniforms.

The Indians rode in on horseback with Chief Micanopy at their head, other tribal leaders and counselors following. It was quite a colorful procession. Brightly beaded tunics glittered in the sunlight while egret feathers decorated their headbands. All rode straight and tall, looking neither to the left nor to the right but staring ahead to where the enemy waited.

The warriors who had been chosen to attend came last and the crowd gasped in unison as they recognized the most fearsome brave of all, Osceola. Beth was more interested in the men riding close beside him. She heard the names — Alligator, Jumper, Wild Cat — murmured among the throng of onlookers but none of Osceola's companions was *her* Indian. Had she really expected him to be there wearing the outlandish mask she knew must conceal his even more grotesque features? In truth she hadn't known what to expect. Just the fact that Osceola had agreed to attend the conference led her to believe anything was possible.

As they passed in front of her, Beth felt a chill run up her spine raising the hairs on the back of her neck. The uncrowned prince of the Seminole Nation haughtily turned his head. His dark piercing eyes looked right at her. In that moment Beth wondered if there could ever be peace between the Indians and the whites, for what she saw was undisguised hatred and distrust. Sighing with relief when Osceola once again directed his gaze toward the table where her uncle rose to greet Micanopy, she was startled to find Robin Hawkins standing at her side. Again she was impressed by his height and the breadth of his shoulders. His face seemed to be carved in granite making his thoughts unreadable. Beth wondered why he had chosen to be an observer when he could have been sitting beside Lance Logan taking part in the proceedings, and after a while she asked him as much.

Like a prophet from biblical times, he replied, "I've done what I was sent to do. It's out of my hands now."

There was no satisfaction in his answer, only sadness and resignation.

"I don't understand you, brother. You urged me to talk to the white eyes. Now you condemn me for what I said."

Hawk stared across the campfire at Asi-yahola. "How can I condemn you for what you said when you didn't say a damn thing?" His harsh words conveyed the anger he had held inside throughout the day.

The tribal elders had done exactly what he had feared they would do. They had listened to the soldiers and agreed to their terms for relocation. The young warriors, including Asi-yahola, made no move to dissuade them.

"I am disappointed in the Black Drink Crier. I did not expect you to give up so easily. The soldiers were of a mind to bargain, to listen to alternatives. You gave them none!" Hawk's jaw hardened as he remembered the smiles on the faces of the soldiers and settlers, the disbelieving look of Lance Logan as the provisions laid out by the military leaders were docilely accepted by Micanopy and his counselors.

Asi-yahola's eyes blazed as he bitterly defended his position. "The only alternative is death. If we stay we will be slaughtered like cattle. I am tired of the bloodshed. I do not wish to see my family die."

"The whites could have been made to see reason," Hawk argued ,though he knew it was too late to undo the damage that had been done. "There is enough land for everyone."

Asi-yahola shook his head regretfully. "That's what we believed ten years ago when we signed the treaty agreeing to remain on the four million acres set aside for us here. But soon the white man wanted the land back. Perhaps he will not covet the land beyond the great river and we can live in peace. We will see."

"If they do not want the land of which you speak then

it is probably not worth having."

Hoping with all his heart that his friend was wrong, Asi-yahola repeated again, "We will see."

Chapter Eight

Only one low-burning lantern kept the interior of the stable from being pitch-black for it was still an hour before dawn. Beth stood in the shadowy dimness taking comfort in the smell of leather and freshly cut hay as she rubbed her hand up and down the white blaze streaking from between Senabar's ears to her nostrils.

Beth had spent a miserable night, first thinking sleep would never come and then wishing it hadn't. She had been plagued with vague dreams that remained just out of reach, buried except for the image that finally brought her back to wakefulness with a start. That she remembered all too clearly for she had seen again the dark face of Osceola as he paraded across the meadow, his obsidian eyes pinning her to the spot on which she stood. There was no doubting his hatred, not only for her but for all of those who would force him to leave his home. His resentment was to be expected. Despite the shiver of fear she felt when he seemed to single her out as the object of his scorn, Beth could not help admiring his regal carriage. Back ramrod straight, the Indian leader held his head high, glaring with haughty disdain at those who would dare attempt to subdue him. She was as astounded as the other onlookers when Osceola stood silently throughout the proceedings as the tribal elders meekly relinquished their rights and agreed to the conditions for removal set down by the white officers. She could not share the ill concealed elation of men like Ralph Tillman who snickered smugly in the wake of the Indians' submission.

Afterward as she listened to her uncle and Davey along with Robin Hawkins angrily discuss the unanticipated acquiescence of Micanopy and his counselors, Beth tried to imagine how she would feel if she were forced to leave her home. Certainly she would not give up without a fight, but then the Seminoles had put up a fight. They had been resisting the encroachment of the white interlopers for as long as she could remember. The result so far had been bloodshed and loss of lives on both sides. Perhaps the new land would be better and at last everyone could live in peace, but Beth had serious doubts. Nowhere could there be a place like the Territory with its wild, natural beauty and plentiful game, its clear lakes and rivers where flowers scented the warm, balmy air and all manner of birds flocked overhead. If ever there were a heaven on earth it had to be Florida, and Beth felt a deep sorrow for the proud people whose destiny it seemed was to carve a new life for themselves beyond the great river.

"It appears the die is cast," she whispered sadly to Senabar whose soulful brown eyes were in keeping with Beth's somber mood.

She would be leaving shortly with Uncle Lance and Davey. After stopping by the McAfees to release Edward from his self-imposed exile, they would head home to begin preparations for the next step in the relocation process. Once word was out, the individual bands of Seminoles would be straggling into the little port settlement of Tampa to await the ships that would carry them to their new home.

The mare raised her head and flattened her ears as the sound of booted feet signaled someone's approach. Beth felt no alarm assuming it to be Davey or his father, for they planned to begin their journey at dawn.

"Well, what have we here? A ray of sunshine before the break of day?"

Beth cringed upon recognizing the odious voice of Ralph Tillman. Damn it all! The man gave her the creeps with his beady little eyes ogling her as if she were a choice morsel on his plate. The last thing she wanted was to be caught alone with him in the stable. Pretending he wasn't there, Beth opened the door of the stall and went in, reaching for the saddle resting atop the half wall.

"Here now, Miss Elizabeth. Let me help you with that," Tillman offered, wedging his bulk in beside her before Beth could protest.

Senabar, not liking so much company in the small area allotted her, whinnied loudly and tried to rear up on her hind legs. Instead she managed to shove the paunchy rancher against Beth until only the heavy saddle kept the two from being chest to chest. Tillman tried to thrust the saddle out of the way, but Beth kept it firmly wedged between herself and the man leering down at her. She felt her stomach lurch. If not for the barrier between them, she shuddered to think what the repulsive old lecher might try to do to her.

"Get out of here, Tillman. You're making my horse nervous!" Beth spit the words at him like a hissing cat.

Tillman continued to grin. "Now, now, Miss Elizabeth. You give me that saddle and I'll handle everything."

Knowing she was probably the *everything* he intended to handle, Beth did as he instructed. She gave him the saddle with a mighty shove against his midsection. Caught off guard, Tillman lost his footing and fell backward out of the stall, landing hard on his posterior. He was no longer grinning.

"Why you little bitch," he sneered, trying to untangle himself. "It's about time you learned who your betters are and I'm just the one to teach you."

Before he knew what was happening, the cumbersome saddle was tossed aside and Tillman was jerked to his feet. A powerful fist sank into his protruding stomach which sent him sprawling once again.

"Uncle Lance! Thank God!"

"Are you all right, honey?" Logan asked without taking his eyes off the nefarious rancher.

"I'm okay," Beth assured though her legs were shaking and her stomach still felt a little queasy.

Lance hauled Tillman to his feet for the second time. "Stay away from my family, you son of a bitch, or I'll make you the sorriest man in the Territory!" Gray eyes as hard as tempered steel backed up the promise.

Tillman straightened his jacket and glared contemptuously at the man who had bested him. "You don't scare me, Logan," he blustered. "My name spells power and influence around here. I've gotten rid of the Indians and I can get rid of you!"

Lance took a threatening step forward causing the boastful rancher to back up two.

"Your name spells 'shit,' Tillman! I'm warning you for the last time! Stay out of my way and don't even

139

think about coming near my niece again!"

Tillman continued to back away, his meaty fists clenched at his sides. "It's not over between us yet. Now that the Indians have learned their lesson, it's time to clean out the traitors that supported their uprising. I'm coming after you, Logan. You and that half-breed son you're so proud of!"

With that Tillman spun on his heels and headed for the open doorway brushing past Davey and Robin as if they weren't there. Beth had no idea how long the two had been standing just inside the stable or how much they had overheard. Only she seemed to notice a third witness to the fracas. A furtive figure slipped out of the shadows and escaped without drawing attention to himself. What, she wondered, did Jesse Tillman truly think of his father's insufferable behavior?

By the time Lance Logan and his kin arrived home, Indians from the many diverse bands of Seminole had begun to trickle into Tampa. The small port settlement was ideally situated at the edge of Hillsborough Bay, a body of water with a deep, natural channel affording easy access to ships sailing up or down the Florida west coast in the Gulf of Mexico.

Makeshift shelters dotted the landscape. Heavyset women with broad features huddled over cooking fires keeping their eyes on the dark-skinned, half-naked children darting hither and yon. Swarthy men with straight black hair clustered around the animal pens talking softly, occasionally casting wary glances toward the fort where watchmen stood guard. Sullen expressions left little doubt as to their opinions of the decisions that had been made on their behalf.

A feeling of unrest hung like a thundercloud over the community, leaving the inhabitants nervous and short-tempered. Beth, who had been forbidden to venture out of the fort until the ships arrived to transport the Indians to their new home, chafed against the restriction which she viewed as punishment for a crime she hadn't committed.

Earlier that afternoon she had overheard a group of soldiers discussing the arrival of Osceola and his followers. As if drawn by a magnet, she had climbed the wooden stairs to the narrow walkway circling the inside walls of the fort. She peered over hoping to catch a glimpse of the notorious warrior and his braves but they were nowhere in sight. In truth, it was not Osceola her eyes were seeking among the crowd of strange faces. The fate of *her* Indian was what drew Beth to the parapet. She longed to see him again, yet dreaded the thought of his being one of the many held captive without chains. But if he wasn't here, where could he be and what could he hope to accomplish by staying in the woods alone? No one man could stand up against the entire United States Army. Beth knew that worrying about him would do no good yet she had been able to think of little else. Hell's bells! She probably wouldn't even recognize him if he were standing beside her!

Now it was twilight and the sounds of daily activity had long since ceased. Only the rustle of the leaves in the giant oak tree nearby disturbed the silence of approaching night as Beth leaned against the fence lightly stroking Senabar's nose.

"I'm sorry we can't chase stars in the moonlight," she crooned softly, "but we won't be stuck in this dismal

141

place forever. I promise."

She spoke more to lift her own flagging spirits than those of the mare. Confinement was becoming tedious in the extreme. How she longed to gallop across the meadow with the wind in her hair!

"At least that awful Robin Hawkins is no longer around to make life miserable. I suppose by now he's halfway back to Washington."

Senabar twitched her ears as the gentle sound of her mistress's voice droned on. "I wonder who he really is and why he came here? Not that it matters. With luck we'll never see him again and that's the most pleasant thought I've had all day."

Her laughter was a melody floating on the evening breeze. Little did she realize what an enchanting picture she made as she stood bathed in the afterglow of sunset. Fascinated, Robin gazed at the vision of loveliness as she stretched to plant a kiss on the horse's nose. He ran his tongue over his lips envying the affection she so freely bestowed on the animal. Stiffly starched petticoats pushed the full skirt of her saffron-yellow gown up in the back as she leaned against the rail fence revealing slim ankles and narrow yellow slippered feet. Red-gold curls piled high atop her head seemed to have captured and held the last rays of sunlight, their radiance undiminished by the encroaching darkness.

In the back of his mind Robin remembered Elizabeth Townsend's remark about her sister's dislike of horses. Was the little chit being spiteful, or could it be that she was so busy trying to be a man she had never taken the time to get to know Edwina? If the latter were true, it was Beth's loss for there was much she could learn from her twin. Like how to fire a man's blood just standing in the half-light. Not that Beth Townsend couldn't send his temperature soaring, but there was a marked difference between "heated passion" and "boiling mad"!

Not wanting to startle her, Robin found a certain contentment just standing unseen in the shadows beneath the tree. He enjoyed watching the camaraderie between the graceful lady and her four-legged companion. Suddenly she turned her head lifting her pert little nose as if she could smell his presence, and Robin found himself walking toward her smiling as he emerged from the umbrella canopy of the huge oak.

"Good evening, Miss Edwina."

Beth clasped her hand over her mouth trying to take a deep breath at the same time. The pressure made her eyes nearly pop from her head.

"You!" she shrieked accusingly.

Robin looked over his shoulder. Surely she couldn't be shouting at him, but finding no one else about he returned his gaze to Edwina, a frown furrowing his wide brow. She did not seem at all pleased to see him again. Then he thought back to the first and only time they had met. He had kissed her and she had run away, but not immediately. And even when she did take flight he had assumed it was because she was innocent and inexperienced. She certainly hadn't appeared to be repulsed by the feel of their lips melding. Yet her reaction to him now seemed more volatile than the occasion warranted. Even in the waning light he could see the high color in her perfect pixie face.

"My apologies if I frightened you." Robin took a step closer.

"I don't scare easily," Beth replied, taking a step back. "It's just that I thought . . . that is, my sister told me you had returned to Washington."

Robin chuckled mirthlessly. "Too bad I don't have pen and paper handy to record *this* historic moment."

"What do you mean?" she asked suspiciously.

Smirking, Robin answered. "For once your omniscient sister is wrong!"

Beth felt her hackles rise.

"Ac . . . tually," he continued, drawing out the word and puffing up rather pompously, "that's *two* mistakes the indisputable Miss Elizabeth has made. I really do wish I had something to write with."

"What do you mean?" Damnation! She was standing here repeating herself like a ninny just egging the arrogant bastard on.

"I mean, my lovely Edwina, not only was your sister under the misconception that I had left the Territory, she was obviously wrong when she told me you disliked horses."

Beth smarted beneath his cocksure posturing. Struggling to hold her temper in check, she nearly choked on the sugary sweetness of her own words as she forced a languid smile. "It's true my sister told me you had left the Territory, Mr. Hawkins, but after all, hope is what dreams are made of."

Before Robin had time to fully appreciate her subtle wit, she let fly another honey-tipped arrow. With a look of adorable bewilderment she asked, "Are you sure she said I *disliked* horses or could she merely have said I didn't *ride* horses? Our speech is sometimes difficult for a foreigner to understand."

Try as he might Robin couldn't remember exactly what Elizabeth Townsend had said. Hell! He couldn't even remember his own name at the moment! Despite her lampooning, he was completely beguiled by this remarkable confection dressed in a gown the color of sunbeams who sugarcoated her acerbic tongue with a voice as melodic as a bubbling brook and a smile men would die for. Pulling himself together, Robin became aware for the first time that the resemblance between Edwina and Elizabeth Townsend was more than skin deep. The realization made him decidedly uncomfortable, for in his dreams Edwina appeared not only beautiful and charming but tractable and obedient the way a woman was supposed to be. Yet here she was valiantly defending her hoyden sister, who he doubted would appreciate her efforts, by verbally sparring with a man who wanted nothing more than to hold her in his arms and taste her petal-soft lips once more.

He could not have ordered a more romantic setting than this: two people alone together as the first stars twinkled overhead, the fragrance of honeysuckle wafting on the warm tropical breeze. Disappointment over not seeing Edwina at Fort King had intensified his longing for her and finding her here in this particular spot exactly as he had seen her that first time had served to heighten his desire. Moments ago he had even allowed himself to imagine that she had been hoping for his return. Instead she had quickly reduced his ardor to irritation and he found himself wanting to strike back; much the way he felt whenever he'd had the misfortune of crossing paths with her sister, Elizabeth. Groaning inwardly Robin berated himself for believing he had found a woman who was everything he dreamed she would be.

It was too dark for Beth to see the myriad of emotions that played across Robin's ruggedly handsome features. She was aware only of the immense breadth and height of him. With his face in the shadows he reminded her of the Indian who tormented her thoughts, and she wondered what the immaculate Mr. Hawkins would look like if he were to cover his face and take off his shirt. Envisioning his reaction should she suggest such a thing, Beth giggled girlishly, her clear blue eyes alight with secret mischief.

Robin fumed. "Would you mind letting me in on the joke, Miss Edwina?"

Beth sobered immediately. "My good humor has nothing to do with you, Mr. Hawkins. I was thinking about someone else. Now what were you saying?"

There it was again, Robin grimaced. This delectable-looking creature opens her mouth and out come words he would expect to hear from her sister. It was most disconcerting.

"I believe we were discussing your sister's horse," Robin reminded curtly, nodding toward Senabar.

Why would a jackass be interested in a horse? Much to Robin's annoyance, Beth giggled again. He looked at her silly smile wondering if she was perhaps a bit simpleminded.

Beth sucked in her cheeks and peered up at him apologetically. "I'm sorry, Mr. Hawkins. I'm not normally so giddy but what with all those savages just outside the gate . . . all I can say is that I am just not myself right now." How she managed to keep a straight face she would never know, but batting thick auburn lashes she managed to look the part of a helpless, frightened female. "Why, I am absolutely terrified, sir, that we might all be murdered in our beds."

Though Robin would prefer her not to use the word

146

"savages," he could understand how a young woman of Edwina's sensibilities, having been sheltered and protected all of her life, might be nervous over the present situation. "Now, Miss Edwina. There is no reason for you to worry your pretty head over something that isn't going to happen." He wished he felt as confident as he sounded. "The Indians came here voluntarily to await the ships that will transport them to their new home. They mean no harm."

Beth's bottom lip quivered. She wondered if she could wring out a few tears but decided not to press her luck. "Thank you, Mr. Hawkins. I feel much safer just knowing that you are here." Why did she continue this role of a simpering half-wit? Surely no one could be fooled by her melodramatic performance, especially a man as perceptive as Robin Hawkins, yet there was no mistaking his desire to comfort her.

Robin not only believed everything Beth said, he was extraordinarily pleased with himself for the way he had coaxed the lovely lady into trusting him. Having recovered from the unexpected shock of seeing him again, Edwina now appeared to view him as her protector. He'd be a fool not to take advantage of the opportunity to kiss away her fears. He reached out and lightly touched her shoulders staring down into her guileless face. She was such an innocent darling he promised himself to go slowly. He would not frighten her away this time.

Knowing he was going to kiss her, Beth held herself rigid. I'll close my eyes and make believe he's my Indian.

Slowly his mouth came down to cover hers, tentatively at first as if he expected her to resist. When she

147

didn't draw away he moved his hands to her back and gently massaged her tense muscles. His tongue came out to brush the velvet smoothness of her full bottom lip with light feather strokes. Beth's eyes flew open as she heard a low moan. She blushed realizing she had made the contented mewing sound.

"Relax, Edwina. I won't hurt you and no one else can hurt you as long as I'm around."

His tender words, like a caress brushing her cheek, buckled her knees and she would have fallen at his feet had Robin not chosen that moment to tighten his grip as he deepened the kiss. It seemed the most natural thing in the world for Beth's arms to wind around his neck as her body melted into his rock-hard frame. His lips slashed across hers no longer hesitantly but fiercely and demandingly. Instinctively Beth returned the kiss twining her tongue around his. But it wasn't enough. She wanted more, but more *what?* Never having experienced the dynamic force of attraction that was pulling her toward a man she despised above all others, Beth was confused by the sudden aching need to merge her body with his. She couldn't think! She couldn't breathe! She was suffocating not only physically but mentally as well. Robin Hawkins was sapping her strength, forcing her to lean on him, something her own independent spirit could never allow.

Determined to break the spell he had cast over her, Beth pushed against his chest with all her might. Robin lifted his head but still held her in a firm embrace, his breathing as heavy and ragged as her own.

"What's the matter, Edwina?"

"Everything, you despicable dolt! Let me go!"

Stunned by the sudden change from passionate lover

to spitting hellcat, Robin dropped his arms to his sides and backed away. He looked at her angry face clearly visible in the light of the moon which had appeared without their noticing and now illuminated the compound in soft, white light.

"How dare you touch me!" Beth hated the tremor in her voice and the tears welling up in her eyes.

Robin knew her desperate struggle to regain her composure was genuine. Edwina Townsend was coldly furious with him. But *why?* She had come into his arms willingly and he had unleashed in her a passion that had jolted him to the core. He wanted her as he had wanted no other woman before, and she had met his advances with equal fervor. What had caused her to change so suddenly?

Beth stared at Robin in wide-eyed horror. It hadn't worked trying to pretend he was someone else. He had held her, kissed her, whispered endearing words, and never had she doubted who he was: Robin Hawkins. He was a sophisticated Washingtonian who was attracted to someone she could never be and would never want to be! But for a brief moment in time, his deep sensual voice and astonishingly gentle caresses had wooed her into believing she really was Edwina Townsend. Sweet, docile, utterly feminine Edwina.

Robin's harshly spoken words brought her back to the present. "What do you mean 'Don't touch me'? I must confess I am unfamiliar with the rules of this little game you are playing!"

In fact, he was more confused than angry. His lack of understanding made him lash out at the perplexing little vixen whose memory had plagued him for weeks on end. "I apologize if I have offended you, Miss

149

Edwina, but if you will excuse my saying so, you were kissing me back!"

Beth flushed beneath his well-directed sarcasm. "You are absolutely right, Mr. Hawkins. It is I who owe you an apology for my behavior. I can't imagine what possessed me to act in such a wanton fashion. I would consider it a great favor if you could forget what happened here tonight for I can assure you it will not happen again."

Without waiting for his reply she turned and walked away with as much dignity as she could manage under the circumstances. Robin let her go. There would be another time, another place. For there was still much to be settled between them.

Beth was ashamed of the way she had permitted . . . no, encouraged Robin to take such liberties. She knew his irritation over her sudden mood swing was justified, but she could hardly tell him he had just kissed a figment of his imagination. She shuddered to think what he would do when he learned the truth. And he would learn it now that he was at Fort Brooke! Even if Eddie were willing to go into hiding once more, which Beth had good reason to doubt since he wouldn't have Maggie to keep him company this time, someone was bound to mention her male twin.

Her only alternative was to leave tonight, and hope that should their paths ever cross again, Robin would have had time to calm down and perhaps even see the humor in her little charade. It was her turn to seek refuge with the McAfees. She would leave Eddie a note and pray he could forestall a search until she was well on her way!

Chapter Nine

"How can this be?" Livid black eyes searched the faces of the two braves as they stood before the man who had led them on raids and skirmishes since the war with the whites began.

"It's true," Alligator insisted. "We heard the soldiers talking and they had no reason to lie."

Jumper nodded in agreement. "Besides they could not know the significance of their words."

Asi-yahola glared toward the fort outlined in the moonlight. "So the whites think to settle us on a tract of land bordering that of our sworn enemy, the Creeks. They must be insane!"

"Or more vengeful than even we anticipated," Jumper suggested.

The Indian leader's expression bespoke his rage at the latest treachery perpetrated by the army. "We can never live in peace with the constant threat of attack at our very door."

Alligator fidgeted nervously. "That's not all," he said in an undertone, unwilling to meet Asi-yahola's piercing glare.

"Speak up," the angry warrior demanded. "What other perfidy can we lay at the feet of this government that claims to have our interests at heart."

"Abraham and his people will not be going with us."

Of the thirty-four separate bands of Seminole scattered throughout the Territory, three groups were comprised of Negroes, escaped slaves who had crossed the border from Georgia and had found refuge among those the plantation owners called "ruthless savages." The slaveholders ignored the fact that it was their own cruelty and abuse that drove the Negroes to take such desperate measures. The three bands were led by an enormous black man named Abraham.

Asi-yahola stared down his long nose. "How can this be?"

"Our dark-skinned brothers are to be returned to their masters where they will be punished for daring to defy those who claim them as their property."

For some minutes Asi-yahola remained silent. Only the rapid rise and fall of his chest gave any indication of the struggle going on within. Finally he said, "We're leaving tonight. Pass the word among our people that any who wish to join us are welcome."

"Where shall I tell them we are going?" The relief in Alligator's voice made it clear that he didn't really care as long as it was not on a ship to some unknown land easily accessible to their enemies.

"Home," came the firm reply. "And if the whites give chase we will disappear into the swamps where they will never find us. Go quickly and quietly. Make our plans known to the others. By morning we must be far from those who choose to deceive us. If our fate is to die, let it happen here; not in some unfamiliar place where our spirits will find no rest when we sleep the long sleep."

Crickets chirped a monosyllabic symphony while the deep-throated croak of a bullfrog added an occasional bass note. Every now and then the splash of a bass could be heard breaking the surface of the creek or a small night animal rustled the heavy underbrush. For one accustomed to the nocturnal sounds of the Territory the dissonance was reassuring.

Beth sat cross-legged staring into the low burning flames of the campfire, her eyelids drooping in spite of her determination to stay alert. Not that she didn't deserve a few hours' rest for she had ridden half the night and all the next day in order to put as much distance as possible between herself and *him*. Yet now whenever she allowed her eyes to close it was *his* image she saw: Robin Hawkins! Damn the man! Why couldn't he leave her alone even in her dreams?

Beth jerked upright and reached for a stick to poke at the dying embers. Why couldn't he have gone back to where he came from instead of intruding into her life once again? What really hurt was that it wasn't *her* life he was interested in. It was Edwina's. Why couldn't he like her as herself? More to the point, when had his opinion of her suddenly become so important? She didn't like him, that was for sure. He was nothing but an arrogant outsider who thought he could come here and within a few short months settle a dispute that had been going on as long as she could remember. Robin Hawkins with his fancy clothes and slick tongue! The thought of his tongue brought back memories of his kisses, so warm and so welcome. Beth felt her face grow hot as she recalled the way her body had reacted to his touch. For the first time in her life she had longed to be what Edwina was: softly feminine and totally at the mercy of the rogue who had held her in his passionate embrace. But Edwina wasn't real and Robin Hawkins could never care for a skinny, unappealing tomboy who preferred horses to household drudgery.

Beth swiped at a tear as a wave of self-pity threatened to overcome her. It wasn't fair! How could a mere kiss turn her emotions upside down and backwards? How could it cause her to question what it was she really wanted out of life? Until now she had been perfectly content to take one day at a time and not worry about what tomorrow might bring.

Beth sniffed most unbecomingly then wiped her nose on her sleeve. What she wouldn't give to see *her* Indian right now. At least he accepted her for what she was even if he did seem always to be getting her out of scrapes.

Suddenly she noticed how quiet the woods had become; no chirping, no croaking, just a black eerie silence. She sensed that she was being watched and silently prayed that it was the masked Indian coming to her once again in time of trouble. Adjusting her eyes to the surrounding darkness, Beth stifled a scream as she felt the gooseflesh rise on her arms. She shook her head lifting her face toward the heavens. "You misunderstood!" she wailed. "I said 'Indian' not 'Indians'!"

Just within the perimeter of light stood at least a dozen fierce-looking braves, their faces painted half red and half white. Directly in front of her, knife in hand, the most fearsome warrior of all glared down at her: Osceola, the Black Drink Crier.

* * *

"What do you mean 'she's gone'? Gone where?" Davey was finding it difficult to make sense out of his cousin's rambling discourse concerning Beth's disappearance.

Inwardly Edward cursed his sister for placing him in such an awkward position. Her short note read like a telegram: Hawkins here (stop) Going to Maggie's (stop) Stall search (stop). Reading between the lines, Eddie concluded that his usually pragmatic twin was thinking with her heart and not her head. He wondered just how involved she was with the man from Washington whom he had yet to meet. How the hell did she expect him to prevent their father from mounting an immediate search even if he could assure him of her destination, especially after what had happened last night? Half of the Indians were missing when the soldiers went to check their camp this morning. Those remaining let it be known with no little relish that the deserters were on the warpath once again. The idea that Osceola and his followers might meet up with Beth did not bear thinking.

Eddie tried to sound nonchalant but he could not keep the worry out of his voice. "I told you what her note said. She decided she wanted to spend a few days with Maggie. You know how Beth is when she gets a bee in her bonnet."

"Damn it, Eddie! She just came from the McAfees a few days ago. Now you're telling me she took off without telling anyone like a thief in the night because she had a sudden urge to see Maggie again?"

Eddie shrugged his shoulders. "She told someone,"

155

he replied with a wounded look. "She told *me!* I found her note under my bedroom door this morning."

His scowling cousin gave him a withering look. "That in itself is suspicious. Where is the note?"

"I threw it away."

When Davey glowered at him, Eddie asked defensively, "Why should I keep a note once I've read it? I'm not an imbecile after all. I can remember what it said, and it said she was going to visit the McAfees."

Davey still wasn't satisfied. He eyed his cousin dubiously. "If you're holding something back, Eddie, you'd better spill it because with the Seminole on the rampage again Beth's life could very well be in jeopardy!"

Just then Davey looked over Edward's shoulder. "Maybe at least we can find out what caused Osceola to bolt. Here comes Hawkins!"

Without turning around Edward groaned, lowering his hat brim as he concentrated on the tips of his cousin's well-worn boots. Davey stepped aside to intercept Robin, leaving Eddie staring at the dusty ground. However, he didn't really notice for he was too busy plotting what he was going to do to his featherbrained sister as soon as he could get his hands on her.

As he approached Davey and his companion, Robin could see the worry on Davey's face. He wondered what further bad news awaited him. Robin had learned too late about the treaty with the Creek tribe that would place them on land adjacent to that reserved for the Seminole. He didn't have to guess why Osceola had rebelled and decided to take his chances by remaining here in Florida.

"Hawkins," Davey greeted with a nod of his head. "Looks like we've got a load of trouble today."

Robin waited for him to explain.

"You remember my cousin, Beth, don't you?"

Immediately, Robin's stomach muscles tightened. No one who had ever come within spitting distance of the little hellion was likely to forget her. He wouldn't want to guess what predicament she had gotten herself into this time. "Yes, of course. I remember Miss Townsend well," he managed to say hoping his voice didn't sound as grating to Davey's ears as it did to his. "Has something *else* happened to her?"

If Davey noticed his sarcasm, he chose to ignore it. "It seems she also disappeared last night."

That got Robin's attention. Beth Townsend was trouble; there were no two ways about it. But the thought of her being abducted by Osceola who, believing he had been deceived was most likely prepared to seek revenge at the first opportunity, made his blood run cold.

"And you believe the Indians took her." To Robin it was a logical conclusion.

"When Hell freezes over!" Eddie scoffed.

The barely audible profanity reminded both men of his presence. Puzzled, Robin stared at the back of the stranger who had so rudely interrupted. He stood waiting impatiently for him to turn around. Knowing there was no way out and feeling it was time to put an end to his sister's little hoax, Eddie did just that. Not only did he pivot to meet the man responsible for Beth's flight but he went so far as to sweep his hat from his head so that the sun haloed his coppery red hair and highlighted the freckles across the bridge of his nose.

"Mornin'," he drawled, scarcely able to contain his laughter at the other man's surprise.

Rooted to the spot, visibly shaken, Robin gaped at

the masculine mirror image of Edwina and Elizabeth Townsend.

Finally taking pity on him, Edward said, "I guess my sister has some explaining to do."

Eventually Robin was able to speak though his voice came out an octave or so higher than usual. "Which one?" he croaked.

Lance Logan and Andrew Townsend disappeared into the woods followed by their two eldest sons. Up until now Robin had thought the phrase "seeing red" only an expression, but his fury was so intense the entire landscape took on a crimson glow. His black brows were drawn together in a ferocious scowl. His jaw was clenched as tightly as his fists, his posture so threatening that two soldiers walking in his direction changed course choosing to give him a wide berth.

From the beginning Beth Townsend had played him false. That she had made a fool of him was enough to justify his wrath, but she had done more than that. *Much more.* For there was no use denying that less than an hour ago he had been totally enamored with the beautiful young woman he knew as Edwina. His frown deepened. He had to give Beth her due. She was a brilliant actress. She was also a consummate liar and a deceitful shrew.

Robin found it hard to believe she had managed to delude him not once but twice. Telling him her *sister* didn't ride horses, making him think Edwina preferred to stay at home playing nursemaid to their siblings, her fear of "savages." Ha! Beth Townsend was as treacherous as a water moccasin and equally devoid of conscience. He had held her, kissed her, and she had protested just enough to convince him of her maidenly innocence before she melted into his arms. Hell, she probably wasn't even a virgin! One minute she was galavanting across the countryside dressed in breeches; the next she was acting the seductress wearing ruffles and petticoats in front of an entire army battalion! No, indeed! Elizabeth Townsend was far from the unsullied miss she pretended to be!

As angry as he was, Robin's ire could not wholly obliterate the hurt he felt inside. His heart was like a great weight in his chest for he was finding it difficult to relinquish his fantasy image of the perfect woman and admit that Edwina was nothing but a fabrication. Too many nights he had lain awake picturing her delicate features and exquisite form. Too many days he had rehearsed what he would say and do once they were together again. Now his dreams were shattered for Edwina was merely an illusion created by a little spitfire who was as cunning as a fox and twice as deadly.

He vowed then and there Beth Townsend would regret her deception. The next time they met it would not be the Robin Hawkins she had toyed with in the past. To his dismay Robin found that his physical desire for the temptress had not slackened, but no longer would he treat her as a gentleman would a lady. She deserved nothing more than to be tossed on her back and taken like a common whore. He intended to prove to her that there was a little bit of the "savage" in every man. And by the time she realized the high price she would pay for her chicanery, it would be far, far too late for apologies!

* * *

"I'm surprised Hawkins declined to join the search," Lance said to no one in particular as the men stopped just long enough to water the horses and wet their own parched throats from a clear stream running perpendicular to the main trail. They had pushed the animals hard all morning and now the sun, having reached its zenith, beat down mercilessly upon them.

"I'd hardly call it a search," Edward remarked pettishly. "We'll find Beth at the McAfees like her note said. And there's no reason why her disappearance should concern Hawkins. From what I've heard, he and Beth didn't get on too well."

Davey chuckled. "You got that right. From what she told me their relationship began with mutual dislike and rapidly escalated to full-fledged animosity."

Edward's expression turned mutinous. "Maybe she has good reason to dislike the man," he countered defensively. "Oh, I know everyone is enthralled with the way Hawkins handles Indians but apparently he's not so adept at dealing with women. According to Beth everything he says to her is critical. He disapproves of her riding dispatch; he disapproves of the way she dresses; he disapproves of the way she talks. . . ."

"He has a point," Andrew Townsend interrupted. "Beth is my daughter and I love her dearly but she has no business carrying messages from fort to fort. She dresses like a boy, and she often uses language unbecoming a lady."

"Damn it, pa! You sound just like Rachel," Edward protested.

Lance Logan crossed his arms over his massive chest. "Hold it, you two! This is no time to be arguing. Beth's feelings toward Robin Hawkins have nothing to do with her disappearance. The important thing right now is to find her."

Edward made a sudden strangled sound. Turning his head he coughed and struggled to regain his breath. After eyeing him suspiciously, Davey turned with the others to mount.

"I still don't understand why she left so secretively." There was hurt as well as worry in Andrew's voice. "Too bad you didn't keep her note," he added glancing over his shoulder at his son as they kicked the horses into a gallop.

They soon reached a narrowing in the trail where they had to ride some distance single file. When the path widened again, low-hanging branches from the nearby trees slowed their progress. Davey took the opportunity to drop back beside his cousin who was bringing up the rear.

A frown marred Davey's handsome features. "I wonder if pa's right?"

"Right? About what?" Edward asked.

"About Hawkins not having anything to do with Beth's disappearance."

Edward managed to keep his expression noncommittal, but he couldn't prevent the heightened color that suffused his naturally ruddy cheeks. "What are you talking about? How could Hawkins have anything to do with Beth's decision to visit Maggie?"

Davey's look was forbidding as he returned his cousin's stare. Edward was the first to drop his eyes.

"You tell me, Eddie. And while you're at it kindly explain why Robin Hawkins acted like he'd seen a ghost the first time he laid eyes on you. Then you can enlighten me as to 'which sister' has a lot of explaining to do. I do hope it isn't little Mandy since she can barely talk," he drawled sarcastically. "After that perhaps you can satisfy my curiosity as to why you never once showed your face at Fort King even on the day of the peace talks. I think *you* are the one who needs to do some explaining and you'd better start right now."

It was more than the implied threat in his cousin's stern voice that convinced Edward it was time to "come clean." Beth might very well be in trouble. If she wasn't now, she certainly would be when Robin Hawkins got hold of her. Despite the fact that she had brought her problems on herself, Edward knew Davey would champion his sister. In all fairness, he deserved to know the whole story.

With no small degree of resignation, Edward began to relate the tale as he knew it.

Beth sat propped against a rough-barked cypress tree outside the range of the firelight. She was bound hand and foot, but things could be much worse. Her arms were in front of her, not behind her back, and the raw-hide strips around her wrists and ankles had not been tied so tightly that they cut off the blood flow. Best of all, she was still alive!

A day had passed since her capture and though she had been forced to ride mounted in front of the unfriendly, copper-skinned brave called Alligator, for the most part the Indians had ignored her. About mid-afternoon they had left the main trail leading to Fort King and turned in a southeasterly direction.

Osceola and his band were abiding by the rules of the hunt, not stopping to eat until well after dark. The old

162

law made sense especially now that they had become the prey rather than the hunters. Beth didn't know why the Indians had left Fort Brooke the same night she had, but she was sure the soldiers would be in hot pursuit.

She gratefully accepted the piece of meat tossed carelessly on her lap as one would throw scraps to a hound. After a twenty-four hour fast she was weak and ravenous. She swatted ineffectually at the mosquitoes who seemed bent on making her itch where she couldn't reach to scratch. She envied the men ringed around the campfire, its heat and light acting as a shield against the pesky insects.

There was some comfort to be found in knowing that her father and uncle would be among the searchers. They would be looking for her, however, not the renegades. Regardless of how convincing Eddie might be in reassuring them of her destination, with Osceola on the loose they would want to see for themselves that she had arrived safely at the McAfees. What would they do when they discovered she hadn't arrived at all? By then the trail would be as cold as she felt right now. Andrew Townsend and Lance Logan might be the best trackers in the Territory, but even they could not do the impossible.

So lost was Beth in her miserable assessment of the situation she did not at first notice that the low, guttural mutterings of the warriors had ceased. When she looked up it was to see the braves sitting cross-legged with backs straight as if frozen in time. Their gazes were focused on their leader; his in turn was directed toward a dark apparition standing at the edge of the clearing.

Beth could barely contain her excitement, for there hovering above them like an avenging angel was *her* Indian. The sight of the grotesque mask covering his face did nothing to lessen the relief flooding through her veins. He had come to save her once again. Holding her breath she waited to see what would happen next.

Osceola glared at her broad-shouldered rescuer, his hatred a tangible thing. "Has the Hawk come to gloat over the betrayal of his brothers?"

His accusation was barely audible yet spoken in a tone so cold and deadly, Beth drew up her legs and huddled closer to the tree for protection. The man called Hawk didn't answer immediately. Instead he turned to look toward the spot where she sat shivering despite the warm night. Beth's hope flared and then died as quickly. Though she could not see beyond the round, vacant openings that served as eyes in the face covering, she knew by the rigid stance of his big body that he was horribly angry. The way the muscles flexed in his powerful arms as he opened and closed his huge fists proved that his fury surpassed any anger Osceola could possibly summon. For reasons she could not fathom, the unmitigated wrath of the mysterious warrior she had come to think of as her own was directed solely at her.

Hawk turned back toward the Indian leader. His muted voice echoed hollowly through the quiet forest. "Often things are not as they seem, my brother."

Beth sensed that his words held some hidden meaning.

"Will you come with me where we can speak privately?" There was no pleading in his voice as he awaited Osceola's reply.

Several minutes passed in silence while Osceola

stared intently at the speaker. His eyes narrowed, seeking the face hidden behind the mask. Finally he stood up and walked toward the opposite side of the clearing to disappear among the trees. He didn't look back to see if Hawk followed.

Chapter Ten

Some distance from camp the two stopped to face each other. As Hawk removed the cumbersome mask, Osceola's attention was drawn as always to his friend's gray-green eyes so at odds with the man's dark hair and brows and sun-bronzed skin. Yet it was more than the color of his eyes that made Hawk unique among the Seminole. Like many of the others he was a mighty warrior, powerfully built, fearless in battle. But more importantly, there emanated from him an inner strength that made men willing to listen to what he had to say. He was intelligent beyond most and had an inherent sense of justice that had served their people well.

Rarely had Osceola regretted his actions or his words, but challenged now with the blinding fury Hawk turned upon him, he would give much to be able to call back his accusation. He knew in his heart that he had done a grievous wrong to the man he called brother.

His chest heaving, Hawk lashed out, "Betray our people? Is that what you believe, Asi-yahola?" The agonized cry pierced Asi-yahola's conscience, making him want to weep for he could not deny the bitter hurt behind the question.

Meeting the other's gaze head-on, Osceola came as close as he was likely to come to apologizing to any man. "My words were spoken in the heat of anger."

"So are mine," Hawk flared back, "but they are words of truth! If anyone has betrayed our people, it is *you!* I knew nothing of the treaty with the Creeks that would place them next to the land set aside for the Seminole, but if I had it would have made no difference!"

To Osceola such an admission was the ultimate in treachery. He reached for his knife but Hawk grabbed his wrist and held it in a viselike grip.

Through clenched teeth Hawk snarled, "I did not care where they put the goddamn Creeks because I never expected the Seminole to leave Florida!"

Black eyes livid, Osceola twisted his arm breaking Hawk's hold. Waving the knife threateningly, he roared, "You meant for us to die here."

Hawk shook his head striving to control his impatience. Searching for the words that would make him understand he said, "My reason for coming back was to help find a way for the whites and the Seminole to co-exist in peace here in the Territory." He paused, staring off into the darkness of the night, seeing a dream that had nearly come true.

A pulse in his cheek began to throb as disappointment heated the blood in his veins. "But you gave up too soon, my brother. You allowed the elders to renounce your heritage . . . our heritage . . . at a time when the whites were ready to make concessions. Can't you see that they are as tired of this war as we are?"

By the time he finished berating his boyhood com-

167

panion, Hawk was shouting, his rugged features strained with emotion, his rock-hard body glistening with sweat.

Laying a calming hand on Hawk's arm Osceola said sorrowfully, "You are wrong, my friend. Though the breadth of this land is many days' ride and the length has yet to be determined, the white man will never accept our presence here. I have no faith in his promises or his treaties. I had hoped in the new land beyond the great river we might find peace, but it seems peace comes only in death. And if I must die, I would choose to die here."

Hawk knew further debate would be futile and, in truth, he had no argument to add. Acknowledging defeat, he asked, "What will you do now?"

"We will vanish into the swamps where the soldiers dare not follow. And if they should . . ." Osceola grinned, "I have heard the gators have a penchant toward tender white meat."

Hawk repressed a shudder for he knew the dreaded man-eating reptiles were only one of the many dangers the fugitives would face in the southern marshes believed to be uninhabitable. There were poisonous snakes, insects whose bite carried the deadly fever, quagmires that could suck the unwary beneath their slimy ooze, humid heat that weighed a man down until he hadn't the strength to go on.

"What of the girl?" Even if it meant doing battle with his lifelong friend, Hawk knew he could not let Osceola take Beth with him. She would never survive the life the renegades had chosen. He told himself his need to keep her alive stemmed solely from his desire to gain revenge for the wrong she had done him.

"She goes with us. She is our hostage."

Hawk straightened to his full height, towering above the Indian leader. "I cannot allow it." His tone brooked no argument. "You do not need a hostage when you are going where none will follow. To take her is to sentence her to death!"

"She is important to you?" There was a certain knowing smugness in Osceola's question.

"Let's say she owes me."

Osceola allowed several minutes to pass as he studied the big man whose ill fate it was to have been born between two different worlds. He pitied Hawk because he still straddled the fence, hoping both sides would come to him and join together in harmonious union so that he could know himself finally as one person. Perhaps someday a way would be found to bridge the gap between the whites and the Indians, but it would not happen in his lifetime. Hawk must choose which direction he would take. If his suspicions were correct, Osceola might be able to help him make the decision.

Reluctantly he acquiesced, "Take the girl. She will only slow us down."

Keeping his feelings well-hidden, Hawk merely nodded. As quietly as a stalking panther he made his way back to camp on moccasin-clad feet.

Beth guessed that not far away her fate was being decided by two men she scarcely knew; men who knew even less about her and didn't care if she was cold or miserable or scared. They were barbarians who murdered, plundered, and kidnapped people for no good reason.

Her Indian was very angry, probably because he was tired of rescuing her from trying situations brought on by her own impulsiveness. She couldn't really blame him, Beth thought, covering her mouth with her bound hands to stifle a wide yawn. Her lips turned down in a pout. It wouldn't hurt him to be a little more chivalrous in this one particular instance. After all, she was only partly to blame. How could she know Osceola would pick the same night to escape?

Beth yawned again, this time not bothering to cover her mouth. The braves had rolled themselves into their blankets close to the fire and one or two were already snoring.

Easing her way down the tree trunk until she lay flat on the mossy ground, she drew her legs up and curled into a tight little ball. It had been a tiresome day and tomorrow would be soon enough to discover what was to become of her. As the embers burned low and an owl hooted overhead, she closed her eyes and was soon asleep.

Hawk crept soundlessly across the clearing, his mask firmly in place. He knelt down and lifted Beth carefully so she would not awaken. He then made his way along a tangled, broken path that led to the cave where his stallion was tied. Only once did his burden stir. Opening sleep-drugged eyes she gazed up at the now familiar visage. She smiled and nestled her face into the crook of his warm, naked arm, and went back to sleep.

As her head thudded painfully against the hard floor of the cave where Hawk dropped her unceremoniously, Beth opened her eyes and sent the bats flying with a bloodcurdling scream of pure terror. Somehow while she was asleep, she had gone blind! No longer could she

170

trace the outline of the trees in the moonlight or pick out the silhouettes of the horses standing side by side. The sound echoed back at her magnified a hundred-fold. Clasping her hands over her ears, she began to weep, certain she had crossed over the thin line between sanity and madness.

Suddenly her hands were wrenched away and she was being shaken until her teeth rattled. "So, little spitfire, the time has come to pay the piper."

The low, raspy voice whispered against her ear making the hairs rise on the back of her neck. The total absence of light disoriented Beth completely. She still couldn't tell if the darkness came from within or without. But she knew who it was that held her in his steely grasp. Even in her muddled state of half-wakefulness she recognized his musky male scent. He had done away with the mask. Though his hoarse voice sounded as hollow as her screams, she knew there was no longer any barrier between them.

"Where are we? Why have you brought me here?" If only it wasn't so dark, if she could just see his face, she might be able to make sense out of what was happening to her.

"Consider this our own private playground where we can play our own private games. You should enjoy this, Miss Elizabeth. I understand you are very good at games."

Beth didn't know what he was talking about but he was beginning to make her extremely nervous with his sly innuendos. She didn't like the way he whispered her name in that silky, sarcastic way.

"Let me go!" she hissed, pulling against his grip, but trying to break his hold on her was useless. "I'm in no mood for games, Mister . . . Hawk!"

His laugh was nearly a sneer as he pushed her down once more, pinning the lower half of her body with one leg as he stretched her arms above her head.

"Oh, but you will like my little game, Miss Elizabeth. It's one I'm sure you've played many times before. But tonight we will follow my rules."

Now Beth was truly frightened. Thrusting her hips upward she shrilled, "Let me up, you bastard! Let me leave!" Every muscle in her body strained against the weight that imprisoned her.

"The only thing I'll let you have is what you deserve, you little vixen!"

Shifting to hold both of her hands in one of his, Hawk grabbed the top of her shirt and gave a forcible yank, ripping it from neck to waist. Beth could feel the cool air sweep across her heated body, chilling her breasts and teasing her nipples to taut peaks. Refusing to give up her vain attempt at freedom, she arched her back and kicked out at her attacker. He simply moved aside to work the buttons on her britches and slide the buckskin down her long, trim legs.

"Nooo! You don't know what you're doing!" she cried. Her pleas, like the tears that had begun to flow, went unheeded as Hawk rose above her, locking her into place with his knees as he freed his swollen manhood.

Despite the darkness, he had a clear mental picture of the wanton temptress seducing the men at the fort, bringing them to her bed, then laughing at their naivete when they pledged their hearts to her. Seething with wrath at so nearly succumbing to her wiles, he lifted her hips and plunged his staff to the very core of her being.

He felt the slight pressure as he split her maidenhead asunder and heard the tormented scream that seemed to go on forever. Instantly he froze like one turned to stone, but it was too late to undo the damage he had done. She had been innocent, this child-woman. He had misjudged her completely. His anguished cry blended with hers as he reared back his head and railed against his own stupidity.

Knowing the pain it would cause her, he withdrew as slowly and gently as was possible rolling away onto his back. What could he say? What could he do? Any words of apology or touch of comfort would be unacceptable. Even if he tried to explain, she would never forgive him. He would never forgive himself. He, Robin Hawkins, known to his Seminole brothers as the Hawk, had committed a vile, despicable act against another human being. He had raped an innocent young virgin. Doing so he had proven himself to be more "savage" than the wildest beast.

Beth's muffled sobs tore at his heart. He felt her pain as if it were his own. Reaching out into the darkness he found the blanket he had left in the cave earlier along with his meager supplies. Tenderly he covered her, tucking the edges close to her shivering body. Moisture formed twin paths running down his cheeks as he felt her flinch at his touch.

"Please, God," he prayed, "help me find a way to make this up to her."

Hawk remained on his knees watching over Beth in the darkness as she moaned softly. He wondered if God would hear his plea. If so, what could he possibly do to right the terrible wrong he had done?

* * *

Dust particles drifted on the air like grains of sand illuminated by sunbeams reaching fingers of light through the cave's entrance. Beth was slow to awaken, her subconscious mind seeming to know she would not like what the morning had to offer. Cautiously she opened one bleary blue eye and then the other. Her gaze took in as much of her surroundings as possible without moving her head. Relieved to find herself alone, she let her lids drop, deciding it might be best if her brain began to function at its own pace rather than confound it with disjointed questions whose answers would make no sense.

Gradually she recalled the terrifying sensation of waking to utter darkness, the gut-wrenching fear when she thought she was blind. But she could see perfectly now, so at least a part of the nightmare was really just a bad dream.

But what about the rest? It was coming back in bits and pieces. *Her* Indian, the one called Hawk, had spirited her away, allowing her to think he was her savior. She could almost feel his arms around her, cradling her tenderly. She had been wrong to trust him, for he had brought her here in a fit of anger. And then. . . . Oh God! Had her gentle protector been transformed into the demonic beast who had assaulted her so savagely or had she only imagined the horror?

Moving her legs, Beth winced. In that area where her thighs came together she felt sore and bruised. All too clearly she relived the moment of excruciating pain, the fear and humiliation she had experienced when he had risen above her and brutally forced himself on her.

"Nooo!" she cried out in shame, her voice repeating

itself as it had last night when she begged him to let her go. Beth sat up, great sobs convulsing her body as she looked beneath the blanket at her nakedness and saw dried bloodstains smeared along the insides of her legs.

A shadow appeared to block the light and Beth clutched the cover beneath her chin, her eyes dilated with fright. It was him! He had come back! Would he continue to torture her or would he simply slit her throat with the wicked-looking knife he held in his hand?

Hawk looked around, having been drawn by her shrill cry, and only when he was satisfied that no one else stood hidden in the shadows of the crude dwelling did he replace the weapon in the sheath at his waist. He motioned toward the clothes folded neatly beside Beth's boots, and turned without a word and left her alone once more.

Beth could not stop her trembling. Had he come because he heard her scream and thought she might be in trouble? Now that would certainly be ironic! Unsteadily she got to her feet. Holding the blanket in front of her like a shield, she kept a wary eye on the narrow opening that led outside. She donned her breeches as quickly as her shaking fingers would allow and threw the buckskin shirt over her head. The hem stopped just short of her knees while the ends of the sleeves covered her fingertips. This was *his* shirt, she gasped, repulsed at the idea that something which had touched his body was now touching hers. She wanted to take off the offensive garment and rip it to shreds, but she could hardly roam about the woods half-naked.

She remembered the cryptic words he had whispered as he held her beneath his sweaty body. Though they still made no sense, Beth resolved to "play his little game" until she could find a way to escape him. If in doing so she managed to leave him with a knife blade stuck midway between those smooth, well-muscled shoulders, so much the better! With her body aching and her heart bent on revenge, she rolled up the too long sleeves, pulled on her boots, and ducked out into the bright morning sunshine.

Senabar stood patiently waiting beside the big black stallion as Beth emerged from the cave. She was glad to see her feisty mare for she didn't relish the thought of riding double with the blackguard responsible for her ruination.

Hawk offered her a tin cup of water and a strip of dried beef but she shook her head, giving him a withering look as she untied her horse and prepared to mount. With one leg in the stirrup, she felt two strong hands circle her waist and boost her into the saddle. She ground her teeth against the acute pain which shot out in all directions ending at the top of her head and the tips of her toes. She exhaled with a hiss, swearing inwardly that the unconscionable bastard would pay dearly for his offhanded treatment of her.

Robin groaned as he saw her expression change from contempt to surprise then to pain. Damn it! He hadn't meant to hurt her! Not ever again! His move to assist her had been the natural act of a gentleman helping a lady. He had failed to take into account what it would feel like to be tossed astride a horse after what he had done to her. His face contorted beneath the heavy wooden mask. One more sin to add to his growing list of transgressions. If his aim was to gain her forgiveness, he was definitely off to a poor start!

* * *

They rode in silence throughout the day always traveling in a westerly direction. Beth quickly regretted her haste in declining the food Hawk had offered. By mid-morning her stomach was complaining loudly, and by noon she had begun to feel light-headed. When they stopped to water the horses beside a shallow, sandy bottomed creek, she dismounted swaying slightly. She knelt to cup the cool, clear water in her hands drinking her fill, then bathing her sun-dried face. This time when Hawk extended a piece of leathery meat her hand snaked out to grab it but he got no thanks in return.

As the afternoon wore on Beth was forced to applaud the Indian's grit. He had had nothing to eat or drink all day, for in order to partake of food or water he would have to remove the ugly mask. It must be terribly hot under there, she hoped, staring spitefully at his broad back held rigid beneath the weight of the disguise. Maybe he will suffer heat prostration and die. Of course, that would deprive me the pleasure of seeing him shot. Then again, when you shoot a man properly, he seldom suffers long. Perhaps hanging would be a more fitting end. But if they allow him to keep his mask on, I won't be able to see the terror in his eyes when he hears the door open just seconds before his neck is snapped. Drawn and quartered? Now there is a pleasant thought!

Beth spent the rest of the afternoon dreaming up ways in which the heathen devil would painfully meet his demise. That night she ate again from her captor's dwindling supply of food. He could not risk leaving her alone while he hunted fresh game for he knew her mule-headedness would push her to try and escape, and he was not of a mind to spend the night searching for her.

Now she sat on one side of the glen staring into the flames that sparked and crackled as Hawk fed dry sticks to the little fire. Beth could feel his eyes studying her from behind the crudely painted cypress bark, putting her at a disadvantage for she could not see his face. He had made no attempt to touch her during the long, hot day. Though she felt uneasy alone with him in the woods, all she could do was hope he would continue to keep his distance. The silence grated on her nerves but she had nothing to say to her solemn companion. Finally she rolled over in the blanket she had draped about her shoulders and let the night sounds lull her to sleep.

Awakening with a start, she felt a moist, breathy whickering against her neck. Beth looked up into Senabar's velvety brown eyes. The forest was quiet as gray streaks of dawn filtered through the thick tangle of trees. Gently nudging the horse aside, she sat up and blinked the sleep from her eyes. Then she turned to survey the deserted campsite. Hawk was gone and something told her he would not be back. She discovered a small leather pouch beside the cold remains of the fire. It contained the last of the dried beef strips the Indian had tucked away. Idly she took a piece and began to chew.

"Well, old girl," she muttered, stroking Senabar's smooth coat, "looks like it's just you and me."

She circled the clearing searching for a clue as to which direction her mysterious captor had taken but she could find none.

"I vote we continue west. What do you say?"

Senabar snorted, nodding her head up and down as Beth tightened the saddle girth. Why, she wondered, had the masked man brought her this far then left her to find her own way? She shrugged dejectedly. There was no point in trying to figure out the workings of the Indian's mind. For better or for worse, she was on her own now. If she kept moving west she was bound to come across a familiar landmark eventually.

She had ridden less than a quarter of a mile when, giving a whoop of delight, she spotted the main trail. She was no more than ten miles north of Fort Brooke. In a few short hours she would be home. There was some small comfort in knowing the Indian called Hawk had not left her until he was sure she could find her way back to the fort.

It was then that the import of what had happened to her began to take hold. She was not the innocent young girl who had impetuously run away just three days ago. She had been taken prisoner by Osceola's renegade band of warriors and had paid the highest possible price for her folly. Much of what had happened to her was her own fault, but she knew her father and her uncle would never see it that way. If she told them she had been raped they would not rest until the perpetrator of such a heinous crime was dead. Hawk deserved to pay and pay dearly for what he had done. Despite her gory fantasizing of the day before, she did not want his death on her conscience. It would be best to make light of what had occurred, bearing the blame for her own foolhardiness. If luck was with her, everyone would be so glad to have her back safely that they would not pursue her captors. And maybe, just maybe, she would someday be able to erase the pain and horror of her experience from her memory.

Chapter Eleven

Things had worked out even better than antici-pated. Beth was greeted with open arms and tears of thanksgiving. The men had arrived back from the McAfees just hours before her own unexpected ap-pearance. They were in the midst of preparing to "scour every inch of the Territory in order to find her" according to an unusually demonstrative Uncle Lance, who squeezed her until she thought her ribs would crack.

Rachel and 'Becca had turned pale as Beth related the story of her capture by Osceola and his braves while little Mandy continued to grin happily having no concept of the danger. She was just glad that her big sister was home again. The boys thought it a great adventure and begged to hear every detail of her es-cape. The men puzzled over the Indian leader's mo-tive in releasing a valuable hostage without making any demands for her return.

Rachel finally shooed everyone away, admonishing the lot for their lack of consideration. "Elizabeth has been through an ordeal and needs to rest. Heaven help us! Sleeping on the damp ground; eating who knows what! Now scatter, all of you!" she scolded as she helped Beth up the stairs.

For the next two days, Beth holed up in her room allowing Rachel and 'Becca to bring her meals and to keep her company. Neither kind lady pressed her with unanswered questions. On the third day, she had had enough! No longer could she use exhaustion as an excuse to escape the inevitable.

Dressed in a simple cotton frock of pale green with a scooped neckline and short puffed sleeves, Beth stole down the stairs avoiding the kitchen where she could hear her stepmother preparing breakfast. She opened the front door without a sound and breathed deeply of the fresh salty air.

Waving a good morning to the young guard on duty at the gate, she headed for the beach. A brisk walk would be just the thing to get her blood circulating after playing the invalid for two long days.

Beth stopped to rest at The Point, a place several miles from the fort where the shoreline jutted sharply right. She sat upon an old fishing boat turned upside down in the loose sand far from the water's edge. White seagulls with wingtips of gray circled noisily overhead, shattering the silence with their familiar, strident cries. Scarcely a ripple marred the surface of the gray-green bay, the soft blend of colors reminding Beth of Robin Hawkins's eyes. She could no longer put off thinking of the confrontation she was sure would come.

Careful to sound indifferent, she had questioned

Rachel about Robin. She told her the man was still at the fort seeing to the affairs of the remaining Indians camped along the wharf awaiting the ships that would carry them to their new home. By now he must know about her ridiculous impersonation of Edwina Townsend, a silly, simpering woman who didn't exist. It galled Beth to know that Hawkins had liked Edwina with as much intensity as he had disliked her. She tried to picture him tipping back her sweat stained hat to kiss her lips, rubbing his hand seductively up and down the sleeve of her dusty buckskin shirt as she rose to meet his embrace on the toes of her scruffy leather boots. *Not likely!* she predicted glumly. Again came the question that had plagued her ever since she began her little farce. Why was Robin Hawkins's opinion so important? Hadn't her deception been based solely on an attempt to escape his censoring gaze and his caustic words? Or was there more to it? Surely she hadn't begun to care for the arrogant ass! Beth shook her head sadly accepting the fact that it no longer mattered what she felt for the handsome stranger. The one thing a man like Robin Hawkins would expect . . . no, demand . . . from the woman he loved was that she be a virgin. Beth knew in her heart that Robin could never accept another man's leavings, especially if that other man happened to be a ruthless, renegade Indian!

Watching from the shadow of a kapok tree, Robin could not see Beth's face, only the thick red-gold curls cascading down her reed-thin back nearly to her waist. The sun dimmed in comparison to the sheen of her fiery tresses. Noting the melancholy droop of her shoulders, he bowed beneath the burden of guilt he felt for having abused her so heartlessly.

Seeing her now, bathed in morning sunlight, full green skirts spread around her feet, Robin thought she looked just as pretty and feminine as Edwina. Then, he chided himself. She didn't just look like Edwina. *Hell, she was Edwina!* He still found it hard to accept the fact that the sharp-tongued little vixen in buckskin was also the sweet young woman he had kissed in the moonlight. How many other personalities were hidden within that willowy frame?

Robin had heard the tale she'd told her family about her capture and subsequent release. He concealed his surprise behind an expression of alarm then relief. For some reason she had chosen not to mention the vile atrocity committed against her person by the Hawk. Instead of mounting a force to hunt the villain down, her father and uncle had voiced their gratitude to Asi-yahola and his band for seeing fit to release her unharmed. Her reluctance to tell the whole truth was a mystery to him. He was sure her family would not only sympathize but would leave no stone unturned in bringing the despicable perpetrator of the heinous crime to justice. Eventually he would learn the motive behind her less than complete depiction of the events that had occurred during her captivity, but for the time being he intended to take full advantage of her unexpected omission.

Discovering the many facets that comprised Elizabeth Townsend's complex nature would take a lifetime, he told himself smiling ruefully. But discover them he would! Robin had spent the past two days and three very restless nights considering and reject-

184

ing ways in which he might make amends for his unconscionable behavior and, in so doing, absolve himself of the monstrous guilt that threatened to consume him. All along, the solution to his problem and hers was right there before his eyes. He argued alternatives but to no avail. He would simply have to marry the ill-tempered spitfire or never know another day's peace. He wondered grudgingly if there might be a certain contradiction in his rationale.

"Good morning!"

Beth spun around at the sound of his voice, crimsoning beneath his knowing smile.

"What are you doing here?" she gasped, wishing she had stayed in her room at least another month!

Beth followed his eyes as Robin looked out over the tranquil water, watching a huge gray pelican circle overhead then dive into the surf emerging with the tail-half of a whiting flapping from its elongated bill. The pelican swallowed, the outline of the still wiggling fish clearly visible as it made its way down the bird's rubbery gullet then disappeared.

Turning his attention back to Beth, Robin noted her high color but chose to ignore it. Instead he said pleasantly, "I was drawn by the smell of the ocean."

Beth sucked in her cheek giving him a dubious look. "This is hardly an ocean, Mr. Hawkins. It's but a bay leading to the Gulf."

"Ah! But isn't it true that the Gulf leads to the ocean?"

"Well . . . yes. But that's hardly the point. You could not have been lured to this spot by the smell of the ocean," she argued inanely.

Robin arched a dark brow. They were disagreeing as usual, but at least they were talking. That was more than he had hoped for. "I stand corrected," he conceded, "but I wonder whom I have to thank for this enlightening lesson in geography? Is it Miss Edwina or could it be Miss Elizabeth?"

Beth stared at the tall, handsome rogue then let her blue eyes drop. Shifting the loose sand with the toe of one slipper, she wiggled her bottom against the boat's wooden planks. She knew exactly how that hapless fish had felt as it fought against the stronger predator. It wasn't Robin's question that made her squirm; it was the way he asked it. There was none of the gloating sarcasm she had expected and he didn't sound the least bit angry. His tone was almost . . . friendly.

He's confusing me! she thought, wondering when he would give her the recrimination she deserved.

After several long moments, she raised her head and wanted nothing more than for the beach to open and swallow her up as she felt unwelcomed tears pool in her eyes. "I am both and I am neither," she answered, trying desperately to control the tremor in her voice.

Damn! What must he think of such a witless reply? For he could not suspect that she was neither the feminine, flighty Edwina, nor the tough, self-reliant Elizabeth. She was now a woman who had been the victim of a vile, despicable act. A woman no decent man would want. How would he react if she told him the truth about losing her virginity at the hands of a savage who had raped her in a pitch-black cave somewhere out there in the woods? Lost in her musings,

186

she sat atop the overturned boat, a picture of misery, as a single tear escaped to roll down one smooth, lightly tanned cheek. She deplored this habit of crying at the drop of a hat!

Robin could read the anguish in Beth's eyes. He could feel her pain as though it were a tangible thing. He wanted to go down on his knees and beg her forgiveness. He wanted to tell her who he was and why he had acted in such a contemptible manner. He knew, however, nothing he could say or do would excuse the way he had so cruelly used her. When the time was right, he vowed he would tell her the truth. For now, he must gain her trust.

He leaned down and wiped away the lone tear with the pad of his thumb. Then he gently took her hands in his and pulled her to her feet. Beth was jolted by the electrifying force that shot through her at his touch.

"Why did you pretend to be Edwina?"

Her eyes flew to his and she was startled by the soft, muted gray of his irises. It was remarkable the way his eyes changed color to match his moods. She tried to pull her hands away but he refused to release her. Shrugging self-consciously she whispered in a barely audible voice, "You would have laughed at me."

"Why would I have laughed at you?" His voice held just a hint of amusement as he thought how childlike and adorable she looked with her hair loose and the sprinkling of freckles across her pert little nose.

"Because I was wearing a dress."

"You're wearing a dress now and I'm not laughing."

"Your voice is laughing even if it doesn't show on

your face. I can hear it," Beth retorted petulantly.

Robin did laugh at that. He couldn't help himself. Before she knew it, Beth was smiling, too.

"That's better," he declared, happy to see her good humor restored. "Now about this dress thing? Why should what you are wearing make any difference? You're still the same person underneath."

With that bit of philosophy, Robin felt his loins tighten, for he suddenly realized how very much he would like to feast his eyes on exactly what lay beneath that demure green gown. He had glided his fingers across her smooth, warm skin in the darkness of the cave. Now he wanted to see her proud, naked body in the light of day.

He was drawn out of his reverie when Beth replied, "It makes a great deal of difference, Mr. Hawkins. Dressed as a woman, I feel vulnerable."

There was no doubting her sincerity. Robin bit his lower lip, preventing himself from reminding her that clothing herself like a boy had not protected her from a savage driven by anger and lust.

"And so you think dressing in buckskins makes you invincible?"

Beth shivered, remembering how totally she had been at the mercy of the unscrupulous Indian. "Not always."

Robin cursed his careless tongue as the light quickly faded from her eyes. "It is my contention that a person should not judge another by outward appearances. I happen to think you are a lovely young lady even when you smell like your horse and hide your beautiful hair under that disgusting hat."

To Robin's satisfaction, Beth giggled. "My, my!

You do have a way with words, Mr. Hawkins." Then she frowned, cocking her head up at him soberly. "Do you realize we have just proved that I am right about the dress making a difference?"

"How so?" he grinned into her impish face.

"Wearing *Edwina's* clothes, I have allowed you to discuss my personal hygiene in a most unflattering manner while I simply blush and giggle. But were I wearing my usual attire, I would have socked you in the jaw, kicked you in the shin, and given you my uncensored opinion of your antecedents. Now what do you think of that, Mr. Hawkins?" she asked imperiously.

"I think you should call me Robin," he answered without hesitation.

Beth stood there, her mouth slightly agape. The speech she had just delivered, meant to be daunting, seemed to have had the opposite effect. Hawkins was apparently too obtuse to understand that she was trying to discourage their friendship for his own good. She was not the "lovely lady" he appeared bent upon charming. And that was another thing. Why, after she had succeeded in pulling the wool over his eyes, was he being nice to her? Surely no man liked to be played the fool.

Studying him suspiciously she asked, "What is it you want, Mr. Hawkins?"

"A chance to begin again," Robin answered. "I'll admit we got off to a bad start and it was all my fault. I'd like to get to know you and, perhaps, introduce you to yourself because I believe you are an extraordinary combination of Edwina, the lady, and Elizabeth, the 'invincible.' What do you say, Beth? Is it worth another try?"

The pleading in his voice nearly undid her. She was as much to blame as he for their "bad start" for she had done her best to antagonize him at every turn. Her pulses quickened as she gazed up at the hope reflected in his ruggedly handsome face. Why couldn't he have said these things before she'd run away? She should tell him the truth right now. Then he would leave her alone and she could take up where she left off, before he barged into her life and turned her whole world topsy-turvy.

Mesmerized by the way his eyes changed from green to gray, she continued to stare at his face, unable to act past this moment. He was such a beautiful man, and for some reason she couldn't begin to fathom he now seemed to like her for herself.

Against her better judgment she found herself agreeing, "Yes, it's worth another try."

After all, she reasoned as they made their way back toward the fort, Robin was only proposing friendship, *not marriage!*

The next morning when Beth came downstairs Robin was there waiting, sitting in the parlor talking with her father as if they were old and dear friends. An empty coffee cup rested on the end table beside the couch which seemed dwarfed by the man's huge frame.

They both stood to greet Beth. After exchanging morning pleasantries, Robin said, "Your father has given me permission to invite you to go riding if you have no other plans for the day."

That a man like Hawkins would ask permission for anything took Beth by surprise. In answer to her quizzical look, Andrew smiled and nodded his head. "Sounds like a fine idea to me. It will do you good to get out in the fresh air, and with Mr. Hawkins as an escort I'm sure you'll be in safe hands."

Robin wondered what the tough army scout with the same fiery red hair as his daughter would do if he knew that his "safe hands" had already defiled Beth's virginal body. Robin might stand a head taller than the older man, but he doubted that would stop Andrew Townsend from trying to beat him to a pulp should he learn the truth.

Beth hurried back upstairs to change into her buckskins. She had mixed emotions about her assignation with Robin Hawkins. Common sense told her she was digging herself into a hole she might have trouble escaping, for there was no denying the man's darkly handsome appeal. But to spend time in his company while giving Senabar some much needed exercise was an opportunity too good to let pass.

It was a glorious summer day, the sun shining down brightly from a cloudless blue sky. They rode like the wind across a fertile green meadow and then slowed the horses to a walk as they entered a dimly lit forest where cypress, oak, and hickory trees melded together beneath a thick tangle of vines. Gray streamers of hairlike Spanish moss hung limply and lifelessly from their branches.

An hour later they came upon a natural spring-fed lake where little black coots darted in and out among the cattails lining the bank. Dismounting they let the horses drink their fill of the cool, clear water, then using their hands as dippers they slaked their own thirsts.

Spotting a bush heavy with ripe blackberries, Beth called gaily for Robin to join in the feast as she picked a handful of the sweet juicy fruit and popped them one by one into her mouth. She took off her hat intending to use it for a bucket but one glance at Robin's horrified expression changed her mind.

"It really isn't that bad," she defended, examining the dilapidated piece of felt with a critical eye.

"That's the sorriest excuse for headgear I've ever seen," Robin stated flatly, coming up beside her. "I may worship at your feet, Miss Townsend, but I absolutely refuse to eat from your hat!"

The levity in his voice kept the moment from becoming awkward. Laughing up at him, Beth held out a particularly plump blackberry which Robin took from her fingers with his teeth. Drawing her hand back as if she'd been burned, Beth searched his face to see if he, too, had been scorched by their touch. Their eyes locked; hers wide with wonder, his flaring with a passion she was too inexperienced to recognize. Before she knew what he was about, Robin leaned down and kissed her lightly on the lips. With a frightened cry she jumped back and would have fallen into the blackberry bush if two strong arms had not reached out to steady her.

Beth's shocked expression told Robin he had moved too fast and he cursed himself for being ten kinds of a fool. Grinning apologetically he said, "I'm sorry, but I have a penchant for purple lips."

Beth rubbed the back of her hand across her mouth, not sure if she was trying to erase the telltale

ENJOY ALL THE PASSION AND ROMANCE OF...

Heartfire

ROMANCES from ZEBRA

After you have read HEARTFIRE ROMANCES, we're sure you'll agree that HEARTFIRE sets new standards of excellence for historical romantic fiction. Each Zebra HEARTFIRE novel is the ultimate blend of intimate romance and grand adventure and each takes place in the kinds of historical settings you want most...the American Revolution, the Old West, Civil War and more.

SUBSCRIBERS $AVE, $AVE, $AVE!!!

As a HEARTFIRE Home Subscriber, you'll save with your HEARTFIRE Subscription. You'll receive 4 brand new Heartfire Romances to preview Free for 10 days each month. If you decide to keep them you'll pay only $3.50 each; a total of $14.00 and you'll save $3.00 each month off the cover price.

Plus, we'll send you these novels as soon as they are published each month. There is never any shipping, handling or other hidden charges; home delivery is always FREE! And there is no obligation to buy even a single book. You may return any of the books within 10 days for full credit and you can cancel your subscription at any time. No questions asked.

Zebra's HEARTFIRE ROMANCES Are The Ultimate
In Historical Romantic Fiction.
Start Enjoying Romance As You Have Never Enjoyed It Before...
With 4 FREE Books From HEARTFIRE

FREE BOOK CERTIFICATE

Heartfire Romance

GET 4 FREE BOOKS

Yes! I want to subscribe to Zebra's HEARTFIRE HOME SUBSCRIPTION SERVICE. Please send me my 4 FREE books. Then each month I'll receive the four newest Heartfire Romances as soon as they are published Free for ten days. If I decide to keep them I'll pay the special discounted price of just $3.50 each; a total of $14.00. This is a savings of $3.00 off the regular publishers price. There are no shipping, handling or other hidden charges. There is no minimum number of books to buy and I may cancel this subscription at any time. In any case the 4 FREE Books are mine to keep regardless.

NAME

ADDRESS

CITY _____ STATE _____ ZIP

TELEPHONE

SIGNATURE

(If under 18 parent or guardian must sign)
Terms and prices subject to change.
Orders subject to acceptance.

HF 108

GET 4 FREE BOOKS

HEARTFIRE HOME SUBSCRIPTION
SERVICE
P.O. BOX 5214
120 BRIGHTON ROAD
CLIFTON, NEW JERSEY 07015

stains of the blackberry juice or the lingering sensations caused by Robin's kiss. One thing she knew for certain. Coming here with him had been a mistake. She was falling under his spell, wanting something that could never be, something she was afraid even to name.

"Come," Robin said, drawing her toward the mossy bank where their two horses stood contentedly nuzzling each other's nose.

Beth allowed him to lead her to the water's edge then sat down cross-legged upon the spongy lichen. Assuming a similar pose, Robin was careful to put enough distance between them to rid Beth of her wariness.

Leaning back on his elbows, he peered up at the powder blue sky. "Were you born at Fort Brooke?" he asked, striving to regain the camaraderie they had shared until his impetuous kiss spoiled the mood.

Feeling better now that Robin had removed himself to a safe distance, Beth chuckled, finding humor in some secret joke. "Far from it, literally," she answered with a smile. "I was born in England. 'Becca is a lady, you know."

Robin scratched his head wondering if he had missed something significant. "Having met your aunt I would never have thought otherwise."

This time Beth's musical laughter filled the air. "You don't understand. What I mean is she's a real lady. A peer of the realm."

Still looking confused Robin waited for her to explain.

"My grandfather was a lord. He owned a large estate in northern England. That's where Edward and I were born. Shortly afterward mama died and papa couldn't live with the memories so he came to Florida to build a new life for himself."

"That must have been hard on you and your brother, losing both parents at such an early age."

Beth was silent for several minutes lost in thoughts of the past. Then she smiled and the sun seemed to brighten. "Not really. As you say we were very young. My grandparents and 'Becca gave us as much love as any parent could."

"What happened then?"

Beth was more animated than Robin had ever seen her as she spoke of the people she so obviously loved, and he longed to keep her talking. "My grandparents were killed in a carriage accident. That's when 'Becca became a lady."

Robin choked, picturing Lance Logan's gracious and beautiful wife. "I doubt your aunt would appreciate your phraseology."

Sighing at the interruption, Beth continued, "At any rate grandfather left 'Becca the title and lands. Then when Edward and I were six she brought us here to live with papa. 'Becca planned to return to England but she met Uncle Lance and you can guess what happened. It took a while but once Uncle Lance confessed his love for 'Becca there was no more talk about returning to England."

The sudden indigestion that unsettled Robin's stomach came from knowing Beth idolized her uncle. Never having had cause to be jealous of another human being, he was hard-pressed to diagnose his strange affliction. But he knew he would give just about anything to have Beth think of him as she did

Lance Logan, to believe he was a man who could do no wrong!

"Now it's your turn." Beth drew her legs up and rested her chin on her knees. "Tell me everything there is to know about Robin Hawkins."

Robin's expression suddenly turned cautious, his long lean body stiffening imperceptibly. What if he told her the truth? His mother had been a full-blooded Seminole Indian, and his father a trapper. He was Hawk, the half-breed who had ravaged her out of spite and misunderstanding. He remembered her face as he had carried her through the woods that night; the trust he had glimpsed in her sleepy eyes. No! He couldn't tell her yet. First he had to restore her confidence in him, but this time it would be as Robin Hawkins. Later would be soon enough to tell her what he had done and beg her forgiveness.

"Hello! Are you there?"

Beth's lightly amused query brought him back to the present. Still balancing her chin on her knees she watched him expectantly.

Forcing himself to relax, he plucked a blade of grass and wrapped it around his finger. "I was just trying to think of something that would equal your entertaining tale, but in comparison my life seems altogether commonplace, even boring."

Looking up at him skeptically, Beth allowed her eyes to roam freely from his raven-black hair tied neatly at his nape to his pristine white shirt, then down the length of his skintight black breeches to his polished boots. "I doubt anything about you could be 'boring.' Why, you're so perfect, I'd wager you don't even sweat!"

As too often happened Beth spoke without giving due consideration to what she was saying. When the full impact of her words hit, mortification overcame her and she buried her head between her legs.

Roaring with laughter, Robin rose up on his haunches and closed the gap between them. He cupped her chin, forcing her to look at him. "I'm afraid you'd lose that bet," he chuckled. Then abruptly the teasing went out of his voice. "No one is perfect, Beth. Don't ever think otherwise," he warned as he gazed intently at her flushed face.

Robin helped her to her feet then they mounted and started back the way they had come. He had gained a reprieve, for Beth seemed to have lost interest in his background. But he knew someday soon she would ask again and he had better have some answers ready. His whole future depended on it!

Chapter Twelve

Each morning for the next two weeks Robin was there when Beth came downstairs. Rachel and Andrew accepted his presence without comment and often invited him to return for supper. The boys hung on his every word and even little Mandy listened wide-eyed as he told them about life in the big city of Washington where powerful men made the decisions that governed their lives.

Together Beth and Robin explored the countryside or strolled along the beach. These were glorious days filled with sunshine and laughter, days Beth wished would never end. Yet as their friendship grew, so did her anxiety. Soon she would have to tell him the truth and then he would leave her. Not a night passed that she didn't lie in her lonely bed and pray for the courage to be honest with the man she had come to love. *Yes, love.* For even if her cowardice forced her to be less than truthful with Robin, she could not deny what was in her own heart. His mere presence made her pulses quicken; the sound of his deep, masculine voice set loose the butterflies in her stomach. Sometimes the way he looked at her with those incredible gray-green eyes caused her to ache with the need to have him hold her in his arms, to feel his warm lips pressed against hers just once more.

Every morning she woke determined to say the words that would put an end to her dreams, and she would find him waiting for her, his handsome face breaking into a smile that was for her alone. Beth would push her conscience aside for she could not bear the thought of losing him.

Robin never wavered in his resolve to marry Beth; however, one thing did change and he was at a loss to explain it. No longer was the need to right the wrong he had done her uppermost in his mind. As he sat in the parlor day after day talking to Andrew Townsend, he found himself keeping one eye trained on the door in anticipation of her arrival. His urgency to see her had nothing to do with guilt. He told himself it was natural to look forward to Beth's company for she was pretty and sweet and the only single woman at the fort. *Hell! Who was he kidding?* True, the sheen of her coppery red curls put the sun to shame, and he had to admit he found her pixie face more appealing than the more classic features some called beautiful, but sweet? Hardly!

Once while riding in the woods they had come upon a fox who had chewed his hind leg off in order to get free of a trap. Beth had cursed a blue streak consigning the unknown hunter to Hell even as she pulled her rifle from its sheath and put the whimpering animal out of his misery.

A few days later they had returned to the fort to find a soldier beating his horse with a riding crop.

Without a moment's hesitation, Beth had launched herself at the unsuspecting offender and managed to blacken one eye and bloody his lip before Robin could pull her away.

No, his Beth was no docile female who would back away from a fight. She had a rigid code of honor and a practical method of dealing with injustice: straight and to the point! He wondered what penalty she would mete out when she learned of his own heinous crime. She was a spitfire and a hellion, and he did not doubt for a moment that his punishment would be deservedly painful. Nothing she could possibly do to him, though, would be worse than living without her.

On the Fourth of July the Logan-Townsend Clan had a picnic and Robin was invited. A long trestle table was set up in front of Lance and Rebecca's rambling house built outside the fort next to a fast flowing creek that cut a ribboning path to the bay. It was obvious that rooms had been added as the family grew, yet the structure had lost none of its original charm.

Remembering what Beth had told him about her lady aunt from England, Robin was surprised by Rebecca Logan's enthusiastic support of the celebration. Whatever her ties had been with the mother country, she had cut the strings cleanly and irrevocably.

Platters of fried chicken, bowls of mashed potatoes, green beans, corn on the cob, homemade pickles, and the lightest, flakiest biscuits Robin had ever tasted, threatened to bow the table. When Rachel handed him an enormous wedge of blackberry pie, he couldn't resist winking at Beth as he assured her step-mother that it had recently become his favorite dessert.

After everyone had eaten his fill, Robin sat in the shade of the porch, with a sleepy eyed Amanda on his lap, enjoying a thin, brown cheroot as he listened to Lance and Andrew discuss territorial politics. Davey and Edward were playing a heated game of horseshoes while the younger boys took turns swinging out over the creek on a rope attached to the thick limb of an oak tree. They would drop into the water with all the whooping and hollering boys were known for.

When the ladies emerged from the kitchen, Robin stood up taking Beth by the hand. "Would you care to accompany me on a walk? After that delicious meal," he said, nodding his thanks toward Rachel and Rebecca, "I'm afraid if I don't bestir myself I may never move again."

Beth answered lightheartedly, "I have no choice but to accept your invitation, kind sir, for I doubt 'Becca wants you as a permanent fixture on her front porch."

Bidding the others a laughing goodbye, they walked hand in hand along the familiar path to the fort, not stopping when they reached the gates but proceeding on in the direction of the growing settlement.

Robin smiled, squeezing her hand. "I like your family."

"I'm glad. They can be rather intimidating at times. I mean there are so many of them."

"That's one of the things I like best. I never had much of a family," he said without thinking.

He was not surprised when Beth took advantage of the opening he had given her. "You've never told me much about your family."

"There isn't much to tell. I was raised by my uncle, a gruff old curmudgeon whose whole life centers around politics. He never married so here I am, no brothers, no sisters, no cousins." Robin gave her a crooked grin.

Despite his disparaging remarks about his uncle, Beth recognized the affection in his voice when he spoke of the man. "And your parents?"

"Dead." There was no emotion in the word, just a chilly finality that dared anyone to probe further. Beth longed to know more about Robin, but for some reason he was not ready to discuss his parents' death and so she let the subject drop with a simple "I'm sorry."

They stopped several blocks north of where the dirt road bisecting the little settlement came to an end. What passed for music from the tinny piano at the saloon down the street could be heard in the distance though it was still too early for the riotous noise of the locals who came nightly to seek a little pleasure after a hard day's work. Looking over her shoulder as the sun dipped below the horizon, Beth marveled at the sky painted with bold brush strokes of melon, lavender, and blue.

"Well, what do you think?" Robin asked, drawing her attention back to him.

With the enthusiasm of a loyal Floridian Beth replied, "I think we have the most beautiful sunsets in the world."

Robin's breath caught in his throat for what he saw

was rare beauty, indeed; but it had nothing to do with the picturesque scene behind them. Beth fairly radiated with youthful exuberance, not a single line marred her smooth, honey-toned complexion. Her sparkling blue eyes danced with delight as she witnessed one of nature's wonders too often taken for granted. The sprinkling of freckles across the bridge of her nose confirmed her love of the great outdoors. Never would she hide from the sun when she could race the wind across an open prairie.

And in that moment, Robin realized that he loved the little spitfire who was both Edwina and Elizabeth rolled neatly into one irresistible package that spelled free-spirited adventure. The truth hit him like a ton of bricks. When he was able to speak he said, "I wasn't asking what you thought of the sunset though I agree it is most impressive."

Beth wondered at the unaccustomed huskiness in his voice. Then her attention was captured by his mercurial eyes which had changed to the color of molten lead smoldering with intensity. His strange expression completely discomposed her. "I . . . I don't understand. You asked me what I thought—"

". . . of that!" he finished for her, gesturing toward a vacant lot which looked much the same as the others that had been staked out in anticipation of future development.

"I think it looks like a vacant lot," Beth answered, her burnished brows raised questioningly.

"Ah! But there is something very special about this particular piece of ground." Robin found it impossible to keep his excitement at bay. "It's mine!"

Beth stared in dismay. "You mean you bought it?"

"Sure did," he replied smugly. "I completed the purchase this morning."

"But why?"

"Because the land agent couldn't get the paperwork completed any sooner."

Beth tapped her foot impatiently. "Damnation! You know what I mean! Why would you buy property here?"

Her thoughts were spinning like a top gone mad. He must be planning to remain in the Territory, she concluded, but how could he expect to earn a living? More importantly, how could she live in such close proximity to the man she loved knowing he would never love her in return?

"I like it here," he defended, disappointed that he had to explain what to him seemed obvious. "It's where I want to plant my roots."

Suddenly Beth felt her stomach lurch and feared she might lose her dinner. An insidious voice whispered from within. "If he stays he'll find out. You won't be able to escape his look of revulsion when he learns of your disgrace."

"B . . . but what will you do?" Hell's bells! She was stammering like an idiot!

Robin experienced a twinge of disappointment that Beth would question his capabilities until he reminded himself that she had no way of judging his proficiency since he had purposely avoided giving her any significant details regarding his background. "I guess I failed to mention that aside from taking me in, my uncle also sent me to the finest schools in New England including Harvard University," he confessed somewhat shamefaced. "I'm a lawyer, Beth, and a damn good one! Between disputes concerning boundary rights and controversies over who owns the wild cattle herds left by the Spanish, I figure I can make a decent living settling claims. So I'm going to build a house right here with an office to boot; then I'm going to hang out my shingle. Robin Hawkins, Attorney at Law. How does that sound?"

"Can't you stop asking me fool questions?" Beth moaned, feeling the pressure building inside threatening at any moment to erupt into full-fledged hysterics. She had wanted to know all about Robin Hawkins but she was learning too much, too fast!

Robin cupped her chin in his hand and raised her head. "I just have one more foolish question to ask." His voice was a caress that made Beth's heart skip a beat. "Will you marry me?"

For one horrifying moment in time, the earth stopped rotating on its axis. Beth reached out searching for something to cling to, knowing that without a lifeline she would fall into the dark void that was infinity. *"Nooo!"*

Robin recognized the raw anguish and the utter despair in her lamentable cry as it echoed through the night. It was the same heartrending entreaty he had heard just before he ruthlessly ravaged her virginal body, the same plaintive supplication that continued to haunt his dreams. Waking night after night drenched in sweat he had vowed never to hurt her again. Yet now his proposal of marriage seemed to have driven her over the edge.

Clawing at his arms like a madwoman, Beth continued to keen and moan. Her face was ravaged with grief, her eyes dilated with the pain of a wounded animal. She wanted to run but she could not let him go. "It's too late!" she bewailed, denouncing the cruel trick fate had played. Then like a tidal wave the tears came, great gushing sobs that seemed to go on forever.

Robin pulled her toward him, holding her tightly within his embrace, refusing to let her drown in her own sorrow. The knowledge that he was responsible for such abject misery in another human being tore at his very soul. Feeling every convulsive shudder of her slender body he shared her pain as if it were his own.

He didn't know how long he waited for her tears to subside but by the time she quieted and tried to draw away, darkness had fallen. Realizing Robin was not about to release her, Beth buried her face against his chest, muffling the hiccups that came in the aftermath of her uncontrollable weeping.

Bending down, Robin whispered softly against her hair, "It's never too late, Beth."

But Beth knew better. She lifted her head and though it was too dark to see her face there was no denying the hopelessness in her voice. "For me it is too late but I wish to God it wasn't so."

She straightened her narrow shoulders, took a deep breath, then stated resolutely, "I cannot marry you, Robin. I can never marry anyone."

Robin knew what it cost her to say those words. What made it worse was that he knew why she felt it necessary to make such an absurd declaration. Yet he could never convince her that he understood without telling her the truth. During the past few weeks she had grown to care for him, to trust him and maybe even to love him a little. Now to see those feelings turn to hate was more than he could bear.

"What kind of nonsense is this?" he chided, giving her a gentle shake. "True we had our differences in the beginning but all that's changed. At least for me. I've come to care for you in a way that's new and different." He paused. "I thought you were starting to feel something for me, too, but perhaps it was just wishful thinking on my part."

Robin's uncertainty tugged at Beth's heart and she rushed to reassure him. "It's not wishful thinking. I lo . . . like you more than any man I've ever met." As soon as the words were out, Beth realized she had fallen into her own snare. It was cruel to lead Robin on when there could be no happy ending for them. "But I can't marry you. God, I don't want to hurt you. It's just that you deserve something I no longer have to give." Damn! She was going to cry again and there was nothing she hated more than feminine tears!

She stepped back and this time he let her go. It would take more than physical force to convince her that marrying him was the only sensible thing to do.

Beth turned, preparing to flee, then stopped abruptly. Every instinct urged her to run as fast and as far as she could away from this beloved stranger who made her body ache with need. But she was no coward. Robin Hawkins had asked her to be his wife and, humiliating though it was, he deserved an explanation for her refusal.

She spun around and collided with his rock-hard chest. Grabbing his arms to maintain her balance, Beth felt the power surge beneath her fingers. The sky was no longer pitch-black for a sliver of moon now cast its dim light on the scene below. Eyes bright with tears, Beth reached her hand to touch Robin's rugged cheek, tracing a path along his stubborn jaw. She could feel the rough stubble of beard that would soon shadow his face which added to his raw virility. She could not see his features clearly. His eyes were dark and hooded in the incandescent moonglow. For one brief moment, Beth was reminded of the masked Indian whose treachery had destroyed her dreams. She could not hold back a shiver of apprehension that rippled through her body. It was as if he were here right now, watching and laughing at her feeble attempts to exorcise the ghost that stood between her and the man she loved.

"Please talk to me, Beth," Robin pleaded, feeling her body trembling in his arms. He wanted nothing more than to erase the horrors of that night when he had so callously forced himself upon her.

Getting a firm grip on herself, Beth leaned back in his arms and said, "Very well. I will talk and I will explain why I can't marry you. All I ask is that you not repeat what I am about to tell you because I love my family very much and would not want my own shame to taint them in any way."

Robin nodded his head, knowing what was to come and powerless to stop it.

"I'm no longer a virgin. I was raped by an Indian." She laughed without humor. "When I ran away from you, I thought the worst thing that could happen was for you to discover my duplicity in pretending to be Edwina, but the joke was on me. Through my rash action I learned the true meaning of humiliation and degradation beyond anything I had ever thought possible."

Her bitter cynicism castigated Robin as nothing else could have. He had sought a way to make amends for his despicable act but up until now he had not fully perceived the crushing blow he had dealt her. The moonlight played upon her delicate features highlighting her tear-brightened eyes, and Robin knew that to lose her would be the ultimate punishment for his crime.

"It doesn't matter, Beth. I love you. I don't care what happened in the past. It's the future that matters now."

His words did nothing to pacify her. "That's the most outrageous thing I've ever heard," she spluttered, suddenly angry that he could not simply accept her refusal and go back to Washington where he belonged. "Every man wants his wife to be pure and unsullied."

Robin felt his own temper flare. "Since you are such an expert on what a man wants I'm obviously wasting my time trying to reason with you. Just go ahead then! Throw our future away because you're too bullheaded to admit that we need each other!"

Beth was taken aback by his ferocity. "I'm just trying to save you from making a big mistake!" she defended staunchly.

"Do I look like I need saving?"

"You look like an arrogant bastard who won't take 'No' for an answer!"

Robin threw back his head and laughed uproariously. He knew once he brought her back to the fighting stage that he had won. "Do you have any idea how adorable you are or how much I love you?"

Without waiting for an answer he caught her to him and whirled around in circles until she was too dizzy to stand alone. "You're right on all counts. I'm an arrogant bastard and I definitely won't take 'No' for an answer. So how about it, Beth? Will you say 'Yes' and make me the happiest man in the world?"

Breathlessly Beth held on to Robin's shirt unable to make heads nor tails of his unexpected reaction to her confession. Shaking her head in dismay, she frowned up into his grinning countenance. "I don't understand. How can you say my virtue, or lack of it, doesn't matter?"

Robin looked at her bewildered face, longing to wipe away the anxiety he saw there. "Listen to me, sweetheart," he implored tenderly. "It was not your fault. You were the victim of an assault and no one can blame you for what happened, certainly not me."

Beth would never have believed a man of Robin Hawkins's temperament could accept her tragic tale with such unreserved sensitivity. That he loved her enough to overlook what she considered a major imperfection in a young, unmarried woman seemed too good to be true. "Let me get this straight. You want to marry me even though I'm no longer a virgin, even though I have been defiled by an *Indian?*"

Robin winced at the emphasis she placed on the last word as though there was an additional stigmatism attached because the atrocity had been committed by a redskin. But he knew Beth judged a man by his mettle, not his race or creed.

"Absolutely," he confirmed. "Now will you say 'Yes'?"

Why should she continue to argue against something she wanted more than life itself? Fresh tears sprang to her eyes as she reached her arms to encircle Robin's neck, but these were tears of joy.

"Yes," she whispered, savoring the feel of him as he covered her mouth with a sigh. He molded his firm lips to hers in a warm, sensuous kiss that promised more pleasurable things to come. Perhaps there is at least one miracle with my name on it, she thought just before her lips parted for his tongue's invasion and she ceased to think at all.

Chapter Thirteen

Apparently there was more than just one miracle reserved for Beth. Less than a month later she and Robin were married by the circuit preacher who passed through Fort Brooke on a regular basis. Somehow during those brief weeks prior to the ceremony a lovely two-story log house had been constructed on the property Robin had purchased. The wedding took place out of doors on the site where the Fourth of July picnic had been held, a place of special significance for both Robin and Beth.

Beth's family welcomed Robin with open arms and sighs of relief. Though they were loathe to admit it, they had often wondered if she would ever find a man willing to put up with her independent nature and volatile temper.

Wrapped in a whirlwind of activity since their engagement, Beth had had little time or reason to probe further into Robin's motives for wanting to marry her. She felt like a fairytale princess who had magically found her prince. Only on rare occasions did she give a thought to the masked Indian, and then it was to wonder how someone she had secretly dubbed her "guardian angel" could have abused her trust so heartlessly. At times she actually found herself hoping he had not been captured or killed by the soldiers who still relentlessly scoured the woods for Osceola and his renegades. Beth attributed her ability to view objectively her unfortunate encounter with the Indian to the many ways Robin demonstrated his love for her. She found it impossible to feel rancor toward anyone when she was so cherished and adored.

While Beth was riding the crest of a seemingly endless wave of euphoria, Robin was mired down in a trough of self-reproach. He knew he was wrong in not telling her the truth; yet he could not bring himself to dash her hopes against the rocks. She was bound to think his proposal stemmed from guilt when, in truth, with each passing day he found himself falling more and more deeply in love with her.

Now it was too late. Beth was his wife and nothing he might say at this point could undo what was already done. He would try his best to be the kind of husband she deserved and heaven help them both if she ever discovered his deception.

"Rather pensive for a man who ought to be celebrating," Lance Logan commented jovially, slapping his new nephew on the back.

Robin grinned. "Post-wedding jitters, I suppose."

"Happens to all of us, son. But you got yourself one of the finest little gals God ever put on this earth. See that you do right by her."

Robin recognized the warning in Logan's words and suspected that if the truth ever came to light he would have a formidable enemy in this rugged frontiersman. He watched Beth across the clearing where she stood beside the heavily ladened refreshment table sharing a joke with her twin and her cousin, Davey. She was as gay and lighthearted as a wood sprite in her long white dress overlaid with layer upon layer of delicate lace. Then her father pulled her aside embracing her fondly. Robin felt his heart constrict as she leaned up to kiss Andrew's cheek, her cherished face reflecting her happiness. Catching his eye she cut a path through the crowd of well-wishers and clasped his arm possessively. For two hours they had danced and mingled with friends and family. Robin was ready to go home and looked to Beth for some sign of mutual consent.

"Well, Mrs. Hawkins, shall we call it a night?"

Ignoring his question, Beth sighed wistfully. "Mrs. Hawkins. It has a nice ring to it, don't you think?"

Kissing the tip of her nose, Robin couldn't resist teasing, "I think you've had too much champagne. You look like a dreamy little girl at her first dance."

"Not my first dance, but my first wedding . . . and last!" she added with conviction.

Suddenly ill at ease as the moment approached when they would be alone together as man and wife, she sought to delay their departure. "Wouldn't you like something more to eat?"

"Most definitely!" Robin affirmed.

Beth glimpsed his rakish leer just before he pulled her into the shadows and devoured her mouth with his. Thinking they were safe from prying eyes, both sprang apart in surprise when a boisterous cheer set the birds in the trees overhead to flight. Robin grabbed Beth's hand prepared to make a quick exit. The urge to have her all to himself within the walls of the house he had helped build, but refused to sleep in without her, nearly overpowered him. But Beth turned back long enough to wave and shout "Thank You" to the laughing people, watching an impatient Robin play a gentle tug-of-war game with his new wife.

"I predict that will be only the first of many occasions when they will pull in opposite directions," Lance chuckled down at his own beautiful, misty-eyed lady as Beth and Robin disappeared from sight.

"Ah," Rebecca murmured, leaning against her husband's side, "but it makes the coming together that much sweeter!"

Beth stood in front of the mirrored dresser nervously fingering the odds and ends that decorated its smooth wooden surface. The reflection in the glass showed the pleasing results of the hours she had spent working with Rachel and Rebecca quilting the white bedspread patterned with morning glories and hemming the matching curtains that hung at each of the long windows in a trellis of deep lavender-blue blossoms. A braided rug in multi-shades of blues and greens covered the hardwood floor.

She had chosen the colors and the light pine furniture with the intention of bringing a breath of springtime indoors. Studying her efforts with the critical eye of one whose confidence is sagging, she wondered if Robin might find the room too feminine for his tastes. She had asked him not to look at her handiwork before their wedding night because she wanted to surprise him. Now she was assailed with doubts and they were not wholly centered on what he would think of her decorating skills.

Picking up her brush she listlessly ran the bristles through the tangle of curls glowing like red-gold flames in the lamplight. Robin had left her at the bottom of the staircase saying he had to take care of a private matter out back but would join her shortly. Knowing he was discreetly offering her an opportunity to undress before he arrived to claim his marital rights, Beth had quickly exchanged her lovely wedding gown for a modest garment that covered her from throat to ankles and shoulders to wrists. Yards of white material billowed around her like the mainsail of a ship. A pale blue ribbon laced its way upward through eyelets starting just below her breasts and ending in a bow tied beneath her chin.

The minutes dragged by and still he didn't come. What if he had changed his mind, deciding he did not want to be saddled with another man's spoiled goods? She envisioned the years of loneliness ahead, locked away each night here in this room designed to depict the Garden of Eden but which without Robin would become her Hell on earth.

When the door opened Beth let out a shriek, the brush slipping from her fingers to land with a dull thump against the rug. "I'm sorry if I startled you. I thought you were expecting me," Robin apologized.

Beth exhaled a sigh of relief as he stepped into the room, his familiar crooked grin reassuring her in a hundred different ways. Her nightmare images disappeared as she watched him survey his surroundings.

"I've found paradise," he uttered, awestruck as he took in every inch of the room that had been only empty space.

Knowing by his expression that he approved, Beth asked anyway, "Do you like it?"

Bending down to retrieve the brush, Robin moved behind her taking up where she had left off. Unlike her haphazard attempts at controlling the fiery tresses, his strokes were sure and firm.

As their eyes met in the cheval glass, he lowered his head to place a gentle kiss on her neck. "I like everything I see except that god-awful thing you are wearing," he chuckled, pulling her back against his lean muscular frame.

Beth blushed as she felt his rigid shaft press against her buttocks. Despite his unflattering description of her tent-like attire, it seemed not to discourage him in the least. As much as she longed to put that other time behind her, she trembled when Robin laid the brush aside and encircled her with his strong, sinewy arms. She scolded herself for being scared. This man was her husband. He loved her. He would never hurt her the way the Indian had.

Sensing her anxiety, Robin turned her around to face him. "Are you afraid of me, Beth?" His eyes begged her to say "No."

Before her mind could form a coherent answer, she moaned truthfully, "Yes . . . maybe . . . I don't know!"

Robin understood her confusion. He had already hurt her shamefully and she had no way of knowing he had vowed never to do so again. In order for their marriage to work he must make her want him with the same intense desire he felt for her. But first he had to find a way to erase the terrible memories that her haunted eyes could not hide.

He urged her down upon the big double bed and sat beside her knowing she was striving to conquer her fear. Choosing his words carefully, he cupped her chin in his palm, forcing her to meet his gray-green gaze. "Loving someone isn't supposed to cause them pain, sweetheart."

Sounding for all the world as if he had been there to witness the dishonor done to her, Beth marveled at his perception. Hoping against hope that he was telling the truth, she confided with childlike honesty, "But the other time it did hurt."

Blue eyes as round as saucers stared up at him for a moment that seemed an eternity. Then Beth leaned forward and placed her petal-pink lips against his mouth telling him as no words ever could that she trusted him completely. "I love you," she murmured as Robin fell backward bringing her with him and then burying his head against her breasts not wanting her to see his tears. He wondered if he would ever be worthy of the love she was offering.

Slowly so as not to frighten her, he stroked her back and gently massaged the taut muscles. She was as tight as a bowstring ready to snap. He knew if he couldn't get her to relax their joining would cause her pain despite his assurances to the contrary. He kissed her forehead, her eyelids, her cheeks, and her nose before settling again on those honeyed lips whose sweet taste sent the heated blood coursing through his veins. He wanted her so badly his body ached with the need to take her then and there. When her lips parted voluntarily inviting his tongue's entry, he struggled to control his raging desire, knowing it was too late to turn back.

Over the past few weeks Beth had tried to envision this moment. She had valiantly fought against the uncertainty that made her heart beat faster and her breathing grow shallow. Covertly she observed her father and stepmother when they didn't know she was watching, envying the special way they sometimes looked at each other as if they were touching without touching. At the same time she couldn't fail to note the way her Aunt 'Becca's gold-flecked green eyes flamed to life whenever Uncle Lance was near. Surely, she told herself, two such levelheaded women could not remain so enraptured by their men if her degrading experience was an example of what happened in the marriage bed. Perhaps Robin was right and it didn't have to hurt or maybe when a man kissed a woman the way he was kissing her it was worth the pain. All she knew for certain was that she hoped he would never stop doing what he was doing.

Robin traced a pattern along Beth's neck with his finger, feeling the tremor of her body beneath his feathery touch. Whether from apprehension or anticipation he could not tell, but her eyes were squeezed tightly shut giving him no clue as to what she was thinking.

"Please look at me, Beth. I want to see your eyes."

Beth found herself staring into the ardent face of the one she had come to love.

"Your eyes are beautiful, you know. Like the sparkling waters of a stream on a sunny day."

Captivated by the deep timbre of his voice and the magic he continued to work with his hands, Beth remained motionless as he loosened the ribbon securing her gown and began deftly to unthread the satin lacing. As if he were unveiling a priceless work of art, Robin parted the soft white material and let his gaze rest on her exposed breasts, small round globes just begging for attention. Feeling his rigid shaft begin to throb, he cautioned himself against moving too fast. Despite the fact that she was no longer a virgin, Beth was still an innocent. Unless he could arouse her own dormant passions they would never achieve their ultimate, mutual fulfillment.

While he planted gossamer kisses along Beth's shoulder, Robin moved his right hand down to her waist then proceeded slowly upward in a zigzag path that outlined each bone protruding from her narrow ribcage and at last cupped one firm breast. He felt her tense as he circled her velvety nipple with the pad of his thumb.

"I want you, sweetheart. I want to be one with you; to plant my seed deep within your womb where it will nurture and grow. But you've got to give me a chance, Beth. Please don't judge me by what happened before."

As strange, wonderful sensations swept over her like a giant wave, Beth yielded to Robin's tender assault, too caught up in a tide of ecstasy to question the meaning behind his supplication. Reacting instinctively to her own needs, she arched her back thrusting her breasts forward. Unable to resist the provocative temptation, Robin bent his head taking one distended nipple into his mouth to suckle it tenderly as his hands slid the bulky nightgown down her slender body until it settled like a cloud on the floor. Beth moaned first with pleasure then with embarrassment as she felt the cool air caress her body and realized she was naked.

"Easy, my love," Robin soothed. Hovering over her, he balanced on his elbows kissing the corners of her mouth. "Don't move. I'll be right back."

With that, he rose from the bed and dimmed the lamp. Then he lifted Beth to her feet just long

220

enough to throw back the flowered spread. He laid her carefully upon the cool, white sheet. Before she had time to consider what he might do next, Robin was stretched out beside her. She wondered briefly what had become of his clothes, but soon she was thinking about other things like how hot his hard body felt pressed against hers.

Starting where he left off, Robin paid homage to her other breast while his hand lightly brushed the triangular mound of red curls at the juncture of her thighs. Any inhibitions Beth might have been harboring evaporated into nothingness as Robin slipped one finger into her most private place, moving to match the steady rhythm of his tongue as it penetrated her mouth.

Each new thing Robin did made Beth's body cry out for more. Inside her head she could hear the roar of the ocean angered by a sudden summer storm. She was terrified at the turbulent emotions he was unleashing in her; yet there was no escaping the indomitable force battering down her weak defenses.

Robin knew she was ready to accept what he had to give. When he rose above her parting her legs with his knee, Beth's eyes flew open as if she'd been suddenly awakened from a sound sleep. Though he felt her body stiffen, she did not utter the protest he expected. Imprisoned beneath him she lay as still as a corpse, wide eyes fixed on his swollen member.

His voice was hushed, reverent, as he entreated, "Relax, darling. Let me in. Let me love you."

As he spoke the soft, persuasive words, he positioned himself and eased ever so slowly into the wet, waiting channel leading to the core of her womanhood. Scarcely discernible in the pale lamplight he watched her expression change from dread to resignation and finally surprise.

Beth willed herself to breathe even as her heart hammered against her chest. Robin had told the truth. There was no pain, just an inexplicable yearning to draw him closer. She searched his face for some clue as to what would happen next. Surely there was more to it than this, she thought disappointedly.

Then Robin began to move. With his arms braced one on each side of her shoulders he pulled away. Feeling only emptiness as he withdrew, Beth reached out to bring him back but he was already driving forward once more. Unhurriedly he filled her then retreated setting a measured pace of pleasure and agony that made Beth sob in frustration. "Please!" Knowing what her body cried out for even if she didn't, Robin thrust harder and faster until his forehead was beaded with sweat and his chest was heaving.

When he could hold back no longer his command shook the room like a thunderclap. "Now, Beth! Come with me now!"

And she did. Beth met him in total surrender but she gave up nothing. Directed by a need that had to be answered, she wrapped her legs around his waist and felt him explode inside her just as she broke free into a new world of iridescent skies filled with shooting stars and rainbows.

Sated as he had never been before, Robin collapsed on top of her, his breath coming in ragged gasps. "My God, woman! What have you done to me?"

Entwining her fingers in the dark swirls of hair matting his chest, Beth pretended to consider before she replied, "I can't be certain but I think what I did to you is called . . ." In Robin's ear she whispered the descriptive term she had overheard Davey and Edward use whenever they returned from a trip to Fort Drum.

Not wanting to believe what he had heard, Robin jerked upright putting an abrupt end to their coupling. Disapproval was written across his stern features as he gritted out, "Damn it, Elizabeth Hawkins! If you ever say that word again I'm going to turn you over my knee and blister your backside!"

Ignoring his threat, Beth frowned at the magnificent instrument that had given her pleasure beyond her wildest dreams hanging limp and lifeless between his legs. "Now see what you've done?" she sighed disgustedly. "You broke it!"

Following her line of vision Robin looked down then burst out laughing. "I can assure you, little darling, it's definitely not broken," he countered, clasping her in a firm embrace.

Refusing to be mollified, Beth challenged him to prove it. And Robin spent the rest of the night doing just that!

Late in August what began as a typical afternoon

223

shower turned into a tropical storm dumping torrents of water on the tiny settlement for two solid days. The creek and the river swelled to overflowing and the main street through the center of town became a quagmire of mud. On the third day the skies cleared and the sun came out again enabling Robin to slosh to the fort through the ankle-deep ooze. Beth was anxious to hear what damage had been caused by the storm. Though they had spent many hours of joyous lovemaking while the tempest raged outside, Robin had begun to feel the walls closing in on him.

As he rounded the corner at the back of his father-in-law's house, figuring Rachel would be in the kitchen, Robin stopped short spotting Beth's little sister sitting on an overturned bucket.

"Hello, Mandy." Flashing a smile, he hunched down beside the precocious four year old who was practically standing on her head as she pounded the water out of a mound of mud with her small pudgy hands.

Twisting her head so she could look at him as she continued to beat a tattoo against the soggy hill of earth, Amanda returned his greeting. "Hi, Robin. I'm glad you're here because I don't have anyone to play with."

Huge sapphire-colored eyes peeked from beneath ringlets of curls as dark as midnight. Even with smudges of dirt streaking her pale, delicately formed face, Robin predicted that Amanda was destined to be a heartbreaker.

"Well now," he said, knitting his brow as he studied the gooey mess taking shape between her high-buttoned leather boots. "Just what game are you playing?"

"I'm making believe." Looking like a homeless waif in her mud-spattered calico skirt, Amanda waited patiently for Robin to decide whether to stay or go on about his business. Although everyone doted on the charming little girl and Amanda seemed to accept the attention of others as her due, she was not prone to whining or wheedling in order to get her way.

"What is it you are making believe?"

Satisfied that she had at least sparked the interest of this good-looking stranger who had married her sister, Amanda explained, "I am making believe this is a birthday cake for Beth and Eddie, but it's only pretend. Momma is making a real one."

The child's face lit up in anticipation of the party scheduled for the following night.

"And what kind of cake is it to be?" Robin asked, hard-pressed to keep from laughing.

Leaning forward and cupping a grubby hand around her mouth, Amanda whispered, "Don't tell anybody but mine is just a mud cake. You don't really have to eat it."

Imitating her pose, Robin whispered back, "My stomach thanks you, princess."

"Your stomach is welcome," Mandy giggled. "Momma's making a chocolate cake with chocolate icing and I get to lick the spoon!" Her jewel-like eyes gleamed as she thought about the treat to come.

"But if I agree to help you make your mud cake, then I should get half the licks," Robin reasoned without cracking a smile.

As Mandy thought over his proposition, Rachel appeared in the doorway, hands on hips. "Amanda Townsend! Just look at you! Come in here and wash up or you can forget about helping me bake this cake!"

Mandy jumped up immediately and skipped toward the steps.

"Wait a minute, princess," Robin called. As she glanced over her shoulder, he said, "Every birthday cake needs a candle." Picking up a twig he stuck it in the top of the round glob of mud.

Mandy took only a moment to weigh the merits of his contribution. "One lick and that's all," she said with finality ascending the stairs in queenly fashion.

Robin laughed while Rachel shook her head helplessly as Mandy disappeared into the house.

"Come on in and have some coffee," the beautiful dark-haired woman invited with a smile.

"Thanks, Rachel, but no point in my tracking up your kitchen floor. I just wanted to make sure none of you blew away in the storm."

"We're fine but a tree fell at Logan's and nearly took Rebecca's front porch with it. Andrew and the boys are over there now clearing away the debris."

"I'll go lend a hand. Is Lance still at Fort King?"

"We're hoping he's on his way back. It would be a shame if he missed Elizabeth and Edward's twentieth birthday celebration. Is Beth all right?"

"Right as rain, if you'll excuse the pun. She's been so busy inside the house these past few days, I don't think she noticed the weather." As he spoke the words, Robin had been thinking about the drapes Beth was making for the parlor, but his thoughts immediately turned to the long hours they had spent in bed isolated from the rest of the world by the forces of nature. The memory was so vivid that his face colored in embarrassment.

"I'm sure she has," Rachel replied, her expression unchanged, but there was a glimmer of knowing amusement in her sapphire-blue eyes.

Robin pulled the brim of his hat lower, mumbling something about Andrew needing his help and quickly took his leave.

Chapter Fourteen

The party was well under way when the door swung open and a trail-weary Lance Logan entered, accepting the enthusiastic welcome of his wife and family. When it was Beth's turn for a hug, her uncle held her at arm's length and admired the new wide-brimmed felt hat Robin had given her which she had been proudly modeling for the others when he arrived.

Rebecca looked at her husband, noting the added lines in his handsome face and the almost imperceptible slump of his wide shoulders. "Come and have something to eat. You must be hungry," she suggested, her smooth forehead wrinkling in concern.

"A little later, honey. Right now I'd like a drink if there's one to be had."

Since Lance was not a drinking man, his request surprised those looking on and convinced his wife that something was definitely amiss. As Rachel hurried to the kitchen to get the bottle of whiskey usually reserved for medicinal purposes, Davey asked the question that was on everyone's mind.

"What's the matter, pa? What's happened?"

"It's nothing important enough to put a damper on this celebration," Lance assured him, reaching for the glass of amber liquid Rachel held out to him and taking a long swallow.

The concerned faces of those he loved most in the world continued to wait expectantly and he knew he was not to be let off the hook so easily. Sighing as he set the drink aside and put his arm around Rebecca's shoulders, he said, "I had another confrontation with Ralph Tillman while I was at Fort King. He accused me of aiding Osceola and his men in their escape and threatened to bring charges against me."

Rebecca Logan's eyes blazed in fury. "That's the most ridiculous thing I've ever heard! The man must be insane!"

"No one in his right mind would believe that!" Davey added angrily.

Already Lance was feeling more like himself. How could anyone be downhearted surrounded by so many loyal supporters? Laughingly he said, "I appreciate your confidence. But to tell the truth, if Osceola had asked for my help I would probably have given it. I've been against the relocation from the beginning."

"As we all have," Beth acknowledged heatedly. "Moving the Seminoles is stupid and unnecessary. There's plenty of room for all of us here in the Territory."

Robin could not speak around the lump in his throat for up until now he had not realized the

229

depth of their compassion toward the people whose blood flowed through his veins.

Annoyed with himself for casting a pall over what was supposed to be a festive occasion, Lance moved to take an empty plate and began heaping it with food he didn't really want. "Hey! Is this a party or a wake?" he asked, striving to appear unconcerned over his recent encounter with the bigoted rancher. "There's no cause for worry. Even if Tillman is crazy enough to bring formal charges, we now have a lawyer in the family who can fight my legal battles for me."

Balancing his plate in one hand, he clapped Robin on the back affectionately. Robin returned Logan's smile but he had the strangest premonition that they had not heard the end of this matter and that defending the man he had come to respect and admire might not be as simple as Lance seemed to believe.

Beth and Robin said very little as they walked home hand in hand, each thinking about the possible consequences of Lance Logan's latest confrontation with Ralph Tillman.

Alone in their bedroom, Beth suddenly felt an urgent need for reassurance. Whirling to face her husband, she blurted out her fear. "Do you think he'll make trouble?"

Robin didn't even pretend to misunderstand. Placing his hands gently on her shoulders he answered her honestly. "I don't know, sweetheart. Tillman is a hothead and a bully, but what makes him dangerous is his unqualified hatred of the Seminoles."

"It's not just the Seminoles," Beth returned knowingly. "Jesse told me his father swore vengeance against all Indians because a band of Creek warriors killed Jesse's mother. Look at the way he treats Davey whose mother was of the Calusa tribe. Now Tillman's animosity seems to be spreading like a disease to anyone who shows sympathy toward the Seminoles' plight."

Robin removed Beth's new hat which she had refused to take off since he had presented it to her hours before. Tossing it on the bed, he gazed down into her dazzling blue eyes. "Of all people," he said with tender bewilderment, "you are the one who should feel enmity toward Osceola and his braves. How can you care about them after what they did to you?"

He wondered if the question stemmed from some perverse need to castigate himself or if deep down he hoped she would say she had forgiven the one who had so ruthlessly violated her.

He saw Beth's features harden. She had tried to understand what drove the man in the mask to commit such a monstrous deed. When no rational explanation came to mind, she endeavored to show mercy toward him. But he had not only abused her, he had stolen what rightfully belonged to Robin and she found it impossible to acquit him of his guilt.

"Only one man was responsible for my debasement. He happened to be an Indian. I cannot blame all Indians for his treachery."

Robin understood and he grieved anew for it was obvious he would have to look elsewhere for absolution. Wishing he had not brought up the past, he drew Beth close. Inhaling the clean, fresh scent of her hair, he steered the conversation back to where it had begun. "Nothing's going to happen to your uncle. I promise," he murmured against her ear. "Men like Tillman are all mouth, spouting threats in the heat of anger but too cowardly to carry them out. It's the quiet ones who keep their feelings hidden that you have to look out for."

As he spoke he cupped her buttocks firmly in the palms of his hands and rubbed his burgeoning arousal suggestively against her flat belly.

Wrapping her arms around his neck, Beth cocked her head at him, all wide-eyed innocence. "Then I certainly don't have to look out for you."

"And just what is that supposed to mean?"

Beth giggled. "Only that since the very first moment we met in Major Caldwell's office you have been exasperatingly open about your feelings. You told me how you felt about my hat, and how you felt about my breeches . . . oh, yes . . . and then as I recall you had a few things to say about my forthright way of speaking."

With a twinkle of amusement in his gray-green eyes, Robin protested, "Those were not feelings; they were opinions."

"When you voice an opinion you are merely putting your feelings into words," she retorted haughtily.

"Which only goes to prove people talk too much!" Before Beth could continue the debate, Robin dipped his head toward hers and captured her lips, putting an end to further discussion.

Several hours later as Robin cradled her against his side, his breathing deep and steady, Beth still tingled in the afterglow of their passionate lovemaking. They had climbed the highest mountain then soared beyond its peak coming together in a climax that surmounted all earthly bounds. As Robin collapsed on top of her, he had whispered raggedly, "Happy Birthday, sweetheart."

His love was a wonderful gift and she suspected she might have one for him in return. Though they had been married for eight weeks and she had not had her monthly flow, she was still afraid she might be mistaken and she didn't want Robin to be disappointed if she was wrong. As of yet there was no sign of the morning sickness Rachel and Rebecca had suffered. Deciding she would keep her secret to herself a while longer, Beth inched closer to her husband hugging her stomach as she drifted off into a peaceful, dreamless sleep.

Beth came slowly awake dragged from the depths of slumber by the sound of distant thunder. Another storm must be approaching, she thought groggily as Robin sat up on the side of the bed groaning and muttering something about people who wake other people up in the middle of the night. Cracking one eyelid open, Beth saw that the first rays of dawn were filtering through the curtains casting a shadowy half-light on the familiar room. The loud booming sounded again only this time she realized it was someone pounding on their front door.

"Stay here. I'll see who it is," Robin mumbled disgruntledly hopping on one foot then the other as he struggled into his pants.

Ignoring his advice, Beth rolled out of bed and snatched up her robe, tying the sash as she trailed along in her husband's wake.

Robin flung the door wide jumping back just in time to miss being hit by Davey's fist as the latter made ready to land another solid blow against the wooden panel.

"I'm glad you're home." Davey let his arm fall to his side and exhaled as if he had been holding his breath.

"Where the hell did you think I'd be at this ungodly hour?" Robin grumbled, quirking a dark eyebrow at Beth's cousin.

Rising on tiptoes to peer over his broad shoulder, Beth asked worriedly, "Is someone ill, Davey?" Then before he could answer, she nudged Robin aside. "For heaven's sake! Stop blocking the doorway and let him in!"

Both men moved at once and Beth pushed the door shut leaning against it for support. She knew Davey would not barge in at daybreak unless there was something seriously wrong. "Let's go into the kitchen so I can put on the coffee," she suggested in an attempt to postpone what was sure to be bad news.

As the men seated themselves at the table Robin said in a tone that brooked no nonsense, "Okay, tell us the news."

"It's about Ralph Tillman." Davey steepled his fingers together resting his elbows on the table.

"Damn it!" Beth slammed the metal coffee pot down on the burner. "He can't be fool enough to think people will believe his absurd accusations against Uncle Lance!"

Davey continued to study his hands. "Tillman won't be making any more accusations, absurd or otherwise," he informed wearily. "Ralph Tillman is dead."

"What?" Beth and Robin both cried out in unison.

"He was shot in the back. A contingent of soldiers from Fort King arrived here late last night. They are *requesting* that pa return with them to answer some questions."

Beth stared at her cousin incredulously. "Do you mean Uncle Lance is under arrest?"

"No, of course not. Pa might kill Tillman in a fair fight but no one in the Territory would accuse him of shooting a man in the back."

"Then why do they want to question him?" Robin recognized the gravity of the situation and knew Davey was trying to shield Beth from the truth.

Shrugging his shoulders, Davey replied disgustedly, "There were a number of witnesses to the argument between pa and Tillman though according to pa it wasn't an argument at all."

"What happened?" Robin prodded.

"Tillman blamed pa for Osceola's escape but pa just laughed in his face. Tillman was so infuriated he attacked pa."

"And?"

"Pa flattened him with one blow. It was self-defense," Davey spoke up daring anyone to say otherwise.

Setting steaming cups of coffee before the men, Beth replied, "Of course it was self-defense. Besides hitting a man is a far cry from shooting him in the back!"

"Then what?" Robin was no longer just a concerned family member. He was an attorney after the facts.

Davey looked blank for a moment. "Then pa came home," he finally concluded.

Robin suspected there was more Davey wasn't telling them. "And your father never saw Tillman again?"

The younger man's chin jutted out at a threatening angle. "No! He never laid eyes on him after that!"

Robin startled both Beth and her cousin as he pounded his huge fist against the table causing the cups to rattle. "Goddamn it, boy! Your father may need my help but I can't give it to him if you don't tell me the truth. All of it!"

Had the situation been less serious Beth would have laughed to hear Robin scolding her cousin like a father would a recalcitrant child.

Contritely Davey admitted. "According to the soldiers, Tillman took off Hell bent for leather after pa vowing to see justice served in his own way. But he never caught up with him. The next day Jesse found his father's body along the trail."

Robin rubbed his hand over the stubble on his chin. "I suppose Lance has agreed to return to Fort King?"

"We'll be leaving within the hour. Pa's as anxious as anybody else to get this mess cleared up."

"I'll be ready," Robin volunteered without waiting to be asked.

Beth had listened attentively to the exchange between the two men. "Don't think you're going without me," she piped up.

Robin looked at her mutinous expression, indecision written on his face. He knew how hard it would be if he insisted she stay here waiting, not knowing what was happening to her beloved uncle. On the other hand, this was no pleasure trip. Despite what she and Davey believed, it was obvious that at least a certain few thought Lance had murdered Ralph Tillman. If possible Robin wanted to protect Beth from the ugly talk she was bound to hear if she went with them to Fort King.

Looking from one to the other, Davey read the hesitation in Robin's face pitted against his cousin's stubborn determination. "You might as well let her join the party," he advised. "My stepmother is going with us."

Robin's eyes widened in surprise. Rebecca Logan was like a beautiful, porcelain doll, so tiny and fragile she looked as if she might break if one stared at her too hard. He could not imagine her

237

withstanding the rigors of the trail.

Again Davey appeared to read Robin's thoughts for he chuckled, "Evidently you've only seen one side of my stepmother. You'll have to get her to tell you about the time she was kidnapped by two unscrupulous trappers who sold her to a band of renegade Calusa bucks."

"And then," Beth added blithely, "you might ask her about the time she was held prisoner by the infamous pirate Jose Gaspar."

"Good Lord!" Robin exclaimed in amazement. There was much he still had to learn about this remarkable family he had married into. "But what can she hope to accomplish by accompanying Lance to Fort King?"

Both Beth and Davey laughed. Then Beth said, "Understand this, husband. You may be Uncle Lance's lawyer but 'Becca will always be his staunchest defender. Let his accusers beware for she's just liable to bring down the walls of Fort King like Joshua did when he fought the Battle of Jericho."

As Robin tried to picture Logan's dainty little wife circling the stockade fence with trumpet in hand, he joined in their mirth. "You win," he conceded. "Go get dressed!"

When they drew their horses up outside the gates of the fort, Robin was still trying to reconcile the things Beth and Davey had told him about Rebecca Logan with what he had seen of the ideal wife and mother who seemed content to stay at home caring for her children and doing her husband's bidding. Beth giggled at his gaping astonishment when the woman in question appeared. Dressed in white fringed buckskins, a white hat, and white leather boots, Rebecca rode beside her husband with all the regal bearing of a true aristocrat. Even her horse was the color of newly fallen snow.

Robin thought she looked just like a diminutive angel until she turned her remarkable catlike eyes on him. The flaming amber sparks he saw put him more in mind of a lioness prepared to meet any foe who might threaten her cubs.

"Lovely morning for a ride," Lance quipped in greeting, attempting to lighten the somber mood. For his efforts he earned a scathing glare from his wife.

Focusing her attention on Robin, Rebecca said, "I'm glad you will be accompanying us; not that I believe Logan will need your expertise as a lawyer. Perhaps together we can discover the identity of the cowardly bastard who killed that low-life scum, Tillman, and dispatch him to Hell where he can spend eternity doing penance alongside his victim."

The manner in which she spoke, softly with her cultured British accent, was so at odds with the words he was hearing, Robin was temporarily stunned and then burst out laughing. "That's a mighty tall order, ma'am."

Glancing over her shoulder at Davey and Edward who were mounted behind her, Rebecca nodded in agreement. "Yes, it is a mighty tall order, but then we have some mighty tall men to carry it out, don't we?" For the first time she smiled, a radiant, confident smile that was contagious.

Without another word the journey began. Lance and Rebecca led the procession, followed by Robin and Beth with Davey and Edward bringing up the rear. To an onlooker, it would have seemed like a pleasant day's outing had it not been for the dozen uniformed soldiers following at a discreet distance. There was nothing in their manner to indicate the broad-shouldered man riding ahead of him was their prisoner, yet Robin suspected that should Logan suddenly decide he wanted to turn back, they would not hesitate to use force to change his mind.

Rachel and Andrew stood at the gates waving goodbye. Though Beth's father had argued to accompany them, he knew the situation between the soldiers and the Indians awaiting embarkation from Fort Brooke had become volatile since Osceola's defection. Someone had to remain to look after the younger members of the Logan-Townsend clan and try to maintain the uneasy peace that threatened to erupt into open conflict at any moment.

They made camp that night beside the river the Indians called Withlacoochee, meaning "little big water." It was a solemn group who sat back as far as possible from the dying embers of the cooking fire, each silently contemplating what lay ahead. The air was humid and heavy without the slightest trace of a breeze to relieve the oppressive August heat bearing down on them. Even the crickets' chirpings and the bullfrogs' croaks sounded lethargic and off beat. The only concession to an otherwise miserable night was the full moon overhead reflecting upon the shimmering surface of the river. Everyone knew it would be difficult to sleep but as the hour grew late one by one they resolutely sought their bedding knowing that tomorrow would be another long, tiring day.

Beth found little comfort in the knowledge that Robin was an arm's length away. She yearned to snuggle up against him but the feel of her sweaty clothes dampened her ardor. Instead she tossed and turned moving the cover aside then pulling it back and over her head to ward off the persistent mosquitoes whining about her ears. Just when she thought she had reached the limit of her endurance a hand clamped over her mouth.

"Ssh!" Robin cautioned. "Don't make a sound."

He pulled her to her feet not giving her time to put on her boots. Barefoot they moved surreptitiously along the grassy riverbank in the opposite direction from where the soldiers were camped downstream. When they were far enough away to risk speaking without waking the others, Robin stopped and drew her into his arms.

"I can't seem to sleep with you so far away," he murmured as one hand trailed a path down her spine spreading tingles of delight to every nerve in her body.

"I can't sleep because it's too damned hot!" Beth retorted testily.

Undaunted by her ill humor, Robin took her shirt by its hem and began lifting it seductively upward.

"What are you doing?" she gasped in dismay.

Amusement lacing his voice, Robin promised with an unusual poetic flare, "I'm planning to cool you off right after I set you ablaze with desire."

Beth's giggles stopped abruptly when instead of removing her shirt, he left it pinioning her upraised arms while he bent to pay tribute first to one outthrust breast and then the other, savoring the salty taste of perspiration sheening her skin. True to his word Robin turned her blood to liquid fire. He slowly slid the close-fitting buckskins over her hips following their descent with his tongue. Grasping her hips as he reached the soft triangular mound of red-gold curls, he teased the sensitive nub encased in folds of sleek, tight flesh.

Beth was caught up in a frenzied burst of carnal passion that threatened to consume her. Throwing back her head, she cried out, her voice muffled by the shirt that still held her a willing prisoner. She pressed her hips forward expelling the sweet nectar he sought to extract with his gentle, persuasive mouth.

Suddenly she was free of the restraint and she threw her arms around Robin's neck as he lowered her to the ground. At some point he had managed to rid himself of his clothing. Now she saw his lean, muscular body silhouetted in the moonlight overhead. He nudged her knees apart and entered her quickly for he could wait no longer. Their climax was swift in coming and infinitely satisfying.

Afterward they lay panting, their bodies bathed in sweat. When her breathing steadied to some semblance of normalcy Beth lifted her head to stare down at the handsome man who was her husband, the man who could without much effort turn her into an unrepressed wanton.

"What about the other part?" she asked provocatively, twirling a damp ringlet of chest hair around her finger.

Robin tried to focus his attention on her question but at the moment all of his concentration centered around his heart and the effort it took to slow its rapid beat. "The next part?" he sighed raggedly. "If I haven't satisfied you after all that you're going to have to give me a few minutes to regain my masculinity."

Beth promptly poked him in the ribs. "I'm not talking about *that!* You promised to cool me off yet here we are still glued together with sweat!"

"Did anyone ever tell you how adorable you are?"

"Yes, you! But what does that have to do with the promise you made? Besides sweaty people aren't adorable!"

How could Robin explain the appeal of a woman who made mad, passionate love to him one minute then immediately launched into a discourse about perspiration?

"Well, my darling, a promise is a promise!" With that he stood up balancing her in his arms, strode to the edge of the bank, and tossed her unceremoniously into the spring-fed waters of the river.

Beth had time for only one yelp before the frigid water rushed up to meet her. She sank below its surface then reappeared coughing and spitting as her toes found purchase on the sandy bottom. Robin executed a perfect dive arcing over her head then cutting through the water like a knife. Watching the spot of widening rings, Beth drew back her arm preparing to send a spray of water in his direction. Instead her legs were swept out from under her and down she went again, but this time she found herself breaking the surface cradled in two strong arms.

As Robin turned in a circle taking her on a magical moonlight ride, she brought him up short by hammering his chest with her fists and demanding, "What if I couldn't swim?"

"You can swim."

"You didn't know that! What if I couldn't?"

"It wouldn't have mattered. It isn't over your head."

"You didn't know that either. Suppose it had been over my head *and* I couldn't swim?"

"Then I would have rescued you, and you would have been indebted to me for saving your life."

Beth gave him a dubious look. "But you're the one who threw me in to start with!"

"Only because you said you wanted to cool off."

"This wasn't precisely what I had in mind," she admitted, squirming against his chest, "but it worked! I feel delicious."

"Yes, you do," he agreed, his voice deep and husky and oh so close to her ear.

Beth wiggled her legs free and stood up clinging to his wet, musk-scented body as she placed her feet on top of his. "I'm not hot anymore."

"I am."

"Oh!"

"Is that all you have to say?"

"No. It came back, didn't it?"

"What?"

"The masculinity you had to regain."

Deciding to answer her question with action not words, Robin lifted her hips, wrapping her legs around his waist as he gently inserted his pulsating heat into her warm woman's flesh. Together they rocked beneath a lover's full moon sending diamond-studded ripples across the glassy surface of the river caught up in their own undulating waves of ecstasy.

Chapter Fifteen

The meeting room was scarcely large enough to accommodate the number of people in attendance. An unsmiling Major Caldwell, flanked on either side by two lesser officers, sat at a table facing the audience while long rows of chairs covered every other inch of space. Each chair was occupied and the temperature inside was easily above a hundred degrees. It was humid, suffocating heat which could quickly drain the stamina right out of a man.

Beth blamed her pounding head and queasy stomach on the fetid odor of so many unwashed bodies but, in truth, the knowledge that things were not going as she had expected was largely to blame for her physical indisposition. They had been assured that this hearing would be conducted as an inquest not a trial, and yet witness after witness had come forth to testify regarding the last confrontation between Lance Logan and Ralph Tillman. Most of the men had been employed by Tillman and without exception they painted a verbal picture of Lance as an arrogant Indian lover who put himself above the law.

Self-consciously Sergeant Rourke described the incident that had taken place outside the barracks weeks ago following the rancher's disparaging remarks about Indians in Davey Logan's presence. Her spirits lifted as the young officer repeated Tillman's foul innuendos and concluded by saying the attacks had been provoked and in his opinion her uncle's actions had been justified. Then to her dismay Major Caldwell had glowered at his subordinate, harshly reminding him that they were not here to discuss opinions but to ascertain facts.

Studying the back of her husband's head and admiring the long raven-colored hair tied back at his nape, Beth regretted her inability to see his face and gauge his reaction to the proceedings. The men from Fort Brooke were seated together in the second row, but Rebecca had insisted on sitting near the back where she would have a clear view of everyone present. Knowing her aunt was hoping that the real murderer, if he were there, might do something to give himself away, Beth had elected to stay with her rather than joining the men. But now she desperately needed Robin beside her, touching her hand to let her know that everything would be all right.

It was Jesse Tillman's testimony that took her by surprise. If anyone had the right to harbor a grudge against the man some suspected of killing his father, it was Jesse. He had been among those who had witnessed the final disagreement between the two men. Yet in a flat, emotionless voice barely audible to those in the back row, he related what he had seen and heard stating exactly what had taken place without a hint of judgment for or against Lance Logan.

He refused to speculate as to what might have happened afterward saying only that he had left the fort to return home the next morning and had found his father's body along the trail.

Beth poised on the edge of her seat waiting for Jesse to describe the fight between Ralph Tillman and her uncle that had occurred in the stable on the morning they left Fort King. One more encounter that would demonstrate their hostility toward each other, but Jesse finished his statement and returned to his chair without making mention of that particular incident. Grateful yet puzzled, Beth fixed her gaze on the unpretentious young man as he took his place among the hard-bitten cowboys who now worked for him.

That night they gathered in the kitchen of the modestly furnished, two bedroom house which was normally assigned to a married officer and his family but happened to be temporarily unoccupied. Major Caldwell had insisted that they use the house during their stay rather than make the five mile trek back and forth to the McAfees. They all took it for granted that his magnanimous gesture stemmed from a desire to keep Lance under surveillance rather than from any concern for their convenience. As soon as supper was over, Edward, undeterred by the long ride, left to visit Maggie.

"I simply don't understand how Baker Caldwell can possibly entertain the idea that you might be capable of shooting a man in the back!" Rebecca's blazing green eyes dared anyone to defend the errant major.

Only her husband took up the challenge. "Caldwell's only doing his job, honey."

"Doing his job? If he were doing his job he would

248

be concentrating on finding the real murderer instead of posturing and posing in front of that bunch of riffraff that just came to see a show!"

Striving to keep things in perspective, Lance said, "You seem to forget. No one has actually accused me of killing Ralph Tillman."

Hands on hips, Rebecca fired back, "Your being asked to come here is accusation enough, and don't tell me there aren't men posted right outside the door to make sure you don't leave without permission."

In fact, no such guards had been stationed but they all knew any movement Lance made would be reported directly to the fort's commandant.

Lance turned toward his new nephew. "Well, Robin. You're the lawyer. What is your opinion of today's events?"

"There isn't a shred of evidence to link you with Tillman's death," Robin answered confidently. "If that bit of theatrics we saw today had taken place in a real court of law, most of what was said would have been declared inadmissible based on hearsay, irrelevancy, and speculation."

Lance laughed, appreciating Robin's unflagging support, then hastened to remind him, "This is the only law we have here in the Territory. The army has as much right to try a man and hang him if he's found guilty as any judge and jury in the more civilized regions of the country."

Robin grinned crookedly. "Whose side are you on?"

Lance and Davey chuckled while Beth and Rebecca glared at them unable to see any humor in the situation.

Suddenly serious, Robin voiced a question that had been troubling him all afternoon. "Did Jesse Tillman's testimony strike anyone as peculiar under the circumstances, or could I be looking for something that isn't there?"

"It certainly did," Rebecca answered coming to stand behind her husband's chair, placing her hands lightly on his shoulders. "Jesse Tillman was totally devoid of emotion. It was as if he was reading a script."

"Hardly the way you would expect a man to act whose father had been murdered," Davey remarked contemplatively.

"Especially," Robin added, "when the man some suspect of committing the murder was sitting right there in the courtroom."

Lance looked sharply at Robin. "Are you saying you think Jesse Tillman had something to do with his father's death?"

"I'm not saying—"

Before Robin could explain, Beth burst out vehemently, "That's the most ridiculous thing I've ever heard!" Her fervent denial astonished even Beth herself, but she had always held a certain affinity for Jesse. Though she considered him weak for allowing Ralph Tillman to run his life, it was that very weakness that made her think him incapable of being involved in such a heinous crime.

With all eyes upon her she sought to justify her position. "Jesse Tillman doesn't have the guts to kill his father."

"It doesn't take guts to shoot a man in the back," Davey argued.

"Besides," Beth went on choosing to ignore her cousin, "Jesse actually withheld evidence that could have proved damaging to Uncle Lance."

"What are you talking about?" Robin demanded, frowning in his wife's direction.

"I saw Jesse Tillman in the barn the morning his father tried to attack me and Uncle Lance came to my rescue. Jesse didn't say a word about it today."

Robin looked at her for a long minute digesting this new information. Rubbing his chin, he finally said thoughtfully as if to himself, "I wonder why?"

Beth answered by stomping her foot. "Could it possibly be that Jesse knows Uncle Lance is not the sort of man who would shoot anyone in the back, and so he sees no point in adding fuel to the fire of speculation?" The explanation seemed perfectly logical to Beth and she resented Robin's continued skepticism.

Smiling like a wolf who had just discovered an untended flock of sheep, Robin nodded in satisfaction. "I think it's very likely that Jesse Tillman knows Lance didn't kill his father. Let's just leave it at that for now."

Before Beth could say more, Robin began briefing Lance and Davey on what they might expect tomorrow when they were called to give their statements. He suggested they answer questions truthfully but advised against volunteering information. Then amid yawns and good nights, each couple headed for their bedroom while Davey returned to the barracks where he would share quarters with the soldiers.

The following day shortly after noon Major

Caldwell read an official statement. It was the opinion of the panel that Ralph Tillman had died at the hands of a person or persons unknown. The adjudication was a hollow victory for Lance Logan. Unless the identity of the murderer or murderers could be ascertained, his reputation would remain under a dark cloud of suspicion and doubt.

It was a subdued group that returned to their temporary quarters to partake of a simple luncheon and make plans for their departure. Only Robin seemed pleased with the outcome of the hearing; try as she might Beth could not understand why. When she had broached the subject with him last night after they retired, he would say only that he had a "hunch" as to who was responsible for Tillman's death. He stilled further questions by kissing her senseless then making love to her until the early morning hours.

Now Beth was so frustrated she could spit! Knowing that some people believed her uncle to be the culprit made her blood boil while her heart cried out for vindication. Surely if Robin suspected someone, this was the time to speak up before they returned to Fort Brooke and gave the true villain a chance to escape. Gritting her teeth, Beth vowed that as soon as she could talk to her husband alone she would somehow convince him to take his suspicions to Major Caldwell.

No sooner had they sat down to eat than an excited Sergeant Rourke appeared at the back door. "Excuse me, folks," he apologized. "Some startling new evidence about Tillman's murder has just come to light. The major would like to see you gentlemen in his office right away."

It was impossible to tell by the young officer's expression whether the "new evidence" would aid or abate Logan's vindication. Judging from his look of perplexity, Rourke probably hadn't even been privy to the information they were about to hear. Rising as one, Lance, Robin, Davey, and Edward excused themselves to the ladies and followed Rourke out the door.

"Well, if that doesn't beat all," Beth fumed, stalking to the window. " 'The major would like to see you *gentlemen* right away,' " she mimicked. "And what are we supposed to do? Just sit here and wait?"

"Didn't you bring your knitting?" Rebecca teased.

Beth whirled to face her aunt. "Very funny, 'Becca! You may be willing to play the patient wife, but I happen to think we have as much right to know what is going on as they do!"

Rebecca sighed resignedly. "I agree with you and I'm no more patient than you are, but the last thing Lance needs right now is for me to make a scene over not being included in their *tête-à-tête*." Going to stand beside her niece, she confided, "Your uncle is more concerned about this damnable business than he lets on, Beth. He has lived his life honestly and believes in fair dealings. To have his integrity questioned has hurt him deeply."

"I'm sorry, 'Becca," she replied through trembling lips. "I'm acting like a spoiled child left out of a game when I should be thinking about how Uncle Lance must feel."

Rebecca squeezed her shoulders affectionately. "It's all right, honey. Believe me, I'm as anxious as you are. But for now the best thing we can do is wait."

Smiling with resignation she added, "It's also the hardest."

By the time they finished toying with their food, they still had heard nothing from the men. Knowing it could be hours before word arrived, Beth suggested, "Let's ride out and see the McAfees. It wouldn't take long and I just don't think I can stand this waiting."

"Beth, dear, I can't possibly leave. When Lance does come back I have to be here." Then she qualified. "I *want* to be here. But there's no reason why you shouldn't go."

Beth looked doubtful. "I couldn't leave you alone."

Forcing a laugh her aunt chided, "I'm hardly alone with a fort full of soldiers around me. I'll be fine. Besides your fidgeting is driving me to distraction, and I did bring *my* knitting!"

"Are you sure?" Beth asked, still hesitant.

Rebecca left the room then returned with a half-finished sock dangling from her fingertips.

"That's not what I meant," Beth argued though she was unable to hide her grin.

"Be gone with you and leave me in peace," Rebecca admonished. "And be careful," she added as Beth kissed her on the cheek.

"Don't worry about me, 'Becca. I'm just going to ride out and tell Maggie and her folks what happened this morning then I'll turn around and come right back. And I know when I get here everything will have been resolved. I can feel it in my bones."

Smiling at her irrepressible niece, Rebecca silently prayed that she was right.

* * *

As Beth rode across the wide expanse of open meadow, for the first time in weeks her thoughts turned to the Indian called Hawk and that long ago night she had spent in the nearby woods under his protection. She wondered if he was still alive and if so where he might be. Then she scoffed aloud, "Why should I care?"

Senabar pricked up her ears at the sound of Beth's harsh denunciation.

"Don't worry, old girl," her mistress reassured confidently, leaning forward to stroke the mare's neck. "We have Robin now, and he's all the champion we need!"

They had nearly reached the far edge of the meadow ringed by a forest of tall, stately pines before Beth heard the drumming noise of a second set of hoofs coming from behind. At first the rider was too far away to recognize and her heart skipped a beat as she hoped it might be Robin following at such a reckless pace. But as horse and rider closed the gap, apprehension replaced disappointment for the man pursuing her was none other than Jesse Tillman.

What could he possibly be doing out here when his ranch lay to the north of Fort King and she was heading due west?

Jesse took off his hat and waved it above his head. "Beth, wait!" he called unnecessarily for Beth had already brought Senabar to a halt.

"Hello, Jesse," she greeted warily as he pulled his horse up short just a few feet from where she sat beside the shaded trail leading into the woods.

Both rider and mount were winded and it took a few moments for Jesse to catch his breath. Meanwhile the horse's sides heaved as the animal blew a spray of mist through its wide nostrils.

Unnerved by the man's sudden appearance, Beth did not wait for him to fully recover before she asked, "What brings you out here, Jesse?"

When he could speak without gasping Jesse replied, "I followed you."

"Why?"

"I had to talk to you . . . about my father's death," he added after a pause.

"I'm sorry he's dead, but my uncle didn't kill him," Beth replied, her chin jutting out at a defensive angle.

Ignoring her remark Jesse asked, "Do you suppose we could walk along the trail a little way? It's cooler in the woods and my horse needs a rest."

Jesse had never given Beth any reason to distrust him and though she would have preferred he just say what was on his mind then let her go, she could not find it in herself to be rude to the young man who seemed to have no other friends.

"I can't spare much time, Jesse," she explained as she dismounted. "I have to get to the McAfees then back to the fort before dark."

"I promise this won't take long."

Beth was ashamed at her lack of enthusiasm for Jesse seemed inordinately pleased that she had not rebuffed him. In silence they walked deeper into the interior of the dense pine forest where the bright afternoon sunshine could not penetrate the thick, vaulted branches overhead. Beneath a heavy layer of decaying needles the ground gave off a musty odor which in combination with the cool, dusky darkness and the solemnity of her companion made Beth long to turn back toward the warmth and light of the meadow.

Apparently Jesse had changed his mind about wanting to talk to her for he had spoken not a word since they entered the gloomy timberland. He was a few steps behind her when Beth stopped, intending to insist they return to where their horses were tied at the edge of the clearing so that she could be on her way. Just as she started to pivot around she heard a short whishing sound. Then a brilliant flash exploded behind her eyes followed by absolute blackness.

"That doesn't mean he's guilty," Robin cautioned as the men entered the house late that afternoon.

A smiling Lance Logan countered, "It may not mean he's guilty but it sure as hell means he's a liar!"

"Who's a liar?" Rebecca asked, coming into the living room from the kitchen and rushing to embrace her husband, not caring that they had an audience.

"Jesse Tillman," Davey supplied excitedly. "A patrol came in this afternoon right after the hearing was over. One of the soldiers was on guard duty the night *before* Jesse says he found his father's body, and he swears he saw Jesse riding into the fort that very night."

Interrupting his cousin, Edward continued the story, "And Jesse came back along the same trail Ralph took when he followed Uncle Lance."

Rebecca stared at the quartet of men who seemed to be taking the news with a variety of emotions. Edward and Davey were jubilant already having determined Jesse Tillman's guilt in their own minds. Logan shrugged his wide shoulders noncommittally, but Rebecca could see hope he was afraid to voice softening his eyes. Robin was obviously playing the devil's advocate trying to keep things in perspective.

"Lying about where he was doesn't prove Jesse killed his father," Robin reminded them, knowing that if Jesse denied leaving the fort it would come down to one man's word against another. In which case, he felt certain young Tillman would have a number of his ranch hands ready to swear he had been here the entire night.

Giving Robin a disgruntled look, Rebecca repeated the questions he had asked Logan the morning they left Fort Brooke. "Just whose side are you on?"

Everyone laughed including Robin who felt things were coming together just as he had hoped. As an attorney, though, he wanted all of the pieces neatly in place before he called for a victory celebration.

Rebecca's next question brought instant sobriety. "What does Jesse have to say?"

"We don't know yet," answered Lance. "They're looking for him right now."

"I sure would like to be there to hear his explanation," Edward grinned, nudging Davey with his elbow.

A knock on the door precluded Davey's reply. Sergeant Rourke stepped inside at Rebecca's invitation.

"Tillman's not in the fort," he informed without preamble. "No one saw him leave but with the patrol arriving and the usual comings and goings it would be easy for him to slip out unnoticed. Major Caldwell has sent some men out to his ranch. I'm sure they'll find him and bring him back."

Having made his report, Rourke departed promising to let them know as soon as the soldiers brought Jesse in for questioning.

"Where's Beth?" Robin asked, surprised that she had not appeared during the commotion signaling their return.

Rebecca's answer brought a worried frown to his handsome face. "She was restless so she decided to ride out to Maggie's. She should be back anytime. Did Major Caldwell feed you?"

Lance chuckled. "The only thing he fed us was information, but I'd call it fine fare."

"Hmph! It's about time he came to his senses and started looking in another direction for Ralph Tillman's killer," she reasoned with all the logic of a wife who believes her husband incapable of doing wrong. "Come in the kitchen and I'll fix you something to eat," she called to the men as she headed into the adjoining room.

During the exchange Robin had paced the room like a caged tiger. Now he said, "Thanks, Rebecca, but I think I'll ride out and meet Beth." His expression remained grim. It was probably foolish yet he didn't like the idea of Beth being away from the fort with Jesse Tillman on the loose.

"Sure you won't have something to eat first?" Rebecca called from the doorway.

"No thanks," he repeated. "Just don't let these two growing boys devour everything in the house before we get back." He nodded toward Davey and Edward but the humor of his words failed to reach his eyes.

Chapter Sixteen

Through a long tunnel Beth struggled to regain entry into the world of the living. The footing along the dark uphill passageway was treacherous. For every two steps she took forward, she slipped back one. But she could see a faint glow at the end of the corridor and she knew she had to reach that point or be forever entombed in this lightless underground Hell which lay secreted just below the earth's surface. Though the vague illumination was still far away, each time she focused on that distant goal the pain in her head became so acute she had to fight the urge to let go and slide back down into the black abyss from which she'd come. She felt as if miniature beings were beating her skull with tiny hammers.

She tried to remember why she couldn't give up but thinking only worsened her headache. It had something to do with Robin: beautiful, handsome Robin whose image floated before her eyes. He would be angry if she didn't come back. She hadn't told him about the baby. Now it might be too late. Unless she could find her way out of here, their child would be consigned to live deep in the bowels of this netherworld, never to feel the warmth of the sun, never to know the wonderful man who was his father. She was close now, so very close. Just a little farther. "Hold on," she told herself. With one final thrust Beth pushed against the darkness and broke through into the blinding light of consciousness lifting heavy lids to survey her surroundings.

"Welcome back."

Beth turned her head slowly toward the speaker whose voice dripped with sarcasm. Forcing her eyes to remain open in spite of the dizzying pain and nausea brought on by the slight movement, she looked into the mocking eyes of Jesse Tillman.

"Why, Jesse?" The words were but a raspy croak. She started to raise her hands to her raw, parched throat only to find that they were bound behind her back. Her ankles had been tied together as well, leaving her feet numb below the tight cord.

She started to shake her head in an effort to clear her fogged brain then thought better of it as her temples continued to throb relentlessly. "I . . . I don't understand. Why?" she repeated, trying to make sense out of this nightmare that had suddenly become too frighteningly real.

Jesse lay stretched out on the ground propped up on one elbow nonchalantly sucking a blade of grass. Anyone watching would have thought he hadn't a care in the world as he eyed the red-haired beauty leaning against a tree just beyond his reach. "The 'why' is simple. You're my ticket out of this godforsaken wilderness."

Beth waited for him to go on but apparently he thought his explanation sufficient. She looked around the secluded clearing wondering where they were. Certainly this was not the trail she had been following to the McAfees. She must have been unconscious several hours for the sun had already dipped below the tops of the trees casting the small glen into the murky gray light of dusk. As the rough bark of the pine tree gouged her back and the ropes bit into the tender flesh around her wrists and ankles, anger overcame fear. Beth lashed out verbally at the young man who would dare treat her so callously.

"Damn it, Jesse Tillman! If this is your idea of a joke it's gone beyond funny! Untie me this instant and let me be on my way!" Her eyes flashed defiantly, but Jesse merely looked at her from beneath lazy lids.

Finally he said, "I'm afraid I can't do that." He actually sounded sorry as he added, "And this is anything but a joke."

Gritting her teeth, Beth fought down the panic that had begun to take hold. Jesse might be weak but he wasn't stupid. Surely he did not think he could keep her here indefinitely, or did he? The situation required a clear head and unfortunately hers could not have been more muddled at the moment. It was then she remembered what Robin had once told her. *It's the quiet ones you have to watch,* and she chastised herself for ever trusting the young rancher in the first place.

Striving to keep her voice calm and her words without rancor, Beth tried again to discover the motive behind his bizarre behavior. "What did you mean about my being your ticket out of the Territory? Surely if you want to leave you are free to go. You don't need me."

Jesse threw the blade of grass aside and sat up hugging his knees with his arms. "On the contrary, Beth, I do need you. I've needed you since the first time I laid eyes on you. Only now you've become vital to my existence."

Beth sighed impatiently. "You're not making sense, Jesse. I'm a married woman. We were never more than friends. But if you don't let me go you will destroy even that."

Jesse threw back his head and laughed. It was like the sound of a wounded animal sending chills down Beth's spine and bringing about her first real touch of fear. When he faced her once again across the short space separating them, his eyes were clouded with memories. He seemed to be looking inward and she suspected then that he was not entirely sane.

"Foolish little angel. You still don't understand, do you?"

Beth shook her head mutely, no longer sure she wanted to hear his explanation.

His eyes cleared suddenly and he searched her face for the truth as he asked, "If it wasn't for my father, would you have accepted my invitation to come to the ranch and share a picnic with me beside the stream?"

The question seemed so irrelevant, Beth was taken by surprise. After a moment's hesitation, she answered honestly, "I don't know. It's hard to picture you out from under your father's shadow."

Beth guessed right away she had said the wrong thing for Jesse jumped to his feet and began stomping the ground as if he were grinding something obscene beneath his boots. "Damn him to Hell! I'm not under his shadow now!" he cried, and even in the fading light she could see the glimmer of tears making runnels down his boyish cheeks. Then he turned, wiping the moisture away with his sleeve. As he did so, his face hardened into an expression of malevolence that made Beth flinch.

"All my life he told me I was weak, that he was ashamed to call me his son. He tried to beat strength into me. When I cowered and begged him to stop he became even more enraged. After my mother died, there was no one to shield me from his cruelty and I was so afraid. I would do anything he asked. *Anything* to forestall the pain of that terrible strap."

Beth listened in horror as Jesse told of the abuse he had suffered, abuse which apparently had not ended until his father drew his last breath. "I'm sorry, Jesse," she said sincerely for she could think of nothing else to say. Her heart cried out for the boy who had never known a father's love. "But what has all of this to do with me?"

"I liked you. My father knew. He could tell by

the way I watched you whenever you came to the fort. He laughed. "Said it took a man to bed a woman like you." His mouth quirked. "Do you want to know something funny, Beth? I never thought about bedding you. All I wanted was to take you on a picnic."

Beth had never felt such pity for another human being. Her own eyes misted in sympathy. "I still don't understand why you won't let me go."

Jesse avoided answering her directly. Instead he kicked at a clump of grass with the toe of his boot and replied wistfully, "I was waiting for you in the barn that morning when you were about to leave Fort King. I was going to ask you again to come to the ranch. Arrange it when my father would be away. I watched you talking to your horse. You were so gentle, so beautiful. You reminded me of my ma. Then my father came." His tone turned vicious. "I hated what he did to you but I wasn't strong enough to stop him. When your uncle arrived I left before you saw me. I didn't want you to think I was a coward."

"I did see you, but I never thought you were a coward," Beth lied, taking him aback.

Jesse stared at her disbelievingly, then his slender chest swelled with pride. Before she could bat an eye, he went down on one knee much like a smitten suitor eager to propose. "You're right, Beth. I'm not a coward. I finally found the courage to do what had to be done."

Beth waited, never guessing what would come next.

"He was evil, Beth. That's why I killed him."

She felt the blood drain from her head, leaving her face chalk-white. Shock rendered her speechless, numbing her brain while her vision blurred making it impossible to focus clearly on the man who had just confessed to shooting his father. The roar of the ocean sounded in her ears like foam-topped breakers rolling onshore at the height of a storm. Surely this couldn't be happening. She must still be caught in the throes of the nightmare that began in the dark underground passageway. Given time the bad dream would run its course and she would awaken with Robin by her side. He would comfort her and the world would right itself once more.

Beth shut her eyes tightly, willing the image of Jesse Tillman kneeling before her to vanish, but when she opened them once more his likeness remained fixed. What started as a weak churning in the pit of her stomach quickly turned into such violent shaking her teeth chattered uncontrollably.

Jesse Tillman's expression changed again. He no longer resembled the poignant youth who had cried out for understanding just a short while ago. His countenance took on an expression of belligerence that dared anyone to condemn what he had done. But it was the look in his eyes as he slowly stood to full height hovering over her like a demon spirit that filled Beth with trepidation and made her realize at last that this was not a dream. For even in her worst nightmare she could not have envisioned the feral glow radiating from his glazed pupils giving off an unholy light. Beth knew she was looking into the eyes of madness.

Swallowing down the bile that threatened to choke her, she whispered incredulously, "You shot your father in the back?"

Her head snapped to the side as he backhanded her across the cheek. She was too shocked by all that had happened in the past few hours to feel much pain, but she tasted the blood from her split lip as it trickled down her chin staining her shirt with drops of crimson.

Jesse looked at her, rage suffusing his face. "Of course I did! I saved your uncle's life! Don't you understand that my father was determined to kill him! You have no right to act as if I am something beneath your contempt!"

Despite her fear, Beth could not suppress her own anger toward the young man she had thought to befriend, the one who had caused her family so much misery. Forgetting the cords that bound her hands and feet leaving her at Jesse Tillman's mercy, she flared back, "You are beneath contempt! Only a coward shoots a man in the back, and if you think my uncle needed your help, you're a fool as well as a coward!"

Her heated words earned her another brutal slap that set the bells ringing in her head. Then her chin was clasped in his cruel grip as he leaned forward, forcing her to look up into his unnerving visage. To her astonishment, he smiled, though it was little more than a baring of teeth. "You're right, Beth," he agreed, increasing the painful pressure on her

267

jaw. "I didn't do it for your uncle. I did it for myself! I never wanted to leave our home in Georgia to go to Texas and I sure didn't want to spend the rest of my life in this tropical hellhole. But pa wouldn't listen. I begged him to let me go but he only laughed and swore he'd keep me here until he made a man of me or died trying." Jesse laughed inanely. "Ironic, isn't it? He did die trying!"

Gathering her wits as best she could under the circumstances, Beth sought to reason with his unbalanced mind. "What's done is done, Jesse. I'm sure Major Caldwell will understand if you tell him how your father treated you. I'll go back with you, testify in your behalf. Together we can get this whole thing straightened out. Then you'll be free to go home."

Jesse raised his arm as if to strike her again but held back. "You stupid, patronizing little bitch!" he sneered. "I'm free now and I intend to stay that way. Oh, I'll get to Georgia all right because I've got you to guarantee me safe passage!"

Beth grimaced. She was to be his hostage until he was out of the Territory. He had it all figured out. With her along, the soldiers would not dare challenge him. She wondered about the timing of his escape. It seemed odd that he would feel such urgency to leave just when the panel of judges clearly had admitted to having no idea who the murderer might be.

As if in answer to her unspoken question, Jesse muttered under his breath, "Too bad the soldier who saw me return to the fort that night wasn't killed chasing those bastard redskins."

It was simple for Beth to put two and two together and come up with the answer to her question, but it was far from comforting.

"It's time to go, Beth. We're heading north." Jesse reached toward her then stopped abruptly, straightening, his body sensing the danger close at hand.

The forest was too quiet. Missing were the usual nocturnal sounds of night animals foraging in the underbrush and owls hooting overhead. Around them there was nothing but silence and the eerie watchfulness of eyes that could be felt but not seen. Hope flared in Beth. Surely by some miracle Robin had discovered her missing and had managed to pick up their trail. Soon she would be free of the lunatic who held her. There was nothing to do now but wait for Robin to show himself.

Drawing his gun from the holster riding low on his hips, Jesse turned in a slow circle straining to penetrate the ever encroaching darkness. Nothing moved yet the air was pregnant with danger. Long minutes passed while Beth tried to become one with the tree at her back. Why was Robin taking so long to make his presence known? Just as she began to think they might both be mistaken and that the uncanny silence was the result of some mysterious quirk of nature, Beth heard something whiz past her ear, followed immediately by an agonized scream that brought her attention back to the man who held her.

Then the seemingly impenetrable tangle of brush

encircling the small clearing was crushed beneath the feet of more than a dozen Seminole warriors armed with rifles; each face painted half red, half white, every eye projected on the one who had unerringly thrown the knife. Beth's blood ran cold as she gaped up at the man who, though not a chief, held firm control over what remained of the Seminole Nation. His dark eyes raked over her briefly, but Osceola gave no command to free her.

She was relieved when he turned once again toward Jesse who was trembling so hard she imagined she could hear his legs knocking together at the kneecaps. Though Jesse and the Indian leader were about equal in height, there emanated from Osceola an aura of power that had little to do with stature and which dwarfed the shaking man standing before him.

"You, white man, have committed a crime that must not be allowed to go unpunished." The authoritative tone of Osceola's voice sent Jesse to his knees.

In a strangled voice he pleaded, "Wait! Hear me out! It's true I killed my father, but he deserved to die! You and your people should thank me for what I did. Don't you understand? He was bent on wiping out every Indian in the Territory."

Osceola looked down his nose at the quivering wretch groveling at his feet. "Your bigoted sire was destined to meet a violent end with or without your help. His death means nothing to me or my people."

Bewildered Jesse Tillman stammered, "B . . . but

if it doesn't matter to you that I killed him, then why do you s . . . say I must be p . . . punished?"

"The crime that will cost you your life has nothing to do with ridding the Territory of scum like your father." The death sentence struck terror in the young man's heart as he swiveled his head left then right, frantically searching for a means of escape.

Tearfully Jesse cried out, "For God's sake! I've done nothing else. Please! You've got to let me go!"

His plea fell on deaf ears. Blood now soaked his sleeve below where the handle of the knife still protruded from his upper arm. Taking a step forward Osceola reached down and yanked the weapon free, paying no need to the earsplitting shriek that rent the air as blade scraped against bone. Jesse grasped his arm in a vain attempt to stem the bleeding as he fell on his side, drawing his legs up in a protective fetal position. "Before you kill me," he whined pitifully, "at least tell me why."

Indignation punctuated each word as Osceola answered, "You have taken that which belongs to my brother." Without further explanation he lifted his gaze to the warriors awaiting his command and said, "Hang him!"

"No!" Beth cried out, tugging against the bindings that refused to give. She reacted without conscious thought, but she might as well have been yelling at a stone statue for all the attention Osceola paid her.

Jesse's horse was brought forward as several of the braves jerked their flailing, kicking prisoner to his feet tying his hands behind him. Beth fought

271

down the panic rising within her as she added her pleas to his terrified bellowing.

"You can't do this! It's against the law! The soldiers will hunt you down if you take this man's life!"

The Indian leader looked scornfully in her direction; his cold, calculating eyes daring her to say more. "Hush, woman!" he ordered impatiently. "You seem to have forgotten that I am already a fugitive whom the soldiers have been ordered to shoot on sight. This man has taken what belongs to my brother and for that he will die. It is the law of my people!"

In spite of the warning, Beth could not sit by and let this unspeakable injustice take place. What could Jesse possibly have stolen that would require his life as retribution? "You have to listen to me!" Wide pleading eyes beseeched Osceola to reconsider. "Whatever Jesse has taken, I'm sure he will gladly return if you'll just let him go. Turn him over to Major Caldwell to be tried for his father's murder, but please, don't take the law into your own hands!"

By this time Jesse had been lifted onto the back of his mount. A heavy rope dangled from the sturdy branch of an oak tree, one end secured to its trunk, the other coiled in a noose around his neck. He was trembling so hard Beth feared he would spook the horse.

"Tell them, Jesse! Tell them you'll give back whatever it is they are after!" Beth knew the Indians meant business. If Jesse didn't speak up now there was nothing more she could do to save his life.

But Jesse remained silent, and the deep timbre of Osceola's voice answered instead. "What has been taken will be returned to its rightful owner," he assured confidently.

Hatred toward the redman who presumed to stand in judgment over him momentarily nullified Jesse's fear. Glaring at Osceola he snarled viciously, "I would not dirty my hands by touching something belonging to a filthy savage!"

Osceola's expression never changed as he lifted his gaze to stare at the defiant young man. Slowly and very deliberately he drew back his arm then brought it forward whacking the horse firmly on its rump. Only in those final seconds, did Jesse Tillman truly believe he would die. His scream of outrage was cut off as the rope tightened then snapped his neck with a resounding crunch.

Beth longed to turn away, but she couldn't. She watched as his lifeless body twitched then spun slowly around suspended from the heavy rope, his chin resting against his chest at an odd angle. Mesmerized by the swaying figure, she wondered what the Indians considered of greater value than a man's life, but it didn't really matter now. It was too late for Jesse. Much too late.

As Robin drew within sight of the McAfee homestead, his worried frown deepened. By now he should have met Beth returning to the fort for she'd had ample time to deliver her news and the sun was already low on the western horizon. Spotting a full-skirted figure beneath the willow tree beside the stream, Robin breathed a sigh of relief before it dawned on him that Beth would not have made the five mile journey on horseback wearing a dress. He could read a disappointment in Maggie McAfee's face that matched his own.

"Hello, Mr. Hawkins. From a distance I mistook you for Eddie." Her love for Beth's twin brother ran deep. Robin could understand how she felt when he had appeared instead of the man she obviously was expecting.

"Evening, Maggie, and please call me Robin. After all it looks like we'll be part of the same family before long."

Maggie blushed, her cheeks dimpling prettily. "Oh, I do hope so . . . Robin. But I wonder if Eddie isn't taking an inordinate amount of time to invite me into the fold?"

Robin grinned. "Patience, Maggie. He'll come around. I just rode out to accompany Beth back to the fort," he explained as he glanced across the yard toward the house hoping to catch a glimpse of his wife.

Maggie's smile disappeared, replaced by a look of bewilderment. "I don't understand. Beth isn't here. In fact, I haven't seen her since the last time she visited Fort King several months ago before you were married. I was hoping she would stop by—"

Robin didn't let her finish. A chill of apprehension shook him to the core. Reaching out, he grasped the startled young woman by the shoulders.

"What do you mean she isn't here?"

Cornflower blue eyes looked up at him mirroring his concern. "Robin, I tell you Beth hasn't been here. What could have happened to her? Where could she be?"

Anguished gray-green eyes framed by thick, dark lashes looked back at her. "I don't know, Maggie, but I intend to find out."

Maggie didn't doubt it for a moment. There was a look of grim determination about the man that eased her mind. She felt sure he would find Beth and take care of whatever trouble her friend had gotten into this time.

Wheeling the stallion around and kneeing him into motion, Robin called over his shoulder, "Tell Eddie that Beth never arrived. I'm going back to pick up her trail."

"Do you want him to follow?" she yelled at his retreating back, but already he was too far away to hear.

Maggie stood wringing her hands praying that Edward would get there soon as horse and rider grew smaller then disappeared completely.

Chapter Seventeen

A campfire burned brightly illuminating the clearing and the grotesque figure hanging limply from the tall oak. Beth fought to conquer the nausea brought on by the smell of roasting meat. But when a young buck approached to offer her the crusty-skinned leg of a rabbit, she motioned him away as she turned her head and gagged. Her hands and feet were no longer bound yet she knew better than to move away from the base of the tree.

Feeling ill and frightened, she wondered dazedly what Osceola and his band of warriors planned to do with her. Would she live to bring her unborn child into the world? Robin was probably worried sick by now and she knew there was little hope that he would be able to pick up her trail. She was glad she hadn't told him about the baby for it would only add to his grief if the Indians decided to kill her.

Unable to hold back her tears, Beth recounted the brief weeks of happiness they'd shared together as man and wife. It wasn't fair that they should now be wrenched apart through death or something worse. She had heard horror stories about what the savages did to their white captives, especially women. Robin had been so kind and comforting when she confessed to being raped by the masked Indian called Hawk. But were she to be ravaged by these painted heathens who had mercilessly killed Jesse . . . she doubted even a man as forgiving as Robin would want her back.

For herself death would be preferable to living as a slave among the bestial redskins. Only the knowledge that her child's life would also be forfeited gave her the courage to go on. Somehow she had to escape and find her way back to Robin. She could not allow it to end like this. Her only chance was to wait until her captors were asleep and hope they would not feel it necessary to post a guard. Then she would crawl deep into the tangled vegetation and hide until it was safe to make her way back to the fort. Tomorrow she would decide which direction to take. For tonight it was enough just to put distance between herself and the heartless devils who seemed bent on destroying her dreams.

Beth allowed her lids to droop hoping the Indians would think she was sleeping. The camp grew quiet. Nothing disturbed the silence except the occasional rustling of a night creature in the bushes and the steady plodding steps of a horse's hoofs moving softly through the woods. Beth's eyes flew open as she listened. She hadn't imagined it. There could be no mistaking the rhythmic beat of the animal's unhurried footfalls. The braves heard it, too. As one they stood up, rifles in hand, facing the direction from which the muffled sound grew ever louder.

When Robin emerged from the forest sitting tall in the saddle, Beth's shock was such that she could not even shout a warning. Before she could recover enough to speak, his hazel eyes locked with hers from across the low-burning campfire.

"At last, the hawk has come for his dove."

Osceola's words failed to penetrate Beth's paralyzed brain. Her heart ceased to beat as she waited, expecting at any second to hear the roar of the rifles that would make her a widow. But the sound of death never came. Looking around the circle of warriors, she finally noticed that the weapons they carried rested loosely across their arms, none pointed at the man she loved and feared for. Robin remained mounted atop Satan seemingly unaware of the danger he faced.

Glancing toward the tree where Jesse Tillman's lifeless body cast a shadow in the firelight, Robin commented dryly, "You've saved the army a lot of trouble. I hope Caldwell remembers to thank you."

It was the first time Beth had heard the fierce Indian leader laugh. The sound was deep and rich filled with genuine humor. "Don't count on it, brother."

Beth gasped as her eyes darted to Robin's unsmiling face but he refused to meet her searching gaze. Osceola had called her husband, "brother." But how could that be? As from a distance the words that had made no sense before resounded in her head with all the impact of sudden enlightenment. *At last the hawk has come for his dove!* No, it wasn't possible. Her heart refused to accept what her mind cried out! Another memory turned her body into a jumbled chaos of emotions. *You have taken that which belongs to my brother. You must die . . . die . . . die!*

The words pounded hollowly in her brain like the words spoken from behind the mask of the man who had raped her. Slowly Beth stood up bracing herself against the tree at her back as the world tilted around her. The half-naked men swayed from side to side in some macabre dance only they could understand. What a fool she had been! How Robin must have laughed at her gullibility. The fire sparked then went out at the same time she felt something within her die. Now there was no light at all on which to focus. As the ground rose up to meet her, she was unaware of the rough bark scraping against her tender skin. Sinking back into the dark oblivion she had tried so hard to escape, she knew she could no longer deny the truth. Robin Hawkins, her husband, her lover, her friend, was also the masked Indian known as the Hawk!

Beth blinked then opened her eyes wide as a cool drop of water rolled down her cheek. Instantly recalling the events that had brought on her faint, she glared up at the man she had loved more than life itself, the man who had violated her, lied to her, betrayed her trust.

"You bastard!" she spat. Her face contorted with

279

fury and disillusionment as she reached out and struck away the damp cloth Robin had used to bathe her forehead. "Get your filthy hands off me! Don't you ever, *ever,* touch me again!"

Beth literally shook with rage wishing she had her gun so that she could shoot the slimy snake who had deceived and made a fool of her since the first moment it had been her misfortune to ride into his trap. She would aim low, *real low,* she thought furiously, as she watched him lean back on his haunches. What pleasure she would derive in blasting his manhood all to Hell! Then he could never again use a woman in the despicable way he had used her! Killing was too good for him! He should be made to suffer the way she had suffered after his brutal attack. The way she was suffering now!

Unbidden tears misted her eyes, but she willed them not to fall. To cry would be admitting Robin still had the power to affect her emotions and such an admission would only add to her humiliation.

Robin groaned inwardly as he saw hatred flame to life, blue eyes darken to the color of turbulent, storm-tossed seas. He had hoped her love for him would be strong enough to forgive past sins, but clearly such was not the case. He sought words that would bridge the wide chasm of misunderstanding that was forcing them apart. Common sense told him that anything he said right now would only make matters worse, but the aching need inside him refused to listen. Bending forward he brushed a loose tendril of hair from her flushed cheek with a feathery stroke of his fingers. Beth slapped his hand away. She jerked her head to the side as she surveyed the small clearing where her world had shattered like a pane of glass, leaving her no protection against the harsh realities of life.

Osceola and his warriors had vanished apparently taking Jesse Tillman's body with them. It was still pitch-black overhead but the fire had been rekindled, illuminating the glade with flickering light. Tongues of blue-gold flames licked upward from the dried wood releasing tiny sparks into the darkness. Like a grim reminder of what might have been, the sparks drifted on the air then disappeared into nothingness. Despite her resolve, a single tear escaped to ribbon a path down her cheek.

Hesitantly, making no move to touch the wife he adored beyond reason, Robin drew her wandering attention back. "Beth, please . . . we have to talk." Gray-green eyes pleaded for a chance to explain, but Beth was in no mood to hear more lies.

Her laughter held a hint of hysteria as it pierced the silent night. "A hawk does not *talk* to a dove. He ruthlessly tears it apart piece by piece until there is nothing left but a few feathers floating in the air. You've played the predator well, Robin. Now get the hell out of here and leave me alone! I want nothing more to do with you!"

Fear of losing her made Robin forget that gentle persuasion worked better on Beth than pure male dominance. "Neither of us are leaving here until I say what has to be said!"

As he grasped her roughly by the shoulders her head thunked hard against the trunk of the tree.

The sound brought Robin up short. "Oh, bloody Hell!" he muttered letting her go abruptly as he sprang to his feet unfolding his long, lean body with the grace of a jungle cat. The last thing he had intended was to hurt her further, but somehow when he was around this titian-haired vixen the discipline instilled in him by both the Indians and the whites vanished.

Beth struggled to rise, not wanting his shadow hovering over her, but the hours she had lain against the base of the towering pine had taken their toll and her legs refused to obey her commands. As she swayed, Robin reached out to steady her then thought better of it when she snarled a warning, clinging to the abrasive bark instead.

"You can force me to stay here and listen," she hissed, her voice filled with bitter contempt, "but never again will I believe your lies! You're nothing but an unprincipled savage, a depraved animal who lives by his baser instincts."

Each breath was labored. Her breasts strained against the thin material of her blouse, as she fought to control her outrage. Remembering how she had freely given herself to the unscrupulous blackguard, she shuddered with revulsion. "It's not just what you did to me though God knows that was bad enough. But I can never forget your face when you rode in here. You actually condoned what Osceola and his heathen followers did to Jesse Tillman; condoned the manner in which they murdered him in cold blood!"

Robin knew she had every right to vent her spleen

and he was prepared to hear her out. Her heated words cut him to the quick but were no less than he deserved. Yet when she began her condemnation of his Indian brethren, Robin's own temper flared. He understood, as she could not, the restraint the warriors had used in carrying out justice by the white man's code of honor.

"Enough!" His harsh command took Beth by surprise. "You have said you would listen to me but so far it is you who have done all the talking. You have said my actions are unforgivable. That is for you to judge even though you have not been apprised of all the facts. But I will not allow you to speak against my people!"

Beth felt her stomach lurch as she thought about the baby growing in her womb, a child conceived in love from a seed planted deep within her by the man who had just called the merciless savages his people. What could he possibly mean?

Robin stared down at her, watching her fingernails dig into the rough bark of the tree. "Just what do you think the soldiers would have done to Tillman if they had caught him here tonight?" he asked, his tone unyielding.

Beth cringed beneath his ferocious scowl but refused to give ground. "They would have returned him to the fort where he would have been given a fair trial," she declared emphatically.

"And then what?" he prodded, his frown deepening.

Backed into a corner, Beth shouted, "All right! They would have hung him!" Her chin jutted out belligerently. "But it would have been for his father's murder, not because of me! Jesse was confused. I was his ticket out of here," she said, repeating the words that had struck terror into her heart. "He would never have hurt me!"

Beth knew what she said was a lie, but her hurt went too deep to allow him to gain the advantage.

Robin's eyes hardened. "I suppose those bruises on your cheeks are a sample of his chivalry."

Beth refused to meet his gaze knowing his point was well taken. Before she could step away, Robin reached out and clasped her chin forcing her to look at him. "Justice was done, Beth, whether you are willing to admit it or not. Regardless of who placed the rope around his neck, Jesse Tillman deserved to die. What you don't seem to understand is that hanging a man for his crime is not the Indian way. Asi-yahola risked losing face among the People by ordering the quick and easy death the whites call punishment."

Robin pronounced the name of the Indian leader as he had long ago when he had come to her in the guise of Hawk. He had warned her then what might happen if she ever found herself alone with the notorious warrior and his braves. Beth knew now the only reason she had been spared ravagement by the hot-blooded young bucks was because they thought of her as Hawk's woman. He had saved her life again, but for what?

Her mind in a tumult of confusion Beth retorted, "Too bad you weren't here in time for the hanging so Jesse could thank you for his 'quick and easy death'!"

Robin retorted impatiently, "My being here would not have made a damn bit of difference. If the braves had chosen to torture Tillman before they put him to death they would have done so regardless of how I felt about it. The reason they followed the white man's rules is because they don't want to antagonize the soldiers anymore than they have already. Believe me, Beth, Asi-yahola is sick to death of this war and the senseless bloodshed it has wrought. All he wants is to be left in peace."

He sounded sincere yet Beth was understandably suspicious of anything Robin had to say. "Then I assume you had nothing to do with the Indians leaving me untouched?"

"You assume wrong!" That anyone else might lay a hand on his wife was unthinkable and Robin's voice reflected his indignation. "My brothers knew it mattered not to me how Jesse Tillman paid for his crimes just as they knew that to touch one hair on your head would seal their own fate!"

Regardless of the unresolved problems between them, Beth felt an undeniable feeling of relief ripple through her as she remembered a time when she had harbored romantic notions of a guardian angel hidden behind a crudely carved cypress mask. More puzzled now than angry, she asked the question that could no longer be avoided.

"That night in the cave . . . why did you do it?"

Despairing blue eyes clouded with painful memories begged him to explain in such a way that she

285

would be able to forgive him for what he had done. Robin knew in his heart there was no excuse for the brutal way he had taken her, an inexperienced virgin who was merely trying to salvage her pride so that she would not appear weak. How could he expect her to understand much less forgive?

Turning toward the brightly burning fire, Robin expelled a deep breath before he answered. "I did you a grievous wrong for which there is no excuse. I allowed my anger to control my actions and in so doing I hurt you cruelly and needlessly."

He spoke in a barely audible monotone but Beth knew him well enough to recognize his anguish. Whatever his feelings they ran deep and troubled him much more than he was willing to acknowledge.

"I trusted you. You made me feel safe and protected even when I could not see your face." Beth's words caught on a ragged sob. "What did I do to make you so angry?"

Childlike in her innocence, she awaited his reply; her gaze resting with longing on his broad shoulders and rigid back, wanting nothing more than to throw her arms around his waist and hug him to her breasts. But there were still too many unanswered questions. Her plaintive cry tore at Robin's heart. Pretending to be Edwina had seemed to him a heartless deception at the time, a ruse for which she deserved to be punished. In retrospect it rated as no more than a harmless prank, but the punishment he had invoked on her could not be undone.

Feeling her eyes boring into his back, Robin knew

286

Beth was waiting for his reply just as he knew she had a right to certain answers. "The morning after you ran away, I met your brother, Edward, and I realized how you had played me for a fool. You seemed such a practiced little flirt disguised as Edwina in your low-cut gown and your sweet-smelling perfume. I assumed you had taken on half the fort."

Beth stood staring at his back in stunned silence. That he could have imagined her distributing her favors freely among the soldiers at Fort Brooke would have been laughable had the consequences not been so devastating.

"You assumed wrong!" She repeated the words he had said to her a short time ago, her tone as frigid as snow on a mountaintop.

"I found that out the hard way," he admitted ruefully turning back toward her, his face ashen as he recalled her excruciating scream of pain when he ruthlessly split her maidenhead asunder.

"But it was too late, wasn't it?" Her voice sounded brittle and detached. Stepping forward she tapped him on the chest with her forefinger. "At least I've given you a chance to explain. You didn't even have the courtesy to tell me what I was *supposed* to have done wrong! And as for deceptions, even now I don't know who you really are: Robin Hawkins, the statesman, the *gentleman,* or Hawk, the Indian who calls Osceola his brother!"

Robin started to speak but Beth stopped him by shoving hard against his muscular frame with both hands. Taken off guard he stumbled backward and had to struggle to right himself before he fell into the fire. By the time he had regained his balance she stood glaring at him with doubled fists digging into her narrow hips.

"It doesn't matter anymore," she declared forcefully. "I don't care who you are! I just want to go home!"

Feeling he had been granted a temporary reprieve, Robin sighed with relief. "We'll leave as soon as the sun is up. I know you've been through Hell today and you're exhausted. Once we get back to Fort Brooke we can talk this whole thing out."

"No!" she shrieked, her composure cracking when she most wanted to remain in control. "I must have time to think . . . about us," she added mournfully. "You will only muddle my thoughts with smooth-tongued words I can no longer trust. I don't want you to come with me."

Robin battled the army of emotions coursing through him as he heard Beth speak the words he dreaded most. He wanted to rail at her, to remind her she had no right to bar him from his own house. She need not know that once a brave married a squaw, the house belonged to the woman. He wanted to beg her forgiveness, to assure her he would spend the rest of his life making up for the wrong he had done. But to do so would make him less than a man. Most of all he wanted to take her in his arms and kiss her petal-soft lips until she yielded to that inexplicable force that had melded their two lives into one, making neither whole without the other.

Robin did none of these things. There was much they still had to learn about one another. It broke his heart to know that she had lost faith in him when even as the unknown masked Indian he had been able to win her trust. He would do so again, but it would take time to heal the wounds he had inflicted. Though it was the hardest thing he had ever done, he would give her that time.

Reluctantly he conceded, "It will be as you wish. Tomorrow I will return you to your uncle at Fort King."

Was there a flicker of disappointment in her eyes at his acquiescence? Robin could only hope that Beth would soon come to realize that their destinies were entwined. If she did not, he had only himself to blame.

Though tired beyond measure, Beth found sleep elusive as she peered over the edge of the blanket to where Robin sat on the other side of the fire. "Tell me one thing," she whispered, trying to see his face in the shadowed light. "Was it guilt over what you had done that made you marry me?"

Robin longed to cross the short distance separating them and take her in his arms while he kissed her doubts away. But he had promised himself to give her time. He must not allow his need for her to influence a decision that must be hers alone.

"Not even guilt could make me marry someone I didn't love. Now go to sleep!"

Satisfied at least on that one point, Beth closed her eyes. She still wasn't sure just who this man was that she had wed. There was much to consider and there were many things to be thrashed out between them, but for now she again felt safe and protected knowing he was near. Her guardian angel was back. Perhaps she would reconsider her plan to return to Fort Brooke alone, she thought, stifling a wide yawn. Tomorrow would be soon enough to decide. Shutting out the problems yet to be resolved, she wrapped her arms around her stomach bidding a silent "good night" to the child resting peacefully within.

Robin remained awake, admiring the sleeping beauty that was his lovely, young wife. Many things he had lived to regret but their marriage was not one of them. Somehow, he would regain her trust and her love. He had lied about taking her back to Fort King. One more transgression to add to the growing list. But he had done so for her own good. Having left a trail plainly marked, he anticipated Lance Logan's arrival on the scene within the next few hours. Had she known, Beth would not be asleep at this moment, and right now she needed rest in order to face the arduous journey back to civilization. It was Robin's intention to wait until he heard Logan's approach, then disappear into the dense, trackless forest, out of Beth's life until she could come to terms with her doubts and decide whether or not he had a place in her future.

Chapter Eighteen

A gentle touch on her shoulder woke Beth with a start just as the first gray light of dawn sifted through the thick tree branches which canopied the clearing. Lance Logan crouched beside her, a worried frown furrowing his wide brow. A horse snorted close by and Beth raised her sleep-glazed eyes to where Davey and Edward stood, awkwardly holding the reins of their mounts.

"Are you all right, honey?" Lance asked, his deep voice filled with concern.

Beth pushed herself up on her elbows and looked around. "Where's Robin?"

Relieved that she seemed alert and unharmed, Lance stood up then stretched out his hand to help her rise. "He's not here and I'd sure as Hell like to know why," her uncle lashed out at no one in particular. "He left us a trail a blind man could follow leading straight to this spot. Now he's disappeared without a trace!"

He put his arm around Beth's waist and gave her a tight squeeze. "When you feel up to it, sweet-

heart, there's a powerful number of questions tha
need answers."

A feeling of desolation threatened to engulf her
as Beth realized Robin had lied again. He'd known
her uncle would follow, made certain he had no dif
ficulty in doing so. He never intended to return
with her to the fort. From the beginning their rela
tionship had been built on a foundation of deceit
With each lie, the foundation crumbled a little
more. Soon there would be nothing left but a pile
of rubble. But even as she mentally tallied Robin's
transgressions, Beth's heart cried out to give him
one more chance.

As she sat beside the campfire sipping a cup of
scalding black coffee, she searched the faces of her
rescuers wondering how much of her story she dare
tell. Each of these men loved her in his own special
way. All had ridden throughout the night to find
her and all looked the worse for wear. She knew her
kin too well to think they might ignore what Robin
had done to her. No, more likely they would hunt
him down and make him pay with his life.

Slowly, measuring every word, she began recount
ing the details of her misadventure. She told them
how Jesse Tillman had lured her into the woods
then rendered her unconscious before bringing her
here on the first leg of his journey north. Davey
and Edward cursed Jesse's villainous assault show
ing surprise, but no sympathy, for the young man
as Beth went on to describe the appearance of Os
ceola and his warriors and the hanging that fol
lowed.

Lance listened without interrupting until she reached the part of her tale recounting how the Indians had fled when Robin appeared. "You did say there were a dozen or more braves in Osceola's band," he reminded skeptically.

It didn't take much to guess what he was thinking. "Y . . . yes," Beth stammered self-consciously. She was not used to sidestepping the truth and knew her uncle was too astute not to detect the flaws in her story. Unable to meet his granite-gray eyes, she suggested uncertainly, "Perhaps the Indians thought there were more soldiers hidden in the bushes. I don't know because about that time I fainted and when I came to there was no one here but Robin. After that I fell asleep and the next thing I remember was you waking me up." Beth prayed for the questioning to end. She knew the man who had been a second father to her was not satisfied with her answers but she hoped to postpone further interrogation until she'd had time to gather her thoughts.

"Sounds to me like you missed a lot of the action," Edward chuckled teasingly. "First you get hit over the head, then you faint, and finally you fall asleep."

"I still can't understand why Robin left you here alone." Davey made no attempt to disguise his censure. His somber expression, so like his father's, made it clear he had not believed her story.

Wanting only to leave the shadowy glen and put the horrors of what had occurred here behind her, Beth searched her mind for a satisfactory explanation. "You've said yourself, Robin left a clear trail to follow. Knowing that you would find me, I imagine he decided to track the renegades and pinpoint their hideout. After all, they are wanted by the United States Army."

Davey grunted. "For a stranger to these parts, Hawkins seems on mighty friendly terms with the Seminole. I wonder if he could bring himself to turn them in even if he locates their stronghold?"

"I'm sure he will explain himself all in good time." Lance Logan's grim expression promised he would make certain Robin Hawkins did just that, and the firm set of his jaw warned that the explanation had better be to his liking!

Dark hooded eyes watched the warrior, Hawk, as he stared broodingly into the blue-gold flames, his thoughts obviously far away. "You are thinking about the woman with hair the color of fire."

It was a statement, not a question. Robin lifted his gaze to focus on the face of his friend, Asiyahola. He saw concern and understanding written in each line and wondered how anyone could call this caring man a savage.

"Hair the color of fire and a temper equally combustible," Robin laughed mirthlessly. "It amazes me how you manage to cope with two wives when just one may prove to be the death of me."

The older Indian chuckled. "My wives are docile. They were taught at an early age to believe a man is a godlike figure to be respected and obeyed in all things."

Robin quirked a brow, for he knew both women and neither struck him as being particularly tractable.

"Besides," his friend added good-spiritedly, "I'm not home much."

"Judging by the number of children I've seen running about your chickee I'd say you are home enough," Robin countered.

Both men laughed enjoying the easy camaraderie they had shared together since they were children. Then Asi-yahola sobered. There were hard words that had to be said, words that could be put off no longer.

"You are right about one thing, brother. Your woman may very well be the death of you." He waited calmly for the other's reaction which was quick in coming.

Robin's body grew rigid, his eyes cold and hard as he challenged his boyhood companion to explain his meaning.

Speaking with wisdom beyond his years, the Indian leader said, "The time has come for you to choose the direction you will follow." Anticipating Robin's reply he held up his hand. "I am not asking you to choose sides for I understand the loyalty you feel toward our people. Your goal is to help us win our freedom, but now you must decide the best road to take in order to attain that objective."

Passionately Robin replied, "I came back to the Territory hoping to convince white men and Indians alike that they could live together in peace. But there are too many like Ralph Tillman; men filled with prejudice and hate who refuse to listen to reason. I see now that the only way we can hold on to our land is to fight, and if I die in the process it will be for a noble cause!"

With an expression of disgust Asi-yahola refuted his words. "If you die it will be because your mind is on that fiery-haired woman instead of the danger we face hiding out here in the woods. You've been riding with us for three days and it's a wonder we haven't all been killed because of your carelessness. Have you forgotten how to move as silently as the panther, how to cover your tracks like the wind, how to sense what you cannot see? I think not! Though you were still a boy when you left us to go live with your uncle, your skills as a warrior were already honed to razor-sharpness. It is not something easily forgotten. Yet you sit your horse like a man in a drunken stupor. You gaze into the fire and dream the dreams of the old, unaware of what is taking place around you."

Robin knew his friend spoke the truth though he was loathe to admit he had allowed his personal problems to endanger the lives of those he had sworn to protect. "What you say is true, my brother. I have acted in a manner unbefitting a warrior, but no more!" he declared vehemently. "I have forgotten none of the skills taught me as a youth and tomorrow I will prove I am worthy to ride beside you."

Shaking his head, Asi-yahola replied sagely, "You cannot will it to be so, Hawk. Until you settle this matter with your woman, you are useless to us. You must return to the one who holds your heart captive. You must seek the trail the gods of the earth and the sun have marked for you." Switching abruptly from the guttural tongue of the tribe to the softer flowing words of the white man, he added, "While you search, think on this. As a warrior you are just one more whose life could be snuffed out when next we meet the enemy. In the white man's world you have an opportunity to influence the outcome of this senseless war. Perhaps it was fate that took you from us, but then again, it could have been the will of a more powerful deity whose purpose was to use you as a means to an end."

"You think I am not worthy to be called a warrior?" Robin cried out angrily, his face ravaged with shame and frustration. He was a white man and an Indian; yet in this moment he felt shunned by both.

Patiently Asi-yahola admonished him as a father would a son though their years were not far apart. "You listen with your heart instead of your soul. I only suggest that there are many ways to fight a cause."

Robin doubted his friend's logic yet he knew until he and Beth came to some understanding, staying here would do his brothers more harm than good. Asi-yahola was wrong about one thing though. His thoughts had not all been self-centered. He remembered what Logan had once said accusing the government of being more concerned about money than human lives. Since nothing else seemed to have gotten the attention of the citizenry, perhaps he should focus on what every man held dear . . . his pocketbook! In his mind he had already formulated a missive pointing out the waste in tax dollars being spent to wage war against a handful of Indians who asked only for a small share of what was rightfully theirs.

"I'll leave at first light," Robin announced, evoking a nod of approval from the dark-eyed man seated across the campfire.

Unable to sleep for thinking of the coming confrontation with Beth, Robin stole quietly out of camp an hour before dawn as the waning moon changed from pale buttermilk yellow to white. The big ebony stallion needed little guidance as he picked his way between the thick forest of trees blending into the dense undergrowth, just one more shadow among many.

Robin let his mind drift, wondering if Beth had had time to consider their relationship in terms of what the future might hold, or if she had already decided his past misdeeds were too reprehensible for her to forgive. It was stupid to have left her there in the woods. She didn't know that he had waited screened behind an impenetrable wall of moss-draped trees and vines until her uncle was in sight. She would think he had deserted her when she needed him most. Who wouldn't under the circumstances? She had asked for time alone to think things through and he had complied with her request. Now he doubted his wisdom in allowing her the opportunity to recount his many offenses without having all of the facts. Perhaps if he had told her about his parents, about the first twelve years of his life, she could have understood his allegiance to the Seminole. But how could he ever explain the war raging inside him, the conflict that tore at his very soul leaving him vacillating between two different worlds . . . worlds populated by men determined to destroy each other?

So lost was Robin in his musings, he failed to notice the stallion's sudden restless prancing and nervous whickering. He heard the rifle's loud report just an instant before his side burst into flame, the bullet's impact hurling him from the saddle into the heavy foliage then down a slight incline where he landed in a narrow ravine.

"What the hell are you shooting at, Perkins?"

"I saw something move, Sarge. I swear I did! Over there!"

"If you're wasting lead taking pot shots at shadows I'll have your hide! Come on, boys, let's go take a look."

Robin heard the distant voices through a cloud of pain so acute he had to take shallow breaths or risk passing out. As his hand touched the sticky wetness gushing from the wound in his side he fought down the rising nausea that came when one saw his own life's blood slipping away. He listened to the thudding hoofbeats of a dozen or so horses and knew it was only a matter of time before the patrol found him. Dressed in buckskin breeches, his bronzed chest bare, with a beaded headband around the raven-black hair falling loose to his shoulders, the soldiers would have no difficulty in identifying him as one of the enemy.

He hoped they would finish what they had started here in the washed-out gully rather than taking him to the fort for execution. Imagining Beth's horror at having to witness another hanging, Robin vowed he would not be taken alive. It was probably a moot point for at the rate he was losing blood the soldiers wouldn't have to shoot him again. That should make the Sarge real happy since the son of a bitch seemed determined to account for every damned bullet his men fired. Maybe he should make a run for it just to irritate the cheap bastard! Maybe not. Somehow he didn't think his legs were up to obeying his brain's commands. It might be better just to lie still and think about it a while longer.

"I'm not lying, Sarge. I know what I saw. There was something moving right here." The voice begging to be believed came from overhead. The soldiers must be standing on the rise not more than twenty feet away.

A stream of tobacco juice spewed through the air staining the grass along the ridge. "Okay, smart ass! If you know what you saw, describe it!"

The officer's challenge brought loud guffaws from the other men, but Perkins refused to back down. "I'm telling you, there was something here and I shot it!"

Eyeing the fledgling soldiers under his command, the sergeant barked, "Ramsey, get down to the bot-

300

tom of this hill and check things out. Maybe Perkins has provided us breakfast."

This is it! Robin thought, wincing as a new wave of nausea rolled over him. It wouldn't be long now. Beth didn't need to worry about him screwing up her life ever again. He'd caused her nothing but heartache since the first day they'd met. She'd looked damned cute riding through the woods dressed like a boy. But she'd sure as Hell better not be carrying any more army dispatches or he'd come back to haunt her. He was going to miss the little hellion, the feel of her warm body molded against his, the touch of her soft lips. . . .

"Aiieee!" The bloodcurdling war cry of the Seminole rent the air sending scores of birds winging from the trees.

No longer sounding so cocky, the Sergeant yelled, "Let's get the Hell out of here!"

Robin was only vaguely aware of the chaos taking place somewhere close by. Determined to escape the raw agony burning in his side, he allowed his mind to recede into a semi-conscious state where physical pain could not intrude. A shadow further dimmed the dwindling light behind his lids. Peeping through mere slits that refused to open farther, he saw Asiyahola standing above him, hands on hips, a scowl on his deeply grooved visage.

The Indian leader's words were lost on the badly wounded warrior who lay at his feet. "I do not envy Hawk's woman," he said to those beside him, "for she will live with his death on her conscience. I will see that it is so!"

For three miserable days, Beth stayed alone in the house except for daily visits by Rachel and Rebecca during which time the two women used every means of persuasion to try and convince her to move back to the fort until Robin returned. Though there were several vacant lots separating the two-storied structure from the commercial buildings along the main street of the growing settlement, the women worried about the ever-increasing number of unsavory characters. Men of low repute came into town for supplies then loitered about drinking their fill of cheap whiskey and sampling the pleasures of the flesh available for a price in the rooms above the saloon.

The morning of the fourth day, Beth awakened with a churning stomach, barely making it to the chamber pot before she lost the undigested remains of the meager meal she had eaten the night before. It proved to be a bad beginning to a day she would long remember.

"It's just not right for you to stay here unprotected," Rachel stated firmly a few hours later as she set her cup down hard against the table, sloshing coffee into the saucer and waving away the proffered honey-glazed bun that Beth had baked despite its noxiously sweet aroma.

It never ceased to amaze Beth when her stepmother got her dander up, for she still remembered that day thirteen years ago when her father brought Rachel home to Fort Brooke. Rachel's parents had been slaughtered by a roving band of Calusa Indians, now a tribe practically extinct. Timid by nature and haunted by nightmares of the gruesome attack, it was only through Andrew's love that Rachel found the strength to face her tragic introduction to the Territory and go on to become one of its staunchest supporters. Proud of the progress they had made in taming the wilderness without spoiling its natural beauty, her stepmother refused to mince words when it came to giving her opinion of the riffraff that drifted into the town who were always ready to take but never to give back what the Territory offered in the way of amenities.

Smiling in an attempt to alleviate the kind woman's concern, Beth placed the plate of freshly baked rolls on the table. "Rachel, this is my home and it's where Robin will expect to find me when he gets back."

"I still don't understand why Robin took off after those renegades that held you captive," Rachel said in a huff, "leaving you alone in the middle of nowhere!"

"The Indians weren't holding me captive . . . well, not exactly. Actually they sort of rescued me." Beth was becoming agitated as she did whenever she was reminded of that fateful night in the woods. Up until now she had managed to skim over the details of her kidnapping by Jesse Tillman and all that had ensued prior to her uncle's arrival. She saw no point in needlessly adding to their anxiety. The ordeal was over. Her body reacted with an involuntary shiver as the image of the twisting body swinging from the limb of the oak tree made her stomach pitch and roll, draining the color from her lightly suntanned face.

Sensing her niece's discomfort, Rebecca Logan stood up, taking Rachel by the elbow. "It's Beth's right to stay in her own home if that is her choice, and I am certain Robin will be back any day now." She spoke with exaggerated confidence as she steered the dark-haired woman toward the door. "Besides, I didn't tell Lance where I was going and you know how he frets."

"Don't be ridiculous, Rebecca! He knows we come to visit Beth every morning; besides, Logan never 'frets'!" Rachel spluttered as she was led unceremoniously down the back porch steps, given only time for the briefest of waves and the promise that they would return tomorrow.

Beth returned to the kitchen where she sank into a chair. Her Aunt 'Becca was acting decidedly suspicious this morning. Up until today she, too, had seemed adamant about the dangers of Beth staying alone. Beth knew that there were no secrets between her aunt and her Uncle Lance. She also knew he was curious about the missing pieces to her story, but so far he had not questioned her further. She wondered if either had guessed that she was pregnant. One look in the mirror revealed the changes already taking place within her. Her thin body had become almost gaunt from lack of appetite and morning sickness. Purple bruises ringed her eyes from the sleepless nights she'd spent pacing the bedroom floor thinking about Robin. Was he still alive, and if so where could he be? More importantly, would he ever come home to her?

Suddenly the unanswered questions and the traumatic events of the past few weeks starting with the inquiry into Ralph Tillman's death and ending with her lonely homecoming seemed more than Beth could bear. Overcome with sorrow she put her head down on her empty arms and wept as if her heart would break. Her deep, pitiful sobs were nearly the undoing of the tall frontiersman who entered the house unannounced and now reached out to offer a comforting hand.

"Rebecca said you needed me." The voice of her beloved uncle affected Beth as nothing else could. Toppling the chair in her haste, she threw herself against Lance Logan's massive chest and continued to weep until his shirtfront was wet with bitter tears.

Lance held her close making no move to stem the flood of emotion Beth had kept buried deep inside since that early morning when he had found her alone in the clearing. Finally she sniffed, then hiccuped, drawing back to look up at him through watery, red-rimmed eyes.

"I didn't tell 'Becca I needed you," she croaked in a voice that sounded unlike her own.

"You didn't have to," he replied, glancing around the empty kitchen as if to make certain no one else was listening. Then he leaned down and whispered, "Your aunt has 'the Sight.' "

Despite her wretchedness Beth cocked an inquisitive eyebrow. "The what?"

" 'The Sight,' " he repeated somberly. "To tell the

truth Rebecca is a witch. A good witch, mind you. She came here from England to make certain we young colonials keep to the straight and narrow path now that we no longer allow the mother country to guide us."

A weak smile teased Beth's lips as she recognized the deviltry glinting in Logan's distinctive silver-gray eyes, causing the weathered skin around the edges to crinkle. "Uncle Lance, she's no such thing and you'd better not let her hear you say otherwise, or she might just turn you into a frog!"

For the first time in days, Beth found herself laughing and it felt good. Not one to wallow in self-pity, she knew it was time to face life head on. After days of keeping her lonely vigil, she had to accept the fact that even if Robin lived, he might choose not to come back to her. There was a special bond between her husband and the Seminole People which she did not understand and would never understand unless he chose to explain. The possibility that she might have to raise her child alone was frightening beyond measure until she looked at the man who had silently seated himself across the narrow table. Then scoffing at her cowardliness she wondered how she could ever have allowed herself to feel so disheartened surrounded by a family of loved ones.

As if he could read her mind, Lance reached across the table and took her hands between his calloused palms, his voice serious now holding no hint of humor. "We all love you, honey. I was joking awhile ago and I'm sorry if I was out of line, but t's so damned good to see a smile on your face for a change."

Pulling her hands back, Beth nervously pleated the crocheted fringe edging the tablecloth. "Oh, please, Uncle Lance, don't apologize. I am the one who should be saying 'I'm sorry.' I know how much I've worried all of you since we came home from Fort King, but I had to have time alone to think. So many things have happened that you don't know about, so many things even *I* don't understand."

Sensing that Beth was at last ready to purge her troubled mind, he encouraged gently, "Do these 'things' have to do with Robin?"

Misty blue eyes met his as Beth once again took his hand in hers seeking the understanding she could always count on. The time had come to unburden her soul.

"Damn the man!" Lance bellowed, pounding the oak-beamed mantel with his powerful fist. "I'll kill the bastard with my bare hands! Just see if I don't!" he swore, turning to face his wife who sat on the brocade sofa. Rebecca waited patiently for him to calm down enough to explain why he had burst through the door as if the hounds of Hell were nipping at his heels and had then proceeded to do battle with the sturdy wooden shelf holding her precious silver candlesticks.

"Since I was the one who suggested Beth might be ready to open up to you about what's been troubling her lately, I would venture to guess your dis-

307

play of temper has something to do with Robin," she stated nonplussed.

Smoldering gray eyes locked with sea-green orbs. "Not *something!* *Everything!*" His accusing words resounded off the paneled walls.

As Rebecca listened in shocked silence Lance repeated what Beth had told him starting with the time she had been accosted by Osceola and the masked Indian en route to Fort King, ending with the news that their niece was pregnant with the blackguard's child.

When Lance finished his bitter harangue, Rebecca appeared more confused than ever. Shaking her head skeptically she said, "Robin can't possibly be an Indian. His uncle is a Congressman, for goodness sake!"

Lance rolled his eyes trying to sort through her inane logic. "Sweetheart, this isn't England! Why, if Florida ever gains Statehood I could run for Congress and no one would think twice about the fact that I have a son whose mother was an Indian."

Smiling proudly Rebecca gushed, "What a wonderful idea! I can't think of a finer man to represent the Territory!"

Suspecting that his wife was deliberately baiting him, Lance roared, "My future role in the politics of the Territory is not at issue here. We are supposed to be discussing Beth."

Innocent emerald eyes sparkled up at him. "I thought we were discussing Robin."

"They are one in the same!" Lance fumed, feeling as if he were conversing with a half-wit.

"Exactly my point," his wife sighed in satisfaction.

"Sweetheart, you're talking like someone a few bricks short of a load."

Rising to stand before her indomitable husband, Rebecca tapped him lightly on his hard-muscled chest. "Just tell me this," she countered indignantly. "Does Beth still love him?"

"What the Hell difference does that make? She doesn't even know *who* he is!"

"That's neither here nor there. How did Beth sound when she spoke of Robin?"

"Sad," Lance admitted without hesitation.

"Good! That means she still loves him."

Lance looked at the silly grin on his wife's happy face feeling his anger deflate like a punctured balloon. "You sound mighty sure of yourself, lady." As he spoke he put his arm around her tiny waist and drew her closer.

"Never more so. All they need is time to work things out between them."

Nuzzling her neck Lance murmured sensuously, "Does that mean I can't kill him?"

Pulling at his full lower lip with her small teeth, Rebecca replied languidly, "Let's give Beth a chance to work things out in her own way first."

"Surely you don't expect me just to stand here and do nothing!" Lance argued without conviction as he cupped his wife's full breast, feeling the nipple peak as he rolled it between his thumb and forefinger.

"Oh, I don't," she purred softly, taking his free

hand in hers and leading him toward the bedroom. "I would never expect a man of action such as yourself to stand about doing nothing."

Soundlessly she closed the door behind them.

Chapter Nineteen

Though sunrise was still several hours away, Beth sat in the lamplit kitchen staring at a lukewarm cup of tea pondering whether or not she'd made a mistake in telling her adoring uncle the truth. There was a decided sense of relief in recounting all the sordid details of what had happened between Robin and herself since that fateful day when he had snared her like a rabbit in a trap, but Lance Logan had made no attempt to conceal his unbridled fury directed at the man who had treated her in such a despicable manner. Had Robin been there, Beth knew her uncle would have shot him on the spot without batting an eye or demanding an explanation. She only hoped that *if* and *when* her husband returned she could keep the two apart until Logan's temper cooled to a slow boil. Luckily her father was on his way to the capital to bring the territorial governor up to date on the Indian situation or she would have had two irate men to deal with.

The noise of dogs barking in the distance scarcely disturbed her troubled thoughts. But a short time later the sound of something scraping across the back porch jolted her from her reverie. Clutching the cup with both hands, Beth waited, eyes as wide as saucers glued to the solid wooden door and the carefully drawn metal bolt which kept her safe from the unseen predators that prowled the night. Minutes passed and nothing happened. Only the incessant singing of the crickets interrupted the silence. Forcing her fingers to loosen their grip on the fragile teacup, she decided it was probably just a curious raccoon who, seeing the light burning, decided to take a closer look. If she had stayed in bed where people were supposed to be at this time of the morning, she wouldn't be quaking in her slippers over the harmless antics of some nocturnal scavenger.

Chiding herself for acting like a nervous ninny, Beth stood up preparing to extinguish the lamp then return to bed to seek a few precious hours of sleep before dawn. She was stopped abruptly by the thunderous burst of splintering wood. As the back door disintegrated into pieces of kindling, the heavy bolt Beth had thought invincible flew across the room to land at her feet. A scream of terror lodged in her throat to be replaced by a weak moan which had nothing to do with fear for her own safety.

The uncrowned prince of the Seminole Nation stood framed against the darkness, his deep-set eyes glowing with anger and resentment. But it was not the sight of Osceola that brought a cry of anguish to Beth's lips. It was the inert form of the man slung across the Indian leader's naked shoulder that caused Beth's heart to hammer against her breast. As the blood drained from her face she watched, mesmer-

312

ized by the crimson drops falling from the wounded man's side, making ragged-edged splotches upon the spotless pinewood floor. She felt her knees begin to buckle.

"Don't even think about fainting, woman!"

Beth snapped her head up as Osceola issued the sharp command. His hostility was a palpable thing. Because she was white? Perhaps . . . but some sixth sense told Beth his dislike stemmed from far more than just the color of her skin. Dark, hooded eyes issued a challenge and despite her trepidation Beth felt herself rising to the occasion, reaching out to accept the gauntlet. Suddenly she was in control again. Osceola might hate her but he had brought her husband home and she would not give him up again without a fight . . . not even to death!

"Bring him upstairs," she ordered, hurriedly leading the way and giving the man she recognized as her enemy no chance to talk.

Beth was not unaware of the gentle manner in which Osceola placed her unconscious husband on the soft feather-down mattress. Here, standing in her bedroom, was the man whose very name struck terror in the hearts of the settlers, the man who had once plunged his hunting knife into a treaty document, laid out upon a table, swearing that any of his people who agreed to the demands of the intruders would face his vengeance. Robin was a white man. At least he had lived among the whites. Yet there was no doubting the genuine concern of the Indian warrior for the one he called brother.

Beth knew this was no time to dwell on such ironies. As she poured water from the pitcher into the

313

basin and began bathing the inflamed area around the bullet wound, the sullen Indian tugged off Robin's moccasins and slowly began to peel down the tight buckskin breeches without being told. Beth drizzled water along the waistband where dried blood acted as an adhesive bonding material to the skin.

When Robin lay naked, his bronzed body a stark contrast to the pristine white sheet, she drew in her breath. Gone was the well-bred gentleman from Washington. Now it was Hawk, the Indian, she saw stretched out helplessly before her, his beaded headband encircling straight, shoulder-length hair as black as a raven's wing.

Tearing her eyes from his handsome face darkened by a shadow of beard, she pressed a clean cloth tightly against the jagged opening in an effort to stanch the seemingly endless flow of blood. With no experience in nursing a bullet wound Beth's panic escalated as she watched the crimson stain saturate the bedding while the wad of linen she held remained scarcely discolored.

"My God!" she cried in horror. "Where is it coming from?"

Osceola was finding it difficult to hold his temper in check. Out of compassion he had ignored danger to bring Hawk back to the one he loved. Now her incompetence might cost them both their lives.

"Damn it, woman!" he thundered. "The bullet went *through* him! Can't you see that the river of blood seeps from the larger hole in his back?"

Cursing herself for ten kinds of a fool, Beth reached for another pad of toweling, wedging her hand between her husband's motionless body and the mattress. Her eyes blinded with tears as she applied pressure to both wounds feeling the material at Robin's hard-muscled back soak up his life fluid like a sponge. She felt her palm grow moist and slick as she swallowed down the bile that pushed upward from her churning stomach.

Never had Beth felt so inept. Here she sat literally holding Robin's life in her hands . . . feeling it slip away between her fingers. In desperation she turned to the Indian who stood aloof, passing judgment on her worth and finding her wanting.

"Please," she begged. "I need help!"

Before Osceola could comment on what he considered a gross understatement, Beth demanded, "You must get my uncle! Bring him here! He'll know what to do!"

When the Indian remained unmoving Beth felt hysteria rise within her. "Surely you know Lance Logan! You must bring him here at once!"

Piercing black eyes bore into her. "I know the man of whom you speak. I am aware of his sympathy for the People. Yet somehow I doubt he will feel merciful toward the Hawk."

Beth, too, had misgivings about how Logan would react to such a summons. She had hoped for the opportunity to discuss with him again the situation between her husband and herself after he'd had time to digest what she had already confessed. But such was not to be. She needed Logan now, and she had no time to waste in trying to convince the stubborn warrior who glared down at her.

With fire in her eyes, Beth lashed out, "Unless you want to see your brother die you will do as I say! It is his only chance!"

Black eyes met blue in a war of wills. A wager on the victor would have been sheer speculation. Lengthy moments went by, then without lowering his gaze Osceola turned and walked out of the room leaving the door open.

Beth grew more frantic with every beat of her heart. Finally she accepted the fact that Robin had been abandoned by the inexplicable Osceola. She debated whether to risk leaving her husband and going for help herself, but she knew he would bleed to death before she could get back. She watched his chest rise and fall, each breath more shallow than the one before, as she continued to press the saturated cloths firmly against his wounds until her muscles cried for release.

Leaning her forehead down upon the mattress she began to pray, a random, disoriented entreaty asking for forgiveness though she could not name her sin. As she implored the Almighty her shoulders shook with unrestrained sobs of abject misery.

"It will do little good to add salt to his wounds."

Beth raised her head at the sound of the deep resonant voice she knew so well. Wiping her tears she managed to give her uncle a weak smile, then closing her eyes briefly she thanked a benevolent God beseeching one more favor: that He guide the footsteps of Asi-yahola, a friend indeed!

After Lance had stitched both jagged openings pulling the red, puffy skin together with sturdy thread, he liberally doused each lesion with disinfec-

316

tant. Though Beth flinched as she watched the antiseptic coat the raw, inflamed tissue, Robin remained motionless sleeping in the arms of Morpheus, the Greek god of dreams, blissfully unaware of what was taking place around him.

"Will he be all right?" Numb with fatigue, Beth's voice sounded dull and listless. Hugging her arms about her chest, she looked to her uncle for strength and encouragement.

Logan struggled to suppress the bitter resentment he felt toward the man whose life he had just fought to save. "He'll live if infection doesn't set in. You'll need to cleanse his wounds often," he said, handing her the bottle of astringent gaining some little satisfaction in knowing how the medicine would sting the tender flesh.

Then noting his niece's sunken cheeks and the dark circles ringing her eyes, Lance offered more than he would have thought himself capable of giving a few short hours ago. "Why don't you get some rest, honey? I'll come and get you as soon as he wakes up."

"No," Beth replied, shaking her head determinedly. "I couldn't sleep. I have to be here."

Seeing that her mind was made up, Lance knew there was no point in arguing. Rebecca had been right as usual. Beth loved this man whose past remained shrouded in mystery and whose future rested in the hands of a far greater power than any put upon this earth.

"Have it your own way," he conceded ruefully. "You always were a stubborn little cuss. I'll be down in the kitchen if you need me. Incidentally," he added, pausing in the hallway, "before your stepmother pays her usual morning visit, I would suggest you remove the headband."

He was gone before she could reply, pulling the door silently closed behind him.

Except for a few minutes spent in whispered conversation assuring Rachel and Rebecca that Robin was holding his own, Beth remained at her husband's side throughout the long, lonely day. Her uncle had returned sometime around noon to check on the patient and finding no sign of fever he again took his leave. Now at twilight, that shadowy intermission between sundown and full dark, Beth dozed in a chair she had pulled close to the bed.

Roused from her drowsy stupor, she imagined someone was painting pictures on the back of her hand using feathery brush strokes. Her arm jerked spasmodically as it rested atop the coverlet. Gradually she lifted sleep-drugged lids to focus on the source of the tickling sensation that had awakened her. Startled eyes widened as she watched a dark finger trace the blue veins visible beneath her skin.

Hypnotized by the slow, seductive movement of that single digit, Beth continued to stare until a low voice rasped hoarsely, "May . . . I have . . . some water?"

Raising her head she looked at the familiar, handsome face. Tightly drawn features bore evidence of the pain he tried unsuccessfully to hide. Beth hurried to fill a glass from the pitcher on the bureau then lifted Robin's head allowing him a deep drink of the cool liquid.

Casting a glance about the room he asked in bewilderment, "How did I get here?"

His voice sounded weak and strained.

"Osceola brought you home early this morning. I'll tell you all about it later," Beth promised, pulling the cover up to his chin.

Robin closed his eyes then blinked them open once more. "Asi-yahola? He got away safely?"

"Yes," Beth answered reassuringly. "You must rest now. There'll be time for explanations in the morning."

Turning her back she walked across the room to put the glass down beside the flowered pitcher. She gripped the edge of the chest of drawers dizzied by a sudden wave of relief. Robin would recover. She could tell by the stubborn set of his jaw. But what then? There remained so many unanswered questions . . . about him . . . about their future. He still knew nothing of the child growing inside her and she decided in that moment to keep her secret a while longer. For reasons she had yet to discover, Robin was torn between her world and that of the Seminole warrior, Osceola. If he chose her, it must be a choice based on love not obligation. She would accept nothing less.

"Beth?" At the sound of his voice Beth thrust her worries aside pivoting to face him once more. "I need you. Come and lie beside me."

Already he was taking control, his words more command than request but it mattered little. For this night at least he was hers alone. Closing the distance between them, she kicked off her shoes and lifted the cover, easing her body down on the bed careful not to cause Robin any undue discomfort. She was physically exhausted and for the first time in days her tormented mind was at peace. A warm hand reached out squeezing her fingers possessively. He had said he *needed her*. If not a total commitment, it was a start. Her eyelids flickered then closed. Tomorrow there were things that had to be said, questions that could no longer go unanswered. For now just having him by her side was enough.

Beth slept soundly, a deep restorative sleep that left no room for the disquieting dreams that had haunted her ever since that terrifying night in the woods. With her eyes still closed against the coming day, she stretched like a lazy kitten only vaguely aware of the heavy weight pinioning her legs preventing her from turning on her side. Frowning in annoyance she reached down and swept her hand along a hard, muscle-corded thigh positioned diagonally across her lower extremities.

She felt his breath stir her hair just seconds before warm, wanting lips began to blaze a trail of need along one cheek, across each flickering eyelid, over the narrow bridge of her nose. Finally he captured her mouth, drinking greedily with the unquenchable thirst of a man suddenly discovering an oasis in the middle of the desert.

His tongue wedged her lips apart pulling and sucking until she responded in kind to a mating prelude as old as time. It was the penetrating heat of his arousal, heat so intense she could feel it burning through her skirt and petticoat that finally brought Beth to her senses.

"Stop!" she cried aghast. "Don't you realize you've

been shot?"

"Through the heart with cupid's arrow," he teased. "Indeed, I've been mortally wounded by the little sprite and I fear only my lover's kiss can save me."

Dismayed that he could joke about his near brush with death, Beth scolded firmly, "If you pull at those stitches Uncle Lance so painstakingly put in, he'll have both our hides!"

Robin drew back to study the adorable pixie face he thought never to see again. "Logan sewed me up?" At her nod he asked warily, "Why? What did you tell him?"

Beth cast her eyes downward which was a mistake. The sight of his beautiful, aroused totally naked body brought an unwelcomed flush to her cheeks. She forced herself to look back at his face.

"I told him everything I know which happens to be damned little!" Her accusing blue eyes mirrored both hurt and recrimination. "Uncle Lance knows everything that has happened between us."

Robin's color heightened then he sighed. "It's a wonder he didn't cut out my gizzard and throw it to the gulls!"

"People don't have gizzards. But I imagine he considered amputating a few other parts!"

"I'm serious, Beth. Why did your uncle save my life knowing what I have done to you?"

The smile faded from her lips, replaced by an expression Robin found unreadable. Her mouth set in a firm line as if she braced herself for a disappointment she would never let show. In the depths of her cerulean eyes he caught a brief glimpse of resignation. Hesitantly, unable to call back the single escaping

321

tear that rolled unchecked down her smooth, flushed cheek, Beth replied, "He saved your life because I told him I loved you regardless of who you are or what you have done."

Robin was stunned by her admission. Never in his wildest dreams had he imagined someone could accept him with the faith and trust his wife had just professed. He felt his own eyes grow moist as he was gripped by an all-encompassing emotion so rare it defied description.

"My adorable Beth," he choked on a ragged sob. "How can I ever make up for the harm I have done you?"

Beth leaned forward until her breasts pressed against his iron-hard chest. Freed from the last vestiges of doubt as he clasped his arms around her, she whispered on a sigh, "You can start by loving me."

And he did. With her help he quickly disposed of the hampering gown and undergarments then she, too, lay naked upon the bed, her eyes darkened with unspent passion. It was a gentle joining unlike the tumultuous explosions of rapture they had experienced in the past. Both were conscious of the raw, new wounds inflicted by the bullet that had ripped through Robin's flesh, but other less visible hurts began to heal as they held each other in a tender embrace meeting as one body, one soul.

Beth lay curled against Robin's uninjured side, her head cushioned by his arm, as she idly fingered the coarse dark hair matting his broad chest.

"Why does Osceola hate me?" she asked, her voice troubled. It seemed the most innocuous of the many questions darting through her head.

Robin picked up a long silken strand of fiery red hair and gazed at its glossy sheen highlighted by the sunlight filtering through the curtains. "He doesn't hate you, sweetheart. He resents what you've done to me."

"What *I've* done to *you!*" Rearing up on one elbow, she looked at her husband disbelievingly.

"I know it's hard for you to understand, but in Asiyahola's eyes my love for you has made me an inferior warrior."

"It's not hard for me to understand," she countered in a deceptively calm voice. "It's impossible!" she shouted.

Blanching in the wake of her wrath, Robin sought to explain. "First I want you to know that I didn't leave you alone in the forest. I waited, hidden behind some bushes until your uncle arrived."

Beth froze him with her icy glare. "Oh that makes *all* the difference in the world, of course. While I sat there cowering like a frightened rabbit you hid in the trees and watched!"

"You didn't cower. You were sound asleep," Robin argued, wondering how every word he spoke seemed to make matters worse.

"That's neither here nor there! Why did you leave?"

"You asked me to give you time. Under the circumstances I felt it was a reasonable request."

"Well it just so happens I changed my mind! I was going to tell you as soon as I woke up but you were already gone!"

It was only a slight exaggeration for she had certainly reconsidered her options.

Her confession brought a smile of regret to Robin's

lips. "I wish I had known, but perhaps it's better that I didn't."

Beth's irritation soared to new heights. "If you had stayed where you belonged, you wouldn't have gotten yourself shot!"

"But don't you see, that was the whole problem? At the time I didn't know where I belonged. Now I think I do."

Beth didn't see at all and she told him so. Clear gray-green eyes searched her troubled face then Robin pulled her closer to his side. "Listen then and I will reveal all the mysteries of my sordid past." There was humor in his voice but Beth recognized a serious undertone as well.

Robin lay back against the pillows looking up at the ceiling. He took a deep breath wondering if, after he told his story, Beth would ever willingly come into his arms again. He spoke softly, pausing occasionally lost in memory. He described his beautiful Seminole mother with dark, laughing eyes and straight black hair that hung below her waist; his white trapper father, a huge man with a gruff voice and a thick brown beard whom the Indians called "Bear." He recalled his early days as a young brave hunting in the woods and fishing in the clear streams with his boyhood companions: Asi-yahola, Alligator, Jumper.

"And you were Hawk," Beth added, clutching his hand, spellbound by the vivid pictures he was painting with his words.

He nodded self-consciously thinking back on the times he had appeared to her as the masked warrior. Then he went on to tell her about the death of his parents followed by the arrival of his uncle who took him to his home in the North. There was no trace of bitterness in his voice. Beth knew that Robin loved and respected the man who had introduced him to the white world, yet Beth's heart bled for the free-spirited young Indian boy who had been uprooted from all he held dear and thrust into an alien society filled with hatred and prejudice.

"Naturally I rebelled. At first I tried to provoke my uncle into sending me home to the Territory. When that didn't work I ran away but he found me and brought me back. His perseverance finally won out and I came to accept what I could not change."

Smiling Beth said, "I'd like to meet your uncle someday. He must be quite a man if he can bring you to heel."

"Remember I was only a small boy at the time," Robin chuckled. "But you're right. They threw away the mold after they made Uncle Martin. He's quite a character. Everything else I've told you is true. I was educated at the finest Eastern schools, invited into the homes of the rich and influential—"

"Introduced to the most beautiful women?" Beth's pique delighted Robin.

"I'll admit the fairer sex played a part in completing my education," he replied smugly.

Beth snorted indignantly. "A major role I dare say! Why did you come back?"

Robin hesitated for it was difficult to explain what he did not fully understand himself. His handsome face took on a faraway expression as he tried to frame an answer. "I guess my heart never really left. Over the years no matter where I went or what I did, I felt my people calling me home. Strangely enough it was

Uncle Martin who finally urged me to return. He had given me the necessary tools to make a success of my life but he knew only I could decide how to use those tools. He understood that I would never be happy until I resolved the conflict raging inside me. He sent me here as a representative of the government to intercede between the soldiers and the Seminole in order to establish a fair and workable peace. He knew in all likelihood I would never return to him."

"He sounds like a brave, selfless man."

"He's a realist, sweetheart, as I am. We both knew my chances of success were next to none which has proven to be the case."

"What will you do now? Continue to fight on the side of the Seminole hidden behind a mask?" Remembering the grotesque disguise, Beth shuddered as a chill of apprehension coursed through her.

Robin shook his head negatively. "There will be no more masquerades, but I will continue to do what I can for my people in my own way. Asi-yahola said I was useless as a warrior because my heart was here with you, not on the welfare of my brethren. I was returning to you when I was ambushed by a patrol of soldiers. If I had not been concentrating on what I would say when I arrived, I would have sensed the danger. Asi-yahola was right."

"That's not true!" Beth defended heatedly, too riled to realize she was arguing against her own interests.

Robin rubbed his foot seductively up and down her calf, amused by her ire, elated by her loyalty. "Does that mean you think I should rejoin Asi-yahola's band in order to prove him wrong?"

"When Hell freezes over!" Beth retorted. "Now

hat I have you back I'm not going to lose you again."

Continuing the stimulating assault on her leg, Robin said soberly, "It's not too late to change your mind. Now that you know the truth, are you still willing to love, honor and obey a savage half-breed?"

With a mischievous grin Beth replied, "I will always love and honor you, my husband, but in truth, I lied about the last part!"

She giggled as he slapped her playfully on her bare buttocks.

"Now I have a secret for you." She drew back so she could see his face more clearly.

"And what might that be, my love?"

Robin knew nothing could possibly add to the peace and contentment he was feeling at this moment. He was wrong.

"We're going to have a baby," Beth whispered shyly.

Stunned by her unexpected news Robin stared openmouthed at the thin, fragile beauty who had just committed herself to him forever. Then overcome by a feeling of euphoria beyond anything he had ever thought possible, he clasped his arms around her burying his face in the curve of her neck.

Beth felt the salty wetness of his tears caress her skin. She knew there was no weakness in his display of emotion for the Hawk would always be her fearless warrior.

Later that same morning a stern-faced Lance Logan entered the bedroom as Robin was finishing a breakfast of lightly scrambled eggs and crusty buttered bread. Handing Beth the tray without so much as a greeting, he ushered her out of the room and closed the door firmly behind her.

After two hours of fretting and stewing in the kitchen without so much as a footfall to indicate what was happening overhead, Beth was ready to give both men a piece of her mind. As she stomped angrily up the stairs she met her uncle coming down and immediately reversed her direction. Lance followed her into the kitchen where she turned to confront him, hands on hips, expression mutinous.

"Well?" she fumed, waiting for him to say something.

After a lengthy silence Logan's weathered face split into a grin. "I reckon he's a 'keeper.' "

Flooded with relief, Beth threw her arms around his neck. Against all odds, two men she loved deeply and completely had reached an understanding and her heart swelled to overflowing. Never again, Beth vowed, would she let anyone or anything come between her and her newfound happiness.

Chapter Twenty

Less than a week later Robin was up and around though he tired easily and sometimes walked with a slight limp to ease the pressure on his injured side. It was mid October and though the days were still warm and sunny, the humidity had lessened considerably and the nights brought a cool welcome breeze from the north.

One evening after sharing supper with the Townsends and Logans, Robin suggested a short stroll along the beach. His mood was more somber than usual, Beth noted as she wrapped a shawl around her shoulders, and she had not missed the furtive glances he and her Uncle Lance had exchanged during the meal. Snatching a crust of bread to feed the gulls, she bid a hasty good night to her family and hurried out the door.

As they walked across the damp, hard-packed sand Beth talked about her plans for decorating the nursery. Robin responded with a grunt each time she paused to look at him expectantly. With a sigh of exasperation she seated herself on a large white boulder and began to break off bits of bread, tossing them to the raucous seagulls circling overhead. She watched as the greedy birds swooped down catching the pieces in their curved beaks.

"You remind me of an Indian I once met who answered all my questions with that same obnoxious sound."

Robin apologized sheepishly, "I'm sorry, sweetheart. I guess I'm not very good company tonight."

Beth gazed out at the darkening horizon where muted shades of pink, lavender and blue melded into gray. "Do you want to talk about it?"

"No, because you're going to be mad as hell, but might as well get it out in the open. There's something I have to do that's going to take me away from you for awhile."

Beth tensed as warning signals rang in her head. She had the man she loved beside her, a child growing within. Yes, life was moving along a little too smoothly. It was about time the props were knocked out from under her. Helplessly she waited for the blow to come.

Robin moved behind her, placing his hands on her shoulders. "I'm going to Washington. Lance is coming with me."

She whirled to face him. "Why?"

"Because someone has to make the men running this government see reason. I had planned to put my arguments in a letter, but your uncle and I both feel it will be more effective if we present our case in person. That way we will be on hand to answer questions and counter objections."

"And just what is your *case?*" Beth asked with an edge to her voice.

Without hesitation Robin answered, "Money. Since the politicians have turned a deaf ear to the humane issues surrounding this conflict with the Seminole, we intend to home in on the exorbitant sum of money being spent to wage war against a handful of people who want nothing more than a small share of what is rightfully theirs."

Beth was moved by his fervor. "Do you think you can convince the Congressmen to put an end to the fighting?"

Robin's voice reflected his steadfast determination. "If we can't, we plan to go directly to the taxpayers who are footing the bill. We'll campaign through the newspapers. One way or another we'll make sure every citizen knows exactly how his tax dollars are being spent."

Beth stood up and wrapped her arms around her husband's neck drawing him close. "I don't want you to go but I understand why you feel you must. I owe Osceola a great debt for he returned you to me; not just your wounded body, but your heart as well."

"My heart was always with you," Robin murmured rubbing his cheek against hers.

"As mine will be with you on the long journey ahead."

It was Beth's way of giving him her blessing and Robin understood what it cost her. He dipped his head as Beth's lips parted allowing entrance to the sweet recess of her mouth. Their warm breaths mingled, their tongues entwined, but it was far from enough for already both felt the loss the next few

331

months would bring. Taking Beth's shawl from around her shoulders, Robin spread it on the sand. He loosened the fastenings of her gown then removed his shirt and breeches as she shimmied out of the dress and petticoats which billowed around her feet. As they undressed, their eyes remained locked in mutual surrender. They clasped each other tightly as a half-moon rose in the eastern sky to silhouette the naked splendor of their bodies. Then Robin lowered Beth to the ground positioning himself above her. He cupped her face in his hands outlining each feature with tender kisses that made her ache with need. She moaned softly as his hardened shaft pulsed against her still flat belly. As he lifted one firm ripe breast to tease the taut nipple gently between his teeth, she bent her knees arching her back in search of the one thing that could put out the flames setting her blood afire, the one thing he continued to hold just beyond her reach.

Robin surrounded each breast with one large, rough-palmed hand massaging them to throbbing peaks. Just when Beth thought she could endure no more of the exquisite torture, Robin lowered his head, his velvety mouth following a winding path around her ribs, over her navel, across her stomach, down to the mound of red curls covering the flower of her womanhood. Parting the petals he drank from the nectar secreted within, squeezing her buttocks in time with the tune his tongue was playing.

Held prisoner by his greater weight, Beth writhed beneath him; her cries of ecstasy blended with the sound of the surf beating against the shore. Wave after wave of overpowering sensation rippled through her. She opened her eyes but the stars twinkling overhead dimmed in comparison to the burst of light that started deep inside and stretched over every inch of her body like a thousand meteors streaking through space. Before her thundering heart could begin to calm, Robin mounted burying his rigid staff in the moist, tight passage he had made ready. He felt her muscles contract enclosing him as she wrapped her legs around his waist. She clung to him with the desperation of one who fears the moment will end too soon and might never happen again. Capturing her lips he plunged and then withdrew as her limbs gripped and then relaxed to match the rhythm he set. Together they climbed, soaring higher than the stars, finally reaching infinity.

They returned to earth on a steadier plane, their energies spent. But Beth continued to hold Robin's body locked between her trembling legs. As if he could read her troubled thoughts, he whispered softly against her ear, "Please don't be afraid, sweetheart. I will come back. Two spirits once joined can never again be separated."

Not for a moment would Beth allow herself to doubt Robin's words, yet she could neither explain nor disregard the chill of apprehension that suddenly swept over her. A vague feeling of portending danger kept her locked in his arms until long after the moon had reached its zenith and the incoming tide had begun to lap at their bare feet.

It took a week for Robin and Lance to make the necessary preparations for the arduous journey. They would cross the Territory on horseback heading northeast to the old Spanish city of St. Augustine. From there they would travel up the coast by ship to Washington.

On October 25th they were ready for departure. The entire clan gathered outside the gates of the fort though the sun had yet to rise above the treetops and an early cold snap had turned the air brisk. The women clutched their shawls against a chill breeze as Beth and Rebecca bid farewell to their men.

Holding his wife in a tight embrace Robin admonished, "You should be inside where it's warm, little mother, not standing here in the wind."

Smiling bravely, Beth leaned back and patted her stomach. "Don't worry. Your son is warm and cozy."

"I envy him being inside you. That's exactly where I'd like to be right now." His gray-green eyes smoldered as he lowered his mouth to hers for one last searing kiss. Then he frowned. "Promise me, sweetheart, that you won't do anything foolish while I'm gone."

Beth rolled her eyes then gave him an impish grin. "Trust me. I've memorized all of the 'do nots' you lectured on last night: 'do not ride a horse,' 'do not climb a ladder,' 'do not trip over the dog' . . ." She paused, quirking a coppery brow. "Hell's bells! We don't even have a dog!"

Robin laughed, chucking her under her impudent chin. "You might adopt a stray while I'm gone and I wanted to cover all the possibilities."

"You did an admirable job of it," she assured, her compliment holding just the right amount of sarcasm to convince him his efforts had been in vain.

Beth caressed his smooth cheek with her palm. Being pregnant does not make me an invalid, darling."

Robin knew his headstrong little hellion would do exactly as she pleased despite his warnings, but he couldn't leave without one final admonition. "At least promise me you will consider the consequences of your actions before you do anything reckless."

"I promise," she conceded though she couldn't imagine why he would think it necessary to caution her. As if he were talking to a willful child!

"Sorry to break things up but that boat we booked passage on has a schedule to keep." Lance was already mounted and sat waiting for Robin to do the same.

Suddenly Beth's stomach fluttered as if the child she carried sensed his father was going away. Unwanted tears shimmered like crystals in her sky-blue eyes as Robin swung up into the saddle. The children shouted and waved as the two men nudged their horses into action.

"We'll be home for Christmas!" Robin called back over his shoulder.

Beth stood motionless watching as they crossed the open meadow then disappeared among the trees.

"Two months isn't such a long time, dear," Rebecca soothed, putting her arm around her niece's narrow waist.

But her words offered little consolation for Beth knew any number of things could happen before she saw her husband again.

"Why do you waste time baking 'em, mama? They

don't taste any better than this," Mandy proclaimed
from her perch atop the kitchen table as she stuck a
pudgy finger in the raw cookie dough rimming the
edge of the big wooden bowl that she balanced in her
lap. Her short little legs crossed at the ankles swung
to and fro; her sapphire eyes surrounded by thick
black lashes sparkled with delight as she licked her
chocolate-coated lips.

"If your mama didn't bake the cookies, the kitchen
wouldn't be filled with this delicious smell," Beth explained, smiling at the dark-haired cherub.

Rachel bent to peek into the oven. "I remember
when you used to beg to lick the bowl, Elizabeth,
though you were a few years older than Amanda."

"I'd still be licking if Mandy wasn't so quick to
grab the bowl first." Beth turned a stern look on her
little sister which brought forth a pleasurable giggle
from the unrepentant child.

It felt good to tease and banter like old times in the
homey kitchen. It was the end of November. Robin
had been gone nearly five weeks, and Beth couldn't
wait for the new month to begin. Her husband had
promised to be home for Christmas and once December was here she hoped the days of separation would
seem shorter like the times between sunrise and sunset
now that winter was approaching.

In truth the days passed swiftly enough but she
could scarcely endure the long, endless nights when
she would lie alone in the big bed, her body crying
out for the passionate release she had known too
briefly. Hour after hour she spent staring at the ceiling, her hands resting lightly on her swelling abdomen, wondering what was happening in the big city

of Washington, wondering why a few powerful men who had never even been in the Territory had the right to govern their lives. When sleep eluded her she found comfort in talking to her unborn child, telling him stories about his handsome father who would soon be home with them. Sometimes the tears of loneliness would come unbidden, but Beth refused to let her spirits sag for long. The baby might sense her sadness and rebel against entering a world where such feelings were allowed to persist.

Beth jumped as the back door was thrust open without warning. Lack of sleep had put her nerves on edge.

"Don't you dare slam it while I'm baking!" Rachel hollered, pointing a wooden spoon threateningly at Edward Townsend who turned and made a show of gently easing the door back into its frame.

Then he grabbed his stepmother around the waist and spun her in a circle, planting a kiss on her cheek as she clucked in annoyance and beat on his chest with the spoon.

"Kiss me, too," Mandy squealed, delighted by her brother's antics.

Releasing Rachel, Edward took a step forward only to stop abruptly when he saw the chocolate mess spread nearly ear to ear. "Not a chance!" he crowed, making a face that brought on more giggles.

Beth laughed as her baby sister tried to pout around the sticky substance gluing her lips together. Edward eased toward the table bending to peck Mandy on the top of the head then retreating quickly before her grubby little hands could reach out and touch him. Satisfied by his display of affection,

Mandy scrambled down and raced to the door where her puppy whined for attention.

"If you want a cookie, Edward, just help yourself. These high jinks really aren't necessary," Rachel scolded fondly.

"It's not food this virile body craves though I can't pass up such a tempting offer," he replied dramatically as he swiped a cookie from the sheet pan Rachel was removing from the oven and plopped it in his mouth. Both women laughed as he fanned the cavity with his hand, his eyes widening as he swallowed the piping hot circle of chocolate.

Beth rushed to the sink to draw water from the pump. Dipping a slight curtsy she handed her brother the glass. "And just what is it your *virile* body craves?"

"A wife!" he answered, blushing until his freckles turned beet red.

Stunned speechless Rachel and Beth regarded him blankly. After a lengthy silence, Rachel shrugged, turning to spoon more dough onto a flat sheet of tin. "Well, you won't find one here," she commiserated without cracking a smile. "Beth and I are spoken for and Mandy obviously prefers four-legged pups."

Their stepmother's unexpected humor served to dissolve Edward's embarrassment and stimulate Beth to speak.

"Eddie, what are you talking about?" Beth already suspected what was to come.

"I'm going to Fort King and I . . . I'm going to ask Maggie McAfee to marry me." He breathed a visible sigh of relief as soon as he finished blurting out his intentions.

Beth threw her arms around her brother's neck. "That's wonderful, Eddie. You'll make Maggie the happiest girl in the Territory."

"About time," Rachel added, smiling and patting her stepson on the back affectionately.

Edward looked from one to the other. "What if she says 'no'?"

Beth knew Maggie was crazy about her brother. Many nights she had buried her head beneath the pillow wishing her friend would cease extolling his virtues and let her get some sleep. But it wouldn't hurt Eddie to worry a little after all the anxiety he had put Maggie through while he made up his mind to settle down.

"If she says 'no,' " Beth replied innocently, "I suppose you will have to make do with that sweet young thing you've got staked out at Fort Drum."

"What? How did you . . . ? Damn! Cousin Davey's got a big mouth!"

Beth watched in amusement as Edward's expression changed from surprise to anger to distress.

"Does Maggie know?" he asked with chagrin.

"Unfortunately poor Maggie has no idea what a bounder you are," she answered, busily transferring cookies from the baking pan to a plate so he would not see her smile.

Edward relaxed then took Beth's hands in his. "Listen, sis. I need you to do me a big favor."

"Anything," Beth answered, concerned by the worried face whose features were so like her own.

"Come with me." His voice refused to beg, but his eyes pleaded for her to say "yes."

Before his words were hardly out, Rachel roared in

protest, "Have you lost your mind? Your sister is going to have a baby. She can't be traipsing around the countryside in her condition!"

Edward had been so befuddled since making his monumental decision to give up bachelorhood he had forgotten that he was soon to be an uncle. Shamefaced he apologized, "I'm sorry, Beth. I guess I was only thinking about myself."

Rachel bent to place another tray of dough in the oven satisfied that the matter had been settled. She jerked about nearly dropping the pan as Beth spoke up, "I'll have to be back by Christmas."

"No, Elizabeth! It's too far," Rachel insisted, wishing Andrew were here to make his daughter listen to reason, but he had gone to Fort Drum and would not return for several days.

"Rachel, dear, it's not going to hurt me to ride to Fort King. We'll take our time." She looked at Edward who nodded in agreement, willing to accept any conditions she stipulated as long as he didn't have to face Maggie alone. "A change of scenery will do me good and help to pass the time until Robin gets home."

"And if we wait much longer the snow will be too deep for the horses," Eddie added, unable to resist a bit of humor.

Rachel turned on him snapping waspishly, "Don't you crack wise with me, boy! Your sister's acting like a pea brain and you're making jokes. If your father was here he'd set the two of you straight!"

Elizabeth and Edward cut their eyes at each other. Both knew Andrew would side with his wife which made it imperative that they leave before his return.

Rapidly changing his strategy Edward gave his stepmother a winsome smile, releasing his breath on a long, drawn-out sigh. "I had planned to bring Maggie back here to spend Christmas with us, but Patrick and Martha will never allow her to accompany me without a chaperone."

"Not if they have good sense," Rachel agreed.

The twins saw her mouth twitch and knew she was weakening. Taking advantage of her slight unbending, Edward pressed on, "If we leave tomorrow we can be home in a week, ten days at most. That will give you ample time to get to know your future daughter-in-law and the two of you can begin making plans for a spring wedding."

There was nothing Rachel liked better than family celebrations. To have Maggie here for the holidays and a wedding in the offing was a temptation Edward knew she would find irresistible. It was not quite as simple as he had imagined for the older woman continued to argue but her counters became more and more halfhearted until finally she threw up her hands in defeat.

"I don't suppose it will do any good to say 'no.' You two could always work your way around me. But if something happens to your sister or her baby it will be on your head, Edward Townsend. You just remember that!" Her eyes glittered like jewels of blue fire and Eddie felt the first hint of misgiving.

Sensing his doubts, Beth quickly stepped between the two. "I'll be just fine and we might even run into Robin and Uncle Lance along the way. Then we could all ride home together!"

The thought which had come to her out of the blue

sent warm, tingling sensations coursing through her body and made her pulse beat faster. Though the distance to Fort King was short in comparison to the miles between here and Washington, it would place her that much closer to the man she longed for with every fiber of her being.

"Oh, Beth! I have to be the luckiest girl in the whole world! I don't know what I've done to deserve a man like Eddie but I swear I'll spend the rest of my days making sure he has no regrets!"

As Maggie pirouetted before her, Beth wondered if her queasy stomach was caused by the baby, the long ride from Fort Brooke, or her friend's nauseating display of enthusiasm.

"I'm deeply disappointed in you, Maggie. I thought surely you'd hold out for someone tall, dark and handsome . . . not settle for a runty little redhead."

"Runty little redhead? Elizabeth Hawkins! How dare you speak of your brother that way!"

As Maggie spluttered in righteous indignation Beth dissolved into giggles.

"I'm only kidding," Beth gasped, choking on her laughter, "but your carrying on is a bit much, Maggie. No man is as perfect as you make Eddie out to be. They all have their faults but we love them in spite of their shortcomings. Let's wait and see how you feel six months down the road."

"I'll feel exactly the same way," Maggie stated unequivocally still in a huff. "Honestly, Beth, I thought being married would soften you, but I see I was wrong. You're as cynical as ever!"

Beth thought back over all that had happened to her since she'd met Robin. Cynical? Yes, she supposed she was but she would prefer to call her attitude "realistic." One thing she had learned was that life could not be judged in simple terms of right and wrong, black or white. It was much more complex than that.

The sound of thundering hoofs stayed any further discussion as the outline of a rider appeared in the distance. Edward and the McAfees came out onto the porch, drawn by the steady drumbeat of the animal's feet. Martha was the first to recognize her son.

"Peter! Peter!" she cried as she flew down the steps and across the yard with the sprightliness of a woman half her age.

Beth rejoiced with the family over their son's safe return. When they learned he had been granted leave from the army until after the holidays, their joy increased tenfold. Only Beth seemed to notice the furrowed brow marring Peter's plain-featured visage as he told them of his extended furlough. How, she wondered, could the military afford the loss of even one soldier with a war going on?

The answer to her question came quite by accident that very evening. After supper when the men retired to the parlor, Martha and Maggie insisted Beth lie down and rest saying they would take care of the dishes. Both women assumed the shadows beneath her eyes were a result of the long trip from Fort Brooke. Actually Beth felt better than she had since Robin's leave-taking. She did not regret her decision to accompany Eddie on his visit, but there was no point in arguing with well-meaning Martha McAfee.

343

In order to reach the room she and Maggie shared she had to pass the open door where the men sat talking before a low-burning fire. Peter McAfee's voice raised in anger brought her up short. She had no intention of eavesdropping on their conversation and would have continued on her way were it not for the name that suddenly exploded in the air: Osceola!

Beth stiffened unable to go a step farther.

"It's just not right!" Peter declared, making no effort to lower his voice until his father cautioned "Now calm down, son."

Even then Beth had no trouble overhearing the younger McAfee's words. "Thomas Sidney Jesup!" He spat the name out as if it were distasteful. "The man has been in charge for over a year now and Osceola has made a fool of him at every turn. The general has become a joke among his own troops!"

"He's not the first." It was Edward who spoke "Every commander they send down here to end the uprising meets with the same results and we're talking about a lot of skilled Indian fighters."

Beth stood back in the shadow of the hallway where she could look into the room without being seen. Peter was massaging his temples between his thumb and forefinger. "It's different this time," he said tersely. "Jesup's career is on the line. He knows it and he's willing to use any trick in the book to get the job done!"

"But to capture a man under an official flag of truce! Surely even the general wouldn't stoop so low!"

Beth's blood ran cold as she heard her brother' stunned response.

"That's where you're wrong, Eddie. Osceola ha

344

agreed to parley with the general day after tomorrow at Fort Peyton south of St. Augustine. Rumor has it that he's sick. I don't know if he's physically ill or just tired of the fighting. I'm home because as far as Jesup is concerned, the war is over . . . or will be when Osceola lands in his trap!"

There was a brief pause then Beth watched as Peter knelt before his father, his voice broken with emotion. "Pa, I know I joined the army against your wishes. I wanted to do something more exciting than plow fields and mind a few head of livestock. But all I want right now is to come home for good. I never really had anything against the Indians. Deep down I think they have more right to this land than we do, and what's going to happen to Osceola just ain't right!"

Beth didn't wait to hear anymore. Her mind whirled with images of the mighty uncrowned prince of the Seminoles led to slaughter, trusting the white man once again and too late finding his credibility lacking. She owed the warrior her husband's life and she vowed to do anything within her power to satisfy that debt!

Purposefully Beth made her way down the hall to Peter McAfee's room, closing the door softly behind her. Without conscious thought she stripped off her gown and undergarments and hurriedly donned the soiled uniform Peter had left draped across the foot of his bed. The pants were inches too big but she managed to hold them up beneath her breasts with one hand as she grabbed a heavy jacket from a peg on the wall. Raising the window she eased herself to the ground then headed for the barn at a run. She spent precious seconds securing the pants with a length of cord then saddled Senabar, crooning to the horse to keep her from whinnying her excitement at the prospect of an unexpected ride out into the night.

Beth walked the mare down the well-worn path a good distance from the house before she mounted. The trail to Fort King was familiar but after that she had only a vague idea as to where St. Augustine might be. Northeast. Of that she was sure, but there were miles to cover and no moon to guide her. *Please let me be in time,* she prayed as she kicked her heels into the animal's flanks, her heart pounding like the thundering hoofs beneath her.

Chapter Twenty-one

Beth rode throughout the night and all the next day stopping only long enough to rest her mount. Her luck held as she circled Lake George then found a ferry to take her across the St. John's river. Gaining encouragement from the boatman who assured her she was heading in the right direction, she took off along the trail at a full gallop.

Around noon of the second day she came within sight of Fort Peyton. As she reined in her horse on the crest of a hill looking down upon the peaceful valley below, she realized to her horror that she had arrived too late. In the distance over a hundred warriors followed by a nearly equal number of women and children trudged along the road flanked on either side by mounted soldiers. One uniformed officer still carried the white flag which had been used to deceive the Indians. Waving in the wind, it bore witness to Thomas Jesup's perfidy. Beth rested her forehead on the pommel and wept with futility as she watched the bedraggled band being led away.

Finally, tears spent, she drew herself up and

nudged Senabar forward. Slowly she descended the hill then crossed the meadow to where a lone soldier stood looking at the departing figures. He turned around on hearing her approach, his eyes widening as he took in her disheveled appearance and the dingy uniform hanging about her slender frame.

Before he could speak Beth asked in a strained voice she could barely recognize as her own, "Where are they taking them?"

Facing the cloud of dust in the distance, the soldier answered, "Fort Marion in the town of St. Augustine." Shaking his head he added disparagingly, "They never had a chance."

Too choked up to acknowledge his reply, Beth turned her horse and followed slowly in the wake of the prisoners.

Her first glimpse of the imposing stone structure once called Castello de San Marcos by the Spanish, who completed the building of the fort nearly a hundred and fifty years ago, set Beth's limbs to trembling. Tapered gray-white walls thirty feet high constructed of huge blocks of limestone loomed above her. Accustomed to the log-enclosed strongholds built by the Americans during the past two decades, Beth shuddered in the shadow of the oppressive fortification. She watched as the warriors were herded across the drawbridge spanning a wide moat then passed beneath an archway into the inner courtyard where they disappeared from view. Indian women and children dotted the hillside on which Fort Marion stood keening and moaning for their loved ones now imprisoned behind walls thirteen feet thick.

Her mind numbed by what had occurred, her body gone weary after two days and nights without sleep, Beth slumped in the saddle unable to decide what she should do next.

"Hey! What'sa matter, soldier?"

Beth looked up to see a young boy, for he couldn't have been more than sixteen, dressed in a uniform identical to the one she was wearing. He eyed her suspiciously. Her delicate bone structure and feminine features were a dead giveaway despite the hat pulled down over her coppery red hair. "Say, lady, what ya doin' in those clothes?"

With more than a tad of annoyance Beth replied sarcastically, "I'm impersonating an army private. It's every girl's dream. If I give up without a fight, will you take me behind those walls?"

The young soldier followed her gaze. "You gotta be kiddin'! There's Injuns in there!"

Beth leaned down, whispering words meant for his ears only. "I know. And one of them happens to be a friend of mine. I have to speak to him."

The boy gaped at her unable to believe what he was hearing. When he could find his voice, he stammered, "Y . . . you have a friend who's one o' them Injuns and you w . . . want to talk to him?"

"What's your name?" Beth asked, seeing no point in affirming what she had already said.

"Wil . . . Wilbur, ma'am. You really want to talk to one o' them Injuns?"

Beth wondered if the lad might be a tad slow in the head. "Actually, Wilbur, the man I need to speak to is not *just* one o' them Injuns.' His name is *Osceola*."

The boy was so flabbergasted he took a step backward and nearly tripped over his feet. His big brown eyes rounded like saucers as his face blanched white. "But . . . but . . ."

"But nothing, Wilbur." Beth fished in the pockets of her borrowed pants and pulled out one of several silver coins she had discovered hidden there yesterday. She flipped it in the air. The boy caught it without thinking. "There's another coin where that came from if you can get me inside those walls."

"That just ain't possible, ma'am. There's guards all over the place."

Beth pulled a pretty pout. "But aren't you one of those guards, Wilbur?"

Shuffling his feet, he replied, "Well, sort of." Then his conscience got the best of him. "To tell the truth ma'am, I just carry notes from the officers who live in town to the major who runs the fort." His face reddened in embarrassment at having to admit he was no more than an errand boy.

But to his astonishment Beth seemed impressed by his confession. "Well then, you're much more important than a guard. Imagine what would happen if those messages didn't reach the fort. Why the result could be utter chaos!"

The youngster's chest swelled with pride.

"I used to deliver dispatches between Fort Brooke and Fort King," Beth confided.

"You couldn't have. You're *just* a girl!" Wilbur' expression registered disbelief.

Weary of arguing Beth snapped impatiently, "I may be 'just a girl,' but I happen to be the girl with another coin to match the one in your hand! Now ar

350

you going to help me or not?"

Squinting up at her he asked skeptically, "Are you funnin' or did you really deliver messages for the army?"

"Do I look like someone who would lie to you, Wilbur?"

After due consideration the youth replied, "Ma'am, you don't look like anything I ever seen before."

Refusing to give up the best chance she had of getting into the well-guarded stone fortress, Beth fished in her pocket for a second coin, holding it temptingly just beyond the boy's reach. His eyes sparkled avariciously. "With or without your help, Wilbur, I will see Osceola tonight!"

She waited not daring to breathe while the youngster stared at the piece of silver clasped between her thumb and her forefinger. He focused his gaze upon the invincible gray walls unable to hide a tremor of fear. "I have to go now," he said, turning back to cast a last longing look at the coin still dangling enticingly before him.

Beth's heart sank. She would have to find another way. But first she needed a place where she could rest while she formulated an alternate plan. She nudged her horse toward the town of St. Augustine located at the foot of the hill.

"Meet me at the end of the drawbridge an hour after sundown."

Beth looked over her shoulder but Wilbur was nowhere in sight. Had she actually heard the words or was it just wishful thinking, her mind playing tricks on her? There was only one way to find out. She would be at the drawbridge at the appointed time.

Beth could not afford a room at the inn. She had only two coins left. If Wilbur had indeed consented to help her, she was indebted to him for one of those coins. The other she used to buy a meat pastry and some sweet tarts from a street vendor who gave her a curious look but made no comment as to her strange appearance. Finding a secluded spot on the bank of Matanzas Bay she ate without tasting the food, knowing her body and that of the child growing within her needed nourishment.

As she gazed out over the calm waters, something caught her attention. What began as merely a speck far out in the Atlantic beyond Anastasia Island, gradually took on the shape of a large sailing ship making its way toward the harbor. She watched the vessel's approach with languid interest peering over her shoulder often to monitor the sun as it dipped below the western horizon. Yawning she stretched out in the grass, pillowing her head on her arms. She had intended only to close her eyes for a few minutes but after two days and nights without rest her body issued commands her mind could not deny and she lapsed into a deep sleep.

She was jarred awake by a man's voice shouting orders some distance away. Through sleep-clouded eyes she saw that the ship she'd been watching now creaked against the dock, its sails furled and tied around the wooden beams stretching upward, their tops invisible in the moonless night. Coming full awake, Beth realized to her dismay that the sun had long since set in the western sky. Lanterns hanging from the eaves of buildings along the wharf gave off circles of light enabling the arriving ship to unload passengers and cargo. She had no way of gauging the exact time and could only hope she was not too late.

Quickly she led Senabar back toward the huge stone structure standing like a silent sentinel atop the hill. Tying the horse to a bush she crept up the slope crouching behind a pile of rubble ten feet from the end of the drawbridge. To her relief the heavy wooden bridge remained down but she could see the outline of a soldier standing beneath the arch just beyond the dark moat.

Beth gasped as an indistinguishable form slithered up beside her. "Where ya been?" Wilbur hissed close to her ear, his nervousness overshadowing his annoyance. Without waiting for her reply he whispered tensely, "Ya gotta let me do all the talkin'. I can get us by Stokes easy enough."

Beth assumed Stokes was the man guarding the entrance.

"Most o' the Injuns are in the courtyard surrounded by soldiers but the one you want is in the 'secret dungeon.' "

"The what!" Panic rose up in Beth like a living thing.

Shushing her outcry, Wilbur explained, "Most people think it's a room where powder is stored but it's really a place where they keep special prisoners."

Wilbur had obviously been busy garnering information while she slept.

"But surely the room will be well-guarded."

"Not likely." Something in the boy's manner made gooseflesh rise on Beth's arms. His next words did nothing to alleviate her growing fear. "He's chained to the wall. There ain't nobody gonna get him out o'

there so you better just be wantin' to talk cause there's
nothin' else you can do."

Beth felt her stomach lurch in revulsion.

"I'll take you far as the door where they got him.
Then I want my money. You won't have any trouble
gettin' out. It's gettin' in that's tricky."

As they stood up and walked toward the bridge,
Wilbur cautioned again, "Remember I do all the
talkin'."

"Howdy, Stokes," he greeted the burly guard,
puffing on a cigar, leaning against the wooden frame
of the bridge.

"Evenin', Wilbur. Shouldn't you be in bed, boy?"
The man's reply was friendly enough, but Beth
cringed tugging at her hat as she felt his eyes rake her
up and down. "Who's your friend?"

"New recruit. I'm showin' him the ropes. Got a
note here from General Jesup for the major."

"Better stay close to the wall. One o' them Injuns
gets hold o' you, ya may come back minus your hair."
Stokes laughed heartily at his own joke as Wilbur and
Beth disappeared beneath the stone archway.

The Indian braves huddled together sitting cross-
legged on the grassy expanse of the inner courtyard.
Occasionally a hushed voice could be heard speaking
a guttural language incomprehensible to the soldiers
who stood ringing the prisoners at ten foot intervals.
No one noticed the two young *boys* pressing close to
the gray stone walls as they made their way carefully
toward the northeast corner of the fortress over which
a circular watchtower loomed high above the parapet.
They passed the sloping ramp used to push heavy
cannons up to the gun deck then crossed in front of

he room where arms were stored. Beth wrinkled her nose. The odor of urine and feces left no doubt as to the location of "the necessary." On they went expecting at any minute to be called upon to explain their presence, but the soldiers' attention was fixed on the half-naked men seated in the square.

As they reached the far end of the enclosure, Wilbur ducked into an open doorway, dragging Beth with him. The room was lit by a single lantern. Judging by the large stone fireplace occupying a section of one wall, it appeared to be a kitchen. Luckily no one was about at this time of night.

Wilbur held out his hand palm up. "This is as far as I go."

Standing in the center of the empty room Beth began to protest. "You said you would take me—"

"Through there," Wilbur interrupted.

"There" was a narrow opening in one wall about four and a half feet high by two feet wide. Beth tried to see into the dark space beyond which she assumed to be a pantry used for storing provisions but she could discern nothing within the gaping black hole. She searched the boy's face wondering if he had played her false but his youthful countenance showed no trace of deception, only alarm at the possibility of being caught with her here. His eyes darted nervously about the room resting on the door they had entered a few moments ago. Deciding she had no choice but to trust her reluctant guide, she withdrew the last coin from her pocket and placed it in his hand. Before she could express her gratitude Wilbur was gone.

Beth had never felt so alone. Trembling from cold and fright she forced her feet to move toward the small opening, steeling herself for whatever lay beyond.

"Damn it! Why now just when we were beginning to see an end to this needless bloodshed?" Robin sprinted down the darkened street like a man possessed. The pounding in his temples was brought on by a rage that had risen up from deep inside him the moment he stepped foot off the ship to learn that Osceola and more than one hundred of his men had been captured by Thomas Jesup under a flag of truce. "I'll kill the sneaky bastard!"

"Like hell you will!" Lance countered, grabbing Robin by the arm and bringing him to an abrupt halt. The older man was tired of running to keep pace with his livid nephew.

"I've worked hard the past six weeks aiding your cause and I don't intend to see you throw it all away in a fit of temper!"

Robin jerked loose from the other's grasp, his chest rising and falling rapidly as he sought to bring his anger under control. Though neither the Congress nor President Van Buren, who had followed Jackson into office, had gone so far as to declare an end to the war with the Seminole, many were having second thoughts about the need to continue the fighting. Public opinion seemed to favor a cessation to the hostilities. When he had reason finally to hope for a fair solution to the conflict, one man's treachery had put the life of his Indian brother in mortal danger.

On first learning the news, Robin had rushed to the house assigned to officers in St. Augustine prepared o do battle with the lily-livered general. He discovered shortly that Jesup had been summoned to the outpost at Matanzas where renewed fighting threatened to erupt at any moment. Logan had barely managed to prevent Robin and the general's aide, who took offense at hearing his commander called a cowardly son of a bitch, from coming to blows. Hurriedly he explained that they had just arrived from Washington and were here in an official capacity to report on the progress of the war, an exaggeration, to be sure, but one he deemed necessary under the cirumstances. The affronted officer had grudgingly issued two passes allowing them entry into Fort Marion. Lance feared unless he could calm Robin down they would probably find themselves clapped in rons before the night was over.

"Listen to me, son. You're not going to do your friend any good by trying to storm that fort single-handed."

Shaking his head as if to clear it, Robin agreed. "I now you're right but I'm just so damned mad I can't think straight!"

"Well you'd better put a lid on that temper of yours ecause Fort Marion's just up the hill."

Robin suppressed a shudder as he stared at the high tone walls rising up from the surrounding river of ater forty feet wide. As they started across the drawbridge a young soldier raced out of the fort running oward them. He bumped into Lance nearly pushing im into the moat as a husky guard hollered, "I arned you about them Injuns, Wilbur. You still got ll your hair, boy?" The guard continued to laugh as ance and Robin reached the archway.

Lance warned his nephew with a glance for Robin appeared ready to shove the man's teeth down his throat. Thrusting the passes beneath the odious guard's nose, he asked where they might find the officer in charge. A short time later they circled the enclosure accompanied by a harried Major Henley who continued to urge them to wait for General Jesup's return before confronting the notorious Indian leader. Lance watched Robin out of the corner of his eye. He saw his jaw tighten as they walked past the prisoners seated in the square. Many of the braves must have recognized the Hawk but none showed any sign that might give him away.

"We have no time to waste, Major," Logan barked impatiently, trying his best to imitate the pompous jackasses he had been forced to share company with in recent weeks. "The sooner we see for ourselves that you have Osceola behind bars, the sooner we can return to civilization." It was fortunate that they had not taken time to change from their "city clothes" of black broadcloth to their well-worn buckskins or Logan's bluff would never have worked.

Major Henley led them into a room where a long table stood before an open fireplace. Taking a lantern from the wall he turned up the flame then indicated they should follow him through an opening so low they had to bend nearly double to enter the adjoining chamber. The sight that confronted them drew decidedly different reactions from the three men.

Osceola sat on the floor, his back against the damp block wall where water seeped down from the ceiling patterning the stone with black runnels. Around his wrists were heavy iron bands with chains attached

358

retching up to rings built into the wall over his head. That appeared to be a young soldier, hardly more an a boy, judging by his slender frame, knelt before e warrior bathing his brow with a rag dampened in e basin of water at his side.

Beth whirled around as light from the lantern illu-inated the room. Her eyes were red and puffy; her leeks glistened with tears.

The demanding voice of Major Henley echoed off e vaulted ceiling. "What the . . . who the Hell gave ou permission to come in here, soldier?"

Following close behind Henley, Robin ducked be-eath the portal then stood up staring in stunned dis-elief at the ravaged face of his wife. "My God! lizabeth!" He crossed the short distance separating em just as Lance Logan entered the room.

It took a moment for Logan to recognize the per-on dressed in military garb sobbing against Robin's hest. "Well I'll be damned," was all he could think to ay.

Holding his wife as if he couldn't believe she was al, Robin looked down at Osceola. The Indian's ves were glazed with fever and he appeared to have st weight. Robin wondered fleetingly if Beth would e able to explain how she had come to be in this ungeon-like cell two hundred miles from home be-ore he throttled her, but he would have to wait to nd out. Right now his friend needed help.

"What is going on here?" Henley screeched. "Who this woman?" How in the name of God was he sup-osed to cope with men from Washington, women ressed like soldiers, and a fort full of savages?

Taking the disconcerted officer by the elbow, Lance

moved toward the narrow aperture.

"If you will be so good as to accompany me ou
side, Major, I'll be more than happy to answer yo
questions," he volunteered with a patronizing a
Henley failed to notice.

"But . . . I can't leave her here," he argued. "She's
woman!"

Placing his hand on the scruff of the major's nee
and leading him forward, Lance replied, "An unfo
tunate trick of nature, Henley. Surely you can't blan
her for that!"

Raising her head to look at Robin through tea
eyes, Beth experienced such a multitude of varyi
emotions she was assailed by a wave of dizziness th
left her clinging to her husband's muscular arms. H
joy at seeing him again was tempered by the know
edge that he was furious at finding her here. Sl
could tell that only concern for Osceola enabled hi
to keep his temper in check. His grip on her shoulde
was less than gentle and the blood vessel pulsing
his temple said more than words ever could. Soon I
would demand an explanation, but overriding ever
thing else was the frightening suspicion that the m:
Robin loved like a brother was dying. Despite the del
she owed there was nothing she could do to save hin
She collapsed at Osceola's side, reaching once mo
for the cloth, hoping the tepid water might reduce h
rising temperature.

Robin knelt across from her placing his hand c
that of his friend, feeling the contrast between tl
cold iron band encircling Osceola's wrist and the d:

heat of the Indian's skin. His eyes were open but instead of the sharp, penetrating gaze Robin knew so well, his fever-glazed pupils seemed to be looking inward.

His rasping voice was scarcely audible. "Tell me, my brother. Were you able to accomplish what you set out to do?"

The question took Beth by surprise. Robin had obviously discussed his trip to Washington with Osceola before setting out. She wondered how many of his frequent forays into the woods supposedly to hunt for game were actually excuses to confer with his boyhood friend.

Robin's rich, baritone voice held a touch of forced humor. "We have managed to stir up a controversy among the country's leaders. They are now reconsidering the position they have taken regarding the relocation of the Seminole. In time I believe they will alter their stand. Public sentiment is on our side." Unable to keep up the pretense any longer, Robin's shoulders shook beneath his burden of sorrow. "Why?" he cried in anguish. "Why did you agree to meet Jesup?"

Pain creased the face of the warrior, pain caused more by heartache than the physical ills he suffered. "The message he sent led me to believe he wanted peace. I should have waited for your return for I have always valued your counsel."

Having experienced the futility of hindsight, Robin straightened his shoulders, again taking control over his emotions. "It matters not now. The important thing is to find a doctor and get you out of here. By the time you are well the government may have decided to end this needless fighting."

Osceola shook his head sadly. "Tomorrow I am t
be transported to Fort Moultrie. The white soldier
are afraid these walls are not strong enough to hol
me." His bitter laughter ended in a choking struggl
for breath. "Jesup believes my capture will bring a
end to the war, but he is wrong. I am only one amon
many determined to remain free. You can best hel
our cause by continuing to use the resources availab
to you as a white man." He saw Robin was prepare
to argue. "Remember what I have said before, m
brother. One more rifle will be but a grain of sand i
the hourglass. Instead you must make your voic
heard above the roar of gunfire."

Beth knew Robin would have to give the situation
great deal more consideration before deciding in wha
way he would choose to fight. When Robin hesitate
to offer Osceola the assurance he sought Beth spok
up, "Fort Moultrie is near Charleston where I unde
stand they have fine doctors."

The Indian turned his head to gaze at her as sh
continued to bathe his heated body with her gentl
touch. "Never let the Hawk escape you, littl
dove."

Beth sat back abruptly. She doubted either Robi
or Osceola knew that "Little Dove" was the name c
Davey Logan's mother, the Calusa Indian her Unc
Lance had lived with until she had been brutally mu
dered by two men who saw her only as a squaw to l
used for their lustful pleasures. Though Beth couldn
explain why, the fact that Osceola had bestowed upc
her the name of the Indian woman her uncle ha
loved long ago, made her feel more a part of the m

362

she had married and of the People to whom he had pledged his allegiance.

He spoke to Robin then, but his eyes continued to search Beth's face from beneath hooded lids. "This woman you have chosen has a caring heart and a touch that caresses like a warm summer breeze, yet she is also endowed with the strength and courage of a warrior."

Beth glanced up to find Robin looking at her intently. Though she could not read his expression, she imagined him to be silently adding a few less complimentary descriptives to the list of attributes with which Osceola credited her.

Throughout the long night they remained beside the stricken warrior, Beth ministering to his needs as best she could, Robin recounting adventures they had shared as young braves. Hours later a dozen soldiers including Major Henley came to escort Osceola to the ship on which Lance and Robin had arrived. Having lost all track of time while buried in the dark hole, Beth blinked against the bright sunlight of mid-morning as she, Robin, and Lance, who had been waiting outside the fort, followed the soldiers and their captive along the wharf to the foot of the gangplank where Osceola walked unaided up the sturdy walkway. At the top he turned, his eyes locking with Robin's in a silent message of farewell.

Robin, frustrated by his inability to help his friend and brother in his hour of need, pivoted around and rode toward a small inn, leaving Lance and Beth to watch the ship weigh anchor then make its way slowly across Matanzas Bay and out into the open waters of the Atlantic.

Chapter Twenty-two

From the innkeeper Lance learned Robin had take a room on the second floor of the small establish ment. Though the thought of a bed in which to l down sounded like Heaven, itself, Beth was not reac to face her husband just yet. As she stood ponderir what she should do next, Logan took her by the e bow and steered her into the dining area set at th back of the inn.

Only after she was ensconced in a comfortab chair with a cup of coffee in her hand did her unc inquire as to the reason for her unexpected visit to S Augustine. His question was neither demanding n accusing for which Beth was grateful, but she kne the interrogation she could expect from her husban would be conducted quite differently.

Calmly she told Lance of Edward's sudden decisic to marry Maggie and how he had urged her to accom pany him to the McAfees. Lance smiled not the lea surprised that his nephew would make such a reques Though Eddie was the elder twin by a matter of mir utes he had always relied on his sister for moral su

364

port. When Beth went on to repeat the conversation she'd overheard revealing the trap General Jesup had et for Osceola, Logan's expression turned grim.

"He saved Robin's life. I had to try and warn him. But I didn't get there in time. And now Robin is furious."

Lance patted her hand sympathetically. "I understand why you did what you did, honey. Robin will, too, once you've had a chance to explain. I'll admit he's angry and rightfully so. You've endangered not only your own life but the life of his child and he doesn't know why. But, Beth, remember this. There's more eating at Robin right now than just his irritation at finding you here. He is trying to reconcile himself to the fact that his best friend will likely die in a strange prison far from home and all alone. He is grieving over what the loss of Osceola will mean to his people, and in the face of all that has happened in the past twenty-four hours, he must reevaluate his own position and decide what role he will play from here on out. It's not an easy thing for a man who just yesterday was filled with hope."

"I love him and I want to help, but I don't know how." Beth wiped away a tear, looking to her uncle for guidance as she had done so many times over the years.

"If you listen with your heart," he advised, "Robin will tell you how best you can help him and he won't have to say a word."

Beth stood at the foot of the bed gazing down at her husband's naked form. His eyes were closed and he appeared to be asleep as she watched the even rise and fall of his chest. The drapes had been drawn across the single window casting the room into semi-darkness.

Such a tall man, she mused, following the length of his long legs which stretched nearly to the wooden footboard. Beth was moved by the similarities between Robin and his Indian "brothers." With his light-colored gray-green eyes shut, the rough chiseled features of his face and the lock of raven-black hair falling across his forehead bore the unmistakable look of his Seminole forebears.

"Come to bed, Beth. I haven't the strength to beat you right now."

Robin's softly spoken words caused Beth to spring back with a start. She wasn't alarmed by the half-veiled promise of what he might do to her once his energies were restored. After that night in the cave Robin swore he would never hurt her again and she knew he meant it. She was simply flustered at having been caught studying his naked body so boldly.

Recognizing her need for him brought a blush to her pale cheeks. She had no right to desire her husband at a time when outside these walls others he cared about were suffering, but she could not deny the aching demand aroused by his nearness nor stem the tide of longing that threatened to engulf her. Quickly she took off her clothes and slipped into bed making an effort not to touch him for to do so would destroy what little restraint she had left. Turning her face to the wall she willed herself not to think and soon she drifted off to sleep. She didn't know at what point two strong arms reached beneath her breasts t pull her into his sheltering embrace, but she awoke late that evening to feel Robin's breath tickling her neck, his leg thrust across her thighs locking her in place.

"Give me one good reason why I shouldn't turn you over my knee and whale the tar out of you?"

Beth froze for there was no disguising the bad humor hovering just below the gently spoken words whispered against her ear. "You might harm the baby?"

It was the wrong thing to say for Robin rolled her over roughly ponning her beneath his rigid form. "The safety of our child obviously means nothing to you," he hissed savagely. "Else you would be home instead of chasing around the country on the back of a horse!"

Beth had never been threatened by such coldly bridled rage. That Robin was holding his anger inside made the impending explosion all the more frightening. He knew only that she had endangered the life of their child. Could she make him see that the chance to save the life of another was worth the risk? At the moment it seemed highly unlikely.

With a sigh Beth admitted, "You have every right to be furious. I have not harmed the baby though I could have. Perhaps you will find that unforgivable, but I beg you to hear me out before you pass judgment."

Without waiting for his consent, Beth began telling him everything just as she had explained it to her uncle hours earlier. Not once did Robin interrupt nor did his unrelenting expression soften even a fraction as he continued to hold her firmly beneath him. She

wondered if anything she said would make a differ
ence or if this time her rash actions had cost her he
dreams.

When she concluded by confessing that her effort
had been in vain for she'd arrived too late to warn Os
ceola of the trap into which he had fallen, she strug
gled to hold back her tears. Though her emotion
were genuine she would not give Robin reason t
think she was playing upon his sympathy by using
feminine ploy. She wanted him to understand wha
had compelled her to act as she had. She wanted hi
approval, but most of all she wanted his unqualifie
love.

Robin remained poised above her. She could fee
the rapid beat of his heart against her breast and sh
longed to look away but could not. She had to b
there to see who won the battle raging inside him,
war as bitter as any fought between two opposin
sides. The hard, accusing eyes, locked with hers
would soon tell her what she had to know. Beth'
shallow breathing could not be blamed entirely on th
solid weight pressing her down into the mattress.

Minutes passed and still Beth waited, praying si
lently for the courage to accept whatever was t
come. Her brows puckered in a frown as she saw
faint spark of light flare to life in the depths of th
cool gray-green orbs she had been focusing on so in
tently. She looked closer. No, she was not mistaken
As she continued to stare unblinking, eyes as cold a
glaciers began to thaw giving way to flames of desire

Only then did she allow the tears to fall, but thi
time they were tears of happiness as she felt Robin'
warm, welcome lips close over hers.

* * *

"Ouch! Go to sleep, my little warrior," Beth admonished, glancing down at her extended abdomen.

During the last two weeks the child's powerful kicks against the wall of her stomach had come more and more often but Beth found the discomfort reassuring for it meant the baby was healthy and anxious to gain entry into the world outside her womb. She turned from the stove to admire the bouquet of colorful wildflowers Mandy had picked and placed in a vase on the kitchen table. It was the season when new life sprang forth, a fitting time for her son to be born.

The back door opened and Beth, expecting to see her husband, was surprised when Lance Logan walked in.

"Something smells good," he said as he dropped a folded newspaper on the table then gave her a brief hug.

Over the past few months, Robin had written a series of articles describing the plight of the Seminole which he had sent to his uncle. Each week one of the articles appeared in the Washington newspaper which Martin Hawkins always forwarded to them by whatever means possible. By the time the papers arrived the news was already outdated. Still Beth found it exiting to read about events that had occurred in such far away places as Washington and its neighboring states. She felt a certain pride seeing her husband's name in print. But today instead of rushing to scan the headlines, she eyed her uncle suspiciously for his mannerisms seemed somehow affected.

"I'm making venison stew and you're welcome to

369

stay for supper but I don't really think it's my cooking that brought you here."

"I've already eaten," Logan admitted, "but I wouldn't say 'no' to a cup of coffee if you'll join me."

Beth poured two cups of the steaming liquid then sat down across from her uncle bracing her chin on folded hands. "Why do I have the feeling you're about to tell me something I don't want to hear?"

Lance shrugged saying evasively, "Probably because you know your old uncle so well."

Alarmed by his unsuccessful attempt to appear nonchalant Beth cried, "Has anything happened to Robin?" She clutched her stomach protectively.

Anxious to alleviate his niece's fear, Logan assured "No, nothing has happened to Robin. Relax, honey It's just that he had to go away for a few days."

Beth jumped to her feet unable to believe what she was hearing. Rachel had said her child could be born at any moment. "What are you talking about? Why would he leave without telling me?" She grasped the back of the chair, her knuckles whitening as the baby landed another blow that nearly took her breath away.

In an instant Logan was around the table, taking her by the shoulders, pressing her into the chair "Now don't get scared, honey. Robin's coming back.

But as her child moved restlessly within her womb Beth found no comfort in his words. "Where has he gone?" she demanded, anger replacing fear.

Instead of answering, Lance unfolded the newspaper and placed it in front of her. She read the date February 15, 1838, six weeks ago! Then a headline midway down the front page leaped out at her: In

370

dian Prisoner Held At Fort Moultrie Succumbs To Acute Tonsillitis. The article went on to describe what little the reporter had been able to glean about Osceola's life focusing mainly on his capture and imprisonment, but Beth was unable to see the words through the blur of tears that clouded her vision.

"Isn't it ironic?" she said finally, her voice choking on a sob. "He led his people in battle, he survived the hardships of life in the wilderness, only to be brought down in his prime by a common throat infection which could have been cured if treated in time. Where is the justice?"

Lance shook his head sadly. "Perhaps what he could not accomplish in life, he will achieve in death. I have faith that the American people will not look upon his defeat as a victory."

"Whatever happens he has won his final battle. At last he has found peace." The knowledge gave Beth comfort. "Robin has gone to his people to tell them the news."

It was a statement, not a question, for she had come to know her husband well during the months since their nightlong vigil at Osceola's side.

"Yes," her uncle confirmed. "But never forget that we are his people, too." He cupped her chin in his rough palm and forced her to meet his steady gaze. "He will be back, Beth. Never doubt it!"

Still and all, Lance decided as he looked into her worried face and troubled eyes, it wouldn't hurt to send Davey to speed Robin along.

After a restless night's sleep Beth welcomed the

new day which dawned bright and sunny, the air filled with the fresh smells of springtime. Relaxing in a high-backed rocker on the front porch, she listened patiently to Mandy's endless chatter as the child played on the steps with the black dog she called Pup, a misnomer if ever there was one since Pup was now the size of a small horse.

"Will the baby be going to the wedding?" Mandy asked, stroking the animal's smooth, glossy coat as his tail thumped a steady beat against the wood. Mandy had talked of little else but Edward and Maggie's nuptials which were scheduled to take place two weeks from Saturday.

Beth massaged her stomach which sat in her lap like a large round dome. "One way or another, honey, he'll be there."

"How do you know he's a he?"

"Because all warriors are male."

Mandy accepted the explanation with unerring faith just as she accepted everything her older sister told her.

As her words drifted in the air, Beth was seized by sharp pain unlike anything she had ever experienced before. She gripped the arms of the chair as the contraction pulled her shoulders forward. Don't panic, she warned herself. Stay calm! Remember you're not the first person to have a baby nor will you be the last. Oh, God! I'm scared to death!

A few minutes later her muscles tightened again, only this time the gut-wrenching agony was even more excruciating than before. As soon as she was able to straighten in the chair, she spoke softly to Mandy who had been too busy blowing in Pup ar to notice her discomfort.

"Honey, I'd like for you to go and get your mama now. Tell her I need her here and that it's very important she come right away." Beth congratulated herself for managing to keep her voice low and steady. The last thing she wanted was to frighten the child.

Mandy looked up from where she sat. Her sapphire eyes widened as she stared at her sister's pinched face. "Oh, lordy! It's the baby!" she shrieked frantically, leaping down the steps and taking off at a run. Beth watched her go, her skirts pulled up to her knees, her short little legs moving up and down like pistons. Pup raced at her side barking loudly and wagging his tail in excitement.

In the meantime, Davey had pushed his horse hard to reach the Indian encampment and deliver his message to Robin. Not waiting for him to catch his breath or find a fresh mount, Robin leaped on Satan's back and kneed the saddleless stallion toward home.

But as he burst through the front door and saw the somber faces of Andrew and Lance, he came to a sudden halt.

"Where is she? Is Beth all right?" Robin demanded. Both men silently pointed upstairs and Robin rushed toward them, taking them two at a time in his haste. Halfway up the stairs, he froze when a blood-curdling scream rent the air. *Oh God! What have I done to her!* He started forward again and just as he reached the landing he heard a lusty squall. The sound stopped and then started again, louder, seeming to echo all around him. Robin burst into the room banging the door against the inner wall. He was brought up short by the sight of his wife lying wan and pale beneath a white coverlet, her face beaded with perspiration, her breath coming in shallow gasps. Purple shadows ringed her closed eyes. She was dying and it was all his fault. His heart thundered in his chest. How could he face life without her? As he rushed to the side of the bed and grasped her limp hand, her lids flickered.

"Welcome home," she murmured, giving him a satisfied smile before her eyes closed again and she sank into deep restful slumber.

Robin watched her chest rise and fall until he was certain she was breathing normally.

"She's fine, Robin. Just tired," Rebecca assured him from across the room. "Don't you think it's about time you met your sons?"

Sons! The impact of the plural hit Robin like a blow. He turned slowly to see Rachel and Rebecca standing side by side each holding a squirming bundle in her arms. Too overcome to speak, he gazed at the swaddled miracles and clutched the hand of his sleeping wife.

Robin rapped softly on the door then entered. Beth sat up against a mountain of pillows propped behind her; an infant suckling noisily at each breast. It was the most beautiful scene he had ever witnessed.

"Doesn't that hurt?" he asked, fascinated by the way the babies pulled with their little mouths and kneaded with their tiny hands.

Beth sighed contentedly. "It's the most wonderful feeling in the world."

Robin lowered himself carefully onto the edge of the bed. "If we keep this up, we will soon have our own tribe."

"What a wonderful idea," Beth replied serenely.

Robin looked at her in surprise. "You mean you would willingly do this again?"

After the way Lance and Andrew had described the hours immediately prior to the birth of the twins, Robin expected her to shy away from any mention of having more children. But blissfully hugging her now sleeping sons, Beth replied with a twinkle in her eyes, "I can hardly wait to get started."

Soon Rachel and Rebecca came to take the boys to the nursery. How, Robin wondered, could Beth look so radiant after the ordeal she had been through? He touched his hand to the fiery curls drawn back from her face with a green ribbon.

Beth's smile faded as she studied her husband's handsome face. He was so dear to her. More than anything she wanted to make him happy but she wondered if his restless spirit would ever be content to stay at home and live the life they had planned so many months ago. As much as it would hurt her, she would willingly let him go rather than see his spirit broken.

"What of the People, Robin?" she whispered, gathering his large hands in both of hers. "What is to become of them?"

Robin looked thoughtful. "Some will give up now that there is no hope of Asi-yahola's return. They will relocate to the Arkansas Territory. But there are others who will never surrender: Coacoochee, Tiger Tail, Sam Jones, Jumper. Even now they are making their way south toward the land of sawgrass prairie and mangrove swamps where no white man will dare follow."

Beth read her husband's faraway expression. "And what will you do now?" Compelled to ask the question yet dreading his answer, she waited, a lump constricting her throat making it difficult to breathe.

Her question took him by surprise but as Robin searched her troubled face he understood. And with understanding came a feeling of overwhelming tenderness and love for this gentle, courageous, firebrand who was *his* woman. In that moment he knew she would sacrifice her own happiness rather than try to hold him if he chose to go. He cocked his head to one side.

Then as Beth began to grow anxious, he smiled a charming, roguish, disarming smile and said, "I believe what I should like to do is spend the next twenty or thirty years raising my sons and attempting to keep my beautiful wife out of mischief."

Any hint at levity was gone as he continued, "I will never cease the fight against prejudice and injustice, especially when it is aimed toward my people, but Asi-yahola was right. Only if I speak as a white man will my voice be heard."

Beth felt her heart swell with joy. "Together we will make certain our children take pride in their Indian heritage and that they grow up to respect all men regardless of color or creed."

Surrounded by a sense of peace and contentment beyond his wildest dreams, Robin reached to embrace her, but Beth drew back sharply, taking his chin between her fingers and turning his face toward the light.

"Darling, what happened to your head?" Frowning she peered at the swollen, purplish bruise above his left eye.

Robin seemed to wither beneath her scrutiny. He spent some minutes studying the braided rug then he admitted sheepishly, "As I was running across the porch last night I tripped over the dog."

Beth could tell his pride hurt more than his wound but as hard as she tried she could not contain her mirth. What began as a stifled giggle burst forth into peals of laughter. Before long Robin joined in.

When at last they sobered, Beth drew him down and kissed his battered brow. "Oh, how I adore you, Robin Hawkins!" As she gently brushed his face with her lips, she sighed contentedly, "My warrior, my love."

After reading newspaper accounts of Osceola's death, Walt Whitman* wrote the following:

When his hour for death had come,
He slowly raised himself from the bed on the
    floor,
Drew on his war-dress, shirt, leggings, and gir-
    dled the belt around his waist,
Call'd for vermillion paint (his looking glass was
    held before him),
Painted half his face and neck, his wrists, and
    back-hands,
Put the scalp-knife carefully in his belt — then ly-
    ing down, resting a moment,
Rose again, half-sitting, smiled, gave in silence
    his extended hand to each and all,
Sank faintly low to the floor (tightly grasping
    the tomahawk handle),
Fixed his look on wife and little children — the
    last.

*Walt Whitman, *Leaves of Grass,* edited by Malcolm Cowley New York: Funk and Wagnalls, 1968), p. 463.

From the Author

Though the Logan family is fictional, Osceola and his braves were real. I have tried to present an historically accurate account of their lives based on many hours of research. For three more years the war against the Seminole Indians dragged on but the men on both sides had lost heart for the fighting. Disgusted with the drain the conflict had placed on the U.S. Treasury and disillusioned with their former hero, Thomas Jesup, American citizens no longer gave the army their full-fledged support. Jesup spent the remainder of his career trying to explain his perfidy. The eight year conflict cost the country more than forty million dollars and the lives of nearly fifteen hundred soldiers.

When at last Colonel Worth declared an end to the hostilities, two hundred braves remained at large hidden deep in the south Florida swampland we now call "The Everglades." Worth, believing no one could survive in the humid, snake- and alligator-infested tangle of vegetation said, "Leave them alone. They will eventually surrender."

But they never did. The descendants of those who refused to give up the land they loved are still there today. Having come to terms with the elements they continue to live much the same way as did their predecessors: the undefeatable warriors of the Seminole Nation.

—Kathy Willis

DISCOVER DEANA JAMES!